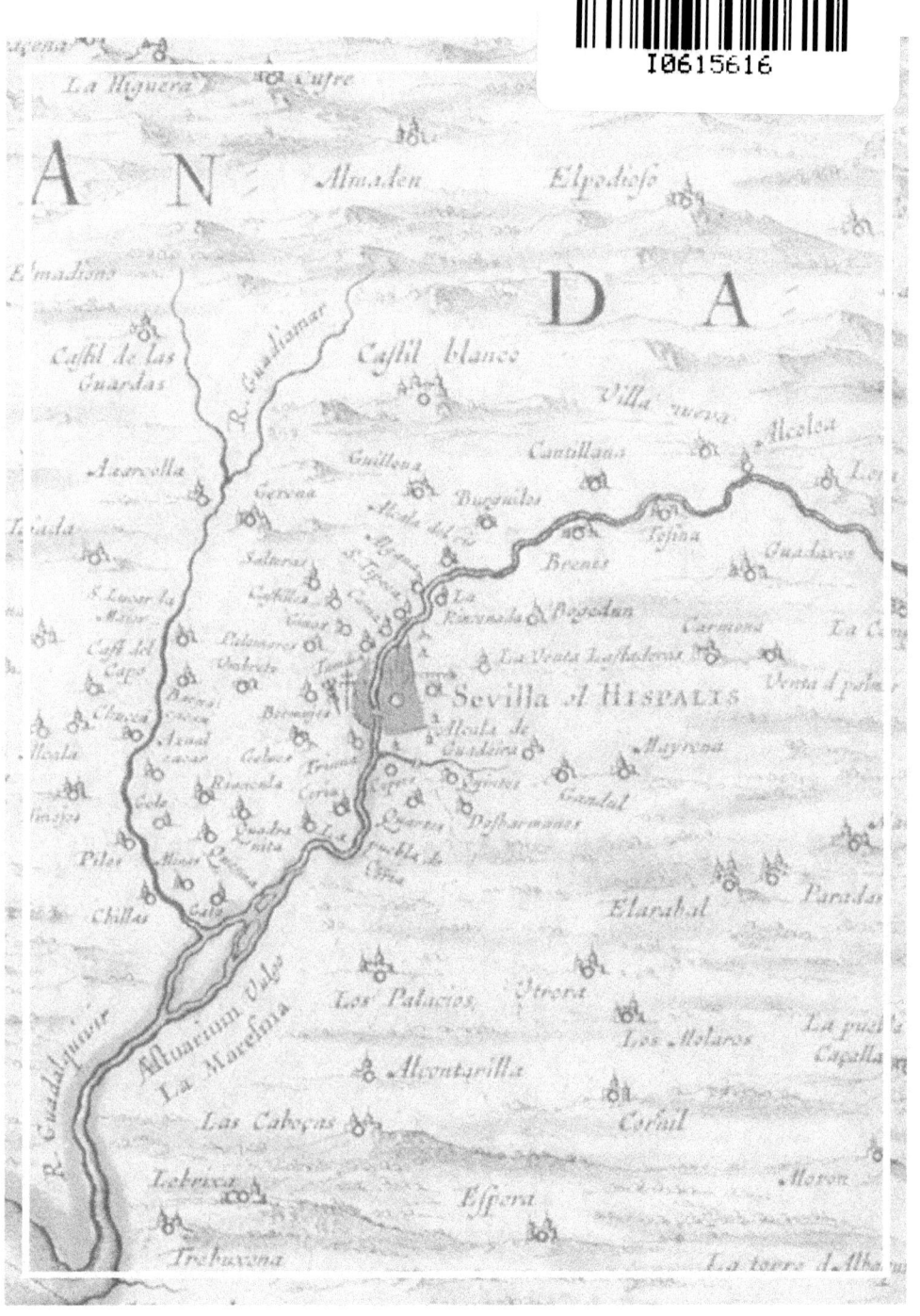

Cass squeezed their hands hard and said, more boldly than she felt, "let's go in." They entered Seville of the thirteenth-century.

# Chapter I

# A Quest

Cass and Thea broke the surface of the water at the same time, just a few feet from each other. They looked at one another through a mist, stunned, speechless. Only when they realized that they were treading water and were being carried along by a rapid current, unable to see where, did they come to their senses. "Over here, Thea," said Cass. "Follow me." With strong strokes and using the current they came to the shore and climbed up the grassy bank. The two teen-aged girls stared at each other in wonderment.

They were completely naked, although the strange necklace around Cass's neck seemed to clothe her. They looked at one another, Thea's blue-green eyes fixed on Cass's dark brown eyes. Thea's pale skin and Cass's darker skin both glistened in the early morning mist. They began to shiver. Cass broke the spell that seemed to have overtaken them when she suddenly raised both hands to the necklace. Reassured by the feel of it, she sighed and smiled faintly, but the wonder remained.

"Are we d-d-d-dead?" said Thea, thinking out loud. Her teeth were chattering from the cold air and from fear, though the fear was mixed with curiosity. Cass made no reply. She shook her head, pinched her cheeks, and shook her head again. They looked about them. The mist was lifting. They could see a strip of the river and its bank and not much else, except each other. Then they heard a voice, and it was addressing them.

"You look lovely. Natural innocence."

Another voice, any other voice, would have sent the girls rushing back into the river, but not this voice. It welcomed and warmed them. The girls squinted through the mist in the direction of the voice. Its owner materialized gradually, becoming more visible until the full remarkable form presented itself five or six paces in front of them. The strange form struck Thea as alien and not connected to the lyrical voice she had just heard. She glanced uneasily at Cass.

Cass was smiling but her eyes were also questioning. To her the figure before them suggested a very tall pitcher: wide at the base, tapering gradually in the middle, and reaching upward with a long, thin neck to the mouth. It was clearly female. Wide hips were covered by a pair of billowing pantaloons which extended to the ankles just above long, narrow, slippered feet. The pantaloons, royal purple silk against the apparition's dusky-gold skin, were the only garment. Above the waist a thin, narrow torso rose to high, small breasts. Above the breasts, the shoulders extended to slender arms, and hands that ended in long, delicate fingers.

"Beautiful," thought Thea.

"Intelligent," decided Cass.

Neither word did the face justice. It was remarkably expressive. Wisdom and mischief danced together. It was a face that would have looked fitting for a deity on her temple wall. The chin, the spout of Cass's pitcher, protruded noticeably but was softened by the full lips and short nose. Above the high forehead the hair piled up in dark curls that were tamed by a shining silver circlet.

The creature's eyes announced that it—she—was friendly for the moment but should not be taken for granted. The girls had never seen such eyes. The irises were shaped like a cat's or like the flame of a candle. They showed various shades of violet. These not-quite-human eyes now scrutinized the girls.

"You are Theadora and you are Cassandra. You may call me Maiden," she said, laughing lightly, eyes flickering. "It is not my true name, but it will serve. Attire yourselves in these," she said briskly as she handed them some clothes. The sudden change of tone from music to business caught their attention. They had been staring at the figure before them as though mesmerized. Thea examined the bundle of clothes, hoping it contained more than just pantaloons. Cass glanced at her bundle but then surprised Thea and herself by curtseying to Maiden. She had, of course, read about girls curtseying and seen it done in movies, but she had considered it old fashioned and somehow demeaning. At the moment it seemed appropriate. She was quite pleased that she curtseyed without stumbling.

As they dressed Maiden spoke. "I am sorry that the beginning of your journey must seem so strange to you. You three have been long in coming, longer than I would have wished. I had to manage the opportunity when it arose."

"Alan! Where is Alan?" Maiden's "you three" startled Cass into remembering. Her brother Alan had been with them before this strange and sudden journey began. Thea backed up Cass's question with a suspicious and questioning look at Maiden.

"Your brother Halán has preceded you, with somewhat less grace than you and Theadora." Maiden pointed to some rocks a dozen yards away in the thinning mist. "You will find him over there. You may take these clothes to him."

The girls looked where Maiden had pointed. They saw a raised hand, a head of dark-brown hair, and a bit of forehead peeping above a boulder. The hand was waving to signal its presence to the girls, but its owner clearly was not about to leave his sanctuary among the boulders. Cass realized that he must be as naked as she and Thea had been, and much more embarrassed. And he was still on his guard but trying not to show it. She walked over, called his name, and threw him the clothes. Alan stood but remained modestly behind a waist-high boulder. He was dark like his sister Cass but taller than she though he was more than two years younger. He had the body of a runner, thin but wiry. Alan put on the strange clothes as quickly as he could figure out how and joined his sister and Thea, keeping a wary eye on Maiden.

"Your brother Halán could not see his way clearly to the shore," explained Maiden. "I swam out to guide him, but he refused to follow me. I had to pull him against his will to the river bank. When we got close to the riverbank, he broke away from me and ran, without even thanking me. Your brother is quite strong," she added as an afterthought. She looked at Alan. From her long throat and full lips emerged the sound, "hmpf," and then a second "hmpf." The first "hmpf" was questioning, the second dismissive. The three listeners would soon come to recognize that Maiden's hmpfs" expressed a range of feelings. The lower the tone, the less pleased she was.

Alan addressed the girls, reacting to Maiden's account of their meeting. "I thought she was some kind of a mermaid trying to drown me," he complained. "And would you tell her my name is Alan, not Hal-On, or whatever she is saying." Both girls laughed, but Alan's behavior reminded Cass of the strangeness of their situation. "I should really be more concerned," she thought to herself. As soon as she had this thought, she realized that it was not an unusual one for her. She tended to regard the unknown as an invitation to adventure, an invitation she generally welcomed despite a certain amount of risk. Bruises, torn clothes, and once a broken collar bone, had failed to dampen her love of adventure. Now she prodded herself, somewhat reluctantly, into a cautious mode for the sake of her brother and her best friend. They didn't always share her tendency.

"I don't mean to be rude, lady... er ... My Lady, but please tell us who you are and where we are," requested Cass. She even wondered, briefly, if this unusual being had put a spell on them, or on her at least, so fascinated was she by Maiden and curious about what was happening to them. "And what is happening to us? Oh, and his name is Alan, as he said, not Halán," she added.

Maiden's response to the name correction was a neutral "hmpf," followed by, "he had best get used to Halán, which is how everyone here will pronounce Alan."

Thea sent Alan a quick look of apology as she addressed Maiden for the first time. "All right about the name," she said, "but how about Cass's question."

"As to what is happening to you, the necklace that Cassandra is wearing holds the answer, as she already suspects," said Maiden in reply to Thea. Cass was unconsciously fingering the stones of the necklace at that moment. She continued to do so, while looking fixedly for some time at Maiden, thinking about what she had just said.

The necklace had belonged to Cass and Alan's Grandmother Esther, but it was clearly from a different era, an older time. Looking at it made Cass think of "heirlooms" and "antiques" or even "lost treasure." It had three square stones, about half an inch on a side and nearly as thick as one's little finger. Each stone was encased in dark gold-leaf with only the top surface visible, protruding above its setting like the rounded crust of a loaf of bread. The middle stone was pale white with a blush of red. The stones on either side were light blue-green with pastel streaks of pink. Small but sturdy gold beads connected the three stones. A short chain of gold links extended from each blue-green stone. One chain ended in a wolf's head, the other in a small circlet of gold. The ears of the intricately fashioned wolf's head were thrust back. Two long fangs strained forward to fasten on its prey, the gold circlet. The necklace, when she was not rubbing it, as she was at the moment, rested smoothly just under Cass's neck. It seemed to have been made for her.

Finally Cass spoke. "Grandmother's necklace saved us from the fire and brought us here." Again she had the feeling of awakening from a dream.

"Of course," exclaimed Thea, remembering. "We were in your house," she said to Cass, "on the third floor, and we couldn't get to the stairs because of the smoke from Alan's room."

Alan now also recalled what had happened. "I came down the hall to get you two when my chemistry experiment blew up and the fire started," he said. "The fire or the smoke at least must have followed right behind me."

"Right," said Cass, speaking quickly as the details rushed back to her. "I had just been showing Thea this necklace that Grand-mother Esther had left to me in her will, along with the mysterious note. The note said something about the necklace transporting its owner, and anyone making physical contact with her, through fire. So, when the smoke started to overcome us...."

"You told us to grab onto you, and then you put on the necklace, Cass" said Thea. She didn't mean her statement to sound like an accusation, but it did.

"We were trapped," answered Cass, a little defensively. "We were coughing and choking and could barely see. I couldn't think of anything else to do. Then I felt the necklace pressing into my hand, and I put it on." She looked at Maiden.

"The necklace saved your lives, and it brought you here, as I directed it to do," said Maiden. "You acted as I expected you would when I used Halán's experiment to start the fire."

"What!" shouted three voices at once.

Maiden ignored the outcry and the three pairs of accusing eyes. "You see, the necklace opens a portal in the presence of fire. With it the bearer and anyone touching her may move—or be moved—in-stantly to another time and place by fastening the necklace around her neck. Fortunately, Cassandra, you had understood that much about the necklace from the letter. In time you will learn much more about the workings of the necklace." She mainly addressed Cass but made sure the other two were listening.

The three companions were still staring at Maiden with shocked expressions.

"No wonder why I wanted to get away from her," snapped Alan.

"She practically killed us, and you two just laughed at me."

"Why?" demanded Cass. Despite her rising anger, she could not keep a note of curiosity out of her demand.

"We could have been killed," accused Thea.

"The necklace and its bearer are greatly needed here. Lives, and even more importantly the beliefs of many, are threatened. I had to risk your safety, maybe even your lives, for the sake of others."

"That's crazy," said Alan.

"You might have asked," said Cass with some heat.

"Did you have to burn the house down?" interrogated Thea.

"The house has not actually burned down, but at least a limited fire was necessary, as I have explained. As for asking, I suppose I could have presented myself at your front door and invited you to travel several centuries back in time to Spain. With the help of your necklace, of course. Hmpf. Your grandmother chose you for the necklace. I have watched you and believe she chose wisely. Now it is time to act."

Maiden's voice had dropped quite low by the end of her last sentence. Several moments of strained silence ensued.

"I see," said Cass finally. "Did Grandmother Esther ever use the necklace?" she asked, her voice a mixture of awe and curiosity.

"Once," responded Maiden. "At first she worried that if she went back a second time she would never return again. She contented herself with raising your mother. When your mother had you, your grandmother watched you grow up from a distance, through your mother's descriptions. She decided to pass the necklace on to you. Unfortunately, she could not part with it during her lifetime. Much time has passed now since her journey. I have been waiting for the new bearer of the necklace, and you are she," she informed Cass. "And you are the bearer's companions," she asserted to Alan and Thea, who met this news with frowns.

"Um, why did their grandmother worry about maybe never returning?" inquired Thea. "You still haven't told us where we are, and how *do* we return home? And where *is* home? Oh...." Thea realized with a shock that she could barely remember anything about her home.

"This place gives me the creeps," complained Alan. He saw and then shared Thea's alarm and wondered both where home was and how to return to it.

"For a short time your memories of your past will be dim," said Maiden, "but you will not forget. In truth it will be of great importance for your quest that none of you should forget your homes and your previous lives. It may help you now to know that you may be able to return to your home with hardly any time passing. Time moves much differently when you have travelled through the necklace. You may be able to accomplish your difficult task here and be back in your home in time to be rescued from the fire there."

"I don't want any part of this," protested Alan.

"I think I may agree with Alan," seconded Thea after a moment's pause.

"Wait a minute," interrupted Cass. "From what Maiden has said, I don't think it would be wise to return right now. I almost passed out from the smoke, and I didn't hear anyone coming to help. The necklace and Maiden saved us, sort of." Alan and Thea quieted down.

"Hmpf," intoned Maiden in a middling low voice. She was about to speak, but Cass headed her off. She could hardly miss the angry flickering of Maiden's eyes, but she also noted a touch of amusement playing about her mouth. "OK," Cass ventured, addressing Maiden, looking directly into her eyes. "We now know how we got here but practically nothing else. You have twice spoken of a quest. Will you now tell us where we really are, and when, and more about this quest?" Cass looked to see if the flicker in Miaden's eyes had burst into flame. Fortunately it had subsided, and her lips stretched into an almost smile.

"As you wish," said Maiden. "You are in the country that you know of as Spain. At present, that is to say, in the thirteenth-century of the Christian era, it has many names. Here in the south, Spain is still known as Al-Andalus. It is the land of the three peoples who follow a sacred book, the Muslims, the Jews, and the Christians. The Muslims, you should be aware, are also called Moors or Arabs and the Christians are known as Franks, but the Jews are always the Jews. When the three peoples are not killing or enslaving each other, they get along reasonably well."

"The river through which the necklace brought you is the Guadalquiver. It flows to the city called Seville whose walls you can now see hard by. It comes from the east, bringing ships with goods from the two other great centers of Al-Andalus, Cordoba and Granada. From here it runs to the great ocean that leads to the edge of the world. At present the city is ruled by the Christians. Fernando the Third, of Castile, conquered it and rebuilt these walls." The three new arrivals took note of these walls for the first time, marveling at the size of the fresh-hewn stones. Until now they had seen pictures of such walls only in books about medieval towns and cities.

Cass's mind conjured up pictures of knights and ladies. "This might not be so bad," she thought to herself. Thoughts of adventure caused Cass to forget that Maiden had not yet answered her question about the nature of the quest. Alan and Thea were not quite as captivated. Still contemplating the massive stones of Seville's walls, Thea inquired, "What can we possibly do here?" She looked at Maiden. Alan simply nodded his agreement and then for the first time looked directly at Maiden, for a brief moment.

"I see you are not as easily distracted, Theadora, as some," said Maiden, looking with mock disapproval at Cass. Cass sighed, looked properly embarrassed, and then waited for the explanation. When she heard it, it was not what she was hoping or expecting. "You, Cassandra, must learn the history and powers of the necklace. In learning its story you will both gain control of its powers and learn about your quest. I am and will remain the guardian of the necklace, but I cannot reveal its secrets or bestow its powers. Each bearer bonds with the necklace in a unique way and understands its secrets and powers in subtly different ways from her predecessor.

"You, Theadora, and you, Halán, will, as I have said already, assist Cassandra." She looked at them and added, "I hope. Her journey may not be less perilous for your company, but it will be less lonely." Maiden paused and waited. Thea and Alan looked from Cass to each other, then awkwardly down at their feet, and finally back at Maiden. Thea's serious look merged into a smile in a way that said, "I trust you." Alan continued his questioning expression. Looking at Thea, Maiden said, "You are a gatherer of facts, I believe, Theadora. There are many facts to be gathered about the necklace in the journey ahead."

"We already know how to travel with the power of the necklace," announced Cass. She had begun to feel a little slighted.

"Hmpf," voiced Maiden skeptically. "Then you must know that the middle stone of the necklace was fashioned by the most intense flame deep in the earth, and that the other two were formed by chill cascading water. Fire and water, the two pathways of the necklace." Maiden watched as Cass and her companions puzzled over her words. Cass, looking embarrassed, fingered the three stones, one by one. "Your task is no easy one. There are those who would destroy the necklace or mislead the bearer and her companions. I will never be far from the necklace, but now that you are here, my main task is accomplished."

"Then you aren't our faery godmother or our guardian angel?" asked Thea.

Maiden laughed so delightedly that Cass and Thea found it impossible not to join in. "Indeed not. I am mother to no one, certainly not to humans. Nor am I a goddess or godmother. Guardian of the necklace, yes and, yes, of its companions." Her musical laughter still echoed in her words.

"Then you are the angel of the necklace," concluded Cass.

"Or perhaps djinni is more correct," guessed Thea.

Again Maiden laughed, causing even Alan to smile. "You are observant, Theadora. I have often been called djinni, less often angel. Perhaps you will be able to decide for yourself. Now it is time you should begin your journey."

Maiden led them to the Great Gate of medieval Seville. "In a short time this gate will be opened for the day. You will not be hindered from entering. Speak but little. Wherever you go you will understand and speak the language. It is a gift of the necklace, and you are now companions of the necklace. Go to the great tower that you will see immediately upon entering the city. Next to this tower is a great church, where a mosque once stood. Seek out Brother Bartolomeo. You can learn much from him about the necklace. He could even tell you something about me, but he may be too shy for that. Fare you well."

Maiden's last words still lingered on the air as she disappeared. A thin wisp of violet smoke lingered after she was gone.

"Wait! You said you would help us," called Thea to the empty space.

"No," sighed Cass, "I'm afraid we are going to have to rely on each other. Maiden will help us help ourselves is basically what she said."

They were alone for the first time since their arrival in this strange land. Until now they had experienced a dizzying mixture of bewilderment and fear, wonderment and excitement. These emotions disappeared with Maiden. They were replaced by a suffocating sense of loneliness, like being away from home for the first time but much worse. They were away from both their home and their own time. As they stood before the huge, silent wooden doors, they could feel their aloneness. Invisible hands seemed to be squeezing their hearts, repeatedly tightening and loosening their grip. Had they been able to recall their homes and families more vividly at that moment, they might have panicked and run back to the river to return to wherever it was they had come from.

Cass was finding it difficult to breathe, but she felt some relief when she reached up to touch the necklace. She noticed that Thea's chest was beginning to heave and that Alan was looking around him with an expression she hadn't seen on his face since he was a little boy lost in a department store. With a singular effort she gained control of herself.

"Hey you two," ordered Cass. She stepped between them and said they needed to face the gate all together. She took them each by the hand, Alan's left, Thea's right. "OK. We can give up right now, go back to the river, and I'll try to get us home. We would be taking our chances with the fire there .... Also with my being able to use the necklace properly. Or we can find out more about this adventure Maiden speaks of." She paused. No one spoke.

At that moment the great wooden doors creaked slowly inward. Cass squeezed their hands hard and said, more boldly than she felt, "let's go in." They entered Seville of the thirteenth-century.

# Chapter II

# The Illuminator

Heartened by Cass's resolve, the companions passed through the gate. They had not taken more than a hundred steps when the road curved to bring them into full view of a palace fortress. Its parapets, equal in height to the city walls, displayed brightly colored pennants waving in the breeze. They were fascinated by its size and faery-tale beauty, but a few moments later, when they caught sight of the great tower, they instantly forgot all about the palace.

The tower was unmistakable. It was tall and square and was crowned by a large bell supported by a wood and iron frame. Atop the frame rose a black metal cross. Lesser buildings clustered around the tower, as though paying it homage. It dwarfed even the palace. They hurried toward it.

On their way through the narrow streets, they began to take notice of the houses and shops and the people who bustled in an out of them on their morning's business. Most of the people were dressed in simple garments that appeared strange to the companions. One boy wore what Alan took to be a nightshirt and tights. Alan made no effort to hide his smirk. Cass and Thea noticed that the women wore ankle-length dresses of coarse homespun, closed up to the neck. They fastened a cord around the waist to keep their skirts from dragging in the dirt, and they sported an array of shawls and kerchiefs which added the only hint of color or style.

"These people are dressed like regular townspeople. I mean not like nobility," commented Thea.

"And look at us," replied Cass. For the first time the companions paid close attention to how they were dressed. They had been too overwhelmed earlier to notice. They stopped on the cobblestone street to inspect each other. Cass and Thea exclaimed their delight in their "frills." Alan voiced an embarrassed "yipes," noticing that he had on the silly-looking tights and nightshirt he had just laughed at on another. Cass laughed inwardly, remembering the much more romantic picture of knights and ladies her mind had presented to her outside the walls.

A few women made their way around them in the narrow street, muttering something about people standing about idly on the cobblestones. Their attention made Alan more embarrassed, but Cass and Thea took no notice. Their spirits were lifting. Even being criticized made them feel that they belonged. They began to relax. Cass was also grateful for the bulky kerchiefs which hid her necklace. She made a mental note that she would have to keep the necklace hidden from view. Anyone seeing it on a commoner like her would assume she had stolen it. Also Cass recalled Maiden's words about "those who would try to destroy the necklace."

With a few final glances at their clothes, the companions resumed their way toward the great tower. They attempted to find the shortest route, but the bewildering network of streets and squares led them so far out of their way that they eventually found themselves approaching the tower from the opposite direction from their starting point. They began to fear they were in a maze.

They escaped unexpectedly out of their maze into a courtyard that finally afforded a close-up view of the tower. They stood, however, not before the tower itself, but in front of a gate to a garden which they would have to pass through to arrive at the tower. The gate itself drew their attention. It was arched in the shape of what looked to them like a large, old-fashioned keyhole, the ones you could spy through. A mysterious series of letters swirled across the wide top of the arch. They passed through this keyhole into the garden. The companions found themselves surrounded by rows of trees, brightly laden with heavy, plump oranges.

"A grove of little suns," exclaimed Cass. "With a fountain in the middle," added Thea. The water from the fountain filled a small pool until it spilled over and splashed into carefully placed stone channels which carried it to the orange trees. The companions forgot the tower for the moment to enjoy the tranquility of the garden, wandering among the trees. This grove of little suns would lift anyone's worries within its walls. Alan, wondering suddenly when he had last eaten, reached up to pick an orange when a man called to him.

"Those are the Bishop's oranges, young man."

"Oh, sorry," said Alan with disappointment as he withdrew his hand.

The man who had spoken was wearing the brown robe of a monk of the Cathedral. He wore sandals. His hood, attached to the robe, was thrown carelessly back revealing a shock of steel-grey hair. "But you do look hungry. Here, the Bishop can spare a few." He plucked oranges for all three companions and one for himself.

While the others promptly set about eating their oranges, the monk only looked longingly at his. He held the glistening fruit close to his smiling face. He squinted so that his eyes were barely visible. Even so they added a glint to his smile. "Since I cannot break my fast until my brothers do, accept another orange." He handed it to Alan who was already licking his fingers from the first orange. He mumbled his thanks while trying to catch the juice dripping down his chin onto the discarded peels at his feet.

Thea stopped chewing as soon as she heard the word "brothers." "Are you by any chance Brother Bartolomeo," she asked. Curiosity competed with respect in her voice.

"By God's grace, I am indeed Brother Bartolomeo, and how may I be of service," he answered, looking inquiringly at Thea.

"How lucky," said Cass. Thea looked at her a little annoyed, remembering that Cass had a habit of interrupting her. "We've come to see you," continued Cass. These two are my friend Thea, Theadora that is, and my brother Alan. I'm Cass, ah, Cassandra." She had already been studying Brother Bartolomeo's face while eating her orange. She liked his face and decided she would trust him. "We are from 800 years in the future and from...."

"A distant place," interjected Thea, while Cass paused. "And closer to 750 years from now," she added. She paused and smiled demurely at Cass.

"Maiden told us you would help us," said Cass. She summarized their story from when they swam from the river, speaking rapidly as though the brother might think her crazy and run off before she could finish.

Brother Bartolomeo made no attempt to hide his surprise—or his interest. He took two or three studied steps toward Cass, squinting diligently at her. He did the same with Thea and Alan. He studied their faces for several moments before asking, "What did this Maiden look like?"

Thea responded promptly. "She says she's the guardian of the necklace, but she looks more like an ancient goddess, Egyptian or something of that sort." Thea smiled at Brother Bartolomeo almost as though she expected a reward for answering his question.

"And where is this necklace now?" inquired Brother Bartolomeo.

Cass hesitated for just a moment and then removed several scarves. With both hands she reached under the collar of her dress to lift and display the necklace. The monk's reaction was immediate. "Come to my workroom," he told them. "She is not with you now?" He paused hopefully for a moment. "But no, she would not be," he answered to himself. He turned and said "Come."

He led them from the orange garden into the building next to the tower. Inside the air smelled musty and felt damp after the garden. To their eyes it was as dark as a moonless night. The rhythmic sound of voices chanting reached them from the distance. "The rest of the brethren are still saying the hours, so be silent and stay close to me." Their eyes adjusted just enough to enable them to follow single file. They turned right at the end of one hall and then left and left again into an inner courtyard alive with sunlight. They had to shield their eyes from the brightness. They filed across the courtyard and into a room packed with enormous books.

"This room gets the best light all through the day, thanks be to God and to his skilled masons and architects," chuckled Brother Bartolomeo. The room still retained a bit of the early morning dampness, but the bright sunlight was quickly dispelling that. Light seemed to come from every direction. It came from two windows facing the courtyard and from two matching windows on the opposite wall. The left wall, the garden wall, had one window in the center. The right wall, the tower wall, had no windows, being the wall shared with the tower. The windows were composed of dozens of small pieces of glass, a few colored, most of them clear, all of various shapes and all held together by thin bands of metal. A glass skylight of the same construction crowned the center of the room. The sun would shine there winter and summer. Directly under the skylight stood a podium on which rested the largest and most beautiful book any of the companions had ever seen. There were other, smaller book stands and benches—Thea counted six of them—located along three of the walls. The tower wall contained shelves with books of all sizes and shapes lying flat. The companions found that their eyes kept returning to the glowing pages of the large book on the podium.

"This is the *Bible of St. Isidore*," said Brother Bartolomeo in a hushed voice, walking over to the central stand. He moved the stool out of the way to make room for the companions. He was gratified by their expressions of awe. The book shimmered. "The colors of letters and drawings are as bright as they were when brand new three hundred years ago. Our artists learned how to do that from our Muslim friends."

"Illuminated manuscripts," whispered Thea. "We are learning about these in confirmation class." She smiled, pleased that her memory was coming back. "So you are …"

"A copier of manuscripts!" exclaimed Cass. Thea remembered that Cass not only had a bad habit of interrupting her but also of completing her sentences.

"Pardon my vanity, My Lady, but I fancy myself more as a book designer and illuminator than a copier of manuscripts. Here, let me show you." He led them to a large flat table by one of the windows where he delicately opened another book of great size and began to turn the pages. "This is *The Book of Hours*. It contains the prayers the brothers must chant at different times of the day. As you can see there is a considerable amount of script. The first letter of key words has a separate design. Framing each page of script are other drawings. Brother Superior excuses me from common prayer so that I can save my eyes to do the lettering and painting. He says the work is my prayer."

He had just turned another page when Thea cried out, "It's Maiden."

Hiding his excitement, Brother Bartolomeo spoke almost casually. "Pray, point out this Maiden."

Alan, who had been feeling excluded, said "there," and pointed to the inside margin of the left page.

"Wrong," corrected Cass. "This one is our Maiden." She pointed to a figure on the inside margin of the right page, opposite the shape that Alan had pointed to. "That other one looks like Maiden but without Maiden's sense of humor."

Alan didn't like the way Cass had corrected him, but he had to admit that she was right.

"That other one looks mean," observed Thea.

"Mean is too gentle a word for her, though I sometimes feel sorry for her," mused Brother Bartolomeo. His three guests wondered at his words, but all eyes remained fixed on the wonders of the manuscript pages before them.

On the wide inner margins of both pages were two brightly colored figures, both about three inches high. Each depicted the face and unclothed torso of a human-like, nymph-like female creature. Where the lower half of their bodies would have been was instead a large vine. It gradually narrowed as it trailed down to the bottom of the page, and then curled around both of the side margins. The head of both figures supported a stone pillar that rose upwards until it was lost in some clouds. Both faces would have been identical except for the expressions, which made them opposites. Maiden's expression embodied well-wishing; the other's bespoke ill-wishing.

Thea broke the spell that filled the room. "Who is the mean one, and what are two naked females doing in your prayer book? I would have expected angels and saints with clothes on."

"Or demons?" smiled Brother Bartolomeo.

Cass couldn't refrain from commenting. "I expect these figures keep the brothers awake at their prayers."

Brother Bartolomeo laughed heartily, looking at Cass with a twinkle in his eyes. He turned to Thea. "If you'll notice, they are each balancing a pillar on their head, supporting the house of God, if you will, both they and others as well. Some do so willingly, like Maiden, others not so willingly, like the mean one, whose name is Bladen.

"I see the others you just mentioned," said Thea. "They have spiked hair and pointy beards. Males. Lots of them but hidden by the vines that come from the females. They definitely don't look like angels."

Brother Bartolomeo looked at Thea. "You say you would expect angels in a prayer book, and you are right. How would you have me draw one." He looked from Thea to Cass to Alan, smiling at their puzzled expressions.

"Alan and I are not religious," said Cass. We are Jewish but not practicing Jews. We have never taken religious instruction. Our father does not allow us to." She spoke matter-of-factly but with a hint of sadness. She brightened and said, "Thea is our expert on religions, at least Christian and Jewish."

Thea took the hint and answered Brother Bartolomeo. "OK, angels don't have to have wings, and perhaps not even clothes. But Bladen? No. No angel ever looked as wicked as that, unless … ."

"Unless it were a fallen angel," replied the monk, completing Thea's point. "The Muslims refer to the good Djin and the bad Djin."

"I thought you called them djinni," interrupted Thea.

"I did," replied Brother Bartolomeo. One is a djinni. Many are the Djin. Your confirmation class probably has taught you that Jews and Christians believe in good and bad angels. All three religions agree that the Djin or angels can take on human form at times so we can see them. Still, what would they look like if we could see them as they are?"

"I see," said Thea, adding, "I think."

"Well, enough schooling for the moment," said Brother Bartolomeo. "Sit down, my friends, here in the sunlight." He indicated the sturdy, polished bench facing the large stand that held the *Bible of St. Isidore.* "My younger students get to sit here and listen to me before they become apprentices," he explained as he pulled his stool over. "I am convinced now that you are sent by Maiden, and I am flattered. I was quite confident when I saw the necklace, but I wanted to be completely sure. I showed you the manuscript with her and Bladen and the others as a test. And to show off some of my work of which I am pleased. Probably too pleased," said Brother Bartolomeo as he lightly touched his right hand to his heart in a gesture of repentance. "Now I will do as Maiden bids and tell a tale that may help you."

Alan surprised everyone by blurting, "Personally I would like to go home now, if you really want to help. Cass has accepted this weird quest, and I guess Thea is with her, but no one has asked me."

Brother Bartolomeo looked intently at him, then at Cass and Thea, who looked at the ground and said nothing. "I am sorry to hear that," he said to Alan. I can help with some information and suggestions, mainly about the necklace, not about going home. But you are welcome to listen anyway. Perhaps something I say will help you to a proper homecoming after all."

Cass and Thea seated themselves on the center of the bench. Even through their rough dresses they could feel the warmth that the wood had absorbed from the sunlight. Alan sat at the end of the bench, partly in and partly out of the sun.

"My tale begins over forty years ago," began Brother Bartolomeo." It was mid-century, 1250. We Christians of Castile and Leon had reconquered this city just two years earlier. I was an archer in the Christian ranks, a young man, not much older than you," he nodded at Alan. After the city yielded to us, I fell in love with it, every pillar, fountain, and arch of it. Lucky for me I wandered one day into the shop of a famous Jewish craftsman named Nathan. There were still many Jews and Muslims in Seville then, so soon after the return of the Christians to power here. Nathan wrought fine jewelry of silver and gold and precious stones. His shop was just a short walk from the Cathedral and tower. Nathan could still remember when Muslims were permitted to worship in a part of the Cathedral when no Christian services were being celebrated. He said that it was proper to share the building since it had been a church, then a mosque complete with minaret, and now was a church again. But that is a different story."

"I loved the jewelry, especially the necklaces," smiled Brother Bartolomeo, looking at Cass. "Nathan knew instinctively that I would be a good craftsman and offered to teach me his trade. I became his apprentice. He was as kind and generous as he was skilled. He liked me, and let me sleep in the storeroom in the shop. I had a steady hand and a good eye, so I learned quickly. We got on well all three years, except for … , but that comes later. When I had extra time, I would roam about the shop and examine all the pieces that Nathan had made or collected, so I could use them as possible models. That is how I first discovered the necklace. It attracted my attention so I studied it carefully."

"Nathan noticed my interest in the necklace one day and told me something about it. 'Jewish work' he said, 'made a thousand years ago, probably more. At that time you Christians were being thrown to the lions, and the Muslim prophet Mohammed was not yet born. Instead of three "People of the Book," Muslims, Christians, and Jews, there was as yet only one book, the *Torah* and one People of the Book, the Jews. Oh, I guess you Christians started writing a few letters back then, trying to figure out what was what.' Nathan laughed as he always did when we teased each other about our religions."

"He told me that the necklace had been found in the ruins of Italica, an old Roman settlement just a few miles north of here. Italica had been the residence of the Roman rulers of southern Spain, which they called Hispania in those long-gone days of the empire. When the necklace was found, there were those who claimed knowledge of it, but their accounts were contradictory. According to some it was a talisman that could change worthless stones into precious gems like its own, or worthless metal into gold like its settings and links. Others said that the necklace gave its bearer unheard of power and made her a great lady. Nathan scoffed at these claims. According to him hard work produces treasure, ability bestows power, and good deeds make one a lady. The people who Nathan determined knew most about the necklace believed that an angel—or djinni if you prefer—dwelt within it. The angel served God and helped the bearer. That made sense to Nathan."

"Finally, one day Nathan told me the legend about the origins of the necklace. And when he had begun that story, I knew that there would be no more work for the rest of the afternoon. As a true teller of important tales, he spoke in a higher pitch and chanted his words. He was a master storyteller as well as a master craftsman. I cannot relate the tale as well as he, but I will do my best to repeat it as I heard it from his lips."

### The Legend of the Necklace

"Many centuries ago the governor of the Roman Colonial City of Italica asked his Chief Minister, a Jew, what he thought about the new religion of the Christians. Was it, he wanted to know, the equal of the Jewish religion from which it sprang? Many of the governor's own courtiers were Romans who had formerly worshipped many gods but had become Christians. Like the Jews, Christians worshipped one God. Now the governor himself was apparently considering changing his allegiance from the many gods of Rome to the one God of the Christians, but he also respected the Jews. He was puzzled. It struck him that the Jews worshipped the same one God that the Christians did and had done so even before the Christians. At the same time the governor's courtiers told him that Christ was a great prophet. He decided to invite both Christian and Jewish religious leaders to his court to explain their religions. When they arrived, however, they argued continuously, which was not useful in the least."

"So the governor asked his Chief Minister to explain the strengths and weaknesses of the two faiths. Understandably the Chief Minister was concerned about how to respond. He was a courtier and thus a politician, not a priest or rabbi. He wanted to speak honestly but without offending his fellow Jews or the Christians at court. He requested three days to consider the question. The governor agreed."

"After much thought the Chief Minister conceived the idea of presenting the governor with a gift that would contain his answer. He commissioned a famous Jewish artisan to create a necklace with two matching stones to represent the Jewish and Christian religions, and with a catch in the shape of a wolf's head to represent the Roman authority. The necklace would show that the two religions were equal and that both recognized Roman authority."

"As the artisan worked, a messenger from God put the thought into his mind that three stones would make a much more impressive gift for the governor. He did not know about the Chief Minister's plans for the necklace. So he added a pale stone with a reddish tint that seemed to lighten or deepen the way the sky sometimes did at sunrise or sunset. This he placed between the two blue-green stones. The middle one he called the Sunstone."

"When the Chief Minister arrived on the third day to collect the necklace on his way to court, he was very upset with the artisan for changing his design for the necklace. He said he would not pay for it. He had had his speech prepared and now would have to think of something else to tell the governor at the last minute. But at that moment a violet light suddenly filled the room. More precisely it was a dance of light that changed shades continuously. Out of the light came a voice that sounded like music. It said that God had entrusted the necklace to a guardian and that the guardian had changed the design. The Chief Minister was to take the necklace to the governor. He would know what to say when the time came."

"When the Chief Minister arrived the court was filled: Christians on one side, Jews on the other. Many on both sides were teachers and religious leaders, but they looked as if they were prepared for a fight rather than for the Chief Minister's explanation. The Chief Minister went to the middle of the room; he bowed to the governor. He told the governor that he had prepared a speech that was very impressive but without meaning. He would now trust in God to speak through him. Here is what he then said."

"At first I came here to say that the two religions, Jewish and Christian, must be equal in every way in the eyes of the law of Rome. Thus you see the two identical blue-green stones joined and held fast by the wolf of Rome that completes the circle. Now I understand better. The Jews came first. They are represented by the Sunstone because they were at the dawn of the worship of the one God. The Christians came later. They are represented by one of the blue-green stones that are called Skystones. The other Skystone prophecies the arrival of a third religion that will worship the one God."

"At this moment one of the teachers, whether Christian or Jew no one could decide afterwards, shouted 'blasphemy.' A war of words ensued, both sides hurling sharply pointed words at the other. The Chief Minister's voice rose above them, silencing them all. 'As you can see, there will sometimes be strife among the three religions. This will happen even though all are related and all worship the one God. This necklace will be a powerful reminder of the unity that should exist. Sometimes it will do more than remind'."

"The governor rose from his throne, smiling. He thanked the Chief Minister and said he had made his decision."

"So ends the legend," concluded Brother Bartolomeo.

"The governor was well pleased with the Chief Minister, with the necklace, and with the lessons it taught. He was both impressed and pleased with the prophecy. He knew full well that he would be remembered because of the necklace and the prophecy more than for any of his decisions as Governor of Hispania, good and wise as they might be."

"But which religion did he choose?" asked Thea.

Brother Bartolomeo smiled. "That was exactly what I asked Nathan. He simply said that that is not important. What is important is the lesson that Jews and Christians serve the same God. And the Muslims as well, now that they are here, as the necklace predicted."

Thea didn't look entirely happy with the answer. Brother Bartolomeo added his own contribution to Nathan's lesson. "The Christians and Jews hereabout are in the debt of the Muslims. The Muslims are the ones who made Seville a great city." He looked at Alan and added, "They are the ones who planted the orange garden and who built the great tower called the Giralda that guided you here." Thea still wanted to know which religion the governor had chosen. Alan, for his part, actually seemed impressed that the

Muslims had supplied the oranges and built the tower. Not only did he like oranges. More significantly he remembered spending happy hours just a few years ago building model towns that always had train stations with high towers. He only stopped doing so when he couldn't interest anyone else in joining him.

Brother Bartolomeo turned his attention to Cass. He could see that she was still thinking about the "Legend of the Necklace." "I know that you must be wondering what you have learned about the necklace that is useful from what I have told you so far. Very little at the moment is my guess. Sometimes knowledge has to ripen before it is useful."

Brother Bartolomeo stood, squinted up through the sun-bright skylight, and told his three new friends that he must leave for a short time, but to await his return. He was barely out of the room when Alan spoke up. "This brother person is nice enough, but I don't think he is going to be able to help us."

"That depends on what you mean by help, Halán," came a voice by the window of the garden-facing wall. Maiden was standing in front of the window. The light coming through made green and red spots that danced about her. Her sudden appearance came as a pleasant surprise to Cass and Thea, who rose to greet her. Alan remained seated but on the edge of the bench. Maiden still made him nervous, especially the way she appeared and disappeared into and out of nowhere. Her comment, of course, was addressed to him. He wasn't actually sure what he had meant by "help." He regretted having said it because it might sound like he would be ready to join the quest.

Cass broke the silence. "I'm afraid Alan might be right. All we have heard so far are legends and stories."

"But he is a very nice person as Alan said," noted Thea. "And we have learned that he knows you and your grumpy opposite, Maiden. Look, he has put you into his book." Thea pointed to the large volume still open on the table. Maiden nodded and smiled at Thea, who responded by blushing slightly.

"Well observed Theadora. Yes, I know about the book. I visit him occasionally. He does not know it, although he may suspect it."

"Poor man," thought Alan.

Turning to Cass, Maiden said, "The reason he is telling legends and stories is because people have always preserved truths in stories so that they will be better remembered. When you need the truths, they will come back to you. In your own time people have become much too literal. Attend well his stories."

"He returns," she said, and she disappeared. Her quick departure left a thin veil of violet light that lingered briefly before dissolving like a mist into the air.

Brother Bartolomeo entered the room a scant moment later with a large wooden tray heaped with fresh, crusty bread with melted butter and honey running down the rounded sides of the loaves. Three steaming cups of milk accompanied the loaves. He placed the tray on one of the apprentice's benches, well away from any of his books, and invited the companions to eat. Brother Bartolomeo moved several steps higher on Alan's ladder of approval. He was already biting into his second loaf before Thea or Cass had half finished their first.

"Slow down. Don't be piggy," Cass said to Alan in a low voice, hoping that Brother Bartolomeo could not hear. They were sharing one of the apprentice's benches. Thea was at another bench, closer to Brother Bartolomeo, who sat near the garden-facing window where Maiden had stood a short time ago. "I wonder if he knows that she visits him," mused Thea as she smiled at the resting monk.

Cass Also looked over at Brother Bartolomeo, where the monk now sat, his eyes half closed, in the warm sunlight. She spoke with only a little bit of bread, butter, and honey getting in the way. "Two questions, Brother. First, you said that Nathan seemed to agree with those who thought there was an angel in the necklace. Did you agree with him? And second, what did Nathan do with the necklace.?"

# Chapter III

# I Am Bladen

The sun must have been almost directly above the manuscript room. It poured through the skylight, chasing away any hint of shadow or trace of the morning's chill. Brother Bartolomeo got up from the bench with a slight groan and a stretch. He pulled his stool away from the manuscript stand and sat down facing the companions, his three pupils.

"And now for the last part of my tale," he announced, "and the answer to your second question, Cassandra, what Nathan did with the necklace." The monk squinted up at the skylight as though looking for something. Then he began with an apology.

"I hope you will not be offended by what I am going to tell you. My emotions overruled my reason at times in my youth. Scandalous," he said, shaking his head and smiling sadly.

Cass was on the verge of saying, "we can handle it," but the sad smile stopped her. Instead she said, surprising herself, "everyone makes mistakes especially when they are young, even future illuminators of sacred books." She glanced at Thea who nodded her head in approval of the remark. Brother Bartolomeo's smile brightened slightly. He began his story.

"For the first two years of my apprenticeship I was busy from first light until sunset, learning the craft and after a time even helping Nathan on some of the simpler commissions. Necklaces were my specialty. He had too many requests for one man to fill and had no other helper but me. Even Christian priests and Muslim imams sought out this Jew to adorn their sacred objects. I was, I think, a help to him. But I became restless. I wrote ballads and sang them in the evenings to the young ladies. Some of these songs I even wrote out in fancy scrolls which I left on selected balconies."

"How romantic," said Thea.

"Perhaps, and innocent enough at first, though the young ladies' parents were not always pleased to hear me or to find their daughters with one of my scrolls. As events proved, they had good reason for their concerns. I became involved with one person, Elena. She became so devoted to me that she would do anything I wished, ignoring the wishes of her parents. She willingly surrendered her maidenhood to me. I fancied myself a benevolent conqueror, even the protector of my gentle foe, as the minstrels were fond of singing."

"When Elena whispered excitedly to me one evening that she was carrying our child, I was thunderstruck. She was overjoyed. Her eyes positively shone with pride. 'He will grow up to be just like you and will take care of us when we are old.' She had no true experience of the world. I was still an apprentice, with no money. Elena's family would doubtless oppose a marriage and possibly send her to a convent. Deep within her she must have known this to be so, but she trusted me as though I were the king himself. Well, then, I had taken advantage of her trust and created this problem; now I would try to find a solution. We would go away. I should have known that I was making a bad situation worse, especially for Elena."

"To make my guilt even deeper, I betrayed Nathan, the other person who was closest to me. God has forgiven me for what I did to Elena and Nathan, though for a long time I thought my actions must be unforgivable."

"Nathan had a habit of working later than usual when he fell far behind in filling his orders. He was working late practically every night during much of the time I was making love to Elena. I now rarely did any extra work for him. He never reproached me. If I came in late, while he bent over his work next to a flickering lamp, he greeted me with a jest about nightingales singing all the night."

"The one service I did perform for him was to clean up and lock up after he left the shop, since he allowed me to sleep there anyway. On that same night that Elena told me she was carrying our child, I returned to find Nathan again working late. As soon as I entered the shop, I knew that I would rob this man who was more to me than a father. Noticing that Nathan was visibly tiring and might not continue working late for many more nights, I resolved to rob Nathan of some of the jewels and gold and flee with Elena the next night."

"The next day I sent word to Elena that she should meet me at the Duke's Arms, an inn near the east gate after midnight. Her chaperone and a trusted family man-servant could bring her to me. We would slip through the gate as soon as it opened at dawn, before her absence was detected, and make our way to Cordoba. She had agreed earlier, after much persuasion, to leave the city with me. Her chaperone, an elderly maiden aunt, liked me and had already trusted me far too much. She wept a bit and complained that I had betrayed her, but she was a realist. She knew that she would lose her position as chaperone no matter what happened now. After Elena was gone she planned to disappear for a while herself."

"After I closed Nathan's shop that night, I selected a number of unfinished pieces of jewelry and some pieces of gold from the cabinet where he kept them. He would not notice that they were missing as quickly as he would spot the absence of the finished pieces or those he was just completing. And though he would wonder where I was that morning, he would never think to check his stock of goods because I was not there. As I was about to leave, purely on impulse, I took the Necklace of Al-Andalus, simply stuffing it inside my shirt. I do not know why. It was too valuable to sell or trade without creating suspicion. Too many people knew of its existence."

"By the time I arrived at the Duke's Arms, I was drenched in sweat, even though it was a cool evening. I was perspiring from worry over what I had just done to Nathan and because of the dangers and uncertainties that I was about to bring to Elena. I was too preoccupied to notice the shaking hand with which the innkeeper handed me the key, or that he avoided looking me in the face."

"The thieves snatched the lamp from my hand as soon as I opened the door to my room. They nearly crushed my skull with their clubs and after stripped me and left me naked in a puddle of blood. For many months I wished that those assassins, which is what they were, had been true to their trade. In their greed for the gold and jewels they neglected to make sure I was dead."

"'That old witch of a chaperone saved herself at our expense,' was all I could think of whenever I gained partial consciousness. Then my head would throb and spin and I would black out again. When I finally regained consciousness, the innkeeper was babbling about not wanting to allow them in, that they would have murdered his children, and 'thanks be' that I was alive. He was worried about me but mostly about the reputation of his inn. So he had let me stay in the room for two days already. He did nothing else for me except to put a dirty rag around my head to stop the bleeding and to bring some watery soup twice a day."

"At the end of the third day, he turned me out with nothing but the same clothes I had been wearing this whole time. They were torn, filthy, and stank of blood and sweat and vomit. Outside the inn, I took a few stumbling steps and slumped against a wall. My head felt as though it had been smashed like a melon. When I touched it, I felt a sticky warmth on my fingers, and then I felt nothing at all. I later sensed myself lying on my back bumping along a road, but I could not tell if I was dreaming or waking."

"When full consciousness finally returned, even though my vision was blurred, I recognized the face looking down at me. It was the face of the chaperone, the 'old witch,' as I had last thought of her. She was wiping my face with a damp cloth. She held me down easily enough when I tried to get up. She had a more difficult time contending with the insults I then rained on her. Finally, impatiently brushing away a tear, she began to tell me what had happened. That is when I first wished that I had died."

"This old woman had tried to get word to me, to warn me to flee alone, to forget Elena. Poor Elena. My love for her had blinded me. I should have seen that she did not have the courage for the ordeal. She confessed to her father at the last moment, pleading for his mercy for the two of us, confident that he would give it. I later learned that he sent Elena to a convent in the mountains, where she had her baby. Elena's father hired the assassins to kill me. Her chaperone went into hiding, but first she sent her man-servant to try to forewarn me. Failing that he was to watch and bring her news of me. He it was that found me at the inn and brought my guardian chaperone to me."

"My new guardian, who seemed to have plenty of resources, assured me that I could stay with her but that the soldiers were looking for me. Nathan had reported that I was missing. He had also reported the theft of jewels and gold, without accusing me. The soldiers were less trusting, however, and were being pressured by some of Nathan's less forgiving customers. 'Or perhaps they are looking for this,' said the chaperone. The necklace. I had forgotten about it completely, but my guardian, as I now always have thought of her, had found it when she washed me and got me clean clothes."

"What I did next was in some ways my greatest crime. I ran away. I told myself that I needed time to regain Nathan's fortune for him. In truth I was too cowardly to face him. And too cowardly to confront Elena's father. I tried to give my guardian the necklace, but she wisely refused it."

"Once I was safely away, I became a vagabond. Eventually it

was the necklace that intervened in my unhappy affairs. I had been wandering aimlessly for weeks, begging for my food, waiting to be killed by assassins or by bandits. Even bandits, it seemed, shunned me, I looked so unfortunate. I was getting ready for sleep one evening, under the stars, as usual. The fire was burning down, and then they appeared, the two Djin you have seen in my manuscript. It was as though they sprang from the glowing embers. Some say that they are forged originally from fire and that it is their element."

"They sat on either side of the fire, studying me, while I looked from one to the other, spellbound, awaiting my fate. We remained so for several minutes. My scant religious instruction told me they were demons, probably sent by the Prince of Demons himself to take me away. Perhaps this was the case with Bladen. She it was that broke the silence."

"'I am Bladen. I will offer you counsel, as will my sister, Maiden, if she will deign to speak without riddles. I am the blunt one. I and others of our kind wish to obtain the necklace you carry in the pouch around your neck. If you prefer not to give it to us, you may choose to destroy it yourself, as you please. In return I promise to deliver your enemy and all his goods, including his daughter Elena, into your hands. Those who attacked you will be brought to justice. These promises I will keep. Think upon them'."

"What she said kindled more than a spark of interest, but while she spoke, I never lost sight of the other one, watching her out of the corner of my eye. Now I turned to look at her. Her mouth seemed to be on the edge of a smile. But, as she said nothing, I was about to turn back to Bladen. Then I heard that song-like voice for the first time. Bladen's voice was flat and dull by contrast."

"'Would you like me to keep you warm as you sleep tonight'?"

"'I knew it,' I all but shouted at her, with something like triumph in my voice. "You mean to warm me if I do what she asked. You are temptresses."

"'No, I will only warm you if you do not do as she asks,' came the reply."

"Though I did not understand immediately what she was saying to me, I again was captivated by the music in her voice and by her smile. Both made me want to trust her. I hesitated. Numerous questions began occurring to me now, but Maiden spoke again with the disconcerting ability to give words to my thoughts before I could. They cannot read our thoughts, but they usually can guess what they are."

"'Do not doubt that she will wholly fulfill her promise, so long as you do what she says. And she is not asking for your soul, only for a necklace that is of no use to you'."

"Those last words pierced my conscience, reminding me that the necklace was not mine but Nathan's. 'Do you not also wish to see the necklace destroyed?' I asked Maiden."

"'No. It has brought about only good for these many centuries. I would like to see it continue its mission, and if it is destroyed, I will have failed in mine.'"

"'And what is its mission? And yours?' I asked."

"'You would not have to ask those questions had you paid closer attention to Nathan's story of the necklace.' She looked at me with those amazing candle-flame eyes."

"Bladen, who had watched silently all this while, seized this opportunity. 'You see, she cannot give a direct answer to your question. Forget her and accept my offer. You have already stolen more than you can repay in a lifetime by yourself. If you simply destroy this necklace, you can restore the price of all that you stole and lost, including a rich replacement for Nathan's necklace'."

"'She will do as she says,' again replied Maiden, in response to the question I was forming in my mind. And then, as though to conclude the debate, Maiden added, 'And you could not be so childish as to believe all that foolishness about the Chief Minister and his heaven-inspired speech and the necklace. Is it not just an old man's story after all'?"

"I was by now catching on to Maiden's sometimes indirect manner of speaking, and I was paying close attention to the meaning of what she did not say but meant. Bladen was right about that at least. Maiden would not answer me directly, but what Bladen did not realize was that Maiden's riddles got my attention and made me think. Then too, her words, and her song-like tone, reminded me of Nathan. I seemed to hear him chanting the 'Legend of the Necklace,' and I smiled at the recollection, and with this recollection came other memories."

"The necklace was a sign of the unity that should exist among all who worshipped the one God. Such was its mission. The Chief Minister and Nathan and now Maiden all said that this was so. Maiden must indeed be the Guardian of the Necklace. I came to my decision. Bladen knew what it was before I even spoke."

"'Fool!' she hissed, her face pinched but still fierce. She made me shiver more than the night did. She burst suddenly into an intense flame that strangely added to the chill of the night. Then she disappeared, leaving behind only a coil of smoke that settled onto the damp ground and dissolved."

"Maiden smiled almost apologetically. She began to glow like a violet ember, just before she too disappeared. Behind her remained only a ribbon of smoke that rose into the night. I sat for a while, musing, relieved. As I rolled into my blankets, I knew that the next day I would begin my journey back to Nathan. Then I thought, as I noticed that my feet were like two pieces of ice, that it would not have been a bad bargain had I accepted Maiden's offer of warmth. But I knew that it could not be, and if it could, it would probably be dangerous to consort with a spirit, however good. I sighed and rubbed my feet together. Several times I almost fell asleep but then my body would begin shaking with the cold."

"As one of these near-sleep moments crept over me, I heard Maiden's whisper and felt her warm breath on my cheek: 'As my sister would, I always keep my word'."

"'I began to protest, remembering tales of men losing their souls to demon women. I looked behind me. As I did not see her and could not feel her body physically next to mine, I quieted down, but I remained tense. Then it began. At first I felt a gradual warming throughout my body. Then it seemed that a cloud of pleasure caressed me, bringing a sensuous tingling all over me. The warmth and pleasure intensified so gradually that I was hardly aware of what was happening before I reached a point when I was convinced I would burst into flame and be consumed like the phoenix. I would die happily. Then the tingling subsided, succeeded by a cooling but finally warming embrace. I slept deeply and long for the first time since I had left Nathan."

Brother Bartolomeo remained unmoving for some moments, with the three listeners respecting his silence. Alan had unconsciously moved closer to the middle of the bench to huddle with the girls in front of the story teller. Thea discovered that a steady stream of tears ran down her cheeks. Cass, remembering something Thea used to say about going to confession, tried to lighten the mood, not very successfully, by telling the monk that she would not give him a penance for this confession. She was more truly supportive when she simply went to him and gave him a gentle hug. Brother Bartolomeo got to his feet: "I must leave you for a while, but I shall return with the provisions for your journey," he said simply and then left the room.

Thea, who had been about to sing the monk's praises for his story and pepper him with questions, instead asked Cass, "What journey do you think he is talking about?"

Before Cass could answer, Alan jumped in: "Home I hope. I'm tired and hungry, and I think I'm catching a cold from my dunking this morning ... or whenever it was. How long have we been here anyway? Someone must have come to rescue us from the fire in our house by now."

"It's tough to keep track of time, Alan," answered Cass, "but I think we have just been here a little over half a day, perhaps just a few seconds at home." Turning to Thea, she said, "I don't know what our journey is. I hope Brother Bartolomeo will tell us. Poor Brother. I'm glad he made the right decision in the end anyway.

Maiden was glad too, it seems."

"I think he made the wrong decision," said Alan. He could have been rich. Even Maiden says so. Oh, and I don't believe Maiden warmed him at all. He must have had a fever and was dreaming. Ouch!"

"Hmpf. Did you dream that, Halán?" asked Maiden, now visible and standing next to Alan.

"You burned my ear with something," complained Alan.

"I merely touched your ear. You will not even have a blister," rebutted Maiden, "Although your right ear will carry a blush mark," she added.

"Maiden, didn't Brother Bartolomeo rescue Elena from the convent?" asked Thea hopefully.

"No, but he did get his son from the nuns. They were happy that the father wished to have his son with him. Then he did what he should have done in the first place. He returned to Nathan, who forgave him, and married one of Nathan's daughters. That made him Nathan's heir, of both his goods and his craft. He and his wife raised Elena's son as their own and had one of their own. After his wife died, he became a monk here. Both sons followed their mother's Jewish religion. They have gone north to the city of Toledo, where one is a scholar and one is a master jeweler. The Jews are most welcome there and do important works."

Maiden turned her attention to Cass. "You called Brother Bartolomeo "poor," but he is a wealthy man, wealthier than most." Cass nodded and smiled to herself, remembering what Brother Bartolomeo had said about getting used to Maiden's way of speaking in riddles at times."

"Thea, who had a puzzled expression on her face, asked Maiden, "Did you say her sons were Jews?"

"Yes," answered Maiden, waiting for the next question that she knew would come.

"But how can that be? He is Catholic, and his wife would have had to become a Catholic or at least have agreed to raise the children Catholic." Thea was quite serious, almost argumentative.

Maiden looked at Thea for several moments. The candles of her eyes flickered dangerously, then held steady. She answered in an even tone. "In the strict sense you are correct. Indeed Christians, Muslims, and Jews all have that same rule for their followers, but they do not apply it too strictly. Perhaps the thirteenth century is more tolerant than yours." Now it was Thea's turn for flashing eyes. Before she could respond, however, Maiden continued.

"Brother Bartolomeo's wife did become a Catholic, sensing that she could help him to become a better Catholic more easily than making him a convert to Judaism. But they agreed that the boys should learn about both religions and then make their own choices. Both became close to their grandfather Nathan and chose his religion."

Again Thea was ready to argue with Maiden. This time it was Cass that cut her off by asking Thea's earlier question: "What is the journey Brother Bartolomeo spoke of? Is it far," she added, sensing that it was more than an afternoon's walk.

"Not far and yet far, perhaps too far for one of you." She looked at Alan who responded by frowning and rubbing his ear that still tingled from Maiden's touch. "Have a care for your brother Halán, Cassandra. He needs more of your help, the kind of help you gave him when he was younger." Cass felt stung by this comment. At that moment she remembered that her mother worried that she had been arguing with Alan of late, or, worse, had no time for him at all. She turned away from Maiden for just a moment. When she turned back, Maiden was gone. She looked fretfully at Alan, but he simply shrugged.

Brother Bartolomeo's footsteps approached. He entered, carrying with him three bundles of bread and cheese and three skins of water with straps so they could be easily carried. "You will look like simple country folk returning from the market. Also, you should all wear these on your head." He handed them kerchiefs with strings that tied under their chins. The girls quickly had them in place.

When they looked at Alan, they had to laugh. He was having difficulty tying the strings under his chin, and they had never seen a teenage boy in a kerchief. He frowned and was about to take it off, but Brother Bartolomeo assured him that no one else would think anything of it.

"Children of farmers learn to keep their hair clean, my lad. Now, you will all leave the city by the east gate. Past the gate stay on the main road for several miles until you come to a fjord where another road crosses the river. Follow this road to the other side of the river and continue straight on. You should arrive at the village well before sundown. Just beyond the village is a hill with just a few houses, a walled-in cemetery, and the ruins of Italica."

"The city in the 'Legend of the Necklace'," said Thea.

"Yes, that is why I believe you should go there. Italica has impressive remains of its Roman inhabitants even after fifteen hundred years. I don't know what you will find there, but since that is where the necklace was fashioned, it is a good place for you to find out why it has brought you here."

"Before we leave, I have one other question," requested Thea.

"Oh, yes, of course," interrupted Cass. "What did you do with the necklace? Oops, sorry, Thea," she added quickly, as Thea reached both hands toward her in a strangling motion.

Brother Bartolomeo laughed. "I see what you are asking, both of you that is. I was wondering when that question would arise. Some time ago I gave the necklace to my younger son. He was my apprentice jeweler. He took it with him to Toledo and keeps it in a cabinet, just as his grandfather did. I hope he does not look for it for a while. If he does, my guess is that he will not find it. No harm though. He knows about its guardian."

"All right, on your way. Enough questions for now," said Brother Bartolomeo. "There are adventures ahead. First, let me give you my blessing." He approached them one at a time. He rested the palms of his hands on the head of each in turn and moved his lips in a whispered prayer. Thea knelt before him. Alan hesitated, then followed her example. Cass first looked directly into the monk's eyes and saw their deep, hard-earned tranquility. She thought how foolish she had been to think him poor in any way. Still standing, she bowed her head for his blessing. Brother Bartolomeo led them out by a different gate, one next to the great tower.

"Climbing this would have been something," said Alan. I wish I could have gone up there."

"Since when have you become so brave?" blurted Cass before she could stop herself. Looking at Alan, she made her face into an apology.

"Right, lad. I had the same thought as you myself when I was your age," laughed Brother Bartolomeo. "From up there you can see all the way to Italica. The Muslims built this tower, with the help of the Jews nearly a hundred years ago. It is called the Giralda because of the winding ramp inside that swings upwards to the top. I have a feeling you will get your chance to climb it one day, Brother Alan." He patted Alan companionably on the back. Alan would later remember the monk's prediction.

The three took their leave, Cass and Thea with affectionate hugs. Alan reached out his hand, but the monk pulled him into a bear hug. It was a couple of hours past noon so the sun would be at their backs most of the way. The air was warm and the road dusty dry. Nonetheless, when they were just a mile or so along the road, they looked back upon Seville with a feeling of regret at leaving. They decided to linger in view of the city and have their lunch. As they broke the bread, the crusts crackled and puffs of warmth escaped to greet them. The cheese was hard and crumbly, but sharp and savory. There was also a sunny orange in each bag.

"I move for a vote of thanks to Brother Bartolomeo," mumbled Cass through a mouthful of food. The other two, without pausing in their eating, nodded their heads in happy agreement.

# Chapter IV

# Where Do We Go From Here?

The companions finished their meal seated by the roadside. A few other travelers passed by on their way to or from Seville. It was the siesta hour, after the noon meal, so most people were seated in a shady spot by the roadside, eating or just resting.

"This was a treat," said Thea contentedly.

"Yes, and now I think it would be a good idea to figure out where we are," suggested Cass.

"In Spain in the thirteenth century," complained Alan.

"You know what I mean," replied Cass. "What can this quest be that Maiden says we are on? And what part does the necklace play? And where do we go from here, other than to Italica, which...."

"Sounds like fun," said Thea. Cass looked at her quizzically.

"Why us?" challenged Alan. Though he meant the question as an objection, the girls took him seriously. It was an important question.

"Because Maiden set our house on fire," said Cass with a smile. "Seriously, because we have the necklace," she answered after a moment's thought.

"How much do you know, or remember, about your Grand-mother Esther?" asked Thea. "How did she come to have the neck-lace? And to leave it to you?"

"I have no idea how the necklace got from Spain in the thir-teenth century to my grandmother's in Long Island in the twenti-eth century. I don't know why us or why grandmother. I know very little about Grandmother Esther. She was my mother's mother." Cass caught a look from Alan and paused.

"Sorry. *Our* mother's mother," Cass corrected herself. "She lived alone. Anyway there was some major break between our dad and Grandmother Esther before I was born. No one would ever talk about it. We never visited her. Mom couldn't even talk about grandmother when dad was around. It's a shame, too, because dad was an only child, and his parents had died young, so we never knew any of our grandparents. We never heard about a grandfather to go along with Grandmother Esther. I always wondered if that had something to do with the break between her and dad. Dad would have wanted to know about family history."

"We don't have any relatives at all, or none that we know of, other than our parents," observed Alan, "not like you with all your Irish and German cousins," he said to Thea. Thea ignored the note of resentment, knowing it was nothing personal.

"But," continued Cass, "in the last few years, I knew that mom regularly got in touch with her mom. I would hear mom on the phone, when dad was not around, making arrangements to meet her. Mom would take the train up to Penn Station, have lunch nearby with Grandmother and come back on the early afternoon train. I think grandmother came down here once, and they had lunch downtown." Cass paused and smiled. "By here I mean Philadelphia, not Spain, of course. When grandmother died, mom went to the funeral by herself. I wanted to go, but I knew that Dad would not allow me to. When mom came back she gave me a pack-age. Grandmother had made sure it would get to the right person. She had printed in large block letters on the paper wrapping and on the box inside, "FROM GRANDMOTHER ESTHER TO GRANDDAUGHTER CASSANDRA. The box contained the necklace and a letter."

"The letter you were showing me the night of the fire," said Thea.

"Right. The letter was a big mystery. At first I couldn't make any sense out of it at all. I spent so much time trying to figure it out that I have it memorized, or at least I did before coming here. OK, I think I have it. This is what she said:

> *My Dear Granddaughter Cassandra,*
>
> *I leave this necklace to you confident that you can solve its mysteries. Perhaps you will discover why I decided not to make a second journey. You are part of the reason. Your mother has told me you are intelligent and a free spirit. I like that. So does your mother, though she might not tell you. I believe that you will discover the full meaning of the necklace and what it requires. If you do, you will help many in their time of great need.*
>
> *I am sorry to have to ask so much of you. There will be dangers where you will go, but you will have a guide, and the necklace itself is a source of hope and consolation, even in the midst of hardship and sorrow. Now that you have the necklace, you can expect to meet the guide soon.*
>
> *I know but little about the necklace, and even that little bit I fear to explain directly. I worry about such knowledge falling into the wrong hands (and I do not mean your father, dear). Here is all I dare say: To fly through time and space, remember this. Choose water only as the way. Starve the wolf. Touch no one; let no one touch you.*
>
> *Your Grateful Grandmother Esther*

"Wow, how did you figure out what to do from that," exclaimed Thea. "It would have been no help at all to me. How did you guess that fire was a portal?"

"It was probably good that I didn't have much time to think," answered Cass. "Flying through time and, especially, space sounded like a good idea at the moment. For the rest, I guessed contraries. Mother had often told me that her mother was a touch person, couldn't talk to someone without touching them. So when her letter said 'Touch no one,' something clicked in my mind about opposites. Water and fire. Starve and eat. No one and everyone."

Thea shook her head as she repeated, "wow."

"I guess dad was right," said Alan with a note of wonder. "He always said your name suited you. Cassandra was that Greek lady who could see the future and solve riddles, a See-something."

"A Seer," corrected Thea.

Cass smiled and bowed to Thea and to Alan, touching each in turn. "Thanks," she said, "but I'm afraid this is about the extent of what we know from Grandmother Esther. "I think her need for the necklace was different from ours. We may have already learned more from Maiden and Brother Bartolomeo about the necklace than she needed to know," she added.

"I don't think so," grumbled Alan. "What have we learned from them, other than…." He stopped abruptly and looked over his shoulder, nervously rubbing his right ear where Maiden had left her mark. "Um, well maybe we have learned something useful," concluded Alan. Cass and Thea both laughed.

"All right," said Cass, "let's brainstorm about the necklace. I'll start. We've learned that we have a lot to learn." They all laughed again. "But seriously, we need the necklace for its powers, but also to help us to understand our quest. OK, you're next, Alan."

Alan frowned but obeyed. "Well, the necklace is very valuable, probably worth a lot of money," he said. Cass groaned. "Just kidding. Besides, Maiden is its guardian and wouldn't let anyone have it if she didn't want them to. There. How's that?"

"My turn," said Thea promptly. "Religion is very important to the necklace. God sent a messenger to put the thought of it into the craftsman's mind. It has a guardian angel. It stands for the three religions."

"And how they are all related," added Cass, building on Thea's insight.

"Correct," answered Thea, "and it is of Jewish workmanship. That's fitting because the Jews are the oldest of the three religions.'

"Yes, the Sunstone represents the Jews," said Cass.

"And Nathan and his grandson that he later gave the necklace to were both Jews," said Alan, drawn into the flow of facts, interesting facts. He paused and looked at Cass: "Everybody has—or had—grandparents except us, Cass. Although I guess you had a grandmother, now that I hear what you've said." Cass had never realized how much her brother missed having relatives. She wondered why she had assumed that not having a larger family never affected Alan the way it did her. Perhaps because he always seemed to be content with his experiments and solving math problems.

"The two aqua stones in the Necklace stand for the Muslims and the Catholics," both descended in some way from the Jews," continued Thea, "which is theologically correct," she added with a look at the others. "It is a source of power for good," she continued. "We just have to figure out how."

"If Bladen and that other gang don't get to it first. They probably know how to use it for bad purposes, or at least keep it from doing good," said Cass.

"Don't forget the wolf," said Alan, "the sign of the Romans."

"The Romans or whoever happens to be the current rulers," suggested Cass.

"Cass, do you remember how we used to get into big arguments about religion and then not talk to each other for days?" asked Thea.

"Yes, and just like our dads," answered Cass. "My dad says that religions have done more harm than good. He doesn't say so in his history classes at the university, but everyone knows that's what he thinks."

"And my dad said that without religions people would be even worse." Thea paused for a moment, thinking. "It was at a dinner one night with both our families. Your dad gave all those examples of crimes connected to religions. I stayed awake half the night worrying. Your dad is very convincing."

"I wonder how our fathers—and mothers—remained friends for so long," replied Cass.

"Oh, because they lived through the war together and saw what happened, especially at the end," answered Thea thoughtfully.

The sharing of memories might have continued, except that the companions were interrupted by a woman from the increasing stream of peasants returning to their farms in the area or the village nearby. "You, boy, you can help me carry some of these goods to the village, if you are going that far. I'll give you a piece of silver."

The voice belonged to a sturdy woman with a baby nestled into a cloth sling resting on her bosom. She was having difficulty managing the baby, a couple of bulging sacks, and a potted plant. The sacks were somehow squeezed between her left arm and her body. The plant was balanced between her right hip and arm. She clutched her baby in both hands. She looked at Alan expectantly.

"We are going to the village, Alan. Why don't you help the lady," urged Thea. The woman smiled approvingly at Thea and then looked meaningfully from Alan to the potted plant. Alan took it from her, relieved to find that it weighed only a few pounds. An hour or so later, as they arrived at the edge of the village, Cass was carrying one of the sacks; Thea was holding the sleeping baby, and Alan had decided that the plant was much heavier than he first thought. The woman gave a small silver coin to Alan, thanking him. She apologized to Cass and Thea that she couldn't afford more.

"If you get tired of visiting the ruins, come back to the village and ask for Alicia, which is my name. I will be baking this afternoon." By now a number of children had arrived to help the returning peasant women. The companions thanked her for the invitation and took their leave.

"That was fun," declared Thea. "I felt like a medieval villager on market day. We must look like we belong here."

"You were very helpful, Alan," said Cass.

"What could I do? She practically ordered me." Cass smiled and thought to herself, as they walked toward the ruins, that Alicia and the other women would not be easy persons to say 'no' to.

In a short time they found themselves in the midst of the remains of the old Roman city of Italica. Most of the buildings had been at least partially torn down and the stone used elsewhere, in the village or in Seville. What remained were mostly the foundations. These showed signs of elaborate patrician estates. An examination of some of the remains revealed that in many cases the floors of marble or mosaic were largely intact. The original roads were fully intact, constructed of boulders carefully fitted together and so huge that they would be in place for centuries to come. A few recent homes had been erected a little farther on, where the ground sloped upward, but the people of the area mostly left the ancient city undisturbed, out of respect or superstition or both.

The companions continued to walk along one of the roads, past the cemetery at the top of the slope, and then down a gentle incline until the road and foundations disappeared into the undergrowth. They turned back, lazily, in the late afternoon sun, still with no more sense of purpose than to further inspect the elaborate floors. As they retraced their steps they had the feeling of visiting an outdoor art museum where the paintings were on the ground instead of hanging on walls. By now—the thirteenth century that is—the works of art had already outlasted their creators some fifteen hundred years.

"Look here." Cass was studying a large mosaic. Pictured in the center was a gigantic bearded figure riding a chariot drawn by some sort of sea monster, most of whose form had been worn away by centuries of foot traffic. In the giant's right hand was a long spear ending in three prongs. "This has to be Poseidon, the Sea God," exclaimed Cass.

"That would be Neptune, the Roman Sea God, since Italica was a Roman Colony," offered Thea promptly. As usual she was correct, but Cass was too interested in the mosaic to be annoyed. Neptune dominated the scene in colorful brown, red, and green stones. Surrounding him in black figures against a white background was every sort of sea creature. Cass and Thea started naming them.

"Sea-horse." "Alligator." "Hippo." "Porpoise." "Fish." "Whale." "Eel."

Forming the outer edge of the mosaic, where the companions stood, were small human-like figures riding pelicans and spearing fish. The effect was so lifelike that the companions could fancy that they were submerged in the watery scene rather than looking on from the dusty dry ground surrounding it.

"I have a crazy idea," said Cass, "but it's worth a try. If we stand on the mosaic, it might act as real water and be a channel for the necklace to take us back to the time when people still lived here. We know the necklace came from here."

Thea, excited by the suggestion, promptly followed Cass's lead, stepping onto the mosaic waves. Alan, who did not share in the girls' enthusiasm, looked both tired and hungry. He made an altogether different proposal. "No. Let's go back to the village and look for Alicia," he grumbled. "In case you haven't noticed, it's getting late." Nothing Cass or Thea said could budge him. Finally in frustration, Cass decided to force him to join them. Slowly, deliberately she undid the necklace and then held it poised, ready to refasten it. Alan shrugged uneasily but did not move.

"It's a stupid idea anyway. You need real water or fire." Alan's voice was partly taunting, partly worried.

Cass picked up on the taunting part, which irritated her all the more because she guessed that Alan was right. Her idea probably wouldn't work. Partly because she was angry at Alan and partly because the idea still attracted her, she went on with it even though her brother still held back. She would later deeply regret her stubbornness. "Last chance," she said. Still Alan did not move. Cass positioned the wolf's fangs over the rim of gold and then pressed the fangs toward each other. They fastened suddenly and firmly around the gold catch, completing the circle of the necklace. Cass instantly heard the rumble of waves and felt herself engulfed in pulsating light. From a great distance somewhere behind her, she heard someone calling her name. At the last instant she reached out and shouted her brother's name. There was no answer.

# Chapter V

# Italica

C ass and Thea found themselves standing by a pile of dirt. A wiry young man was digging a ditch, with his back to them. Thea was still holding on to Cass's arm but now let go. As the man threw another bucket of dirt onto the pile, he caught sight of the girls. He put his bucket down and mopped his forehead. Looking up at Cass, he spoke as though he already knew her. "I did not hear you come. Am I late for...." He stopped abruptly, stared at Cass intently for another moment, and then he apologized. "Excuse me. I mistook you for someone else." He smiled a greeting to Cass and then to Thea, but he quickly turned his attention back to Cass, still with a hint of dismay in his eyes.

The girls could not at first respond. They were just beginning to realize that Cass had guessed correctly. The water displayed in the Neptune mosaic had acted as a portal. They had gone back to a time in Italica when it was still inhabited, but they were not sure precisely when. "Roman times," thought Thea with a kindling of excitement. Cass, on the other hand, was regretting that she had acted hastily, without making a plan first. She became aware that they continued to stare at the man without responding to his greeting. First putting her right hand to her throat to check that the necklace was secure but covered, she spoke. "I am Cassandra and this is Theadora," she said. She used their full names to make a proper impression. Then not knowing what else to say, she explained, rather lamely: "We were watching you work."

"I am Jonathan," the man replied, observing them both. He noticed how different the two were. Theadora's coppery red hair, blue-green eyes, and fair complexion indicated to Jonathan that she was probably a barbarian from the north. Cassandra was a couple of inches shorter and olive complected, with dark hair and eyes to match. He marveled at how much she resembled his own Mara. He noticed that Cass and Thea were both wearing sleeveless linen shifts. Cass also wore a veil around her neck and shoulders, out of modesty or taste, or both, assumed Jonathan.

Observing that the two young women began to fidget under his scrutiny, Jonathan inquired, "Can I help you? If you are looking for someone, you have come at a bad time. No one else has been here all morning. The mistress left so that she would not have to watch me tearing up her courtyard." He smiled easily, his teeth showing white against his deeply tanned face. "And she took all the female slaves with her, so you cannot be gossiping with them."

Hearing this, Cass and Thea promptly overcame their shyness and any lingering sense of disorientation.

"We are not slaves," corrected Thea.

"And we are not looking for gossip," retorted Cass, "but if we were, why should you think it a waste of time?" She was clearly rebuking the man before her, but she could not get really angry. He was much too pleasant in looks and speech for that.

"Well spoken," replied Jonathan with an approving laugh. "I am properly put in my place."

"Are you a slave?" asked Thea.

Jonathan's face eased again into a ready collection of smile lines. "You would think so, judging from this messy task. But no, we Jews are free workers. Today I am a plumber. Normally I am one of the builders, working on the amphitheater, but this citizen"—he cocked his head at the house—"has influence, so I have been assigned to do some work on his private property. No, I am not a slave, but I admit that at first I thought that you were," he said, addressing Theadora. From where do you come?"

"From Seville," chorused Thea and Cass in perfect time.

"From over there, a few hours' walk," continued Thea, pointing in what she guessed—correctly as it happened—was the General direction of Seville. She realized as she spoke that she did not even know if Seville were there in whatever time they had happened into. Jonathan, however, accepted her explanation without question.

"And you can help us I hope," added Cass. "We have gotten separated from my brother. Have you seen a boy of fifteen that looks something like me?" She had been worrying about Alan for some moments now.

"No, but I can assure you that if I had seen him, I would remember. I am relieved to hear that you are under your brother's protection, though." Cass frowned at this notion and was about to make a retort, when Thea explained with a half laugh.

"Under Alan's protection? More the other way around. Cass is our leader." Now Jonathan looked both uncertain and concerned.

"And why does that bother you?" demanded Cass. Then she caught herself. "I'm sorry. Never mind me. We could use some help, and not just to find Alan. Please tell us what year this is and where we are."

Jonathan found the questions strange, but he also recognized the anxiety in Cass's voice. He looked at the two young women with increasing concern. "They really seem to be quite lost," he thought. Then he came to a decision. "I do not know where you are from. I know of no place named Seville. Most importantly, you do not understand your situation. Of course I will help you."

"To start with, you are in Italica, patrician city of the Roman Colony of Spain. A short distance from here is the commercial city of Hispalis, which is probably the same as your Seville, according to what you told me, Mistress Theadora."

"Yes, they must be the same," agreed Theadora. "It was called Seville when we were there."

Jonathan shrugged at this but continued his explanations. "We are in the tenth year of the reign of the Emperor Hadrian, who was born here in Italica."

"Hadrian," repeated Cass.

"He's the one who built the wall in England, sometime in the second century A.D.," explained Thea.

Cass for once was grateful for Thea's encyclopedic memory. "Then we are at least in the same century when the necklace was made," she said hopefully to Thea.

"The necklace that you are wearing, that you were checking on a few minutes ago?" asked Jonathan. Noticing Cass' nervous smile, he reassured her. "Do not worry. Your necklace and whatever secrets you seem to be hiding are safe with me."

"The necklace is perhaps something else you can help us with," said Cass. "We've been told to learn everything we can about it. We have come here hoping to find its maker and its owner. Its maker was a Jew."

"That is typical," responded Jonathan. "A Jewish maker and probably a Roman owner. Speaking of owners, I had better finish my job here. Then you must come home with me for lunch, and we will address your questions."

"Thank you," replied Cass. "That will be wonderful." The mention of lunch made her think again of Alan. He had wanted to return to the village for some of Alicia's baking. "Thea...dora and I will look for my brother while you finish."

"No, no," said Jonathan immediately, adding "please, ladies" and a smile when the two companions turned back to him. "I said before that you do not understand your situation. I should have explained right away. You are strangers here. You might be stopped and questioned by the patricians or the soldiers, and that could lead to difficulties. I will tell you more later. But for now stay here on the patio. I will not be long."

The girls agreed to wait. While Jonathan finished his work, they discussed the situation.

"Well the water in the mosaic worked," said Thea to Cass. They looked at each other, the same thought occurring to them both in an instant. They looked down at their sandaled feet. Brushing away some clods of earth from Jonathan's digging, they discovered the mosaic. "Sea horses," exclaimed Thea.

"Alligators," echoed Cass.

"Cass, we are in the exact same spot!"

"But eleven centuries earlier, during the reign of Emperor Hadrian." Cass's voice held a note of awe. "What Dad would not do to be here. But I wish we could find Alan."

"Maiden will watch out for him," Thea said. "That's what Guardian Angels are for. Besides, for some unknown reason, she likes him in spite of himself. I can tell."

They now heard Jonathan's voice and realized that he had probably been talking to them for some time while he worked in the ditch. "It will be the finest amphitheater outside of Rome itself," he concluded with pride. He paused from his labors long enough to point towards what looked like stone walls rising and facing each other from two nearby hills. "It occupies a good deal of the valley. You can just make out parts of it, the upper seats."

"Very impressive," thought Cass, looking where Jonathan directed, but she remained quiet. Thea admired the distant construction aloud, prompting Jonathan to provide additional explanations while he started cleaning his tools. Cass did not want to prolong Jonathan's task. She was anxious to continue their quest—after finding Alan. Nonetheless her surroundings attracted her attention. She allowed her gaze to wander. The patio was the back porch of the villa, connecting the main house to some gardens with gravel walks lined by white stone pillars. To one side of the patio stood the statue of a woman, a goddess, guessed Cass. The sculptor had paid unusual attention to details of dress, depicting the flowing gown drawn in snugly under full breasts and a mantle draped in folds from the shoulders to below the waist.

Cass admired the garden, walks, and especially the statue, but she soon became restless once again. She turned her attention back to Jonathan and Thea. As she did so, she noticed Jonathan cleaning a dirt-encrusted piece of pipe. It was of an unusual shape, the opening reminding her more of the open end of a jacket sleeve. Jonathan had scraped away the dirt and crust of age to reveal some markings. Cass had to look closely to make them out. "CAAI," she recited aloud.

"Those letters stand for 'Colony of Italica of the Divine Augustus,' in the old Latin, of course," explained Jonathan. "That means that Caesar Augustus was emperor when this pipe was made, so it is over a hundred years old."

"Caesar Augustus," exclaimed Thea. "He was emperor when Jesus was born. This is amazing."

"He was also the emperor who tore down the Temple in Jerusalem," said Jonathan matter-of-factly. "Jews build. Others tear down. Look at this pipe. For more than a century it carried warm water for the baths of the patricians who lived here. Good workmanship I call that. If you look more closely beneath those letters, you can see the initials 'sn' and next to them the outline of a shofar, a ram's horn used by Jews at religious celebrations. The pipe-maker, whose initials were sn, was Jewish."

"Indoor plumbing and hot water?" asked Cass in some surprise.

"All of these villas have such plumbing and have had for many years. In the village and in the city of Hispalis, only the public baths have it. My part is finished here. I have replaced that pipe, but I am keeping this old damaged one as a reminder of the workmanship and the worker. That is his immortality, you see." Cass looked at Jonathan and recognized that he was smiling but quite serious. She was impressed by the accomplishment of the earlier workman who had proudly left his mark on his work, but she was more impressed by the sense of connection that Jonathan shared with this long-dead 'sn'. She also sensed that he wanted her to join that connection.

"Hard to believe isn't it," remarked Thea. "Jonathan was explaining to me how the lead pipe is buried under the patio. When water flows through it picks up the warmth from the patio surface and carries it to the baths. The stone patio, including the mural, absorb the heat from the sun."

As they left the villa, Cass asked, "were your people always such great builders, then?"

Looking pointedly at Cass, Jonathan said, "our people are not the architects, but, yes, we are and have been the stone masons and the carpenters and pipe fitters and the laborers. But some of us are not as skilled as others," he laughed, looking at his mud spattered leather apron. "Jews have always been builders," he continued. The Second Temple was one of the wonders of the world before the Romans leveled it. Augustus, as you said, Mistress Theadora. Now we build for others, instead of having them destroy our buildings." Jonathan spoke without any anger. Cass, however, recognized an edge to his tone, perhaps implying that his people's work would remain long after the Roman rulers were no more. Cass also had recognized that Jonathan had included her in "our people."

Jonathan lapsed into silence, thinking he had perhaps sounded too boastful. Cass and Thea respected his quiet, having a great deal to occupy their own minds. Cass was taking note of the roadway. It was the exact same road that the companions had encountered in the thirteenth century when they first arrived in Italica. Only now it was eleven centuries earlier, and the stones were a bit smoother. Looking fixedly at the road reminded Cass of Maiden's riddle about their journey: "Not far and yet far, perhaps too far for one." This thought brought back her anxiety for Alan. She hoped that Thea was right and that Maiden was watching out for him. But she also remembered Madean's other words: "You will have to rely on yourselves and each other." Cass would have preferred to search for Alan, but she knew they had to be patient and be guided by Jonathan.

While Cass was thinking and worrying about Alan, Thea was busy examining the people they encountered along the way. Some were strolling leisurely, others hastening to some appointment or task. Of the strollers, most were women of various ages, dressed almost as elegantly as the goddess statue that Cass had pointed out to her before they left the patio. Their hair was braided or done up on top of their heads, held in place by silver pins and combs. They were attended by other women whom Thea knew must be household slaves, dressed more simply than their mistresses, but still elegantly. She realized that the light gray tunics she and Cass were wearing were plain, even in comparison to those worn by the slaves.

Thea took particular note that the women were invariably accompanied by at least one adult male. She also noticed that most of the people hurrying along looking busy, were men, alone or in the company of other men. They, like the women, wore comfortable, loose fitting tunics, but they wore no jewelry. The younger men typically wore plain tunics that came to the knees and were held in by a belt at the waist. Some of the older men wore free-flowing tunics or mantles bordered in rich purple or gold. An occasional soldier passed, armed with a breastplate and with a skirt of leather strips over a cloth undergarment.

"I can see why Jonathan thought we might look out of place here by ourselves," Thea observed to Cass. Even as she made this comment, however, she noticed that they had arrived at a market square where the patricians and their slaves mingled with villagers and farmers from the area. "Aha! Here we are. At least some of the people here are dressed like us," she noted as she recognized that she and Cass were dressed in the village women's ready-for-work style.

Cass couldn't help being drawn into Thea's fascination with their surroundings and, for a time, away from her concern about Alan. She examined the villagers and farmers. She was struck by

the thought they, their descendents that is, would still be here centuries from now, long after Italica had fallen into ruins and the
patricians were all but forgotten.

Jonathan asked them to stay close to him as he led them across
the square and into a side street for some way. Simple, square houses, tiny by comparison to the villas, lined the clean, narrow street.
The girls recognized that the square both joined and divided the
village and Italica. Jonathan stopped before the entrance to one of
the tidy houses just a few minutes from the square. He poked his
head inside and announced their presence. "Mara, we have guests."
He gestured for the girls to enter. It was a simple, one-room dwelling. To their left differently colored strips of material marked off
the living and sleeping area. It reminded Thea of pictures she had
seen of tents in a desert. The remaining space was occupied by a
large table that suggested frequent dinner guests. Beyond the table
another doorway, this one covered by a curtain.

"Welcome to our home, friends," answered a woman's voice
from beyond the curtained door. "I will join you as soon as I have
damped down the oven." The house was kept dark and cool, but the
voice assured them of a warm welcome and announced someone
young and vivacious. The voice, however, did not prepare them for
the person that now came through the curtains. Thea openly stared.
She was speechless. Cass rubbed her eyes, then laughed, then made
the second curtsy of her life, in Al-Andalus. She almost felt as
though she were curtseying before a mirror. She knew that Mara
was what she would look like ten years hence.

Mara laughed and returned the curtsey. "I have heard that it is
a good sign to find one's double," she said. Her laughter was due in
part to the looks of astonishment on the faces of her two guests, as
well as the pleased expression on her husband's face at not giving
away his surprise. It was also an expression of her pleasure at seeing
her own good looks in Cass's. "But come sit down, and thank you
for bringing the plumber with you." She smiled in gentle mockery
at her master builder. Cass recognized the tone as one that her

mother used to prod her father back to reality when he was being smug.

At lunch Thea and Cass discovered how hungry they were. There seemed to be plenty of food, even with two extra people at the table. When they had nearly finished the meal of bread, fish, vegetables, and fruit, Jonathan began the conversation. "Cassandra and Theadora are strangers, who recently came from Hispalis. How they came to be there or from whence, I am not certain, nor am I going to inquire. I am satisfied that they are honest and in need of help." He explained who Alan was. He also mentioned the necklace, which intensified Mara's already deep interest. Then he stopped and looked at Cass.

Cass knew that Jonathan had set the stage for her to ask about the necklace. She focused on the details she thought might be helpful in identifying the necklace if possible. "Supposedly the necklace was made at the request of the Chief Minister to the Roman Governor. The Chief Minister was Jewish, which I guess is why he went to a Jewish artisan for the necklace." Cass would have told their whole story, including answering Jonathan's implied "from whence" question. To do so, however, would take too long, and Jonathan already had made his own surmises about them and seemed satisfied. The information about the Chief Minister did not appear to be of much help. Mara and Jonathan knew the Jewish community of both Hispalis and Italica well, but they knew of no Jewish Chief Minister, though they noted that there might have been one before their arrival. Knowing that a Chief Minister of the Governor had commissioned the necklace might still help them to find it, or to find the maker.

"Cassandra, if you will show this necklace to Mara, she may know something of its maker," suggested Jonathan. "No piece of jewelry has escaped her attention in the two years we have lived here."

Cass, who was sitting beside Mara, removed her scarf to reveal the necklace adorning her neck. "A shame that you must keep something so beautiful hidden, especially since it compliments you so well," said Mara to Cass, who blushed. "It looks Jewish-made, but I do not recognize the particular style," continued Mara. "I will make inquiries among my friends and among the craftsmen. And I will ask about your brother."

"As will I," said Jonathan, "when I get back to my work at the amphitheater, which is where I must be going now. Try not to worry. We will find him if he is in Italica or here in the village. A word of caution, My Ladies. Do not go back to Italica. Here in the village is safer for you, although you will probably be asked questions even here. Tell anyone who asks that you visiting Mara and me. Cassandra, that will be no problem for you since you and Mara are practically twins. Theadora, you stay with Cassandra. Let her do the talking."

"That will be normal," laughed Thea. "Sorry, couldn't help myself," she added to Cass.

"I repeat, you will attract attention even in the village here, Theadora. Be careful." Jonathan was on his way out the door as he spoke this warning.

"What difficulties was Jonathan referring to?" Thea asked Mara.

"Well, first that you look like a barbarian from the north, and second that you are young and attractive," answered Mara. "Those are the difficulties. Most barbarians are slaves here in the south, and women with red hair and fair complexion are especially prized by the Romans. Some citizen could easily claim you as a runaway slave."

"Oh," said Thea somewhat nervously.

"As a slave?" asked Cass. She was dismayed.

"The Romans do not make slaves of the people here in Spain. Most of the population has become Romanized and is protected by imperial law. Slaves are taken only from peoples beyond the boundaries of the empire, or from those who rebel against Rome. There are still a number of tribesmen to the north who resist the Romans, and Theadora resembles their women strikingly. So heed

65

well Jonathan's warning."

"Now, I suggest we go first to the street of the artisans. Then I will take you to see if Jonathan has found out anything from the other workmen. Also you must see the new amphitheater. The patricians will think you are the slave of one of my customers, The-adora. A friend and I are dressmakers." The three women set off with high hopes. Cass's sense of adventure was fully restored as they set out.

Their inquiries, alas, proved fruitless. None of the craftsmen knew about the necklace, nor had anyone seen a stranger resembling Alan, though it was possible that they could have mistaken him for one of the boys of the village. The girls were disappointed. Moreover Thea was feeling the effects of the sun and the heat. Mara suggested they return to her house to rest, instead of visiting Jonathan at the amphitheater. Cass was further disappointed by this suggestion. When they did not find Alan in the village, she had decided that he must have gone to explore the amphitheater. She was herself curious to see it. Looking at Thea, however, and seeing the red blotches on her face, she agreed to the delay.

They retreated to the protective shade of the house. Cass and Thea stretched out on mats on the cool, clay floor, while Mara lay down behind the curtain in the corner. Cass lay awake, while listening carefully until she heard Thea's steady, deep breathing. Restless, she crept to the curtain and peeked under it. "Both asleep," she concluded to herself. She hesitated just for a moment before she slipped quietly out of the house.

Cass had dismissed Jonathan's warning, or rather she had mentally sidestepped it. "If people are used to seeing Mara in the city, they will think I am she, as long as they don't get too close. Anyway Thea is the only one who would be in danger." As she expected, no one stopped her or gave any sign of suspicion. The amphitheater was off limits to anyone but the workmen—and Mara, when she was coming to see Jonathan. Two soldiers were on guard and the entrance. Seeing them, Cass wished she had brought a jug of water or something else she could say was for her husband. She arranged her scarf as a veil so that it covered head and arms. She had seen that Mara wore long sleeves. Then she tried to adopt a smiling but modest expression as she approached. The soldiers returned her smile and never blinked.

Cass was impressed with the amphitheater from the moment she stepped into the entryway. She thought that this is what it must feel like to enter a canyon between two rock walls. Beyond the entryway was a field as large as a football field, but oval rather than square in shape. Rows and rows of seats surrounded the oval, making a gradual ascent to the top row, which was protected by a parapet. The outer coliseum walls were what Cass had seen from Italica. The grand scale of the place fascinated her. She imagined the people who would appear here. Thinly clad runners, a lone runner with a flaming torch, charioteers, wrestlers, orators, actors. She could hear in her mind the cheering by the sun-drenched spectators. Thea, who did gymnastics and loved to run, should be here, thought Cass, and she felt a momentary twinge of guilt. She had already seen a number of workmen about half way around the oval, working on the wall separating the stands from the field. Jonathan was the last person she wanted to see just then.

Cass turned and went back midway through the entryway. She had noticed two side passages with ramps leading up, she presumed, to the seats. She took the ramp to her right and found herself in a high passageway behind the seats. "Just like a football or baseball stadium, except nicer," she decided. The spacious insides of the coliseum were both practical and pleasing. There was a carefully designed waiting area, smaller passageways leading to the lower seats, and ramps and stairways to the upper tiers. A memory flashed across her mind. The Penn Relays at Franklin Field at the University of Pennsylvania in Philadelphia. "It's just like that," she thought, except, again, nicer.

Cass fell under the spell of the place so completely that she lost track of the time, and of her original purpose for being there.

Fountains and statues in niches seemed to be everywhere. As she roamed the passageways or sat in the lounge areas, she imagined handsome people in light summer garments coming in to escape the sun during an intermission. The inner spaces of the amphitheater were designed to provide light higher up and shade below. It was partly for this reason that Cass failed to notice that the light was rapidly diminishing. She finally made this discovery when she found herself squinting to make out the features of a statue when she was just a few feet away from it.

Cass walked quickly through one of the short passageways to the seats to check on the workmen. They were gone. She ran back and this time nearly ran into the statue she had been staring at. Her heart started to race as she realized that she had lost track of time and that she might easily get herself lost before she could find her way out. "Now you've done it," she told herself, partly to calm herself as she began making her way back along the main passageways. She had gone only a few feet when she saw something that made her stop abruptly. She was sure that a statue had moved. It was in the middle of the passageway about twenty feet away, directly in her path.

Cass remained unmoving for what seemed forever, feeling a tightness in her chest. She looked back over her shoulder, but there was only darkness and an untried passageway. The statue had not moved again, and Cass persuaded herself that it never had. She took a deep breath and started forward. Keeping as close as possible to the inside wall of the passageway, she made her way very deliberately, eyes, straining in the increasing darkness. She was a few steps past the statue and beginning to breathe again, when she heard the sound of someone or something moving behind her.

She was about to scream and run, when she heard the voice.

"Cassandra."

Cass could not mistake the voice, though it was less song-like than usual. "Maiden, thank goodness, but why did you scare me so?"

"Because while you have been indulging your love of exploring, Theadora has been searching for you. Alone."

Cass immediately realized the significance of the "Alone." "I'll go find her right away," she said in a strained voice.

"Hmpf," was Maiden's response, in a deep tone. "It is a bit late to do that. She has been taken to the home of a wealthy citizen, just as Jonathan warned might happen if you were so foolish as to go about Alone. You seem to have lost both of your companions, and you their leader."

"What can we do?" cried Cass. Maeden's words stung her deeply, but no more so than her own guilt feelings.

"Return to your friends. They will help. I and some of my kinsmen will also keep watch. Go now."

# Chapter VI

# Barbarian Nobility

Thea had awakened about a half hour after Cass had slipped out. She was refreshed but, apparently, alone. She guessed correctly that Cass had gone exploring. She knew that Cass was restless and had agreed to taking a nap solely for her sake, to avoid the afternoon sun on her fair skin. "She probably went to see that amphitheater. That's where I wanted to go," thought Thea. She started toward the doorway and then hesitated. She clearly remembered Jonathan's repeated warnings that she should not go out Alone. "I could run and maybe catch up with her before she leaves the square," she decided, hastily getting up and heading for the doorway. She assumed that Mara had gone with Cass. Unfortunately she neglected to look behind the divider of colored strips of material. Had she done so she would have seen Mara sleeping and perhaps curbed her impulse to try to catch up with Cass.

She soon questioned her hasty decision. She had barely arrived at the market square when she realized that people were staring at her, making no effort to conceal their interest or surprise. But Thea stubbornly persisted, continuing on. When she was about half way across the square, she noticed a patrician gentleman and a soldier coming directly toward her. She panicked, turned and began to run. She had barely started when she heard a voice trumpeting, "Stop the slave!" She never got back to the relative safety of the side street before numerous hands reached out and took hold of both her arms.

The patrician had seen her and summoned the guard, intending simply to ask her why she was in the market without her mistress. He was a kindly gentleman and acted at least partly out of concern for Thea's safety. The guard now asked him if she were his slave. "No, not mine," the citizen responded truthfully, "but I will take her along with me and find out to whom she belongs." Thea, alternating between panic and irritation, tried to explain that she was visiting Jonathan and Mara, and that she did not *belong* to anyone, but, of course, they did not believe her. The guard accompanied them to the citizen's home. Thea, telling herself to stop trembling, tried to make the best of the situation. At least she had not been arrested, or she did not think so. She felt confident that Cass, Mara, and Jonathan would find her soon.

The patrician delivered her into the care and supervision of his wife. "Perhaps we are the beneficiaries of someone's loss in another province, at least until they come looking for her," he said to his wife. They both asked her about her masters, where she was from, and many other questions. But Thea could do little more than give her name, her full name of Theadora Leiterman. To all other questions she replied meekly that they would not believe her if she told them. The couple acted friendly, which reassured Thea. The woman had been intrigued by Thea's full name, recognizing it as both Germanic and Roman. She also understood that at the moment Thea was both frightened and bewildered. She decided not to press her with further questions.

She clapped her hands twice which quickly summoned a short sinewy boy of no more than ten. "Jaimie, take Theadora to the house servants' quarters and find a place where she can be quiet for a while." Turning back to Thea, she said, "rest for a bit and we will talk later." On their way to the servants' quarters, they encountered a number of other slaves. Everyone smiled and looked very sympathetic, but no one spoke to her. Everyone, however, greeted Jaimie with and word and a smile.

"No one is permitted to speak to you," said Jaimie, including me. We have been told that you are a runaway slave. It's against the rules to speak to a runaway until the master or mistress gives permission," he continued. Thea was to learn that Jaimie was a favorite with everyone, especially the mistress. He frequently broke various rules, for which he received regular but not very severe punishments. He quickly found her a small but pleasant cubicle in the women's slave quarters. He then returned with a cup of water. "Drink this," he said, "and do not be worried. This is a good house. Maybe you will not have to go back to the place you ran away from."

When he left, Thea felt grateful for his friendliness. His jauntiness helped her to compose herself to try to think of what to do. If the boy returned, she decided, she would ask him if he could get a message to Cass. Luckily later that evening he did return, with her meal. He laughed when Thea asked the favor as though she were asking him to risk his life.

"I am not afraid. At most I would get a few strokes on my legs for leaving without permission, but they would have to find me out, and that is not likely. I am Jaimie. Ask anyone about me," he boasted. "It is well known among the slaves that I can go anywhere in Italica without being found out by the masters or the soldiers. But it will have to be when you are talking to the mistress. I overheard her saying that she wants to see you after you have eaten. Just remember to talk until I have had time to go to your friends and come back. I am leaving now but will return to bring you to the mistress." He smiled and made a hand gesture that Cass interpreted as meaning "good luck." Thea dipped a crust of bread into the bowl of broth that Jaimie had brought her. She ate slowly and waited.

Later that evening, after Jaimie led her to the mistress's chamber, he squeezed her hand to reassure her. "Keep the mistress talking," he whispered and left.

"Come, come closer, child. I am not going to boil you in oil. Tell me. What are you fit for?"

"Pardon me?" asked Thea.

"What have you been trained to do?"

"Oh!" Thea was anxious to make a good impression. "I can make cookies from scratch," she said blurting out the first thing that came to her mind. The mistress laughed. Thea was relieved and a little embarrassed.

"Then tomorrow you must start your chores in the kitchen, though I think cook will have other jobs for you than making cookies from what you call scratch." Thea expected more questions. Instead the mistress looked like she was poised to clap for Jaimie, who was supposed to be standing just outside the chamber.

Alarmed Thea blurted out, "mistress, no!"

The mistress stopped suddenly. Her hands were still raised, ready to clap, but they remained where they were, practically framing the mistress's face. Her expression indicated that she was not used to being addressed so abruptly. There had better be a good reason.

"Sorry, my Lady, but now I remember. The answers. To your questions." Thea, who had been undecided about what story to make up about herself, decided at that moment to tell the truth. "I will tell you where I am from …if you promise not to laugh." The lady's expression softened into a smile; she nodded for Thea to sit on a cushion near her and begin. Thea got the impression that this is what the mistress had wanted all along.

At first haltingly but gradually with growing confidence, Thea related the seemingly implausible truth, starting with her arrival from the future by means of a charmed necklace. She noticed with relief that the mistress was listening attentively. Thea almost started to enjoy herself. She carefully omitted naming Cass or Alan, but she did not intentionally omit any detail of their adventures. She also revealed true details from her personal life, such as being both a ballet dancer and a flute player. The mistress said nothing about Thea being a dancer, but she said that she would like to hear her play the flute.

As she ended her narrative, she knew she had given Jaimie more than enough time. The mistress had been a good audience. She had smiled and nodded occasionally. Thea could detect no skepticism. Now the lady looked down at her in a thoughtful way and remained so without speaking for several moments, while the storyteller awaited the verdict.

"You have an interesting story and an interesting name, Theadora Leiterman. It seems that some god has sent a messenger named Maiden to look out for you. You are a bright and accomplished young lady. This much is clear from your story. Also, your name tells me that you are the daughter of barbarian nobility friendly to Rome. Only a barbarian who is an ally of Rome, or at least respects Rome, would call his daughter Theadora, and Leiterman means 'leader' in German. You say that you are not a slave. We shall see, but for the present, and for your own good, we are going to treat you as a valuable and expensive slave. I have my doubts about this strange future world of which you speak. I expect that we will have many tales from you to while away our dark winter nights. You are a born storyteller."

Thea felt like she had just gotten an A on her first exam in Italica. She was so pleased with this praise that at first she wondered why Jaimie was making curious faces at her when she finally noticed him in the doorway on the left. With a start, she realized that he had probably been trying for some time to get her attention. She thanked the mistress for her kind words, skipping over her doubts about some of the details. She rose to her feet, giving Jaimie his entrance cue.

"I came, Mistress, but hearing the new slave's story, I waited."

"You see, Theadora, I said you were a good storyteller," said the lady. To Jaimie she said, "take Theadora back to her quarters. I suggest you behave yourself. Very likely she will be in charge of you before long."

"You certainly have pleased the mistress," Jaimie said with a new respect in his voice. "Why not stay with us?" But Thea was anxious for news of her friends. "They will come for you tonight. I shall watch for them and bring you to them when they are here." For a moment Jaimie looked uneasy. "It can be dangerous. Soldiers keep close watch through the night, and they are not as kind as the master and mistress."

"Thanks, Jaimie, I'm sure it will be fine." Thea later huddled down into the blankets, counting herself lucky that the women slaves each had a private cubicle. She knew now that many of the women slaves would sound the alarm out of loyalty to their masters. "And with good reason," she thought.

She had been falling into and out of a shallow sleep for some time when she felt Jaimie shaking her. He whispered to her to be silent and follow. She grabbed hold of his night shirt. For the next few minutes she felt as though she was the seeker in a very serious game of blind man's bluff. The few minutes seemed more like an hour to Thea. She followed Jaimie blindly, barely risking to breathe. She heard nothing other than the blood thudding in her ears. When Jaime's foot crunched on the gravel she nearly screamed. They were just off the outer edge of the patio.

Next moment she was muffled from the head down in a cape, as someone whispered heavily: "hush." Whoever had her now obviously did not want her asking any question. Firm hands guided her on either side. Thea guessed that Jonathan and Mara were her guides. They paused, hesitated. Thea heard a husky shout, followed a few seconds later by a second but quite different shout. She discovered that she was half running, half stumbling now between her guides. Sounds of loud voices and running followed them. What she heard next tingled her scalp and raised the hairs on her neck. It was an unearthly shriek that pierced her ears. It was followed by an eerie, high-pitched laugh.

The laugh stopped abruptly. Their pace slowed slightly. Thea felt the cape being removed. She breathed in the refreshing night air, cooling her from her face to her lungs. They continued to run but less clumsily now that Thea did not have to be led. At first she could see nothing but two shadowy figures, one on either side. Then her eyes focused, confirming what she had supposed. Her guides were Jonathan and Mara.

Still they ran. "This must be the village now," thought Thea. They passed what might have been the front of Jonathan and Mara's house. Then she noticed another figure running with them. Cass! They slowed to a trot when they left the village behind. Looking over their shoulders, they could still see the torches of the soldiers looking like so many fire flies darting about in the dark. When even these points of light disappeared from sight, the four of them finally stopped. Thea collapsed by the side of the road. No one had enough breath to speak, but Cass sat next to Thea and embraced her. Though darkness enveloped them, they could see the moon-light shimmering on the river below. Across the river and in the distance, they could see the glow of the watch fires of Seville.

"We will build a small fire down by the river and wait with you but only for a short time. We must return before dawn. And you should not delay over long in removing yourselves further from Italica," cautioned Jonathan. Cheered by the small fire built by Jonathan and Mara, the four adventurers prepared to share their stories. Each took a sip or two from Mara's wine skin. Mara gave them each a packet of bread and cheese for later. Thea began her story. When she had finished, Mara congratulated her on her re-sourcefulness. Then Mara took her turn as narrator.

They had been greatly relieved, Mara began, when Jaime brought them Thea's message. They immediately made their simple but daring escape plan. She and Jonathan were to take charge of Thea once Jaime got her past the patio. If they were caught, they would rely on their good standing and on the good reputation of Thea's master and mistress to save them. They would say that Thea was Cass's personal slave whom they were reclaiming. "I am glad that we did not have to use that story," said Mara with a smile. "It was a pretty thin stew. Jews do not normally have slaves, and Cass looks like my little sister, very much the young Jewish girl."

"We nearly had to rely on that thin stew," said Jonathan with a chuckle. "For some reason, after the four soldiers of the watch had passed the house, they returned. They caught us out in the open. I was not even going to run, but then there was some other disturbance that distracted the watch. Someone was shouting at them and waving a torch. So we ran. One or two of the soldiers may have started after us. I could not tell, but then came that hellish howl, and we were forgotten."

"That howl came from one of Maiden's kinsmen. I saw them," explained Cass. "I was waiting in the doorway of your house, Jonathan. As I stood there in the shadows, a crowd of them rushed by. Most of them looked like males, quite different from Maiden. They had long hair that seemed to sprout from all over their bodies. I couldn't be sure but their legs might have been animal legs. They looked like goats walking on their back legs. Like satyrs, I guess. One of them noticed me. He came over and leered at me, pointing that arrow-shaped chin and beard at me, just the way Brother Bartolomeo painted them. Maiden had promised that her people would be watching. They seemed to be enjoying themselves."

Cass had been speaking animatedly. She stopped, now seeming uncertain of what else to say. She took a deep breath. "Thea, I'm really sorry. And Jonathan and Mara, I've caused you so much trouble." Cass felt awkward but relieved by her confession and apology. Thea hugged and held her while Jonathan and Mara looked on smiling.

"We wish you could have been with us longer," Jonathan said to them. Then to Cass he said, "even if Thea had not been taken into custody yesterday by the Roman master, it would not have taken long before someone else would have suspected her and reported her. Slaves such as she are highly valued."

"Rightly so," piped up Thea, prompting laughter that lightened everyone's mood.

"Well, if God ever blesses us with offspring, I hope they are like you two," said Mara. She and Jonathan embraced them both and started to leave.

Mara turned back for a moment. "Oh, yes, I nearly forgot in all the excitement. When I went to look for Cass after my nap this afternoon, I heard everyone speaking of great news for the Jews. The Roman Governor of the province has appointed one of our people from Cordoba, a city not far from here, to be his new Chief Minister. I will pay close attention to see if this Chief Minister commissions one of our artisans to make a necklace."

"Now, go, you two, with God's blessing," concluded Mara as she and Jonathan moved off into the dark.

"Cass, you heard Mara. Now we know that Nathan's story is real," exclaimed Thea.

Cass took little comfort in that knowledge. "We might have found out much more if we could have stayed," she lamented. "We can never go back there. We'd be arrested before we knew it. First I lose Alan. Now this. I may be the biggest obstacle rather than the leader of this quest."

"Hmpf. At this moment, it seems that you might be correct," spoke a familiar voice, after an initial sound that was half sigh, half growl.

"Maiden!" Both girls exclaimed together. She was sitting across from them by the fire. She did not look pleased. Cass noted the displeasure, and her own rush of joy at seeing her evaporated.

"I know," said Cass. "I haven't done much that has helped anyone."

"Again you might well be correct," said Maiden reprovingly. "Fortunately your failures have not been fatal, but they have had serious consequences. Because you allowed your anger at your brother to distract you, you did not direct the necklace, as you could have done, to take you back closer to the time of its making.

Because you left Halán behind, he has suffered greatly. And when you finally went to look for him at the coliseum you were the cause of Theadora's capture."

"It wasn't her f...," began Thea, but Maiden quickly stopped her with a gesture.

Cass, looking more and more downcast, simply nodded her agreement with Maiden. Thea said nothing further. She saw how the muscles of Cass's face tightened and twitched. Thea recalled seeing Cass do this only one other time. That was when Cass's dad shouted at her when they were young for leaving Alan at the park because he would not come home with her.

"Even from such mistakes something good can come. Halán is hurt, but you can heal him with the help of Theadora and the necklace. He has learned much from his ordeal." Here Maiden turned to Thea. "You also, Theadora, have learned something useful about yourself, I believe. Storytelling, as I have said before, is valued here. Music as well." Maiden smiled, much to the relief of the girls. "Also I can see that you have already forgiven Cassandra, if indeed you had ever faulted her for leaving you. Therefore I can do no less," she said, turning again to Cassandra.

"I don't deserve your forgiveness, but I thank you for it," said Cass a little stiffly. "But, please, Maiden, where is Alan?" she asked, her voice becoming anxious.

"You will have to discover that for yourselves. I and others have helped him where we could, but he needs you," said Maiden. She looked long at Cass, both stern and sad. Then her expression softened. "You might have learned more about the necklace and even met the Governor's Jewish Chief Minister had you used the necklace better. But then you would not have met Jonathan and Mara, or my kindred for that matter," said Maiden, with a breath of a laugh.

"Indeed," said Maiden, noticing Thea's and Cass's hesitant smiles, "you have had an adventure and survived. All is not lost." Looking at Cass, she went on. "Well, what did you think of my kinsmen?" Cass realized that she was quite curious to hear her answer.

"A little strange," replied Cass at last. "I might have thought them to be up to no good if I hadn't recognized them as your kinsmen."

"Many humans make that same mistake, which indeed is not always a mistake." Maiden looked at the two humans in front of her. The fire had by now burnt down to glowing coals. She walked across without being burnt by them and barely disturbing them. In fact the fire rekindled itself in her footprints. She put a hand on each of their heads. "We will meet again," she assured them and then stepped back into the flames, which turned from red to violet, and then she disappeared. The girls stared for several moments at the glowing coals.

Thea stood and broke the silence. "You see," she said, "we have learned some things, about ourselves and our mission both. So you have to stop feeling so guilty."

Cass sighed. "All right, but what I heard was that my actions had some good and some bad results. That doesn't mean I wasn't stupid and thoughtless. I was. You, Alan, not aiming the necklace for the right time."

"I didn't quite get that part. We went where we wanted, didn't we?" said Thea.

"Yes to where; no to when," replied Cass. "If I wasn't trying not to leave Alan behind at the last minute, I would have been able to take us closer to the time the necklace was made. We could have been there and back to look for Alan in a short time." Cass paused and looked up at Thea. "There and back, that's it," she exclaimed, reaching out to Thea. "We can find him. That's why Maiden repeated the point about concentrating and directing the necklace. She was angry with me, but she also wanted to give me the clues so that we could figure out for ourselves how to find Alan."

"I got it." Thea nearly shouted with excitement. "We—you that is—can take us directly to Alan in his present time by focusing on him with the necklace."

"I—we—can do better than that. We can go to him, his exact time and place, and bring him back here to our time. He has been hurt and is in danger." Cass was standing next to Thea now. "OK," said Cass, "stand by my side, Thea, and think of Alan. Now move with me. Thea did as Cass asked. Shoulders touching the two of them stepped onto the faintly glimmering ashes of the fire. Cass repeated two words, "Alan; return," in a husky whisper, three times, each time with more urgency, as she undid and then refastened the necklace. Suddenly Alan stood between the girls. He was encrusted with dirt and blood. "Alan," exclaimed both girls as he collapsed into their arms.

# Chapter VII

# Vandals

For many minutes Cass cradled Alan in her arms as Thea looked on anxiously. Alan wandered in and out of consciousness, muttering incoherently or calling out in pain or delirium. Cass did not have to understand what Alan said. She could sense the depth of his hurt. Thea wiped away as much as possible of the dirt and blood caked on his face and head and wherever his body was exposed. She used water from the river and tore material from the bottom of her tunic. When he remained conscious long enough, she coaxed him to swallow a little water and wine mixed.

Thea finally persuaded Cass very gently to put Alan on the ground so they could both tend to him while he slept. The only whole garment they had to remove from him was a blackened soldier's cloak that was saturated with the smell of smoke and fire. By the time they had finished ministering to him, they had used a good portion of their tunics to make bandages and compresses. Most of Alan's wounds looked nasty and likely to leave scars but would not maim or impair him permanently, except for one.

His right hand was a shapeless lump of burnt flesh. It had ballooned to more than twice its normal size. Ugly deep streaks of red showed where the charred skin had split open. A green liquid oozed from some of the cracks. Thea wrapped the hand in a wine-soaked cloth as gently as possible, but she could tell that Alan had no feeling below his elbow. She decided not to share this discovery with Cass who was busy across from her, impatiently brushing away her tears. It occurred to Thea that she had never seen her cry.

"Of that wound he will not soon heal, unless...." Maiden paused.

The girls looked up at her, too concerned with Alan to be surprised at the sudden reappearance. "What happened to him," demanded Cass sharply. "You said you looked after him."

"As I told you then and have told you often, Cassandra, I can help only within limits. You must find your own way to your destination, and you must rely on each other on the journey. Halán's life was and is in your hands. Had you not acted as you did just now in bringing him back, he would have died there in a short time. I had not thought he was so bad. I saw you rescue him and returned to see how he fared."

"Maiden, he might lose his arm," cried Thea. She doubted that even Maiden could help.

Maiden knelt next to her and took Alan's mangled limb in her left hand. Then she turned to Thea. "Place your hands on his wound," she said. Thea looked at Maiden doubtfully but said nothing. She then placed her hands on the swollen and oozing cracks of Alan's injured limb. Maiden recognized the doubt mingled with pity in Thea's face. Next Maiden looked across to Cass. "Cassandra." Cass stared at her, still upset with her. Maiden did not blink. Cass slowly placed her hands so that they overlapped with Thea's, leaving only a small space of charred skin uncovered. Maiden placed her right hand there. Within seconds a purple light began to glow outlining their hands. Cass and Thea felt a painful shock in both their hands but held on. Alan moaned loudly and thrashed about, but he remained unconscious. The girls and Maiden still managed to hold onto Alan's hand. At a nod from Maiden they now pulled away. They stared. Alan's lower arm, hand, and fingers were perfectly normal. A thin purple coloration evaporated from the healed skin as they watched. Only on the inside of the hand did the girls notice any trace of Alan's ordeal, which was as yet a mystery to them. White lines, barely visible, stretched across the fingers and scored the palm.

Cass looked up at Maiden. "Forgive me, again."

"I simply channeled the energy from Theadora's emotions, and yours," responded Maiden. "As for forgiveness, it is yours, again. One thing more. We have begun the healing of his outward wounds. Only he will be able to heal the wounds within, but he will need help there also." Cass and Thea both nodded agreement. "Insist that he tell you all of his story. Everything. He begins to stir."

Cass and Thea returned their attention to Alan. His eyes were opening and closing as though he were awakening after a deep sleep. "Cass. Thea. The fire. What happened." He stared at his right hand. "Maiden! I saw her in a dream. She offered me a two-edged sword, blade first. When I tried to hold it with my bad hand, she pulled the sword away, cutting through the dead parts." He looked up at the girls and tried to see past them. "She healed me didn't she? Where are we and where is she?" None of them was surprised that she was gone. Curling above the ashes of the fire, a wisp of violet smoke gave way to the bright sunlight that was just appearing above the horizon.

Cass and Thea took turns answering Alan's questions.

"Cass stepped into the embers of the fire to bring you back to us."

"Thea helped me, and she helped Maiden heal your hand."

"We are about half way between Italica and Seville, Hispalis they call it now," said Thea.

"But we can't go to either place because they will be looking for a valuable runaway slave with red hair." Cass's sense of humor was returning. It helped to lift their spirits. All three started asking and answering questions at once.

"Where have you been?"

"And who or what nearly killed you?"

"We escaped."

"We met a Jewish couple."

"Are we still in Brother Bartolomeo's time?"

"And Romans, Patricians."

"Cass looked exactly like Mara."

"I was captured."

"I was a slave."

"No, we are in the second century A.D. Hadrian is emperor."

"Cass and Thea, nearly out of breath, looked at the bewildered expression on Alan's face and smiled. "I don't think this is going to work," said Cass. "We had better tell you our story first. Then you have to tell us everything." The girls could barely check their curiosity about Alan, but they forced themselves to take their time and recall the details of their own exploits. Alan listened to all they said as though he were listening to two teachers to whom he would have to recite back the lesson. He smiled twice, once when Thea told of her story-telling session, and a second time when Cass told about her reunion with Thea after the escape. Otherwise he looked as if the story actually caused him pain, particularly the descriptions of the beauties of Italica and the kindness of its people—slaves, workers, and masters alike.

While they told their stories, Cass and Thea watched Alan carefully. Both knew that something had happened to change him. They had never seen him so subdued and attentive. They completed their account with Thea speaking fondly of Jaimie and the mistress, and Cass of their debt to Jonathan and Mara.

"So you have been to the second century for one day and one night," observed Alan. So much had happened that Cass and Thea were both astonished to think that it had all occurred in such a short time. "Your experiences make mine seem all the more terrible. You'll see why, if I can tell it right. I don't have your knack,

Thea."

"Just start at the beginning," prompted Cass.

"We'll help you with lots of questions," offered Thea, "such as how did you get separated from us to begin with?"

"Oh, that's easy enough to figure out. I was standing just off the mosaic of the sea god. When I saw you begin to disappear into a cloud of light, I stepped onto the mosaic. I probably could have joined you, but I hesitated." Alan paused, looked a little sheepish. "I guess I thought I could stop you, or make you come back. I wanted to go home, as you remember. When Cass called my name, I finally stepped into the cloud, but you were gone. I was only a few seconds behind you, but those seconds turned into centuries, as you will see." He paused to gather his thoughts.

"The coliseum was there, Cass, but it was far from new. It was pretty rundown and not used much, except for training civilians, the few who were left, how to act as soldiers. The citizens could have used your plumber too. The sewers worked, but the other water systems were broken. Most people got their water from a couple of public wells. A number of villas were empty, with grass growing over the paths. The workers and artisans had left. It was a deserted village. The barbarians, who were invading from the north, were supposed to be very generous with the artisans, prized them in fact. But evidently the Jews—artisans like your friend Jonathan—didn't want to be prizes, and when the Jews left, the other craftsmen left."

Alan stopped and stared into the distance, his thoughts far away. For the first of many times, Cass and Thea had to recall his attention to his story and prompt him to continue.

"Were you still on the sea-god patio?" asked Cass.

"Yes, and it was a hot, dusty morning. A girl, a little younger than me, maybe twelve or thirteen, walked out of the main house and stared at me for a moment. She and the others I saw later dressed just like the people you described, Thea, though their clothes looked worn. She wasn't surprised or frightened that I was there. Her name was Cecilia, and she was as pretty as her name, prettier even. She pretended to be a soldier on sentry duty. 'Declare yourself, Roman or barbarian.' I said I was lost. 'Of course you are,' she said, 'and a little grumpy too, but harmless.' She was teasing me, but in a nice way. She reminded me of you, when we were younger, Cass." Cass winced at the unintended meaning; she had not paid Alan much attention as they both got older.

"She took me into the house and introduced me to her mother as Alan the Refugee, as though I had a special title. The lady was not surprised. Other refugees stayed there for days at a time. She said I looked lost and held my face in her hands, then kissed my forehead." Alan looked at Cass here. "Like mother did when we were small." I stayed with Cecilia and her mother for six days."

"Six days?" asked Cass.

"What?" exclaimed Thea.

"I thought that would surprise you," said Alan. "That's why I asked you how long you had been in the second century. Your one day and night seem to have been the equal to my six. And I was in the fifth century. When I asked Cecilia's mother, she told me it was the year 410 of the Christian Era."

"Didn't Einstein have a theory about the relativity of time?" asked Cass. "But go on with your story," she urged.

"OK. Since I was now in Italica, I was expected to join the city militia. All the boys my age, and even younger, and any of the men who could walk and hold a sword went to the coliseum for training. The other men of Italica were in the field fighting the barbarians elsewhere. They called the barbarians Vandals," which I guess is fitting with all the destruction they caused. We all learned how to use the short sword, a bow, and a spear. Our instructors watched how we did and then assigned us our main weapon. Mine was the short bow for close range. My instructor, a wounded veteran like the others, said I was a born bowman. In fact he called me Alan Bowman." Alan smiled at this memory. He was getting into his narrative now and did not need further coaching.

"Each evening when I returned to the villa there were new

refugees who were too tired to keep running. They spilled over from the house to the patio and gardens. At night in the house you couldn't move without tripping over someone. Cecilia and her mother worked magic with their few supplies. They and a few servants—they didn't refer to them as slaves as your mistress did, Thea—shared their small stores of food and took care of the sick and wounded. Cecilia and her mother were devout Christians, as were most of the Romans of Italica, but they didn't ask people their beliefs when they took them in. Cecilia said that her mother had sold all her jewels, even her jeweled cross, to buy food and medicine."

"One night Cecilia and I slept outside in the gardens, away from everyone else. The house was crowded and stuffy, but we lay under the stars, talking. Cecilia said that she had planned to be a church woman and not marry, but now she had changed her mind. She would consider marrying me, if I could avoid being grumpy. She spoke with such assurance, I actually believed for that night that it could happen. That night was the best—and last—night's sleep I have had."

"We were jarred awake next morning by a messenger running through the city shouting, 'the Vandals!' So the evacuation began. My instructor took command. All the women, children, and wounded were to go to Hispalis. Cecilia and her mother left. Cecilia gave me a hug and said, in her confident commander's voice, 'your orders are not to get killed.' I thought I would never see them again, and I wish I hadn't." Alan paused but only briefly.

"The militia—boys, old men, and the not-too-seriously wounded—would hold Italica as long as possible as a rear guard. No one said anything about our getting to Hispalis, or anyplace else. We were going to fight with guerilla tactics, house to house, burning everything as we fell back. When possible we could choose to fight from our own houses. I was to start on the roof of Cecilia's house. Before we took our positions, the instructor-commander called us together. He ordered a moment of silence and suggested that we pray. Then he spoke his final words to us."

"'Remember what you have learned, young soldiers'—he talked a lot like Brother Bartolomeo—"concentrate on two things: your weapon and your opponent. Nothing else exists. The rest will take care of itself. The empire is in retreat, but it is not defeated. We must hold our ground.' The commander paused, saluted, and then added. 'Long enough'."

"I should have felt proud. I used to daydream about being a Roman soldier, but this was real and I was scared. Lucky for me we worked in pairs. A boy named Tonio was my partner. He was old enough to have been in the field with the men, but his father wanted him to stay to help with the defense of the city. He gave me one of his father's old army cloaks."

"We saw the Vandals coming for a good half hour before they reached us. That watching and waiting was almost worse than what came later. No, I think it was worse. The barbarians had learned a lot from fighting the Romans for so many years. It would have been hopeless, even if they hadn't been such good fighters. There were so many of them, thousands to our few hundred. Some marched, others rode their ponies, until they were only a quarter of a mile away. Then they stopped and rested—at attention—for what seemed like an hour, standing in the sun. I noticed a few of our younger boys sneaking away. The barbarians' plan was to scare us, and it worked. When they began the attack, thousands of them, all screaming, many more defenders ran away, this time both men and boys."

"I would have run too, except for Tonio. It was…." Alan broke off. He shuddered involuntarily, then went on. "It was terrible. The horsemen rode across the fields straight for Italica, crashing like a wave, unstoppable. They poured through the city. Tonio was shooting arrows like a mad man while I watched them pass."

"Shoot or we won't hold them long enough for the women to get to Hispalis,' Tonio ordered."

"When they charged back through the city, I shot as fast as I could. You aim for the horse's neck. Horses are more valuable than the riders and chances are that the riders would be killed when the horses stumbled or fell." Again Alan faltered. When he resumed, he sounded both angry and sad. "I hit at least two horses that I'm sure of, poor animals, and the riders never moved from where they fell. I killed them." He sounded like he was accusing himself.

"But, Alan, you were fighting for your life," interjected Cass.

"And for the women and children and wounded," added Thea.

Alan looked at them gratefully but shook his head. "The horsemen were too vulnerable in such close quarters. They found that out, so they left and let the foot soldiers take over. The soldiers marched with shields locked in front and overhead to protect against our arrows. Tonio said they learned this tactic, called the 'turtle,' from the Romans. The turtle came right up to the edge of the city and then charged. That was our signal to light the torches. It was reassuring to see how many of us there still were. Torches marked many roofs. Bonfires crackled in the main squares. We had jars of burning oil that we crashed on the streets like bombs, when their soldiers were near enough."

Alan stopped and held up his right hand, showing his palm with the network of white lines, thin as sewing thread. "That's when I did this. I burned my hand. My whole arm was on fire for a while from some oil that I spilled when I lifted a jar of it over my head to throw down below. I lost all feeling in my hand, which was lucky in a way. When I pulled back on the bowstring, it cut into my hand, but there was no blood, just red lines where the flesh pealed back."

"If we could have held them until nightfall, some of us might have been able to slip off. But they went from house to house, villa to villa, after the fires died down and flushed us out. There were too many of them. We were out of arrows. Tonio fought with his sword until they cut him down. I picked up his sword with my left hand, but they easily took me prisoner. I guess they admired us for fighting so hard. We were supposed to become auxiliaries, to fight with them."

"We were well enough treated, the twenty or so of us who were left alive. Their surgeon said the hand might have to be cut off later. He was an old Roman who had been captured by the Vandals years before. He put some ointment on my hand and wrapped it in clean strips of cloth. I felt nothing from the elbow down. That night they made offerings to their gods and actually shared their personal rations with us. Around the fires they told stories about old heroes and brave enemies. They drank to our health."

"I could almost admire them, except for what happened next day. Hispalis was more of a commercial center than a fortress town like Italica. It didn't have strong fortifications, not like later in Brother Bartolomeo's day. I guess his people learned their lesson from what happened to the Romans. But they didn't even make use of the little protection the city offered. The Vandals had their main force, including all the horsemen, cross the river near Italica. They approached on the Hispalis side, from above the city. They were not visible from the city because of the hills. There was no tower in Hispalis then. A smaller detachment, the foot soldiers, marched along the path across the river from Hispalis and then made crude log rafts to cross just below the city.

Instead of waiting, the Roman soldiers came out from the city, hoping to prevent their landing or to push them back into the river. But by this time an advanced contingent of barbarian horsemen had moved up undetected. They took advantage of the Romans' exposure and surprised them out in the open. Caught between the horsemen and the foot soldiers the Romans didn't have a chance. The fight was over in no time. The town itself was easily overrun only a few hours later when the rest of the Vandal army arrived."

"Hispalis was totally defeated, and this time there were no orders to take prisoners. The army surgeon told me about the Vandals' style of warfare. Our little militia at Italica had been considered an army, an honorable enemy that fought well and could supply recruits for them. The garrison of Hispalis had been annihilated, and its inhabitants were the spoils of war. Captives would have been extra baggage for an army on the move. All I could think of were

Cecilia and her mother."

"They had brought us Italica captives with the first detachment of foot soldiers. We watched everything from across the river, where we were kept under guard. We didn't want to watch then or later, but we couldn't help ourselves. It was like being in someone else's nightmare. The smoke and flames, the shouting and screaming, the crush of swords and shields. Still worse was to come."

"That evening the barbarians brought us into the smoldering city. They were heaping the dead bodies on top of brushwood in the main square to burn them. They made us sit and watch these preparations and the tearing down of what remained of the city. Everything, every building, had been emptied out. The men and children must have been killed quickly. The women were...." Alan choked up and had to pause before he could continue. "If they were lucky they were killed right away. I only hope that is what happened to Cecilia and her mom. It seemed like it would never end. The barbarians were still dragging the few surviving women out of their hiding places and...and killing them."

"Then I saw them. A Vandal soldier passed within a few feet of where I was sitting. He was carrying two limp bodies like they were piles of dirty laundry, one dangling and bouncing under each arm. I couldn't tell if it was them, but the thought jumped into my mind that it could have been. I shouted and tried to get up, but a guard smashed me down with his fist. I must have passed out."

"The next thing I remember is feeling someone whispering in my ear for me to get up and run. He practically lifted me up and pushed me along for a few steps. The guards must have been busy. I turned and got a look at my would-be rescuer. I think it was one of Maiden's kinsmen that you described, Cass. He was hairy enough and had the pointed beard. In that moment that I saw him he seemed to catch on fire, but he just jumped around, grinned, and howled."

Alan stopped. He seemed to be struggling with his thoughts. "I'm not sure what happened next," he said. "Everything got confused."

Cass and Thea were staring at Alan with alarm and fascination. They would have spared him any further details of what happened, but they remembered Maiden's warning to have him tell everything. Still, Cass could not bring herself to press him further, perhaps guessing what had happened next. Thea, however, persisted.

"Did you get away from the barbarians," she asked Alan.

Alan looked up, startled. "No. Yes. I don't know. That must be when you brought me here."

"Alan, something happened before we got to you," said Cass sadly, reluctantly. Thea's question had prompted her to speak. "What was it?"

Alan took a deep breath, then let the air escape slowly between his cracked lips. "I threw myself into the fire," he said quietly. "They were all dead, everyone who had been so good. Tonio cut down. Cecilia and her mom burned. I thought I would never see you again." He began to cry, quietly. Cass continued to hold him, pressing him carefully closer, to comfort him. And herself. They remained that way for a long time until Alan's weeping subsided. Alan, without moving his head from Cass's shoulder, spoke again quietly. "Then you brought me back. I had hardly landed in the fire when you were there. Both of you," he added looking up at Thea.

At length Cass got up and gently helped Alan to his feet. She kept his healed hand in both of hers. "Maiden had her people watching out for you, though it's difficult to know just how they are doing that," said Cass. "It's amazing. Maiden and her kinsmen must have guessed at that point that you would throw yourself into the fire. You had to be in contact with fire, too, as Thea and I were." Cass paused. "Please forgive me. If anything had happened to you I would never forgive myself." Thea approached and put her hands on theirs. Cass looked at her and said, solemnly, "I'm getting lots of practice at apologies."

Alan looked at his sister, his eyes glistening, perhaps still with tears of sadness, perhaps with tears of gratitude and love. "I did it to myself," he said, "with my own stubbornness. I kept fighting against you and being here. I was a brat."

"I've been taking you for granted for way too long," said Cass. Alan squeezed her hand tightly. "Ouch, where did you get that grip?" said Cass." Alan just smiled.

The companions lingered for some moments longer. Finally Thea released her grip, stepped back and looked at her tunic, or what was left of it. She had gotten into the habit of smoothing and brushing it with her hands. She did this now. "Hopeless," she concluded. "I suggest we wade out into the river. Can you walk, Alan?" In answer, Alan, with Cass holding onto him, began to walk to the river.

As they washed, Thea continued to focus on practical matters. "We'll have to look for food. We finished the last of Mara's supplies ages ago."

"We'll look for food in another age, I think," replied Cass. "I doubt that we have anything further to learn in this century, about the necklace or ourselves. How about going back to just before Brother Bartolomeo's time to find out who had the necklace before Nathan."

"Can we do that?" asked Alan.

"Yes," answered Thea. "Cassandra the Seer can now direct the necklace with her mind, by concentrating on some details of place and time."

"And Thea is being modest. She figured out that the bearer of the necklace can go to someone's present time and place by focusing on that person, without knowing time or place," said Cass. "I think that it must work best if there is an emotional or spiritual link between the person and the bearer. What I don't know for sure is if both the person and the bearer have to be in contact with water or fire."

"So how are you-we-going to be able to go back to Seville *before* Brother Bartolomeo's time?" asked Alan.

"Brother Bartolomeo told us that the tower was completed not long before the Reconquest by the Christians. He also told us that the east wall of the mosque-church was added by the Christians. Remember he complained that it blocked their view of the orange grove. So we will focus on the tower and on the mosque and on the orange trees without the wall between them. That should have us arriving at just about when we want."

"Bravo," said Thea, impressed.

"Wash carefully," said Cass jokingly, as she threw a handful of water at Thea. "We don't want to arrive looking messy." She splashed water on her face and neck. Her hands brushed against the necklace. It was becoming part of her, like a sixth sense. She realized that she was gaining more control of its powers. She felt renewed. "Everyone ready?" she asked.

"I wonder what kind of clothes we will have," said Thea by way of saying yes.

Alan, looking at the few tattered rags that remained to him, said only, "let's go."

Rather solemnly, as though they were enacting a ritual, Cass unfastened the necklace and gave instructions. "Each of you put a hand on one of my shoulders." They complied. "First, think of us standing in the river across from Seville. We can see the tower. Now imagine the orange grove near the foot of the tower. Imagine that we can see inside the mosque because there is no wall separating it from the grove. There are no altars or crosses, just open space. Again, now think of us across the river, looking at the tower."

Cass refastened the necklace. The companions were surrounded by a cloud, inside of which they felt immersed in particles of dancing light. Then the cloud disappeared.

# Chapter VIII

# Am I Not Dhu Khiffil?

The companions found themselves standing in the marshy edges of the Quadalquiver River across from the city of Seville.

"Nicely done, Cass," exclaimed Thea. "Seville looks pretty much like it did when we first arrived."

"We are just across the river from where we first swam ashore." Cass spoke in a pensive voice. With her right hand she was patting the familiar outline of the necklace underneath her veil. "And you're right. The city looks the same. But I do not think that we are. It seems so long ago."

"Look at those walls. If only they had been there … ." Alan's voice trailed off. He was remembering his last visit to this city, as a captive of the Vandals. But the scene before him cheered him up quickly. The walls were of thick stone and at least twenty feet high, with frequent battlements from which pennants waived welcome to those who came in peace and defiance to all others. Beyond the walls rose the upper part of the tower, like a giant looking leisurely out over its domain. "Something about the tower is different," he remarked.

"Right," responded Cass. "No bell. That came later, with the

Christians." Instead of the bell, there were four gold-coated balls, one on top of the other, all resting on top of a tiled dome. The first and largest looked like a giant pumpkin. The next three were smooth surfaced and progressively smaller. "I think I like it better this way," concluded Cass.

"That would mean that we are here before the Christians re-conquered it and made the mosque into a church," observed Thea.

"That's what I am hoping," replied Cass.

"Well let's find out," suggested Alan. "There are plenty of rafts for us to choose from."

The companions, observing what other people had been do-ing while they were talking, untied the mooring line of one of the sturdy log rafts and pushed off toward the opposite bank. Alan and Cass pushed with the two poles, one on either side of the raft, while Thea sat in the rear. She noticed and admired Alan's clothes.

"You look quite handsome, Alan," she said, "right out of *The Arabian Nights*. The necklace has done very nicely for you." Alan was wearing a black and gray striped robe, with a sash around the waist. On his head was a kind of turban, a neatly fitted cloth of gray that hugged his forehead and swept back to his shoulders, giving him the dashing appearance of a desert Arab. He pretended not to hear Thea's compliment, but he smiled, and even blushed a little.

The girls' appearance was somehow neither plain nor ornate. Their robes were long, black and formless. However, they each wore a veil. Each, like the robe, was black but of a light-weight material, almost sheer. It covered the head and fell in ample folds over the shoulders. Thea soon discovered a way of fastening the right side to the left so that the veil covered the face below the eyes. Wearing the veil in this manner had several effects. The wearer could breathe without taking in dust and particles of sand. She could practice modesty by covering her beauty. And, as Thea now demonstrated, she could, if she wished, draw an onlooker's attention to her eyes, in Thea's case large and blue-green eyes, which the veil could set off in striking fashion. Curiously, the veil endowed its wearer with both modesty and attractiveness. Also, of course, with a sense of mystery.

Cass smiled as her friend experimented with the many different ways of wearing the veil. Cass thought, with mounting excitement, that the clothes were an indication that they had probably arrived, as intended, before the return of the Christians, but she could not yet be certain. At that moment, Alan startled both girls with the announcement, "The legend Maiden told us is true. Look by the river bank. The Tower of Gold is covered with real gold." From his vantage point on the right-hand side of the raft, Alan had been studying the tower as it gleamed in the sunshine, wondering what caused it to shine so brightly. He got his answer as they approached the near side of the river, where the tower guarded that approach to the city. Each of its twelve sides was adorned with twelve-foot square sheets of pure, glittering gold.

"Then we are definitely here before the threat of the Reconquest," said Cass softly. "They would never have left those sheets of gold for the Christians. We arrived when we wished," she said to Thea and Alan. "More importantly, we know how we did it."

"So we are going to meet the people who built Hispalis—I mean Seville—into a wealthy city. I would have guessed it would stay deserted forever after the Vandals sacked it," said Alan grimly.

"The builder people would be the Muslims whose coming was predicted by the necklace in Nathan's story," noted Thea. "The Christians called them Arabs or Moors. This will be exciting."

Alan guided the raft to the river bank where there was a post to secure it to for the next users. After fastening the raft, they started walking toward the city's main gate, the one by which they had entered once before.

"These soldiers look much more orderly than the barbarians who destroyed this place." Alan indicated the soldiers stationed on the walls. Some wore turbans similar to his. Others wore helmets that were part turban, part steel that came to a point. A guard stood at attention outside the gate. He had metal armor strapped to his shoulders and chest. He was holding, or holding on to, a wooden shaft taller than himself that ended in a steel-tipped point. By his side hung a long curved sword. The companions stared at him as they passed, but he kept his attention fixed straight ahead, as though disdaining to bother with persons of such little consequence.

Unlike their first visit, they had no trouble finding their way to the great tower. There were fewer houses, and they were not as tall as those that would come later. They approached from the southwest and found themselves in a square in front of the tower. Water bubbled up from an opening at the top of a marble pillar and splashed happily into the pool of water at the base of the fountain. A low wall, also marble, circled the pool, inviting the strangers to rest a while. The companions perched themselves on the wall, enjoyed the warm sun, and examined their surroundings.

The tower itself was bright in its newness, the red brick sharply contrasting with the white marble pillars and balustrades that adorned the seven open archways ascending, evenly spaced, to the top. "Brother Bartolomeo told us that the Moors built this tower, with Jewish help, about a hundred years before his time," said Thea, breaking the spell that had settled on them. "That would mean that we are at about the end of the twelfth century or beginning of the thirteenth. Isn't it strange to think of him being here a century from now...?"

"Working on his books," said Cass, completing Thea's thought.

"And giving sunny oranges to hungry, frightened strangers in need," Thea cut back in and smiled at the memory. "Gentle and wise," she thought to herself, "and with some dark corners that he did not hide from us, as though telling us his confession."

"I remember that he told me that I might someday climb this tower," said Alan. "But before I do that, please explain to me what our being here now has to do with our mission."

Cass noticed that for the first time since they had begun their quest, Alan said "our" mission. She was more than a little pleased. "Good question," she said aloud. "According to Brother Bartolomeo, Nathan got the necklace from someone else here in Seville.

I thought by visiting the century before Nathan's time, we might find more clues about the necklace. Remember that Maiden told us that we would learn what our mission was by finding out everything we could about the necklace."

"Follow the yellow gold necklace," contributed Thea.

"What more is there to know about the necklace?" Alan continued his questioning, encouraged by Cass's approving replies.

"That is what we have to find out, and I am hoping the necklace, or Maiden, will help us. We got this far." Cass sounded content to let matters—or the necklace—take their course at the moment.

"Look there." Thea was pointing to the side of the tower, to their left. Two young children appeared to be sneaking up on a gray-bearded man who sat cross-legged on a rug on the ground, dozing in the sun. The man was leaning up against the wall just around the left corner of the tower. The children passed stealthily directly in front of the sleeping man and then disappeared into what must be the main entrance of the tower.

In a short time the children emerged into the light on the balcony of the first archway. The three companions waved, prompting the two children to duck quickly back into the shadows. At the next higher level, however, they waved hastily before darting on. They repeated this action as they ascended to each of the next five archways that faced the fountain, and then waved triumphantly from the seventh and highest archway.

"Uh, oh. Trouble." Alan, who was climbing the tower vicariously, gestured toward the base of the tower. "We may have given them away."

The keeper of the gate had awakened and arisen from his mat. He had seen them waving to someone and was approaching them. The children disappeared well before the man crossed the fifty feet of cobblestones and directed his gaze toward the top of the tower. He turned now to the three companions, bowed slightly, and said, "Peace be upon you. Welcome to Seville. Strangers are gifts from Allah." The kindly gentleman looked back up the tower, just catching sight of two heads before they ducked back into the archway. "Grandchildren are also Allah's gifts to us, but they are sometimes full of mischief, going where they have been forbidden. They will have to be punished. Do not try to dissuade me."

The companions sensed that this threat of punishment was meant more for their benefit than as a prediction of what would actually happen to the grandchildren. They also remembered, how-ever, the formality of the guards they had seen and did not doubt that some of them could apply much stricter sanctions to the chil-dren than would their grandfather.

"Sir," said Cass, "Allow us to get them for you before anyone sees them."

"Yes ," immediately seconded Alan.

"Right," said Thea, but much more hesitantly. She did not like any heights higher than her knees.

The elderly man narrowed his eyes and made a stern face at Cass. "Am I not 'anyone,' although the grandfather of these offend-ers? Am I not Dhu Khiffil, Master of the Tower Gate and Muez-zin, Caller to Prayer? And is not Allah all seeing?" The companions had the feeling that this speech was more weighty than the situ-ation called for. It told them lots about the speaker, however. He seemed to be enjoying his own performance. Indeed, having made his speech, Dhu Khiffil resumed his more customary expression of gentleness, though his voice retained a note of concern.

"I fear I am too old to catch those infidels, and if the Captain of the Guard, who is also my son, discovers them he will chide both them and me. So, I accept your offer. But those two are sly ones. Watch out for their tricks." Again Dhu Khiffil attempted to assume a stern expression, but now it simply prompted smiles from the companions. Alan began jogging toward the tower. Cass and Thea followed. The Master of the Tower Gate shuffled along well behind them, shaking his head and muttering in a plaintive voice, "Rested my eyes for two heartbeats, and see what they do to their grandfather."

What began as a search for the two small 'offenders,' soon became a pleasurable excursion for Alan and Cass. Thea followed Cass, clinging to her robe. Alan led. They quickly discovered something very unusual about the tower. Instead of steps inside, it had a ramp, a spiral ramp. The tower was square on the outside and round on the inside. Dhu Khiffil later informed the companions that the name of the tower, Giralda, derived from an ancient root word meaning round. The spiral ramp was wide enough for three people to ascend side-by-side, although Alan was now ahead on his own. The ceiling was high enough for someone to ride up on a horse. That thought actually occurred to Thea. "Why is not Dhu Khiffil or anyone else riding their horse to the top. Why am I here risking a possible high-altitude disaster?"

They came to the first arch facing the fountain square. The archway was flooded with sunlight. As they continued their ascent, they discovered that the tower had archways that opened on all four external sides. From the inside, each opening simply occurred a little further along the spiral ramp. And each offered a fresh and interesting view. After the fountain, there appeared, in succession, the tops of buildings, the orange grove, and the mosque itself. Each of the seven spiraling levels offered a higher observation point enabling the climbers to see greater distances. Alan, at least one rotation ahead now, marveled to see the land beyond the distant hills. What especially fascinated Cass was that each archway was of unique design. Some consisted of double arches separated and supported by an ornamental marble pillar. Others had projecting balconies and marble railings, and some even had seats on which the Muezzin could rest periodically. Thea, by contrast, refused either to look at or through the arches.

Cass had become so absorbed in the sights, and Thea in staring at Cass's robe or the ground, that both had forgotten the children, one of whom now ran full tilt down the inner curve of the ramp and stopped just in time to avoid bumping into them. The young girl whispered, "Young Ladies," and made a sign to Cass and Thea to stay in the shadows by the outer wall and to make no noise. She was apparently the hider in a game of hide and seek. A moment later more hurrying footsteps approached, but with stops and starts. This must be the seeker, and when he passed them by, the little girl dashed back up in the opposite direction. She had just disappeared from sight when she let out a scream. Alan, laughing, appeared around the bend, firmly holding the hand of the now shy little girl. The boy, who might have gotten away, remained with his captured comrade, awaiting their sentence.

I will free you both," said Alan, "if you give me your word of honor you will go immediately to surrender yourselves to your grandfather." Both children gave sighs of relief when they heard "grandfather." Also both approved of Alan's grand manner of speaking and gravely gave their word. After they started off, Alan invited the Young Ladies to accompany him to the top of the tower.

"You can go up a ladder to a walkway around the top of the main part of the tower," he explained. "The children apparently do not go up there. They must have hidden against the wall, and I passed right by them on my way to the ladder." Cass readily accepted Alan's invitation. Thea looked wishfully after the children, but they had disappeared on their way down, so she followed Cass and Alan.

The view from the top of the tower was breathtaking. Even Thea admitted it was "magnificent," though she stayed well away from the balustrade that guarded the edge of the rampart. People would be able to hear the Muezzin from miles away in all directions. In case of attack, they could be forewarned days ahead of the enemy's arrival. "If such a tower had been here when the Vandals approached, there would have been no ambush, and maybe the city could have been saved, even without the new walls." His tone was sad, but not, Cass noted, edged with the deep sorrow that had marked it earlier that day when they had arrived and first viewed the walls.

Thea surprised the other two by actually taking a half step

toward the guard rail facing the east. "Somewhere over there is where Brother Bartolomeo was supposed to meet Elena. Before he was a Brother, of course."

"And over here, we have a garrison of soldiers looking a bit unfriendly." Cass indicated the guards by the south gate. They were waiving to them rather insistently. "I think we should go back down," she warned. She was right. By the time they reached the ground, a soldier—an important one by his looks—was talking, with lots of gestures, with Dhu Khiffil and the children, who were hiding their faces in their grandfather's robes. As they approached, the companions heard the soldier's voice clearly.

"Father, those children will grow up without a proper respect for the law. You spoil them. And then you send three curious strangers after them." Here he paused and bowed slightly to the companions and said, "Peace be with you," but he did not sound like he meant it.

"Young friends, this is Mushua Baba, my son and the Captain of the Guard." Dhu Khiffil held up his arms for attention." He gazed upward and spoke:

"Justly he attacks my negligent flaw—
Clap them in irons, my valiant Mishua."

Dhu Khiffil was wrinkling his forehead, but finally he smiled. "Not too bad, but, of course, it is not a true rhyme," he said to the companions.

The captain threw up his hands despairingly and took his leave of his father and the companions. Only when he was out of sight did the two little ones emerge from the protective folds of Dhu Khiffil's robes, obviously relieved that their father had gone. "These two law breakers are Salik and Shelah," announced their clearly proud grandfather. "Run home swiftly," he told them, "and tell your mother that there will be three guests to honor our table this night. And remember, you are still my prisoners and bound not to return to the tower for … some time."

Without fully realizing it, Cass had been studying Dhu Khiffil since their arrival at the fountain in the square. She took special note of his expressive face and voice. His face was thin and long, ending in a trim, salt-and-peppery gray beard. His eyes were large and sharp and blue, protected by lashes and bushy brows. He had an unusual nose that could make his whole face comical, but only if his eyes permitted. It was a long nose, with a narrow tip that hooked downward and came almost to a point. "Like a sea-gull's beak," thought Cass.

Whenever he spoke, his tone and manner were as impressive as his words, and sometimes deliberately more important. His tone of voice ranged from polite formality to warm affection, from sternness to good humor, from self-mockery to self-pity, from plaintiveness to wonderment. Accompanying each tone were meaningful gestures, the nod of the head, the narrowed eyes, the half-smile, even the shuffling feet. He easily succumbed to laughter, often directed at himself.

And when he recited lines of verse, which he did whenever possible, it was a performance to be remembered. Cass could still see the outstretched arms and the distant gaze. His high-pitched but pleasing musical voice still echoed in her mind. She guessed that this was the voice Dhu Khiffil used both for reciting poetry and for calling the people to prayer. He was, as he said, Muezzin.

"Sit and tell me your story, my friends," he invited, ushering them to the wide marble wall of the fountain, where they had earlier sunned themselves. None of the companions had the slightest hesitancy in accepting his invitation. Although they had just met him, they trusted Dhu Khiffil instinctively and completely. They kept nothing from him. With three memories to rely on, the companions included even the smallest details of their now numerous adventures. Thus it was that shadows were lengthening into late afternoon when they finished.

The square had filled with people in this cooler portion of the afternoon, but they respectfully avoided interrupting the group and never tried to overhear what was being said. No one thought it unusual that a group of young people like the companions would speak at such length with an elder of the community, especially when the elder was also the Chief Muezzin of Seville.

Dhu Khiffil had listened attentively, and he had observed. He never once questioned or doubted that the companions came from a still-to-be-discovered land centuries in the future. He readily devoted all of his attention to them personally. He heard in Cass's voice the attachment she felt for Jonathan and Mara, and he heard the sorrow she felt for her companions' misfortunes, especially Alan's, and her part in causing them. In Thea's flushed cheeks, he recognized her pride in being called "a born storyteller" by the Roman Matron. He was moved by Alan's pain of body and sorrow of spirit as he watched him clenching and unclenching his right hand and looking around the square as though he might be witness, once again, to a human bonfire. And, unmistakable on all of their faces when they spoke of Brother Bartolomeo, Dhu Khiffil saw smiles that would easily expand into affectionate laughter. Affection was also one of the ingredients he detected in their voices as they spoke of Maiden. Respect and awe were two other ingredients.

"So you have met the Djin, and one of them is your guide. Then you are singularly honored. Your Maiden clearly is also a healer." He took Alan's hand and studied the faint white lines that still scarred it. He smiled then at all three with an expression of added respect. "The healers are the most powerful of the Djin, Also the most helpful. As for the necklace, many legends exist about charms and enchantments that have been placed upon such a treasure, and it is often the case that the maker is a Jew, as with your necklace. I know of one such legend, which I shall share with you tonight."

"There are Jews living here now? Where?" asked Cass. "And what is the date of now?"

"Ah," replied Dhu Khiffil with a long sigh and a glint in his eyes. The companions already knew the signs of a verse in the making. "You come at an auspicious time, my friends,

600 years less five since the Prophet's hadj

> To Mekkah, Mohammed's pilgrimage;
> 1200 years less two since Jesus' birth
> Our Tower is risen from the earth.

"Bravo," proclaimed Thea.

"1198 on the Christian calendar," proclaimed Cass as she and Alan joined Thea in applauding Dhu Khiffil's verses.

"I must confess that I had already composed those lines for the recent dedication of the tower," said Dhu Khiffil, who nonetheless beamed with pleasure at the praise. "As for where the Jews live, they reside wherever they choose, as is proper, at least during peaceful times," answered Dhu Khiffil. "Most of them choose to live in the neighborhood of the royal palace not far from here." He waved generally toward the east corner of the square opposite the tower. He gave another long sigh, but his eyes were sad. "When some of my extra-strict Muslim cousins—they call themselves the True Believers—become overzealous, the Jews feel more secure being close to the palace."

"There are many artisans in the Jewish barrio, who work on everything from houses to earrings. They helped us greatly with the mosque for a number of years, and the tower too, which is practically new, not yet four years old. The old Romans helped us also," said Dhu Khiffil, with the twinkle back in his eyes, "even though they were long since dead. They perfected the Roman arch, and we Arabs learned how to set the feet of one arch standing upon the shoulders of another. Without such double arches neither mosque nor tower could have reached their heights. The Jews also contributed to the arches by showing us how to cut and fit the stones at different angles."

Dhu Khiffil's voice was getting higher and his gaze more distant as he continued to speak of the tower. The companions once again were not surprised, then, when he broke into verse. "To my grandchildren I say,

> Tell your children of our great Tower—
> Single building, …"

He paused, his brow wrinkled, eyelids closed so tightly that the bushy brows looked like two caterpillars. "Single building,…three builders, … three peoples, … hymm."

"Four peoples' power?" offered Thea somewhat timidly.

"'Power.' Excellent!" cried Dhu Khiffil, looking at Thea with wide-eyed approval. Then he turned his gaze back to the tower: "Single building, three peoples' power." He paused for just a slight wrinkle of his forehead and then continued. "Yes, Muslims, Romans, and Jews. The Jews…."

"But shouldn't you count the Christians also, Dhu Khiffil? Brother Bartolomeo said that there had been a Christian church on this site before the mosque," persisted Thea.

"Oh, yes, you are right," replied Dhu Khiffil. "Very proper that you should speak up for the Christian Franks, young lady," he said with a shrewd look at Thea. "As the necklace tells us," he added, turning to Cass. "Therefore, ahem:

Tell your children of our great Tower—
Single building by four peoples' power."

"Now, as I was saying, the Jews have preserved their skills since your friend Jonathan's time. We could visit their neighborhood tomorrow. I have a merchant friend who lives there." Dhu Khiffil had been shading his eyes with his hand. He shifted his gaze from the tower to the setting sun. "The time approaches for me to proclaim the hour of prayer. Please wait for me here."

Watching him shuffle across the square toward the tower entrance, Thea again wondered why Dhu Khiffil did not use a pony or burro to ride to the top.

"I wonder why they don't have someone younger to go up there." Alan was having similar thoughts about Dhu Khiffil's difficulties in climbing the tower ramp.

"I am sure it is a great honor to be the Muezzin and Keeper of the Tower Gate," responded Thea, "reserved for very important persons."

"He is a wise man," commented Cass. "He knows more about

the Angels—Djin I mean—than we do, and he has never met any. I think we can learn a lot from him."

"He seemed to see hidden meanings in our stories," acknowledged Alan.

"He reminds me a lot of Brother Bartolomeo," added Thea.

Several people had now joined them in sitting about the fountain or taking water from it. The companions felt a bit shy and became quiet observers. Of the scores of people in the square, some were passing through, some simply milling about. The men had beards, and their bronzed complexions contrasted with the white or gray cloth that covered their head and shoulders. The dominant feature of the women was their striking eyes, large circles of black marble set in the creamy ivory of their skin, the little that showed. The small portion of white in the eye itself was partially concealed by a droop of the lids away from the nose. Both Cass and Thea admired these striking women.

The youngsters were miniatures of their elders, except that the boys lacked beards and the girls had no veils. Thea noticed that a few men stood out as different from the others. They dressed more like the people of Brother Bartolomeo's day, in long shirt, trousers, and some with a linen cloth on their head, covering in at least one case, curly blond hair. She guessed that these were Franks. Descendents of Alan's northern barbarian Vandals. Thea took note that there seemed to be no women of the Frankish complexion. To make sure of this, she threaded her way through the crowd, carefully not to lose sight of Cass and Alan. Her Italica experience made a good story, but she had had enough of being on her own. She also made a mental note to be sure her veil covered her hair and hid her blue-green eyes; she did not want to be singled out. Again. She noticed that while most people had now stopped moving about and stood with an expectant air, the Franks—all males—were leaving the square.

Thea's observations were interrupted by the first splendid notes of Dhu Khiffil's high, vibrant voice singing the evening salutation from the top of the tower. For a passing magical moment no other sound could be heard. Most, though not all, of those present in the square bowed and moved their lips, praying in unison with Dhu Khiffil's singing, all facing in one direction, with their backs to the sunset. Cass followed their example and motioned to Thea and Alan to do the same. She thought it would be prudent to do so, but also she was responding to the compelling note in Dhu Khiffil's song and to the enchantment of the moment. Thea hesitated for a moment, then smiled at the bowing Cass and did likewise, although a little less deeply than the others. She was able to look over the backs of the people around her. She was shocked and almost cried out when she looked a little to her left and directly into the face of Maiden's opposite, Bladen.

# Chapter IX

# The Earthly Garden

"Mom and Dad should see us now," said Alan to Cass, as evening prayer ended.

"I was thinking exactly the same thing," laughed Cass. "We would for sure get the 'prayer is private' lecture from Dad and a shrug and a 'let them find their own way' reply from Mom."

Thea hurried over to rejoin them. She looked worried, her veil unfastened and forgotten. Without preamble, she announced, "I just saw Maiden's evil twin Bladen."

"Are you sure?" exclaimed Cass.

"Yes, there were only three people between her and me. I was doing my half bow and sneaking just a peek over the backs of the people in front of me. She was staring at me with those dreary, frightful eyes, just the way Brother Bartolomeo painted them, evil looking. She is gone now, or hiding somewhere in the crowd," concluded Thea, looking around her, still distressed but more composed. She noticed Dhu Khiffil just emerging from the Tower Gate. "Here comes Dhu Khiffil. Should we tell him about Bladen?"

"Not right now. Later, when we are not in a crowd," answered Cass. "Maiden warned us about her sister Bladen. The two of them are alike in a couple of ways. Neither one can force us to do anything against our will, nor can they directly cause us to achieve or lose our quest. Maiden can help us, but she can't lead us by the hand. Bladen can put all kinds of obstacles in our way to trip us up, but she cannot harm us, at least not physically."

"OK, but she gives me the shivers," said Thea.

"Me too," said Alan, "but Dhu Khiffil is nearly here," he cautioned in a whisper.

The companions turned to greet him. He was walking briskly, they noted, moving with a bounce rather than his earlier shuffle. As he approached, he tilted his head back slightly over his shoulder and looked up at the tower. The companions recognized that he was concentrating on a line of poetry. He reminded them of a seagull poised on a current of air, just before setting off on a long graceful glide. He began to recite:

"That was food for the spirit, my guests.

Now, for the body, 'tis time for a feast… umm… fest."

"Perfect," said Thea encouragingly, happily turning her thoughts away from Bladen. Dhu Khiffil looked at her . He smiled gratefully and motioned for the companions to follow him.

He led the way to an area of streets lined with shops and so narrow that only two could walk abreast and still leave room for someone going in the opposite direction. Shops of every sort were bursting with goods that spilled out into the street. The companions spent a good deal of time stepping over and around oranges and baskets of silks and ceramic pitchers and even birds in cages. They stopped and started and swerved to avoid bumping into the increasing numbers of people. As often as not they were unsuccessful and finally surrendered to the good fellowship of the crowd. People seemed to expect to jostle and be jostled. They eventually left the thickest part of the crowd behind and finally stopped in front of a low wooden door in a high stone wall. It was not an especially inviting entrance.

But through the door was an entirely different world. It was as peaceful as the streets had been bustling. The companions followed Dhu Khiffil into an open courtyard, in the center of which was a sizable goldfish pond of an unusual rectangular shape. They studied it as they walked around one end.

"It's the tower," exclaimed Cass, pointing to seven square stones that marked each level.

"You're right," affirmed Thea solemnly.

"You could go up that one by yourself, Thea," laughed Alan. She didn't mind at all, remembering that it had been a long time since he had teased her that way.

But the pond was not the only wonder of the courtyard. Colorful tiles, still warm from the sun welcomed their feet. Lemon and orange trees, plants and shrubs, delicate pink and red and white blossoms greeted them with an exotic array of colors and sweet aromas. A second story with balconies added an upper level of smaller plants and hanging vines. Dhu Khiffil waited appreciatively as his guests surveyed the yard and house. "Welcome to the house of Dhu Khiffil. The earthly garden is to remind us of the heavenly one for which we long."

Hardly had he finished when his two grandchildren were hugging him, one on either side. And after them appeared two women, one about Cass's age and the other a few years older. Cass knew she was staring at them, but she could not help herself. "Beautiful. Different," she was thinking.

"And these are the two other treasures of my household. My son's wife Tirah," said Dhu Khiffil, introducing the elder of the two, "and my daughter Zarah," he added with a smile.

Cass continued to stare, even after the introductions. "The veils they wear in public must be so that people do not stare," she thought. Being indoors, the two women wore their light, colorful veils around their necks and draped over thin robes, under which billowy blouses and skirts were visible. Both had long dark hair to match their almond-dark eyes. Their cheeks bloomed with a healthy redness that accentuated their light honey-colored skin.

Their lips too were notably red.

"I beg your pardon…I mean, hello. I am Cassandra and this is Theadora," stammered Cass, noticing that her companions were also silently staring, "and this is my brother Alan." Zarah bowed while Tirah welcomed them warmly with the traditional greeting, "peace be with you."

Cass was saved from further embarrassment by the arrival of the Captain of the Guard, who was looking much less forbidding than he had when they met him earlier in the day. Shelah and Salik ran to him, totally unmindful of their mischief earlier in the day. Their father swept them up, one in each arm. They each kissed him on a cheek and then wriggled free. The Captain greeted Dhu Khiffil with a bow. He then bowed to the companions. He seemed much more pleased to see them here than at the tower and greeted them heartily.

"Our guests honor the house of my father."

Dhu Khiffil then formally introduced the companions to Mishua Baba in a manner that showed how carefully he had listened to their story and how well he understood what he heard. He bowed slightly toward Cass first. "Cassandra, the bearer of the necklace of great power, and Seeker among the Jews." Next he gestured toward Thea. "Theadora, the Maker of truthful tales, who shares the beauty and virtue of the Christian women who dwelt in Al-Andalus even before our ancestors came to these shores." Finally he walked over to Alan, stood before him, and placed a hand on each shoulder. He looked into his face, with a mixture of compassion and friendliness, for several moments. "And this is Alan whom I now name Idris, Halán Idris, the Wanderer, for he is like us Muslims and travels the lonely desert in search of an oasis of the spirit."

Mishua Baba looked at each in turn and nodded as though confirming his father's statements. Cass smiled and nodded back. Thea blushed and bowed. Alan bowed formally and then stood straight, as he remembered Tonio doing when the Roman Officer inspected them. All three wondered at Dhu Khiffil, at how well he understood them. The Captain of the Guard studied Alan with a look that combined sympathy with a soldierly appraisal. He was impressed both by what his father said about Alan and by what he saw in the young man's bearing. But now Tirah took command, for it would soon be time to eat.

"Zarah, we have kept our guests here long enough without offering them water to wash the dust from their feet. Show Cassandara and Theadora where they may wash and refresh themselves before dinner. Halán Idris, you will go with my husband and father."

"Washing up. Lovely, and it gets everyone out of the way before dinner," thought Thea.

Twenty minutes later everyone reappeared in the courtyard. The young ladies had enjoyed washed up in luxury in a steamy bath that was large enough to hold five or six adults. Cass and Thea sat on the smooth stones of the bottom, their heads just clearing the water. They, quite naturally, assumed that there could only be one such bath in the house. Now they looked at Alan in a superior manner, as though they knew a deep secret.

"How did you like washing up?" Cass asked him.

"Very much," replied Alan, struggling to keep a straight face, "but probably not as much as you two, by the sounds you were making." He could no longer repress his laughter, when he saw their smiles turn to questioning looks.

"You heard us?" asked Thea.

"I had a bath too, answered Alan, "right next door to you."

"There's more than one bath?" asked Cass.

One bath, but the men's and women's sides are separated by a wall only one brick in thickness. You two were shouting and splashing loud enough to be heard through ten bricks."

Thea and Cass laughed good naturedly. "The best bath I have ever had" said Thea.

"It was wonderful," said Cass, turning to Dhu Khiffil. "Your baths are like heated pools for swimming."

"And when Zarah put in the flowers and perfume, I felt like a princess," added Thea, looking at Alan to see if he too had gotten such royal treatment. Alan just smiled.

The companions seemed so energized by their baths that Dhu Khiffil was moved to compose a verse about the origins of Arab baths.

> "Another gift of the Romans, my friends,
> Those builders of great renown..., great ends... trends...
> amens... hmm.

No, that will not do at all," bewailed Dhu Khiffil, "and it started out so well."

"Never mind, father. Come and bless our food and all of us," said Tirah. To this Dhu Khiffil readily agreed and led the way to the dining room.

This room, just off the courtyard, was cool in the evening, yet was still lighted, though faintly, from the lingering flush of the summer twilight. Oil lamps already flickered, and through a large doorway the fire was visible in the kitchen, glowing on the open hearth. Thea and Cass craned their necks, as they passed to get a look at the kitchen. They saw a great hood covering most of the room and funneling into a chimney. A wood fire under the center of the hood was flanked by stone benches. On the wall behind the fire were shelves. These held the dishes that would shortly be marched triumphantly to the table which the family and guests now approached.

On the table silver dishes and crystal goblets rested on a white cloth, catching and playing with the light from two four-branched candelabras. Dhu Khiffil sat at one end with Cass and Thea on either side of him. Alan sat to Mishua Baba's left at the other end, with his two captives, Shelah and Salik, across from him. Tirah and Zarah would sit in the middle, on either side of the table, when they were not serving. Dhu Khiffil spoke a blessing, praying that all who partook of the meal would be joined in a fellowship of the spirit and a celebration of the gifts of Allah.

Then the feast began. From start to finish, the meal resembled a slow and graceful procession. When the hungry feasters sat down, a loaf of bread was already at each place, and large platters of dried fruit—apples, oranges, and peaches—had been set at either end of the table. The bread and fruit simply whetted everyone's appetite. Next in line appeared a thick steaming soup, with chewy groats and tender bits of meat. Right behind the hot soup came pitchers of snow-cold water and two bowls, the size of sugar bowls, each containing a pale powder.

The companions watched as Shelah and Salik each reached avidly for one of the bowls, spooned a little heap of powder into their goblets and added water. Shelah's goblet turned a sunny yellow, Salik's a deep orange. Salik had his goblet practically to his lips, when an 'ahem' from his grandfather reminded him of his manners. He waited, fidgeting, as the others followed his and Shelah's example. Then they all drank.

"Orange juice," announced Cass.

"Lemonade," claimed both Thea and Alan.

"Ambrosia, the drink of the gods," pronounced Dhu Khiffil. "Or at least that is what the unenlightened ancients used to say," he explained to his grandchildren.

The procession of food continued. Following the soup, the main dish arrived in the form of individual bowls of shredded breasts of chicken in a savory white sauce of milk, rice, and flour. When she had wiped her plate clean with a piece of bread, Thea, with a pang of regret, thought the meal was over. She thanked Tirah and Zarah. Cass did the same, adding that every taste bud in her mouth was tingling with gratitude. Alan expressed his thanks by announcing that he was filled to the bursting point.

Tirah and Zarah smiled, went into the kitchen, and returned, each carrying a tray full of an assortment of pastries, some with sugar sprinkled on top, some containing a fruit filling, and some that were plump with a thick cream. Zarah placed her tray down deliberately in front of Alan. After a glance around the table, he reached for one of the cream pastries, to the amusement of all. It seems his bursting point had just expanded. And now the procession did truly end, with the arrival of fresh fruit.

Little conversation occurred during the meal, unless one considers the clatter of crystal and silver and the delighted 'umms' and 'ahs' to be a form of communication. Conversation of a different sort began after the pastries. Cass was surprised and pleased that it was her brother who began by formally thanking their hosts for all three of them. She had noticed how much at home he clearly felt in this house. It was also clear that the males took care of the polite formalities of speech.

"We have not eaten so much or such good food since our first visit to this land," he said, sounding a little like Dhu Khiffil. He spoke particularly to Tirah and Zarah, who smiled with pleasure at the compliment from Halán Idris.

But it was Mishua Baba who responded to Alan. "In the *Koran* the Prophet Mohammed says that one who does not feed the hungry traveler has no religion. You have come from afar, as I understand."

"Yes, so we have heard," said Zarah, sitting next to Alan. She asked if he would share with them the story of his previous experience in their city. Alan readily agreed and began speaking of their first coming to Seville and of Brother Bartolomeo. The first time he paused, however, Zarah politely interrupted. "Please, Halán Idris, my father has told us that you visited Seville when it was called Hispalis. I would love to hear of Hispalis." Alan flushed with confusion. He looked to Cass and Thea for help. But before they could say anything, Dhu Khiffil spoke.

"My family would be honored with this story, but I fear it is too painful for you, Halán Idris. I told Zarah that you lost loved ones in Hispalis, but I did not explain how. Perhaps it was wrong of me to mention this. Zarah has, I fear, a romantic imagination, but it is also a very sympathetic one."

Hearing himself addressed in this manner by the kindly Dhu Khiffil, Alan felt that he was among family who valued what he could tell them. He had not felt this way for some time. He agreed to tell his story. Dhu Khiffil was pleased, as much for Alan's own sake as for the instruction of his children and grandchildren.

Alan spoke with hardly a pause: of Cecilia and her mother, of Tonio and the battle of Italica, of the ambush of the Roman army at Hispalis and of the fate of the citizens that followed, a fate that included Cecilia and her mother. He spoke of the Djin, of throwing himself into the fire, and of being rescued by Cass and Thea. When he finished, there was complete silence until he spoke again. "I had been a reluctant visitor to Al-Andalus before Hispalis happened," he confessed, "but no longer," he concluded. Cass assumed that he meant that he had embraced their quest, but she would have liked to hear him say that.

Solemnly Zarah thanked Alan. She reached across him and took his right hand in both of hers just as Maiden and Thea and Cass had done, as though to add her own healing skills. Alan responded with what Cass was certain was the deepest shade of red ever to show on his face.

The young ladies were asked for the story of their time in Italica. Thea told most of it, but Cass insisted on relating the parts involving her foolhardy behavior that resulted in leaving Alan behind and having Thea arrested as a slave. Dhu Khiffil added his commentary on Maiden the healer and the other Djinn, mainly for the benefit of Shelah and Salik. Then he spoke of the necklace, which is what the companions had been waiting for.

As the companions had come to expect, he started with an apology. "I fear I may have but little to tell to travelers such as you, other than a bit of legend about the necklace, as I promised you this afternoon. First, I must thank you for reminding us in your narratives that the necklace signifies the harmony that should exist among Jews, Christians, and Muslims who are related in belief. Here in Seville our ancestors from each religion have together built a great city, and over the centuries the blood of each has mingled with that of the others. Yet the promise of the necklace has not yet come to pass. Our peoples too often fail to be true to our ancestors' hope for living in harmony." Dhu Khiffil paused and smiled. "They had a most poetic word for this togetherness. They called it *convivencia*." Dhu Khiffil's expression turned serious again. He looked meaningfully at Zarah as he said, "even cousins have failed at *convivencia*."

Zarah took her cue from her father. "As my father speaks of strife among cousins, so it is with me. I love Abul Feda, who returns my love, but because our family is from a different clan than his, we may not marry. His people are warlike and fiercely loyal to their own clan. They would not accept me. If we marry we will have to go the great city of Toledo in the north where such differences do not matter so much. As the waters from different streams converge there to make the Tagus, the greatest river in the land, so do persons of many differences come together to make a city of greatness and hope."

"And may Allah help us and you in making your decision, my daughter," prayed her father.

"And now I will share with you, my guests, my meager offering. It is a tale of an antique and magical necklace. This tale speaks of a later chapter in its history. I believe it can be no other than the necklace you possess.

### Dhu Khiffil's Tale of the Necklace

"The story tells of a Jewish goldsmith named Malachy who lived here in Seville some three hundred years ago. He was a hardworking, upright man, but he never succeeded in his trade. Thus he could not attract any promising apprentices to help him to make his name known. When he first came to Seville, he had, perhaps unwisely, purchased a rare necklace, one made by a fellow Jew but not in any of the traditional styles for which Jewish craftsmen are famous."

"As his fortunes worsened, he began to take the necklace out of its secure place each evening to admire it. It was one of his few consolations, but when he became so poor that he feared he would lose all, he asked himself one evening while gazing at the necklace, 'Should I not sell this treasure?' 'No, master,' came a reply. Before him stood a djinni. She was an evil djinni, but Malachy could not tell this from her face, which was empty of emotion. She told him that he would become successful if he would promise to destroy the necklace after he had made his fortune. Some tell of a good djinni who attempted to persuade Malachy not to destroy an object of such beauty. Better to sell it to a worthy buyer whom she would help him find."

"Malachy liked this second djinni better, but he was desperate. Unwisely, he agreed with the evil djinni. She warned him that if he did not keep his promise to destroy the necklace he would be worse off than before."

"In less than a year Malachy became the most famous and richest of his trade in the city and even far beyond it. All the skilled apprentices hoped to join him. But he was no happier now than before. Too late, he discovered that he preferred the necklace to fame and riches. No matter how many times he tried, he could not bring himself to destroy it. And so it happened as the evil djinni said that he lost everything in a great fire. Everyone except Malachy thought it was a strange fire, for it burned only his house and shop. His neighbors' houses on either side of his were not even blackened by the flames and smoke. No one was harmed, not even Malachy, who explained that he had been warned in a dream by a good djinni who awoke him with her singing."

"After the fire, Malachy had nothing left, except the necklace, which he kept always close to hand. In fortune he was worse off than before, but inwardly he was relieved and felt happier than he had in years. He decided that the necklace must be an object of great importance, too great to belong to one person, so he put it into the hands of his Rabbi who was a wise and holy man and also learned in matters of magic."

"Malachy found that he had not lost everything after all. Many of his friends and his customers, when they heard of the fire, came to commission new work from him, and they paid him well and in advance. Malachy became even more famous than before. He was especially known for making bracelets and buckles adorned with precious stones of a purple hue."

*Here Ends Dhu Khiffil's Tale of the Necklace*

"Your necklace is, based on what you have told me of Maiden and Bladen, the same the one the Rabbi kept for a time in the synagogue. The legend of Malachy the Goldsmith does not tell of the later fate of the necklace, but I know of someone who may be able to help you when we visit the Jewish barrio tomorrow. He once told me of a necklace given by a Rabbi to General Yusuf when the General and his followers of Strict Believers occupied Seville about a hundred years ago."

After Dhu Khiffil concluded his story, the dining room was again quiet. Mishua Baba nudged his two children, who rose a bit sleepily from their places and went round the table, kissing each person on both cheeks. Then they went for a final hug and a blessing from their grandfather.

"The feast lacks only for a verse or two before the children go to bed," said Dhu Khiffil. "I will compose the first line and Theadora will complete the couplets." Thea smiled a bit nervously but nodded agreement and looked intently at Dhu Khiffil.

"Allah is great, is good, is generous,
God has blessed us, has united us.
The earth and All its bounty praise God
The heavens and All its lights glorify God."

Everyone repeated each couplet after the composers. The feast and the fellowship were, for them, complete.

The next day, as he had promised, Dhu Khiffil escorted the companions to the Jewish neighborhood. Mishua Baba invited

Halán Idris to accompany him on his daily round of inspecting the defenses of the palace. Alan hesitated, but only for a moment. He would have been delighted to the see the castle and the Palace Guard, but he thanked Mishua Baba and told him he was honored but felt it his duty of accompany his companions. The Captain of the Guard smiled his approval, saluted Alan, and was gone. Alan knew he would long remember being saluted by the Captain of the Palace Guard of Seville, as he set out with his companions and Dhu Khiffil.

The Jewish barrio reminded Cass of a honeycomb. The main streets were similar to the streets in other parts of the city, lined with protective walls, behind which nestled cozy homes. All of the shops seemed to be on one main street, yet none of the shops actually opened onto that street. A door, a gate, or a narrow alleyway provided entry to clusters of shops where jewelry-makers, smiths, weavers, tile painters, and other artisans made or sold their wares to merchants, traders and travelers who crowded into the narrow spaces. Alan and especially Thea would have liked to examine the shops, but they had to hurry to keep up with Dhyu Khiffil, who, with Cass close behind, wove his way through the friendly crowds exchanging greetings. He seemed to know everyone.

Dhu Khiffil led them to a particularly large shop that occupied one whole side of a square of shops. Once inside, he introduced them to a large, robust man, Benjamin the Merchant.

"Benjamin, chief merchant of Seville, give greetings,
To the companions, our guests for a time too fleeting."

"Well spoken, friend," said Benjamin, as he put one arm around Dhu Khiffil's shoulders. "You are in good form today. Have you been taking lessons from your guests?" He bowed to the three companions and addressed them. "Allow me to show you my wares." His shop was itself a small bazaar with numerous little shops. Thus Benjamin's "wares" contained the creations of a variety of skilled craftsmen. Some were apprentices. Others appeared to be more like junior partners. All greeted Benjamin the Merchant warmly.

Their host insisted that the companions each select a gift. Thea removed her veil and replaced it with an elaborate headpiece that she had been eyeing. It was made of colorful red cloth and had a gold band from which hung six gold-colored discs. Cass picked only a light kerchief. Alan was undecided so Benjamin finally selected a curved dagger with an ornate case and tucked it into the sash at Alan's waist. "It would not be of much good in a fight, but it looks good on you," he said to Alan. Alan thanked him. Benjamin bowed, then led them past a standing suit of armor and through a curtain to a small room where cushions dotted the bright rugs that covered the ground.

"I come here to rest," he said. "The armor guards my retreat. Even merchants have sometimes to rest. Please tell me about yourselves and how I may serve you."

Benjamin had tea and biscuits served, and for a third time in two days, the companions told their story. They did not tire of doing so because each retelling helped them to better understand their adventures and to think of what might be ahead of them. Each had become practiced in his or her part. They took turns as though they played roles in a drama. Cass concluded by repeating what Dhu Khiffil had told them about General Yusuf getting possession of a necklace. "Dhu Khiffil thought you might know something further about that necklace," added Cass, with a smile and nod for Dhu Khiffil.

"And no doubt you recited a few verses of poetry that you 'borrowed' once again from the great Jewish poet and sage Samuel Ha Nagid, you old pirate," said Benjamin to Dhu Khiffil. "I use Samuel's proper Jewish name," added Benjamin to the companions.

"Borrowing, like imitating is a way of honoring the authors who went before us," responded Dhu Khiffil to his accuser. "May I say the following, however, in defense of my borrowing from your great soldier, romancer, Vizier and poet, Samuel Ibn Nagrela. Of course, I use his Arab name. He had an Arab heart," explained Dhu Khiffil.

"Of war and the mind, of nature and wine
Nagrela wrote. Sweet as grape of the vine
Are his songs to all who love romance.
Yet I imitate only his style so elegant…ah, of elegance…
hmm."

"'Elegant' is good," said Thea. "Imperfect rhyme is perfectly
fine," she added with a mischievous smile at Dhu Khiffil. Cass and
Alan seconded Thea's judgment by applauding. They could tell that
this debate over a famous Samuel had a long history.

Dhu Khiffil's face brightened. He bowed. "And now," he said
turning to Benjamin, "it is your turn, my old friend." Dhu Khiffil's
voice had just the slightest note of challenge in it, as if to say, "see
if you get a round of applause." So Benjamin began his tale with a
smile.

*Here Begins Benjamin's Story of the Necklace*

"I hear many tales from customers and fellow traders here and
also when I travel to far places. How much of these tales is true I
do not know, but, yes, I have heard of such a necklace, and one of
the most reliable stories involves the same General Yusuf about
whom our esteemed Dhu Khiffil has spoken. Abu Jacob Yusuf was
a great General and later became the Caliph of Seville. At first
he was unfriendly toward the Jews, even though Jews helped to
construct the mosque he caused to be built. As a way of gaining
the General's toleration for the Jews, a Rabbi, who had in his keeping a mysterious necklace, suggested giving the necklace to him as
a gift from the Jewish community. The Rabbi was both wise and
clever. Having learned some of the powers of the fabled necklace,
he thought of a plan to ensure success. He would get help from his
ten-year-old daughter Sarah."

"Many objected to the Rabbi's suggestion because the Jews
treasured the necklace, but in the end they decided that it was better to lose the necklace than to lose their homes. General Yusuf

accepted the gift, but at first, as the Rabbi had expected, it did not change his behavior towards the Jews, whom he continued to persecute. So the leaders of the Jews, including the Rabbi asked to see the General. Yusuf already treasured the necklace, so he granted the audience to the Rabbi and the other leaders of the Jews, and to little Sarah, the Rabbi's daughter. The Rabbi explained that the necklace signified the cooperation that should exist among worshippers of the one God. General Yusuf was highly pleased, but not as the Jews had hoped. Instead, the General said to them, 'That is exactly what we believe, that all true believers should be one, and that is why we will require you to become Muslim and why we will exile or execute all others. It is the will of Allah.'"

"Hearing this, the leaders of the Jews trembled, except for the Rabbi and Sarah. They had foreseen the General's reaction. The Rabbi answered the General by explaining to him that the true meaning of cooperation is that all can respect the beliefs of others even without agreeing with those beliefs in every single detail. The General was becoming very angry and was about to send the Rabbi and the other Jews away, or, worse, to prison. But before the General could speak, the Rabbi, with Sarah, bowed respectfully and began backing away, taking care not to step into the gold fish pool. The Rabbi was pretending that he thought the audience was at an end. Sarah followed him. As though it were an afterthought the Rabbi mentioned, 'of course, the magic djinni of the necklace serves its master as well as its mission.' The Rabbi emphasized the words, 'magic djinni.' in a loud voice. The General, naturally, commanded that the Rabbi remain and explain this 'magic.' Just the Rabbi and his daughter. Yusuf even dismissed his courtiers and soldiers. He loved the idea of magic."

"The Rabbi did more than explain it. He demonstrated it. He instructed the General to give the necklace to Sarah and to hold onto her robe. Yusuf did as he was instructed, not even hesitating to step into the pool. The next thing he saw was a vast expanse of desert as they stood in a shallow wadi. Seconds later they were back in his palace. So amazed was the General that he agreed to change his policies towards the Jews, and maybe even toward the Christians. They would not be equals with the Muslims, of course, but they could follow their own beliefs. And so it came about that a time of peace and harmony reigned in Seville and it continued so, even increased after the General became Caliph. The people, especially the Jews and Christians, were grateful to the Caliph and to the Rabbi."

"The Rabbi was practically always at the side of the Caliph, having become one of his chief counselors. Whenever the Caliph wanted to travel through the necklace, he called upon the Rabbi and Sarah, and later, Sarah's daughter. It seems that the necklace works its magic only for a Jewess. Either that or the Caliph feared magical travel and wanted a female along to ensure that the Rabbi would be careful." Benjamin laughed loudly at this last statement. "Excuse my little joke. But it is true. The necklace might smile upon a male Jew who possesses it, but it seems to work its magic only for a Jewish female." He looked directly at Cass.

"And when Caliph Yusuf died, the Rabbi became counselor to Yusuf's son. The son of Yusuf became even greater than his father. His name was Al-Mansur. He was known as 'Protector of Believers' and 'The Victorious.' He it was who began the construction of the great tower, a fitting minaret for the mosque of Yusuf his father. During all of that time, cooperation among the three peoples prevailed throughout Al-Andalus. That time came to be known as the *Convivencia*. It was believed by Muslims that their Caliphs had a magic carpet. Al-Mansur would be in Africa one day, tending to his kingdom there, and the next day he would be back in Seville. And he could watch over his northern frontier seemingly without ever leaving Seville. And Sarah's daughter became his chief wife."

"When Al-Mansur died, he was, alas, succeeded by a cruel and greedy Caliph who once again persecuted the Jews and Christians. He was harsh even with his own people. As he started to lose more and more land to the Christian Franks from the north, he became harsher still. The Rabbi, now very, very old, disappeared, and with him the necklace. He feared that the Caliph would try to use its powers wrongly, or even to destroy it. He decided that the necklace should be hidden for a time. All of these happenings occurred not many years past."

*So Ends Benjamin's Story of the Necklace*

The companions sat in silence, reflected on what they had heard and learned. Alan then broke the silence. "I wonder what would have happened if the bad Calif had tried to use the necklace in battle."

"Probably nothing, young warrior," said Benjamin, with a smile. "No story speaks of the magic of the necklace being used in battle except to escape from it." Benjamin produced another of his short bursts of laughter at being so witty. He quickly became serious again. "In fact one or two stories speak of the necklace producing an end to a battle, even if it meant sacrifice or surrender rather than what is usually considered victory." He paused and looked at Cass with an expression of uncertainty and concern. Then his usual smile returned, and Benjamin rose from his cushion. "But come, my friends, I have spoken overlong and know you must be about your business."

Dhu Khiffil and the companions followed Benjamin out of his sanctuary. As they passed the suit of armor, the merchant stopped suddenly. He reached for the helm atop the armor, removed it, and handed it to a surprised Cass. "You did not choose a gift worthy of my reputation as 'chief among merchants,'" he said to her. "Please accept this helm. Perhaps it will protect you. May Yahweh let it be so." Cass looked into Benjamin's eyes as she accepted his gift. She knew what he was thinking. Being mistress of the necklace was wondrous but also perilous.

After taking their leave of Benjamin, Dhu Khiffil and Thea chatted as they walked. Alan and Cass followed, Cass preoccupied with her thoughts about Benjamin's story of the necklace. As they entered the square in front of the mosque and great tower, the companions were surprised to see a small troop of four or five Frankish soldiers resting their horses by the fountain, while a few Moorish women drew water from the fountain. Dhu Khiffil explained that the Franks must be the bodyguards of some Christian merchants who were in Seville for business, which was not unusual.

As the companions and Dhu Khiffil approached the fountain, four of the soldiers greeted them in a friendly manner. The fifth, who had been talking with one of the women, now turned an inquiring eye on them. He moved away from the fountain and gestured for the others to follow. He was apparently their captain. As he spoke to his men several of them glanced toward the companions. Their friendly manner was gone.

Dhu Khiffil quickly realized what was causing the change. Thea had forgotten to replace her veil. The fancy headdress, the gift from Benjamin, hid neither her red hair nor her blue-green eyes. In fact it put them on display. The soldiers mistook her for a Christian in captivity to Muslims. The soldiers were looking around them, uncertain of what to do, but clearly weighing the possibility of rescuing Thea. Dhu Khiffil whispered his fears to the companions and said he would call the Guard.

"No," responded Cass promptly. "We do not want a fight. Alan, Thea, we must leave. Come on, quickly," she exclaimed. She hurriedly embraced Dhu Khiffil. Thea and Alan, bewildered, did the same and began running after Cass.

"May our One God be with you," said Dhu Khiffil, "and the magic djinni too," he called after them. The companions heard him but could not see his smile nor the sparkle of tears in his eyes that somehow complimented it.

Cass was the first to reach the edge of the fountain. She threw herself onto the rim and swung her legs over, and plunged them into the water. Thea lifted her robes with one hand and launched herself into the fountain with her other hand on the rim. Alan lunged over and into the water and came up sputtering. Cass handed Thea the helm. "Grab onto me but leave my arms free," she commanded, noticing out of the corner of her eye that the soldiers were now moving toward them. A Muslim woman was speaking to the Captain and pointing at them. "Bladen," gasped Cass, catching a glimpse of her eyes.

Cass tore off her veil, grasped the wolf's head on the necklace and unfastened it. She paused for just an instant as the Captain of the Franks rushed toward her, reaching out to seize her. She hesitated. She feared that he might reach her and did not want to transport him with them. But when he suddenly pulled up and stopped, she joined the wolf's head to the ring catch, making the necklace whole again.

# Chapter X

# The Alcazar of Seville

"I don't understand!" exclaimed Thea, who had quickly hopped out of the fountain, again pivoting over the rim with one hand. She watched as Cass lifted her feet from the fountain, swung herself around the rim, and put her feet down on the cobblestones of the Courtyard of the Fountain. Neither of them took much note of the fancy, though soggy, leather slippers that encased their feet, which they could barely see in any case in the faint pre-dawn light.

"I don't know if I understand either," said Alan, as he splashed his way to and over the fountain wall. "Why did those Frankish soldiers get so nasty-looking all of a sudden?"

"Bladen again," announced Cass. "She was the one talking to the Captain. All she had to do was draw his attention to Thea and mention the word 'slave.' The Franks thought they recognized a fellow Christians from the north. With Bladen's prompting, they decided to act on their own. Dhu Khiffil was about to call the Tower Guard to protect us, but that would have made matters even more 'nasty,' to borrow your word, Alan. Thea, you forgot to keep covered up."

"You are right. How could I do that? I am either being captured by Romans or freed—unsuccessfully, thanks to you—by Franks," said Thea plaintively. "Sorry."

"Not all your fault. We did not remind you either," said Cass. "That lovely red hair of yours and those blue-green eyes are the culprits. It seems that Christian men are sensitive about their women being enslaved, and I have gotten the strong impression that Moorish men have long been partial to red-heads."

"That all sounds very romantic I suppose, in a way," observed Thea, "rescuing a Christian lady at the mercy of the Saracen. But I am sure that I did not look like a lady in distress, and Dhu Khiffil was the only Muslim man in sight."

"What I still don't understand," said Cass, "is why the Captain of the Franks pulled back all of a sudden when he was about to reach for me."

"I can explain that," answered Alan. He drew out his curved, ornamental dagger, the gift from Benjamin, and held it in front of him. "I pointed this at him."

"Hmpf," intoned Maiden. "Well done, Halán Idriss, Wanderer. I bid you good day," said Maiden as she approached the companions through the thinning morning mists. Alan did not quite know how to react to such praise from Maiden, usually his chief critic. He did his best to appear composed, even nonchalant. He nearly succeeded, formally bowing his greeting to her, but at the last moment, he surrendered to his considerable pleasure at her words of praise. He straightened up, smiled broadly, shrugged a bit, and said, to most everyone's surprise, including his own, "I treasure your compliment, My Lady."

Maiden, who was not at all surprised, acknowledged his words with a nod. She turned to Cass and Thea, who had been surprised not so much by what Alan said but by the way he had said it. "Grown up," thought Thea. "Courtly," mused Cass.

"Good morning, ladies. It is the dawn of a new day, or had you not noticed." Unlike Alan, Cass and Thea had made no show of formality. As soon as they heard her voice, they had immediately hastened to her side and waited impatiently while Maiden spoke with Alan. "You have brought a friend, I see, Cassandra," said Maiden. Cass was puzzled until she saw that Maiden was looking at the helm, the 'friend,' on the rim of the fountain where Thea had left it. "May your gift prove as useful as the dagger of Halán Idris," Maiden continued.

Cass walked over to the fountain and picked up the helm, laughing. When she returned she began plying Maiden with questions. "You know that we have visited Benjamin the Merchant?" she asked Maiden, and then answered for her. "Of course you do. We have learned much from Benjamin and from Dhu Khiffil, but we have not had time to think about it all." Cass looked at Thea and Alan, who agreed with her. "And," continued Cass, "you brought us to whatever time this is, did you not? I had no chance to think of where and when to go, as I closed the catch, so I focused on you and thought, 'Maiden, you decide.' Why are we here, and when?"

"I am pleased with what you have learned thus far. You may find that you now understand more than you realize, or that you can express in words as yet. The stories you have heard and your adventures in Seville have told each of you much about yourselves, as well as about the necklace. You had a good instructor. History remembers Dhu Khiffil as a wise counselor as well as a poet and Muezzin." As Maiden spoke, the companions, slightly surprised, realized the extent of what she said. They had indeed learned much about themselves, though they could not yet put into words what they learned or how it pertained to their quest. They also realized at that moment what a good listener Dhu Khiffil had been, how he had gotten them to share their personal stories.

Maiden turned to Thea, once again seeming to read her thoughts. "And you, Theadora, composed poems with one of the most famous Arab poets of old. You should be proud." Thea glowed with delight. Maiden's light-heartedness buoyed them up, inviting another flood of questions. The one clear fact was that they were still in the Courtyard of the Fountain.

"How far have we travelled in time this time, and in which direction?" asked Alan.

"What happened to Dhu Khiffil," put in Thea, "and to Zarah and Tirah and Shelah and Salik, and....?

"And how did it happen that Bladen turned up so suddenly?" inquired Cass. "I know you said that she could not harm us directly, but she came pretty close to causing serious trouble through those Franks. She makes me jittery—and angry."

"I saw her the day before as well," volunteered Thea. "She scares me."

"Ah, yes. Bladen. Her taking action is a good sign. She is becoming concerned that you could actually succeed in your quest," replied Maiden. "Up to now one of your chief defenses has been her rather low opinion of my selection of a bearer of the necklace, and her companions." She added a smile to her cheerful tone, as she looked fondly at the three of them for some moments. When she again spoke, however, she had become pensive. "Now that my sister is not so sure of her first impressions, you will need to be ready for more 'serious trouble,' ahead, Cassandra. And companions," she added.

"As for your question, Thea, I will tell you of Dhu Khiffil and his family, but briefly, since we have but little time to tarry," said Maiden, briskly now. "Dhu Khiffil lived to a ripeness of years. He had the joy of seeing his grandson, Salik, become his successor as Keeper of the Tower Gate and Chief Muezzin of Seville. Zarah left Seville within the year of your visit and joined her beloved Abul Feda in Toledo. Mishua Baba and Tirah lived a long life and died, happily, fortunately just before the wars of the Reconquest of Seville. Shelah never married but governed the household of her brother Salik who had many children. Some of these—too many—died in defending the city before it fell to the Franks fifty years after the completion of the great tower, and your visit."

"In answer to you, Halán Idriss," said Maiden, "three hundred years less nine have passed into the future for you. It is 1491 of the Christian Era, and the Christian Reconquest is nearly completed. Al-Andalus will soon be no more though its spirit will remain.

Now, I must leave you for a short time. Someone approaches yonder."

The companions turned to see who was coming. A lady in a very fancy outfit and a gentleman, in only slightly less ornate attire, had entered the square, evidently taking a leisurely morning stroll. The new arrivals were clearly surprised to see that someone had arrived in the Courtyard of the Fountain ahead of them. They acknowledged the presence of the companions with just the slightest inclination of the head.

"Gone again," said Cass, who was looking back for Maiden. There was a note of disappointment in her voice. "She did not explain why she brought us here, to 1491 I mean."

"Oh, Cass, how beautiful," said Thea. "Just look at your dress." After seeing how the strolling couple was dressed, Thea had finally examined their own finery.

"Both of you, look at you," said Alan, who was noticeably impressed.

Thea and Cass wore dresses of the same style as the lady they had just nodded back to, though not as richly. Gowns was perhaps a more accurate term than dresses. They were long and weighted with fabric, trimming and ruffles. White lace veils and dark blue cloaks kept them warm but still displayed the fronts of their gowns. Cass and Thea, however, pulled their cloaks about them more closely. They had been standing still for some time, and they now felt the chill in the air despite the morning sun that was peering hazily at them. Besides the hems of their gown, as well as their slippers, were still damp.

"I am surprised we made it out of the fountain in these," said Cass, "but look at you," she exclaimed to Alan, who had flattered the ladies for their attire. Alan wore a soft, blue floppy hat, quite jaunty, and an open, ankle-length cloak under which there was a shorter, blue robe that reached to the knees. Visible from the knees down were close-fitting, bright blue stockings, which disappeared into ankle-high leather shoes. These latter were definitely still damp. "You look handsome, brother," said Cass, as though she had made a discovery.

"Just like the courtier angels in the painting Brother Bartolomeo showed us," exclaimed Thea.

"Except for no flowers on your hat, though" teased Cass. "But nice legs."

"Maiden said she would return shortly," said Alan to get attention away from how he was dressed.

Seemingly on cue, a "hmpf, hmph," sounding almost like a laugh, came from under Cass's cloak. Cass was so startled that she nearly dropped the helm she had been holding in her left arm. Fortunately she juggled but did not drop it. She lifted it with great care up to eye level to look inside, through the slits in the visor.

"Maiden!" she announced gleefully, "like a djinni in a bottle."

Maiden was reclining on the curved portion of the inside of the helm, which made for a convenient couch. "I have decided to stay with you for a time, at least until you have safely settled into the palace. Benjamin's gift enables me to be your secret guide. Not that anyone would dare to challenge you. As you have noticed, you are dressed as Spanish nobles, suitable for courtiers. And you speak like them, but you have to learn to behave a bit more courtly so that you do not arouse suspicion." Maiden paused, smiled, shrugged. "For now watch how your fellow courtiers act and do likewise. When those who are doing their morning promenade here in the Fountain Courtyard return to the palace, follow them. And, Cassandra, kindly carry this helm as though you were the one inside."

Cass replaced the helm in the crook of her left arm, under her cloak, carrying it as she would a baby. As she completed this arrangement, she thought she heard a muffled but melodious laughter. She could not repress a laugh of her own and looked at Thea and Alan expecting them to join her, but something else had attracted their attention. They were staring as though hypnotized. She followed their gaze. She uttered a barely audible "oh." Before them bathed in the early morning sunshine, were the walls and arches and flying buttresses of a huge new church. It stood where the Mosque-Cathedral had been, just behind and to the west of the great tower. In the darkness and then the pre-dawn mists of their arrival, and with the excitement of Maiden's appearance, they had taken little account of their surroundings.

"Huge, larger than the palace," exclaimed Alan.

"Larger than the Mosque-Cathedral. It must be the biggest Cathedral in the world now," pronounced Thea.

"The Christians have conquered indeed," said Cass, with a mixture of awe and nostalgia.

"Maiden just told us that the year now is 1491, but I wonder when they built this place," said Alan.

"They probably started right after Seville fell to the Christians in 1248," said Thea promptly. It had to have taken a couple of centuries."

"Maiden has always been clear on dates. She wants us to be aware of them," mused Cass. What do we know of 1491"?

"Columbus," offered Alan.

"About to set sail, searching for the passage to India," added Thea.

"And nearly the completion of the Reconquest," said Cass, still musing. "That means that the Christians will soon rule the whole country. What will that mean for the Jews?" she asked, looking at Thea.

"Bad times," said Thea uncomfortably, "a far cry from the way things were during either Dhu Khiffil's day or Brother Bartolomeo's. But at least the orange grove is still in the same place," she said with a sigh. She was pointing to several orange trees visible just to the east of the great tower. "The earthly garden…,"she began.

"To remind us of the heavenly," concluded Cass, with just a faint smile of apology for interrupting Thea.

"The great tower is nearly the same, too, mainly just a bell instead of the four gold balls," offered Alan, on a hopeful note. He had detected the sadness in his sister's voice.

"'Built by four peoples' power," said Thea, recalling Dhu Khiffil's verses.

"I think we are about to go into action," noted Cass, getting her companions' attention. Most of the people out walking—there had been a steady stream of them—were now leaving the Courtyard of the Fountain. They were heading in the direction of the royal palace, the Alcazar. The companions joined their fellow nobles.

Leaving the square, they entered a wide street that curved away from the Cathedral. As they rounded the curve, they saw the palace walls straight ahead. These walls were different from the more picturesque but less imposing ones the companions had seen the first time they had entered the city, the Seville of Brother Bartolomeo. These walls were gray, at least thirty feet high, and had ramparts wide enough at the top for soldiers to march four abreast. A shoulder-high castellated wall protected the outer part of the ramparts. The periodic openings gave defenders ideal spaces for loosing their arrows or stones or boiling oil at any attackers.

The openings reminded Thea of a story about a dragon her dad used to tell her when she was little and losing her front teeth. "Like a gap-toothed dragon," she observed. "I hope it is friendly," she mused.

"Anyone trying to scale that wall would have to have a forty-foot ladder and a lot of luck," noted Alan more seriously, impressed by the defenses he saw.

"Functional," admitted Cass, "but I preferred Mishua Baba's walls."

As they approached the large arched gate, the companions, Alan in particular, took note of the soldiers on guard. He approved of their uniform, a white mantle over chain mail or light plate armor. Emblazoned on the tunic was a red castle keep, symbolizing the Province of Castile, and above it, as though leaping over it, was a golden lion, symbol of the Province of Leon. These were the emblems of Queen Isabella of Castile and Leon. Alan was not yet aware of the meaning and importance of these insignias, but he admired them. Nor did he miss noting the belt that neatly circled the mantle at the waist, and from which hung a broadsword. He even noticed the metal cap that sat smartly on the head.

The companions, having reached the palace gate, found themselves alongside one of the soldiers on guard. Had they kept on going with the flow of nobles entering the gate in knots of three and four, they would have aroused not attention at all. Instead, the companions paused and looked at the soldier, wondering if he would challenge them. The soldier, after studying them for a moment, frowned visibly and took a step in their direction. He pulled back, however, when an authoritative voice rang out that seemed to come from an older woman who was just then passing Cass on her way through the gate. "Hurry, my Young Lord and Ladies, you are expected." Now it was the soldier's turn to look guilty. The companions, confident and unchallenged, passed through to the very large outer courtyard of the Moorish-built Alcazar, now one of the homes of the Christian monarchs.

Cass patted the helm hidden under her cloak. "Thank you, Maiden." Then she looked over the courtyard. This area appeared to be primarily for conducting business. Soldiers, including, surprisingly, several turbaned Moors, milled around as messengers, and court clerks bustled about. The courtiers were just passing through. Cass slowed down to examine the ornate arches of the wall ahead of them. She would have stopped for a moment, but just then a voice rang out—again.

"Hurry Along. You really are expected, and try acting like you belonged."

The companions attempted to obey Maiden's command. "Hurry up and act natural. Easier said than done," thought Alan as they passed quickly through one of the arches that Cass would have liked to examine more closely. They arrived at an even larger courtyard. Sunshine flooded all but a few corners of this space and reflected off the bright yellow walls. Thea decided that it should be named the Gold Courtyard. It was impressively large but, other than the 'gold' walls, quite plain, providing a simple background for the elegant courtiers who were milling about in groups, conversing. The companions gazed, or rather, gaped around them, definitely not looking like they belonged.

Cass and Thea now realized that their clothes were quite plain in comparison to the elaborate outfits worn by most of the others, both men and women: dresses of brocade flowers; cloaks, capes and hoods trimmed with fur; tunics of every color of the rainbow; short surcoats with heraldic beasts—lions and eagles and, most often, unicorns; stockings as silvery as full moons or yellow as suns; and jewelry as sparkling and as abundant as stars in the night sky.

While Cass and Thea were thus preoccupied, Alan was showing off his knowledge of soldiering, unaware that no one was listening to him. "This smooth surface of flat stone would be ideal for marching," he said. "The soldiers are probably garrisoned nearby. They...."

Cass unintentionally interrupted Alan. "These courtiers live in a different world from the one made up of the peasants and the monks we met the last time we were in Seville and that was less than a hundred years ago. They look like the pictures in the history books, the ones I expected to meet the first time."

"Right, the history books speak less of peasants than of the nobles," said Thea. "I agree with you. I think I felt more at home with the peasants," she added, looking more critically at her clothes. "We must look like the country cousins to these courtiers."

Both Thea and Cass were beginning to feel self-conscious. Even Alan had become silent as a young man approached and addressed Cass.

"Welcome. I have been waving to you from across the courtyard. It is difficult to get the attention of anyone here at the best of times, and with the King and Queen being in residence, our numbers are double, as you can imagine. But here you are. I am Sebastian, at your service." He bowed and included Thea and Alan in the gesture. Cass and Thea immediately felt more comfortable. Unlike most of the other courtiers, Sebastian was dressed richly but simply and in good taste. His clothes and his manners suggested that he was more important, and certainly busier, than they were. He repeated his verbal 'welcome' with a warm smile. "The steward told me you would arrive today. He did not tell me that you would add such brightness to the morning."

"Thank you for the compliment," answered Cass. She managed a slight curtsey, her self-consciousness now completely gone. "Are you sure you have the right persons?" she asked, hoping very much that he did.

"I trust that I do," he replied, "if you are the Ladies Cassandra and Theadora, and you, sir, are Master Alan."

Thea made a slight but polite curtsey and nod; Cass curtseyed again, this time more deeply and slowly, her most graceful curtsey thus far; Alan bowed and smiled happily.

"Ah, you see I am correct. Now we have to sort you out. Alan, Julian is looking for you, to show you to the squires' quarters. He was just with me. Yes, there he is." He waved to another man of his own age and drew his attention to Alan. "You are in the hands of the Sergeant of Squires," he told Alan. "My Ladies, would you come with me?"

# Chapter XI

# Ladies In Waiting

Cass, with Thea close behind, followed Sebastian through what seemed to the two new-comers to be a solid wall of people. While Sebastian seemed to glide effortlessly through the crowd, Cass and Thea found themselves entangled in flowing skirts or capes, their own or others" and heard themselves repeating, "pardon, pardon." No one seemed to notice the clumsiness of the new arrivals. Most often a gentleman bowed courteously in response to their "pardon," and insisted that the fault was entirely his own. Several of these gentlemen, the younger ones especially, paused to stare appreciatively at Cass and Thea, so openly that the ladies were quite red in the face before they escaped from the courtyard.

They finally did escape by way of a staircase lined with ornate tiles. They climbed several flights of stairs and made their way down a long corridor. Sebastian stopped before a heavy wooden door and knocked. The door was opened promptly by a smiling, bright-eyed girl. Sebastian introduced Maricarmen. She was perhaps about the same age as Alan, although it had become increasingly difficult to tell the ages of the companions of late, especially in this new setting. Had Brother Bartolomeo seen them now, he might have told them that they looked "more mature." The young woman curtseyed gracefully and naturally, "like a dancer," Cass thought. She and Thea returned the curtsey, both pleased that doing so was becoming almost spontaneous. As he parted from them, Sebastian said he looked forward to seeing them often, perhaps even the same evening in the palace salon.

His new charges barely had time to assure him that they hoped to see him that evening before Maricarmen exclaimed, "Oh, may I see it please?" Cass's cloak had fallen back, revealing the helm. Before Cass could prevent her, Maricarmen had it in hand and was examining it. When she set it down on the window seat facing outside, the companions realized that Maiden had gone. "That will be for protection against bad spirits," said their new acquaintance, who now gave her attention to Cass and Thea.

"I had not thought you would be so old. You must be older than the Lady Francesca," she said to Cass and Thea, before catching herself and placing her hands over her mouth. "Oh, I am sorry, My Ladies. That just slipped out. I hope I did not offend you," she said apologetically. When Cass and Thea's laughter reassured her that they were not offended, Maricarmen began rattling away about helping them with preparations. The ladies understood portions of what she said, catching words like "journey," "dresses," "veils," "the Queen," "the Duke."

Finally Cass held up her hand. "Maricarmen, what preparations are you talking about?"

"Yes, this is all new to us," said Thea. "We were told to learn as we go," she added, which, of course, was the truth.

After showing mild surprise at their lack of information, Maricarmen happily explained, chatting away in considerable detail. She was interrupted frequently by questions from the two companions, if only to slow her down. Cass and Thea were to become members of the household of Lady Francesca and accompany her to Cordoba, in a few weeks time, for her wedding. Alan would be a squire in her service; they would be Ladies In Waiting.

"Lady Francesca," Maricarmen explained, "is an orphan, a ward of Queen Isabella's, who was a childhood friend of Lady Francesca's mother. The Queen found the right match for her, just recently. And once she makes a decision it is soon done. Believe, me, I know. I usually attend Her Highness when she resides here in the Alcazar." Maricarmen paused and smiled at her two attentive listeners with a touch of pride at being their instructor. "The wedding will take place in Cordoba on December 31, so there are little more than three weeks to gather suitable attendants and prepare for the journey."

"What is today's date," asked Cass.

"Why, November 30," answered Maricarmen. But I forget, you have come from some distance and probably have lost track of the days."

"Some distance indeed," noted Thea.

"Well, you will learn everything there is to know in the next three weeks. I am to help you. My room is just across the corridor. Call on me at any time. You will be quite busy and have many questions about becoming a Lady's Companion, but it will be fun. You will likewise then become Ladies of the Queen's Court yourselves. People will address you as My Lady." Turning her attention to more practical matters, Maricarmen observed, "I must say you had enough baggage sent." She indicated the two large trunks which the companions had been using as seats. "And now we have time to look around, if you like."

Cass and Thea nodded, wordlessly, rather dazed at their roles. In fact having roles to play was a new and different experience for them since entering Al-Andalus. They were used to telling people who they were and what they were about. As Cass considered their present situation, she remembered once again that she had placed the companions, herself, Thea, and Alan, in Maiden's hands for this most recent journey of the necklace. She also remembered that Maiden had not answered her question about why here in the Alcazar with the court in residence, and why now.

Thea too was thinking about their new roles. They quite pleased her. She and Cass were after all members of the royal household, apparently nobility, minor but still nobility, from some distant outpost, in training to become official Ladies. They were at the moment trailing along behind a young woman, Maricarmen, who waited upon the Queen of Spain when Her Majesty was in residence in the Alcazar of Seville.

"I think we must have graduated," said Cass to Thea.

"What?"

"I think Maiden feels that we have learned enough about ourselves and the necklace. We are ready for the main part of the quest."

Thea was about to reply when they found themselves back in the Gold Courtyard where numerous courtiers still lingered. Further talk of their quest would have to wait.

"What is everyone actually doing?" inquired Cass of Maricarmen.

"They are here to wait upon the Queen or the King—supposedly," answered Maricarmen, grinning back at Cass. "But they spend most of their time showing themselves off, flirting, and gossiping. Today the chief topic of gossip is speculation about the surrender of Granada. With Caliph Boabdil el Chico here and both Monarchs present something important is happening, but I hope the gossip is wrong about the surrender of the Moors. I guess I should not say that. Anyway, do not let the courtiers worry you. They are harmless, at least most of them are." Both Cass and Thea were impressed with their guide's friendly disrespect for the courtiers.

"The Queen is not holding court this morning, so we can go into the inner palace." Maricarmen gestured to the right, where a triple arch showed the way.

In the weeks to come Cass and Thea would be able to absorb what they now saw, but this first encounter defied their senses and imagination. They simply could not take it all in. They dream-walked through marble courtyards, past bubbling fountains, along dazzling halls, and under countless arches, and they stared at ceilings that portrayed the heavens filled with moon, stars, sun, and a spectrum of colors. Their minds formed pictures so rapidly that the ladies afterwards could not be sure if they had seen or only imagined them. They retained a few dominant images, however: pale-white, blue-veined marble that seemed to breathe and to pulsate with the warmth and brightness of the sun; wood polished and of the color of honey; carvings decorated with inlaid gold leaf; glowing tiles of green and azure; pillars and arches one after another in seemingly endless succession.

As though awakening from a dream, Cass and Thea found themselves next to Maricarmen in the Queen's private courtyard. Here above the rows of pillars, above the triple arches on every side, the walls rose, unbroken to the royal balconies forty feet up. The four walls were works of the sculptor's art.

Thea at first thought of the courtyard walls as elaborately decorated wedding cakes. When her mind rejected this picture, it remained blank for a moment and then was filled with three pictures in succession: a sea full of fishes; a field filled with flowers; a sky full of stars.

Cass's mind was gradually able to grasp the basic design molded onto the walls. It was a though an ancient and enormous vine had wound its way in conscious patterns, crisscrossing itself without ever tangling or snarling. Scattered throughout the loops of the vine were stars, fishes, sea shells, and flowers.

Maricarmen offered them a much simpler appreciation. "Truly, the walls proclaim the glories of creation and the greatness of its Maker."

"The artists must have worked for years on these walls," said Cass. "And it is going to take me more than three weeks to look at it all."

"And for me to find my way around," added Thea.

Maricarmen was enjoying the awe-struck reactions of her pupils. "It is much nicer than it was a few years ago, before the Moorish artists were brought in to restore it. The Queen wanted to recapture the beauty the Moors had been famous for when Seville was theirs before the Reconquest."

"Are there now no Muslims living in Seville, other than artists?" asked Cass.

"A few, in one neighborhood, but they are mostly businessmen who help us trade with their countrymen in the south. A few more, the artists, builders, and gardeners, are in the service of the Queen. There are some in the provinces who work as farmers and herdsmen, but they are very poor and not likely to get ahead like these in the city." Maricarmen paused in her recitation, then added, in what Cass and Thea decided was a wishful tone, "and there are the Mariscos. They are of mixed Christian and Moorish blood. Their ancestors were Moors who converted to Christianity. Some, maybe even most, were probably forced to do so at first but then decided to remain Christian even when they did not have to."

Maricarmen spoke with such positive feelings about the Muslims that Cass was encouraged to ask another question. "Do Jews still live in Seville?"

"Yes, some artisans and traders, like the Muslims. Some Jews have even been courtiers in the distant past. But not nearly as many Jews live here now, not since the great purges."

"Purges?" asked Thea.

"Pogroms," said Cass slightly more sharply than she intended. She went on in a more controlled voice, "killing whole communities of Jews." Thea nodded her understanding.

"Yes," agreed Maricarmen, "though I have not heard that word. A hundred years ago we Christians blamed the black plague on the Jews. That was ignorant, of course, but many believed it. They started persecuting Jews, even killing them. I am afraid the greatest purge started here in Seville."

"What of the city of Toledo in the north," asked Thea, remembering the children of Brother Bartolomeo and of Dhu Khiffil. "Are there Muslims and Jews there?"

Maricarmen rewarded Thea with an immediate brightening of

her face. "Oh, yes. Toledo will always be home for Muslims and Jews as well as Christians. There is a saying that no one people can ever claim Toledo, for its treasures of art and books and gold are so plentiful that one or even two peoples have not sufficient hands to hold them. But come. It is getting chilly standing here. We shall see the gardens."

"Gardens" sounded rather tame, even dull, after what the ladies had just seen in the Alcazar. They were mistaken. Leaving the inner courtyards and patios, they first re-entered the Gold Courtyard, which seemed to be the main crossroad of the palace. They then entered a passageway on the opposite side of the square from their staircase. After a short walk along a cobblestone path, they turned and entered a tunnel on their right. In semi-darkness, they again walked for a short space, then passed through a curtain of vines and leaves, emerging at a point overlooking vast gardens. Once again Cass and Thea were reminded of Dhu Khiffil and of his words about earthly and heavenly gardens.

Before them and on both sides were many distinct gardens each with its special attractions. Rows of hedges or shrubs along with stone or gravel pathways marked the borders of the separate but interconnecting, rectangular gardens. The ladies could see that the arrangement of the gardens somehow mirrored the pattern of the varied courtyards and patios of the palace. The builders and designers had applied their art to stone and flower alike.

Cass and Thea followed Maricarmen down two sets of steps next to a square goldfish pool so large that it could have held fifty human swimmers. The overview they had had of the pattern of gardens now gave way to a detailed close-up of the first garden, the one closest to the palace. It was a walled-in area of tile paths, fountains, statues, and neatly trimmed shrubs. This garden spoke to their senses. The splash of water mingled with the song of hundreds of birds. The mild air carried the sweet scent of blooming plants and the freshness of evergreen cuttings.

"Moors made these gardens centuries ago, so it is right that

Moors are now fixing them up, just as they are repairing the palace. We females are supposed to use just this enclosed garden unless we are accompanied by a male," said Maricarmen, making a face that meant, "how foolish." "I think three of us make for protection enough. We will go further…that is, if you want to," which, of course, they did.

Cass noticed a light heartedness in Maricarmen that seemed to increase the farther they got from the palace buildings. The garden they now came into had no walls that one could see and had an untamed appearance.

"My friend and I call this the 'wild garden'" said Maricarmen. The paths were of gravel or dirt. Fountains and statues were fewer, and these few seemed to have grown out of the ground. "This is a garden for exploring," stated Maricarmen, "and here is a good place to start." She led the others to a large but shallow pond in which was an island with what appeared to be an ivy-covered mound the size of a small house. On closer inspection, the mound proved to be a huge boulder. It was very large and pitted and looked like it must have dropped out of the sky. The lower half, partly submerged in the water, was hollowed out into what looked like the entrance to a cave.

"Inside the cave is a stone goddess of fertility," explained Maricarmen.

The ladies stood by the edge of the shallow pond, peering across a fifteen foot expanse of water to the opening in the rock where the statue rested in a current of water. Even in the relative darkness within the rock and despite a covering of mold or green mildew, they could see the large breasts and strong arms of the goddess. The face had a seductive smile which struck both ladies as familiar.

"Shall we wade over to get a better look?" asked Thea, and without waiting for the others, she kicked off her slippers, lifted up her dress, and splashed across in her stocking feet. Cass followed, but not before she glanced at Maricarmen, who held back, as though she were afraid, which struck Cass as rather strange. As Thea and

Cass bent over to peer into the hollow, two male figures rushed out at them from the darkness, shouting.

"Trespassers!"

"Sacrilege!"

# Chapter XII

# Yusuf And The Squire

Alan remained where he was, as Cass and Thea followed Sebastian. He did not have to wait long.

"You are Alan, yes? I am Julian, but you will address me as sir. Come with me please."

Julian was courteous in a businesslike, military way. Alan did not mind. In fact he found it flattering to be addressed by a person of such bearing and authority. He followed Julian through the same passageway from the Gold Courtyard that Cass and Thea later took to the gardens. Julian pointed out that the gardens could be reached through the tunnel on the right. The barracks were straight ahead. Alan wanted to inquire why they were going to the barracks, but he did not, for fear that he would somehow be unmasked as an imposter. He wanted a chance to see where the Guardsmen lived before that happened.

They marched along a cobblestone pathway. There were horses in the stable to the left. "What beautiful animals," thought Alan, "and twice the size of the Vandals' ponies." A hundred yards farther on, they came to a large, three-story stone building. He brushed shoulders with men and boys in different uniforms. The few who wore the distinctive black and white of the Guards caught his special attention. The squires and other new recruits had their living area on the top floor. Julian assigned Alan to a bed in a large room that contained nine other beds. There was a trunk at the foot of his bed and laid out on top of it was the plain brown uniform of a squire. Alan was just deciding that it was time to explain that there must be some mistake about who he was when Julian called across the room.

"Yusuf, be a good fellow and show the squire around. I have to see to the other new squires." Turning to Alan, Julian said, "Yusuf knows every corner of the palace. His father has just rebuilt it." Julian pointed to the only other person present in the room, a boy of about fifteen, the same age as Alan. Then Julian left without further ceremony.

"Are you going to be in the Guards?" Alan asked when he turned to the boy named Yusuf. The other laughed.

"Only by a special favor to my father am I even allowed to train with you squires and wear the brown uniform. No, they would not permit a Muslim to serve in the Guards, though I have often heard that in past times Christians served in the Royal Guards of Muslim Princes."

"Christians fighting with Moors? Even against other Christians?" Alan was surprised and intrigued.

"Yes, and sometimes Moors against other Moors," replied Yusuf. "One of the heroes of our chronicles is the Emir of Valencia who many years ago defended his Spanish homeland against an invasion by Moors from Africa. Christians and Spanish Moors fought together, and the Christians came to honor the Emir, calling him 'El Lobo,' the Fox, because of his cleverness. But that was many years ago," concluded Yusuf a little sadly.

This story fired Alan's imagination. "I wonder if I could be a Guard," he said aloud.

"I doubt it," responded Yusuf promptly. Only a few of the squires will qualify to become Guards. And even fewer, if any, will be selected to become a Queen's Guardsman. They are selected only from the higher Spanish nobility. Most of the squires here are training for duties elsewhere, in a smaller palace or nobleman's court. But why would you want to become a Guard here anyway? They have little freedom and many duties. And you have been specially honored as it is. You are to go with the Lady Francesca as a Lady's Squire, are you not?"

"I do not know. Am I?"

"So one of the other squires told me, but the Alcazar is a palace of rumors. Come with me and we will find out and look over the grounds at the same time."

On the way to the gardens Yusuf explained, in answer to Alan's polite questioning, that his father was an engineer and the supervisor of all the builders and artisans working on the palace. Yusuf spoke with pride.

"Where I am from we have many palaces like this one, though not all are as large. In my city of Granada we have the greatest palace of all, the model for all others, including this one. Some day you must visit us, and I will show you our great wonder. But I am forgetting...." Yusuf ended abruptly. Alan was about to ask him what he was forgetting when he noticed that the young Moor had to compose himself. He seemed either angry or on the verge of tears, or both.

"Forgive me," Yusuf said apologetically. "But I have heard just today that something we Moors thought to be impossible might be happening. The surrender of Granada. Our King Muhammad, or Boabdil as you call him, is here in the Alcazar, meeting with the Queen and King. If the rumors are true, it is a very sad day for us. Boabdil will have to go into exile somewhere, and then we will have no Protector of the Believers. And what will happen to Granada where Muslims have lived for seven hundred years? Allah must be very angry with us."

Alan did not know what to say or do. Yusuf tried to shake off his sadness. "Father says, Allah will provide." When he mentioned his father, Yusuf's face brightened. He explained that since his family was of Moorish nobility, he and his father were permitted to live in the Alcazar. The two of them had been at the palace for over two years now, and Yusuf had been living in the same quarters as his father until a few months ago. "Come," said Yusuf, "let us continue the tour." He had regained his composure.

As they descended some steps, with the fish pool on their left, Alan noticed a low tunnel to his right and looked in.

"The old dungeons," said his guide, seeing where Alan was looking. "I have never seen anyone imprisoned there. It would be too terrible. I have heard some frightening tales from the squires about rats bigger than the palace cats." Yusuf shuddered and moved on, as though a draft from the dungeons had caught him and might pull him in. They walked directly to the gate leading to the garden. "This is my favorite garden. My friend and I named it the wild garden. It contains the best hiding places." Yusuf smiled a little shyly at Alan when he mentioned hiding places. Then, impulsively, he took Alan's hand and said, "Since you are my new friend I will trust you. I will show you where my companion and I hide, even now sometimes."

Alan quickly caught his friend's enthusiasm for the wild garden with its secret hiding places. "You could be gone for days, without being discovered?" Alan asked.

"And nights if you wished," replied Yusuf. He led Alan to a section of the outer palace wall. Leaf-covered vines draped the wall like a rich tapestry. Yusuf pulled on one vine. After a few tugs a whole section of leafy tapestry pulled like a door, revealing a hollowed-out space about the size of a bed. "We call this our nest. My friend would not like me to show it to you," said Yusuf. Again Yusuf was slightly embarrassed as he put the door of vines back into place. "Now I will show you the goddess' cave."

Alan and Yusuf were already exploring inside the goddess's cave when they heard the ladies approaching. "Yusuf said, "we must remain hidden," but first he went to the edge of the cave and carefully looked in the direction of the approaching voices. Alan was surprised then to see him take a scarf from around his neck and place it carefully, where no one would see it unless they knew where to look. He came back to Alan and explained what they were to do. The ambush was ready.

Thea and Cass screamed and raised their arms to cover their heads from an attack. The next moment they heard laughter, from Maricarmen and from their attackers. The ladies now became the attackers, splashing and beating Alan on his back and shoulders as he continued to laugh. "That was not very funny," scolded Cass, although by now both she and Thea were laughing, or at least smiling.

"And who is your accomplice?" demanded Thea, "besides Maricarmen, that is," she added, looking accusingly at their guide.

"This is my friend, Yusuf," said Alan. Cass was happy and sad when she heard Alan say "friend." He had called Cecilia "my friend" also. That was the only other time she could ever remember him using that expression.

"And this is my new friend, Alan," announced Yusuf to Maricarmen.

Maricarmen greeted Alan warmly, as Cass and Thea did Yusuf. The companions now recognized to whom their respective guides had been referring as their "friend." As the five of them strolled back toward the palace, Maricarmen was able to confirm that Alan indeed was to be one of Lady Francesca's squires. This news pleased the companions, most of all Alan, who beamed.

"Remind me to thank Maiden for...." He stopped when he caught Cass's warning glance. But Yusuf and Maricarmen had not noticed. They mostly noticed each other. It did not take the companions long to realize that the friendship between Yusuf and Maricarmen was special. What was charming, thought Thea, was that they were quite unselfconscious about it.

As the group neared the walled-in garden and the palace just beyond, they detoured slightly to where men were working.

Christians and Moors labored together, to finish blending the wild garden with part of the walls of the enclosed garden. Here they met Yusuf's father, Alzarad, who greeted them politely but briskly because he was busily occupied overseeing the work.

"If I turn my back, the mortar turns to dust," he said dryly and only half jokingly. He returned to his work and the young people continued on to their assigned quarters in the Alcazar.

# Chapter XIII

## Palace Romance

As Maricarmen had predicted, the ladies quickly fell in with their duties, which at first were light enough and left them plenty of time for themselves. Lady Francesca made a fuss over them for a few days. She had never had her own personal attendants, other than the Matron. Unlike the elderly Matron, her ever-present Maiden-Aunt and chaperone, Cass and Thea were close to her own age. If Lady Francesca had asked about their ages, she would have learned that she and Thea were the same age, both a year younger than Cass.

They might have become friends, but Lady Francesca, under the guidance of the Matron, had developed a haughty attitude, which discouraged telling ones age or much else of a personal sort. She regularly managed to remind her Ladies In Waiting to know their place—below hers. She expected them to take turns performing certain practical duties, like helping their mistress dress and un-dress, which she did at least four times a day. She also expected them to entertain her, especially when she tired of conversations, which she did rather quickly since she had come to frown on ordi-nary news, much less gossip, again influenced by the Matron, who said talk of such a common sort was unbecoming for a great lady.

Still Lady Francesca came to appreciate her Ladies In Waiting. Thea quickly gained favor with her mistress by mastering the flute-like instrument called a recorder. It was much easier for her to play than her flute at home had been. Lady Francesca was so pleased that she told the Queen of Thea's talent. The Queen in turn invited Thea to play in the palace salon on the special evenings when the Queen joined her courtiers at one of their regular entertainments. Playing the recorder, Thea accompanied some of the other ladies, who sang. The Queen was pleased, which led to her attending more frequently. After the music and singing on one such royal evening, Thea offered to tell a story. The Queen nodded her approval. Thea made up the story from the words in the ladies' songs about knights and ladies, kings and queens. From that evening forward, if the Queen were not in attendance or did not request a tale from Thea, Lady Francesca asked her to do so back in her own rooms. She came to rely on Thea's performances as relaxing diversions from the business of preparing for the wedding.

Cass found this arrangement to her liking. Maricarmen had taught her how to do fancy needlework, at which she quickly became expert. She would do needlework as Thea played or told tales. Her work also caught her Lady's attention. Cass was soon asked to design a small tapestry for Lady Francesca's bedroom. Now she was able to boast to the Queen of both of her Ladies In Waiting. The fact that the Queen was impressed raised Lady Francesca's reputation in the eyes of the court.

On most mornings Lady Francesca, accompanied by Cass and Thea and two Palace Guards, walked in the outer gardens. On two occasions they ventured out into some nearby streets of the city, and once they visited the Courtyard of the Fountain. Aside from the church, the orange grove, the great tower, and, of course, the fountain, Cass and Thea saw little that reminded them of their earlier visits other than the style of architecture, particularly the ever-present courtyards and gardens.

It was a pleasant enough existence. None the less, Cass and Thea looked forward to siesta time each day when Lady Francesca retired to her room for a few hours after the mid-day meal. While most residents of the palace were resting, the two ladies, joined by Alan, Yusuf, and Maricarmen, explored the gardens or revisited the courtyards and elegant patios of the inner palace. They developed an elaborate game of hide and seek, with Yusuf and Maricarmen as the hiders. At first the three seekers rarely found them, but as they learned the geography of the Alcazar, they surprised the hiders a couple of times. Cass and Thea also had some free time in the evenings after the entertainment. Lady Francesca retired earlier than most other young nobles. The Matron advised her that plenty of rest and avoidance of exertion enhanced her beauty.

Cass and Thea were thus able to join other courtiers in the salon for conversation, even occasional gossip (of the elevated sort of course), or to listen to an impromptu tale of adventure and romance, or to a late ballad or two. Thea was able to relax and listen. Occasionally she and Cass visited the small library where they were the only females, creating a disapproving stir among a majority of the palace's scholarly and clerical members, but eliciting encouraging smiles from at least a few of these types.

Alan was a quick study as a novice squire. Yusuf regularly boasted about him to the ladies. "At first," related Yusuf, "a clique of the more aristocratic squires who are training to become Guards made fun of Alan, especially after they learned that he did not know how to saddle a horse. They called him the 'bare-back rider' and 'farm boy.' But when we started dueling practice, only a few of those elites could afford to tease him without coming away with a mark from the flat of Alan's sword on them. And after they saw him with the bow and arrow, the taunting stopped altogether. A few grumbled something about the bow not being the true nobleman's weapon, but no one said it to his face. Besides being better at arms than they are, Alan is bigger than most of them. He has become something of a hero to the other squires who have been getting tired of the superior attitude of the elites." Cass and Thea had almost forgotten about Alan's military training in Italica under a Roman officer, however brief it had been.

Alan returned Yusuf's praise, especially for his skill as a rider. "I would never have learned to ride if it were not for Yusuf's private lessons. And I never will ride as well as he. They are making a mistake by not letting him become a squire, but 'Rules are our life's blood'." Everyone laughed as Alan mimicked Julian's favorite daily advice to his young squires. In her pride in her brother's abilities, Cass for the moment forgot her concern about something he had said to her recently. He had confided to her that he envied the Queen's Guardsmen because they were professional soldiers and formed a tight-knit group. Alan's wish to share in this comradeship of soldiers had struck her as contrary to his friendship for Yusuf and to the memory that he still carried of Cecilia and what the Vandals had done to her. For the first time since coming to Al-Andalus, Cass thought of her Philadelphia friend Robert, who came from a Quaker family. Robert had told her of his paradoxical admiration for soldiers and his opposition to war. She worried that Alan did not seem to be aware of a similar contradiction.

She worried about him, but her worry diminished when she saw how well he was doing and how much Jusuf admired him. Something else distracted Cass from her concern about him. She was watching the growing flirtation between Thea and Sebastian. From their arrival at court Sebastian had paid particular attention to Thea. "Just good friends," is how Thea described their relationship, when Cass asked her. Cass had observed that Sebastian behaved courteously to her but showed greater interest in Thea. It was not long in fact before Sebastian sought out Thea every evening, even venturing into the library on the pretext of looking for some maps. Whenever Thea and Cass joined the other courtiers in the salon, Sebastian promptly appeared at Thea's side. He proved to be a talented musician, singing pleasantly to Thea's accompaniment on the recorder. At other times he played his lute and composed verses in the current fashion of love poetry. A few of the lines caused Cass to blush once or twice. Thea on one occasion responded to Sebastian's lyrics by improvising an adventure story in which a woman played the part of the hero, rescuing the man by her needlepoint skills rather than feats of arms, to the delight of the courtly ladies.

The Queen was present for most of Thea's storytelling, including the one about the rescue through needlepoint. Queen Isabella had formed a decidedly high opinion of Lady Theadora. The Queen was also quite aware of the courtly romance between Sebastian, one of her own Guardsmen, and the Lady Theodora. She approved. Two such talented courtiers would naturally find one another attractive, and such romances were, of course, public and well monitored by the Queen through her attendants. The fact that the two at times played religious music suitable to the Advent season further pleased the Queen.

It surprised no one when Queen Isabella assigned young Lord Sebastian and Lady in Waiting Theadora the task of providing the entertainment to honor the arrival of Duke Antonio Leon de Cordoba. The Duke had arrived from Cordoba the previous day with members of his household, including a number of soldiers suited to his position. He ruled Cordoba in the name of the King and Queen. He was also a friend of the family of the young nobleman who was Lady Francesca's fiancé. He and his retainers would be the official escort of the Queen and Lady Francesca for their journey to Cordoba a week hence. The Queen announced to the court the news that the next evening there would be a special entertainment by the Lord Sebastian and the Lady Theadora in the Duke's honor.

The salon was the Queen's favorite room in the palace, so she chose to conduct both business and pleasure in this bright, high-ceilinged room that was large yet not so large as to lose a sense of intimacy. It was a cozy room, with thick red drapes that added to its cheery warmth. It was rectangular in shape, with arched entryways midway on the two longer sides. On most evenings the palace residents moved chairs, stools, benches, or just cushions into casual arrangements for talking or listening. But this evening was different. The Queen would be hosting Duke Antonio Leon.

Thea and Sebastian planned to sit at one end of the salon with the chairs and benches facing them in curved rows. There was a narrow passage to cross from one high arched entrance to the other, but people who came late would have to make their way along the folds of the drapes, to stand at the far end of the salon. Or, if they did not mind being viewed by half of the audience, they could just stand in the archways. But on such an occasion who would come late?

Thea and Cass—who was the more nervous of the two—with help from Sebastian and Alan, were setting up for the performance as the courtiers started to fill the area. "Is this all right?" asked Cass. "Will you have enough light? Can you see? Where will Sebastian be? Do you…."

"Everything is just fine, Cass," interrupted Thea. "You, however, are not, and you are making me nervous. Sit down. Over there." She motioned Cass to a bench by the wall in the second row. "Sit!" she repeated, as Cass was about to move her chair.

The music that Thea would need fitted nicely on the bench in front of her stool. Sebastian could look over her head and also receive his cues by watching the motion of Thea's recorder. Lights came from two tall candelabras on either side of the performers. Alan joined Cass in their favored second-row seats, in case there were any needs for them to tend to. The room was now filled except for the first two rows. A hush descended except for the rustle of ladies' formal gowns as the courtiers rose. The Queen was approaching. She entered from the performers' left. Women curtseyed and men bowed from the waist as she made her way to an unpretentious and comfortable, high-backed chair near the center in the front row. Lady Francesca sat to the Queen's left and Duke Antonio Leon to her right. Other important people claimed the remaining chairs and benches of the first two rows. Since the rows curved toward the performers, Cass and Alan at the end of the second row had a view of the royal person, the performers, and a good portion of the audience. "Ideal seats," whispered Cass to Alan. "We can watch to see how the audience reacts," she added anxiously.

She need not have been concerned. Thea performed beautifully, as Cass remembered she always did before audiences, whether by herself or with a group. Sebastian who had lived all his life in one or another of the royal courts, was perfectly at ease. His presence as well as his voice pleased the audience. It was during the second song, when Cass was just beginning to breathe a sigh of relief, that she noticed the stranger leaning against the pillar of the arch to the left of the players.

The stranger had expected to be bored, and thus came as late as he could. Now he was regretting that he had missed the first song. While enjoying the second piece, his gaze moved about, lighting first on the performers with a critical eye. The young singer's handsome face expressed both confidence and pleasure in his singing. The young woman who accompanied him was as beautiful as she was talented. Her red hair was escaping from under her headpiece and framed her face, the blue-green eyes, the light complexion, the short nose, and the purple lips now pursed over the mouthpiece of the recorder. "Frankish ancestors," mused the stranger to himself. His gaze was drawn to a second woman seated to the right of the performers and to the left of the Queen's party, in the second row. Here was a more familiar beauty of Al-Andalus. Dark. Dark hair, skin the color of honey but with a hint of roses, eyes deeper than midnight and more mysterious. His eyes moved to the young man sitting next to her. "Related by blood, quite obviously," he quickly decided, but he got no further. The dark lady nudged the squire and when the stranger looked back at her, her midnight eyes were fixed on his own. He shifted his gaze a little too abruptly; he had been caught in his attentions.

Cass looked at Alan and nodded toward the archway where the stranger was now intently focused on the performance. She noticed now that he was dressed in the household livery of the

Duke de Cordoba, and yet he did not seem to blend in with his uniform or with the other members of the Duke's party. He was unusually tall and thin. Dark curls covered his head, and an equally dark beard covered most of his face and elongated the chin. His complexion was tawny. "He must the Duke's counselor, or maybe even a magician," thought Cass. "Not your typical courtier."

"He has been staring at us," whispered Cass to Alan, but neither of them dared say anything further, not wanting to cause a distraction. Cass shrugged and forced herself to concentrate on the music. She noted with some relief that the late arrival seemed careful not to look at her again, as if to atone for his earlier boldness. In fact the stranger was at that moment scolding himself for staring, or rather for letting himself get caught doing it.

It was not until they were back in their room, long after the end of the entertainment, that Cass had the chance to describe to Thea the mysterious "counselor" who had been staring at her and who seemed at first to be threatening but then simply mysterious and out of place.

"You have made a conquest, it seems to me," was Thea's reply. "Otherwise how could he have been paying attention to you when I was there, not to mention the Queen," laughed Thea. Her laughter distracted Cass from her mystery man. Nor did she let that last comment pass.

"Oh, and do you think he could see you with Sebastian draped over your shoulders like a shawl pretending he could not see the music from where he stood. Thank goodness at least he did not try to recite one of his saucy love poems."

Thea again laughed instead of objecting to Cass's attack. She put one hand to her forehead in a melodramatic pose and proclaimed, "Alas are we never to be alone?" Putting her other hand over her heart, she continued in exaggerated Sebastian-like tones. "Your eyes are stars, your teeth pearls, your cheeks marble, your lips rubies."

Not only Cass, but Lady Francesca and the Matron, and some

of the other courtiers as well, were aware of Thea and Sebastian's 'friendship.' Indeed most such romances were quite public and tolerated, within bounds. Rarely were two young people of the opposite sex left alone after the age of twelve. The Queen was very strict about this rule. The reason the matrons visited the bedrooms every night to say goodnight to each maiden in the palace was not just for courtesy. It was a way for the Queen to make sure that her young courtiers were behaving themselves and not getting carried away by their emotions. So Sebastian's attentions to Thea were, at least at the beginning, simply a pleasant pastime for both young people, part of the elaborate game of courtly romance. That is why Cass, at the moment, could not embarrass her friend, try as she might, about losing her heart.

"Actually we had our first argument today," said Thea, who did not seem particularly worried about it. "All I asked was had he noticed how close Maricarmen and Yusuf were. At first he just scoffed at the idea. But as he thought about it, he realized that I might be right, and then he became quite serious. He said that if he were sure that they were in love he should report them to the Queen. That is when he explained to me that he is an officer of the Queen's Guardsmen, the ones that travel wherever she goes. He told me that she is more than strict about any liaison between a Christian and a Moor. I said they were too young to be serious, but if they did become so, could they not get permission to be betrothed. Sebastian was completely shocked. He said it would be unlawful, even if Yusuf converted to Christianity. He was still a Moor."

"Cass," continued Thea, "if I did not know Sebastian better, I would think he was prejudiced, not just because of different religions either. That I could at least understand." At this moment Thea looked over at Cass who was listening intently. "I guess the right religion was what we used to argue over, is it not, and I would get so upset with you for not becoming a Catholic, or at least a practicing Jew. I am—I was—pretty much of a prig about religion

I guess."

Cass smiled at her. "Yes, I remember. But you do not sound nearly so sure of things as you used to. I am glad, it complicates your world, but we will talk more tomorrow." Cass managed to yawn and smile simultaneously. "Great performance, Lady Theadora. Excellent! Do not you think so, your royal Highness," she added, mimicking Lady Francesca's tone.

Tired as she was, a few thoughts crept into Cass's mind before sleep overtook her. One was her growing sense of curiosity about the mysterious stranger, who seemed so interested in her. She admitted to being pleased at his evident attentions. Other thoughts were more disquieting. Sebastian clearly liked and admired Thea. If he became upset over a possible romance between Maricarmen and Yusuf, the other courtiers would probably react even more negatively."

# Chapter XIV

# The Mysterious Stranger

The companions, now including Sebastian, were, of course, not alone in observing the closeness between Yusuf and Maricarmen. The courtiers who paid them any attention, which were quite a few, were conscious that Yusuf and Maricarmen were now past the age of twelve, and of an age when such a friendship would normally not be permitted to continue. Few said much about the relationship, at least publicly, because the Queen continued to show favor to Alzarad and, notably, to his completing the rebuilding of the Alcazar. Alzarad himself, however, had been increasingly uncomfortable with the situation. Cass and Thea became aware of his concern the day after the entertainment during one of their last walks in the gardens. They were with Sebastian and Alan. Maricarmen and Yusuf had gotten far ahead and were no longer in view. Alan, who at first had always joined Yusuf and Maricarmen for these daily walks, now was more often in the company of Sebastian. As the companions returned to the palace from the wild garden, Alzarad approached them rubbing his hands on a cloth. Cass noticed that his face looked careworn.

Alan and Sebastian needed to return to their duties. They

exchanged greetings with Alzarad and continued on into the Al-cazar. Cass and Thea stopped to talk. "You should not work so hard, sir," said Cass. This palace has been growing for centuries, so it need not be completed tomorrow."

"You are right, My Lady, but even when the work is going its best, I worry that something will go wrong before we can finish. Sometimes I think Allah is not pleased with me. Also…." He hesitated for a moment before going on. "Also, we have been too long away from our people. You have become good friends to my son in these last weeks. You have seen him with the maiden who is his friend of long duration."

"Do you disapprove of their friendship too?" protested Thea, thinking of Sebastian. She then remained silent, realizing she had said more than she intended.

Alzarad sighed and nodded. "When we first came to court, the two were little more than children. They are of similar rank, and it is, or was, fashionable under this Queen to overlook the differences between our peoples in ones so young. They joined forces immediately, like fellow countrymen in an alien land of grownups. They have been inseparable ever since. My approval or disapproval is not the issue. They are at an age when friendship often blossoms into love. Perhaps it already has," he said looking at Thea. "There was a time, now past, when a love such as this might have been possible. I doubt not that they each have more than a drop of the other's blood. But such relationships are not permitted any longer, nor do I think that they ever will be again."

Again he looked at Thea. "From what you just said, others have already noticed their closeness and raised questions. I feared this and regret I did not act sooner." He lifted his hand gently to silence Thea, who was about to protest. "The Queen is unbending about this," continued Alzarad. No exceptions. She has been unusually patient in this instance, partly because she is so anxious for me to continue here until the renovations are completed, but that may not be soon enough.

"What if Yusuf were to become a Christian," blurted out Thea in frustration.

"Even so, the Queen—and others—would be suspicious of him, as they have become of others. She and the king have already appointed special investigators called Inquisitors. They examine reports about Jews or Muslims who may be posing as Christians in order to gain privileges or to marry wealthy Christians. So, you see, Yusuf and Maricarmen have no future together. I tell you all this because you are friends of both of them. I hope that continues to be so. Now if you will excuse me, I fear my workers are wondering where I am."

"I see," said Cass pensively. "That does sound serious."

"Well I think it is shameful of us," said Thea.

Alzarad smiled sadly, bowed, and took his leave. The ladies, having curtseyed, continued on their way. "But it is not at all fair," complained Thea again, still angry, as they climbed the steps by the golden fish pond.

Cass resisted the temptation to remind Thea that there was a time in their other life when she would have frowned on a Catholic girl even dating, much less becoming attached to a non-Catholic. She was pleased with Thea's change, so she simply noted, "It is the way matters stand in Al-Andalus just now, I fear. Those 'Inquisitors,' the name alone sounds frightful." Thea nodded and sighed. This conversation with Alzarad would become a painful memory before they left Seville, and later. That very evening Thea and Sebastian had a more serious quarrel over Yusuf and Maricarmen. They did not part happily. It took a minor emergency to bring them back together.

The fallout between Thea and Sebastian went unnoticed by most of the courtiers. Lady Francesca and her household were now fully engaged in the final preparations for the journey to Cordoba two days hence. Cass and Thea had little or no time to think further about Yusuf and Maricarmen's attachment, though Cass did make an indirect attempt to warn Maricarmen the evening after their conversation with Alzared. While Cass, Thea, and Maricarmen were folding and packing Lady Francesca's wardrobe, Cass hinted at the taboo against marriages between Christians and Muslims, or for that matter between Christians and Jews. Maricarmen talked unselfconsciously about the laws separating Christian and Muslim, but without any awareness that they had anything to do with her and Yusuf. "Either she has forgotten that Yusuf is a Muslim or she is unaware that they are in love and are no longer children," thought Cass." There the matter rested for the moment.

The ladies saw little of Alan. He too was busier. He received final instructions and special sessions of advanced training. Technically, as the squire of Lady Francesca's household, he had primary responsibility for protecting her, with his life if necessary. On this journey, of course, the Queen's Guardsmen and the Duke's men would be present in considerable numbers. Alan had trained hard. He knew he had attracted the attention of his instructors, even of the demanding Julian, who had complimented him once. But instead of making him feel good, the compliment only aggravated Alan's feeling of melancholy. He worked even harder.

Yusuf had come to recognize his friend's moods and to give him time to work his way out of them, but on this occasion he took Alan aside while he still had the chance. "My friend, my father says that if you frown too much your face becomes permanently sad. Please let me help you. Let us talk. We will soon be parted."

Alan looked at his friend. At first he said nothing. Then he blurted out, "I want to become a member of the Guards. I am as good as or better at arms than most of them."

Yusuf put a hand on Alan's shoulder and looked at his downcast eyes. "I thought so. As my father would say, 'Life is a stingy master, but even worse, a blind one.' Life does not reward according to merit," Yusuf explained, "but according to birth or some other chance event. Otherwise you would be destined to be a captain of the Palace Guards. But my father has another saying. 'If you teach a blind man a new path, he may choose it if it is less bumpy than the old path, and he may even thank you.'"

Alan thought about Yusuf's hint, wondering if Julian would be open to a new path. He decided to find out. Later that same afternoon as he came from the training field, he rode up to Julian, took a deep breath, and asked permission to speak. Julian inclined his head by way of permission.

"I would like to be made a member of the Guards."

"Impossible," snapped Julian.

Irritated at this, Alan lost his reserve with Julian. "In fact I am offering myself to the Queen as one of her Guardsmen." He saw that Julian was shocked into silence. He struggled to control himself but decided that he had nothing to lose now. "I have been told that I am nearly as good as the squires training to be Guards"— this was good diplomacy since, as he had said to Yusuf, Alan was better than most of them—"and I would like to have the chance to try. The Queen might be happy to honor Lady Francesca by having her squire also be a member of the Queen's Guardsmen," he added hopefully. Julian gave Alan a cold stare, but he replied in his usual businesslike tone, as though reciting a verse from the training rules.

"Guards, and in particular the Queen's Guardsmen, are selected only from the oldest and most noble families of the country." He glanced a second time at Alan, almost sympathetically, and added, "you are not of such a family." Dejected, Alan was turning his horse away when Julian surprised him by continuing, as though it were his duty. He sounded like he was reciting a memorized lesson. "It has happened in the past, but rarely, that some unusual service earned a lesser noble a place in one the Guards units. But such occurrences are sung about by people like your friends Theadora and Lord Sebastian." Recalling some of those heroic songs, Alan, pensive, dropped back further. He returned to the barracks and looked for Yusuf. He needed to talk again, but, to his surprise, his friend was not there. He then sought out Cass and Thea, but no one knew their whereabouts. He returned to the squires' quarters and threw himself on his cot.

Cass and Thea had left the Alcazar only minutes before Alan came looking for them. Their work for Lady Francesca had been completed for that day. They had surveyed the chests and boxes surrounding them. "That is as much as we can do for the moment," said Cass. "We need a change of scenery. Follow me."

"Good idea. We owe it to ourselves," replied Thea, who followed her out to the hallway. Cass took her by the wrist and hurried her along.

"Where are we going?" asked Thea.

"Do you need to see Sebastian first?"

"No. We are still not talking, so I would just as soon not see anyone at the moment."

"Good," said Cass, "I mean good that we can just slip out. Before we leave Seville I would like to try to find the house of Dhu Khiffil, or at least visit that part of town. I have been thinking about Dhu Khiffil, maybe because of our conversation with Alzarad about Yusuf and Maricarmen. Dhu Khiffil was always speaking and writing verses about different people living and working together."

"Yes, what was that word he used that he thought was so musical? Conventus, or ...."

"*Convivencia*, living and working in harmony, especially the people of the three religions with the one God," said Cass. "I remember it because he was convinced that our necklace had something to do with *convivencia*."

"Yes, as did the Giralda in Dhu Khiffil's poetry," said Thea. Then she laughed lightly, fondly remembering the Chief Muezzin of Seville. "The tower was accomplished by 'four peoples' power.' At first Dhu Khiffil said the Romans, Jews, and Arabs, but then he added the Christian Franks. I told him how Brother Bartolomeo believed that part of the Tower and the mosque were built on the foundation of a Christian church."

"But there were difficulties even in Dhu Khiffil's day, and even among Muslims," replied Cass. "Remember that his daughter had to go to Toledo because she wanted to marry someone from a different Arab tribe?"

"True, but still, Brother Bartolomeo was able to marry a Jew when he was a young man in the century after Dhu Khiffil," said Thea.

"Marriage between a Christian and a Jew now would not be wise, probably not permitted even if the Jew were one just in name only." She paused for a moment and took a deep breath. She hooked arms with Thea. "You are worrying about your argument with Sebastian, are you not? I have a good feeling about Sebastian. You will make up. The two of you can be creators of harmony," said Cass with a laugh. "Let's explore," she said, as they crossed the outer courtyard to the main gate. There was still more than an hour before the gate would be locked, though the guard gave them a mildly disapproving look as they went through.

They knew the general vicinity where Dhu Khiffil's house had been located, but when they got there, the layout of the neighborhood was different: newer, larger, and unfamiliar. They found themselves in streets still filled with people, including a sizable number of Moors. "This must be the barrio where the Moorish traders or servants of the Queen live, the ones Maiden spoke about," said Cass. "Could it be possible that Dhu Khiffil's descendants still live here? Two hundred years later?"

"Well, as you said, let us explore. At least this is probably where they would be if they are still in Seville," replied Thea.

The two companions turned down several twisting side streets, stealing glimpses of the gardens visible inside the open doors in the walls lining the streets. They lost track of the time and where they were. With darkness approaching, Cass finally said what had begun to worry them both. "We are lost." Cass was upset with herself. "How could we expect to recognize the house, even if his family still lived in it. I cannot recognize a thing," she fretted. "Sorry that I brought you on a fool's errand. I just hope we can find our way back," she added as she looked sheepishly at her fellow explorer.

Thea, however, seemed not to be listening to her. She was looking right past her with a quizzical expression that was just beginning to give way to a smile. "Look there. That fountain and courtyard look awfully familiar, Cass," prompted Thea.

They hurried over to the open doorway to peek in. In their excitement they entered the courtyard without a second thought. "You are right," announced Cass, rewarding Thea with a hug. "It is the fish pond in the shape of the Giralda."

"And all around it the 'earthly garden to remind us of the heavenly,'" added Thea, returning the hug. They both laughed, until someone spoke.

"A nice sentiment and from unexpected guests," came a clearly male voice. Cass and Thea froze, unmoving, now holding onto each other for encouragement. "My apologies if I startled you. You honor the house of my fathers." The voice was polite and reassuring. The ladies parted and looked. Coming toward them was a tall, shadowy figure.

"It is you," said Cass, with a sigh of relief. "The Duke's man at the entertainment, except that you are dressed as a Moor now."

"At your service, of course, My Ladies. I would ask you to enter, but we must return to the palace at once to arrive before the gate is locked. I was just preparing to leave. May I escort you?" Before they could say anything, the Duke's man removed his headdress and robe in two quick over-the-head motions.

A bit later that evening, Cass and Thea were excitedly telling Sebastian and Alan about their adventure.

"His name is Ibrahim Leonides," said Cass. "Originally it was just Ibrahim. He added Leonides in honor of his master the Duke, Antonio de Leon. He said we may call him Ibrahim Leonides.

"He is related to Dhu Khiffil's family, which makes him Muslim, but he also has Jewish ancestry, and he has been baptized a Christian. A model of *convivencia* in one person," said Thea.

Alan and Sebastian were both seated on Cass's bed, watching and listening, as Cass and Thea paced excitedly back and forth firing one detail after another at their listeners. Like Alan, Sebastian had gone to look for the ladies earlier that evening. He then sought out Alan. Both became anxious when the Ladies In Waiting were still nowhere to be found and the gates were about to be locked. In fact the two young men were waiting just inside the main gate when the ladies arrived, barely in time but at least accompanied by one of the Duke's men. The guard studied all three with an expression of mingled irritation and relief.

"Just in time," Sebastian had called out, not disguising his concern and with no trace of his argument with Thea. The guard had quietly commented, "Better than some others," shaking his head, but no one took any note of what he said, except for Ibrahim Leonides.

"He is a historian. No, a chronicler," Cass corrected herself. She laughed and added, "he claims that 'chronicler' is another word for 'gossip,' which is an honored position, especially in the household of a nobleman. According to him, Duke Antonio Leon de Cordoba employs him because he has contacts everywhere and keeps track of important gossip, especially court gossip. The Duke wants to make sure he is the first to hear about other families, but especially about his own family, past and present members."

"He is both Moor and Jew by ancestry, but he says he is a realist, so he is officially a Christian. He actually considers himself a skeptic in matters of religion," noted Thea. She was still trying to sort out the many sides of their new friend.

"He asked us questions about where we are from and who our families are," said Cass with a glance toward Sebastian. "I had the feeling that he already knew everything there is to know about us. So we answered his questions directly, and asked just as many of our own, and he answered them all."

"It seems," said Thea, "that a story of three companions who travel through time with a magical necklace has been handed down in Dhu Khiffil's family and even among other Muslims to this day. But...."

"But Ibrahim Leonides had never taken the stories literally

until he saw us at the entertainment. Even then it took him awhile to put the puzzle together. Excuse me," she added to Thea. Cass had not completed one of Thea's statements for some time. She was clearly excited.

"Apology accepted," returned Thea. "Ibrahim Leonides says we must all meet together. He wants to know more. "He might even include us in his chronicle," added Cass. "According to him we have arrived at a key time in the history of Al-Andalus and all of Spain. "That made me think of our mission, so I asked him to explain."

"I told him that all we knew about 1492 in Spain was that Columbus sailed from here and discovered the New World, which, of course, he did not know because it has not happened yet," said Thea.

"One of the biggest issues, he says, and I had the same question, is what will happen to the Jews and Muslims now that Granada, the last Muslim stronghold, is about to be occupied by the Christians," noted Cass. "There has been a great debate going on for months at court about it. A famous Jewish leader, a counselor of the King's, speaks for permitting Jews and Muslims to stay in Spain."

"For *convivencia*," added Thea. She raised both hands as a victory sign and then, arms still held high, joined hands.

"Exactly," said Cass, smiling at Thea's enthusiasm.

"King Ferdinand encourages the debate to try to keep at least some of the Jews, and maybe even some Muslims in the kingdom," said Thea hopefully. "He says that they enrich it in many ways."

"But a priest, who is counselor to the Queen, leads those who speak against keeping Jews and Muslims. They must leave, he argues, for the sake of a unified, Christian Spain," said Cass with a sigh. Ibrahim Leonides is worried that the 'unified' side will probably win out and make Spain a very drab place."

Cass and Thea both sat down on Thea's bed. They were finally winding down. "I think this debate must have something to do with our mission. This is the time that Maiden—and the necklace—chose for us. How are we to help the Jews and Mus-lims? Are we to try to persuade the Christians not to expel them?"

"How could we possibly do that?" asked Thea.

"Only one of us has even the slightest chance of influencing the Queen about that," said Alan, looking at Sebastian, then glancing back at Cass and Thea. "And that does not include the three of us from the future, who have accepted this quest."

"Whatever is required, I pledge my help," offered Sebastian, "even if doing so goes against some things I have previously taken for granted." He addressed these words to Cass but then looked at Thea. They smiled at one another a little awkwardly. Looking back to Cass, he asked, "But can you explain a few mysteries for me, such as what you told Ibrahim Leonides about yourselves, and how you seem to know the future, and what is the necklace and who is Maiden?" Sebastian paused. He had other questions to add but decided to stop for the moment until he got some answers.

Cass and Thea laughed at Sebastian's bewildered expression. Even Alan had to smile. The three companions looked at each other knowingly. They had revealed themselves to Sebastian totally and without hesitation. Each on their own had begun instinctively to trust him completely.

"Allow me to answer Sebastian," said Thea, holding up one hand. "After all I am the storyteller." As she began, the color rose in her face. She was both blushing and excited to be sharing their story finally with Sebastian. Thea covered the highlights of their lengthening story. She concluded with Maiden and the powers of the necklace. Cass held the necklace up to view, but without tak-ing it from around her neck. Sebastian's expression changed from bewilderment to concern.

"But why you three? What can you—we—do? Will you have to return to this future of yours?" he added after a slight pause.

"The necklace," began Thea. She then paused and looked at Alan and Cass.

"You are doing fine," said Cass. "We will help fill in some of the blanks."

"Yes," agreed Alan.

"Cass and Alan's grandmother gave Cass the necklace," continued Thea. "It was Grandmother Esther's decision—and Maiden's. It was as though they saw a connection. They did not ask Cass. She was chosen. Cass is the bearer of the necklace, and Maiden appointed Alan and me to be her companions. You are the first one to volunteer, Sebastian."

"My Grandmother Esther had become more of a keeper than a bearer of the necklace for a long time. According to Maiden, the necklace is needed more urgently once again. As bearer, I, with the help of the companions, must find out what that need is and try to fulfill it. That is why 'we three,' or now we four. We can only continue to follow where the necklace leads, and Maiden, which is the same thing. Maiden comes and goes mysteriously. When she last visited us she was in the helm." Cass looked over to the window casement and exclaimed, "But where is it? It was here this morning."

Alan, who had been listening but saying nothing now spoke. "When we came to your room looking for you earlier this evening, Maricarmen was with us. I remember her holding the helm. Perhaps she borrowed it."

"She was so preoccupied she could have taken it with her without realizing it," said Sebastian who had now regained some of his natural composure. "With our worrying about you, and now these tales of marvels, we have not yet thought to tell you. Yusuf will be going with us to Cordoba." At the "us," Sebastian noted that Thea blushed and frowned at the same time, betraying her mixed reactions. She was pleased to hear that Sebastian would be along, but she was on her guard as to why Yusuf would. Sebastian quickly continued. "Alzarad has decided that Yusuf should return to Granada to separate him from Maricarmen. I am afraid it has been decided. The Queen agrees." Sebastian looked at Thea and added, simply, "I am sorry." Thea knew that he was apologizing for his earlier lack of sympathy for the plight of Yusuf and Maricarmen. He was seeing them now through Thea's eyes.

"We learned about Yusuf from Maricarmen, who was coming to tell the two of you," said Alan to the ladies. "She was distraught. No one knows where Yusuf is. All three of you had disappeared."

"And he is still missing?" asked Cass anxiously.

"I hope not. Everything that can be done to find Yusuf is being done," replied Sebastian kindly. "We should take our leave now. Tomorrow will be a busy day with the final preparations for the journey. I trust we will have better word of Yusuf." Sebastian knew that the ladies were tired and that they would want to digest the news about Yusuf. "Good evening, My Ladies."

Alan followed Sebastian to the door and then paused. "I will see if I can find Yusuf, if he is still missing," he said before turning to leave.

Cass and Thea were saddened by the news, which added to their emotional exhaustion. Cass soon fell asleep. Thea followed her, but not before she remembered Sebastian's question about would the companions have to go back to their own time and place. She remembered that they had not answered that question. Then she too slept. Both were awakened suddenly.

# Chapter XV

# The Face of Bladen

Loud noises and hysterical weeping startled Cass and Thea out of their deep sleep. Cass hurriedly blundered from her bed to the door and opened it a crack. She saw two soldiers, one on either side of Maricarmen's door across the hallway. They looked eerie in the flickering light of their torches. One of the Palace Matrons was supporting a sobbing Maricarmen, at the same time as she was fumbling with her keys trying to unlock the door.

"What is happening?" Cass demanded. "What are you doing to Maricarmen?"

The Matron shook her head brusquely in response. "Back into your room and lock your door." One of the two soldiers motioned with his torch, clearly meaning that Cass should obey the Matron. She did so, reluctantly.

Not long after Cass and Thea had climbed back into their beds, they heard a sharp knocking at the door. Cass again made her way to the door. It was the Matron and the two soldiers.

"Does this belong to you?" she asked Cass. One of the soldiers held out the helm under the torch for Cass's inspection.

"Yes," replied Cass.

"And do you know where it was?" quizzed the matron.

"Yes, Maricarmen borrowed it from me," lied Cass easily.

"Did she also tell you what she wanted it for?"

"No. I did not think to ask her."

"Because your friend used it to trick me into thinking she was in bed."

Cass was on the verge of smiling at this trick, but the Matron's expression made her think better of it. "She is upset more at being tricked than at Maricarmen's attempt to sneak out and perhaps to run away," thought Cass. Aloud she said, "I see. In the dark, anyone would think the helm was a person's head, would they not?" This was the right thing to say.

"That is so yes," said the Matron as she looked defiantly back at the soldiers. She now became almost chatty, and Cass at first just wished she would go away. But then she heard her say with some satisfaction, "It is mostly that Yusuf's fault. He will spend a chilly time in the dungeon tonight." With that the Matron finally left, after giving Cass the helm. Cass leaned against the door after she closed it.

"Put Yusuf in a dungeon! How can they?" said Thea in a stunned voice. She and Cass could still hear Maricarmen weeping. Not even thick wooden doors could mute the sobs completely.

The night's happenings affected nothing in regard to the wedding trip, except that it kept most of the courtiers busy with speculation. Some thought that the runaway attempt had been foolish, with no chance of success. Others judged that had the couple been able to join a group going south, where many Moors still lived and farmed, their plan might have had a chance to succeed. Many wondered at how Maricarmen could wish to run off with a Muslim. But all agreed, whether they said so or not, that the attempt had captured their imaginations.

Cass and Thea kept to themselves. They had so many tasks that it was mid-afternoon before they could go looking for Alan. They found Sebastian, or rather he found them. He once again expressed his regrets about Yusuf and Maricarmen, particularly to Thea. In response to Cass's inquiry about Alan, he replied that Alan was still at the practice field. With somewhat mixed feelings, Sebastian added, "Your brother, My Lady, has challenged the entire barracks and has beaten everyone who has accepted, and with their choice of weapon."

Cass was not pleased with this information. "That distresses me, and I think he knew more than he was willing to say about Yusuf and Maricarmen last evening. Now it seems we will not be able to talk with him until after the banquet tonight."

But Cass was wrong. They were unable to talk with Alan at all that night. The banquet was formal, with most of those attending sitting at two long side tables. The Queen, Lady Francesca, and Duke Antonio Leon and two of the Queen's favorite courtiers sat at the High Table that formed a bridge between the other two tables. The unmarried men and women were on opposite sides of the bridge, as the Queen intended. The Duke delivered a toast honoring Lady Francesca and her betrothed and, of course, her guardian Queen Isabella. Her Majesty acknowledged the toast and followed with a brief but eloquent speech about marital responsibilities—and about happiness."

Cass and Thea looked at each other when the Queen finished. "I suspect that if all wives had the authority and respect that the Queen has, there would be more happiness and less flirtation among married courtiers," said Cass.

"You just read my mind," whispered Thea, nodding her head for emphasis. The Queen was announcing that the travelers were to retire early so they would be ready to begin their three-day journey early in the morning.

"At least we found out what happened to Maricarmen," said Cass, when they got back to their room and prepared for bed. Cass had made this discovery at the dinner table. Finding herself next to one of the Queen's Ladies who had a reputation as a gossip, Cass had struck up a conversation with her. When Cass asked the lady, as casually as she could manage, if she had heard any word about Maricarmen, the lady had been more than happy to share her inside information. The "poor girl" had been sent back to her parents already. It was felt that her being deprived of court life for a while was sufficient punishment. "And besides," added the lady, "it was mainly that young Moor's fault."

Thea was sitting on Cass's other side, away from the Queen's Lady. Cass could sense Thea tensing at the lady's patronizing tone and placed a firm left hand on her friend's arm just in time to head off a sharp retort. Cass had continued her conversation. The Queen's Lady clearly knew—and relished—many of the painful details. About Yusuf's fate there had been a number of ghastly rumors at first. "Torture, the dungeon, banishment, forced labor, enforced military service," recited the lady with some relish. But she acknowledged, a little more genteely, that the Queen would not have imposed any such measures on Yusuf. He was young, which always excused much in her eyes. Also the Queen held Alzarad in high esteem. When Alzarad requested that Yusuf still be allowed to be taken to Cordoba and then be permitted to continue on to Granada, the Queen agreed readily.

"That woman you were speaking with at dinner would have been happier if the Queen had tortured Yusuf," said Thea as she climbed into bed. "And I do not understand the Queen. She respects Alzarad as an Arab nobleman. Why would she not allow Yusuf to be Maricarmen's friend even if they did become romantic? And then to put him into that awful dungeon that Yusuf hated. Sebastian agrees with us," concluded Thea, as if that clinched her argument.

"The Queen has not been schooled by you the way Sebastian has," said Cass. "Nor does she have the same attachment to you that Sebastian has," added Cass. "You have become an advocate, and a good one, for *convivencia*, Thea. Sebastian is on our side because of you. I would call that a pretty good accomplishment." Cass blew a kiss to Thea and then blew out her candle. "Get some sleep.

We will be on our way at daybreak."

In the early dawn the line of horses passed through the eastern gate of the city and set out on the Cordoba Road. Cass promptly tried, with numerous twistings and turnings, to locate Yusuf and Alan. She could not find Alan, but she spotted Yusuf at the very end of the column riding between two Guards. She and Thea were in the middle of the column where they were under strict orders to remain. Although the King's Peace, enforced by the local nobles, protected major roads, added precautions accompanied the Queen on her travels. Unfortunately the extra security made it impossible for Cass or Thea to speak with Yusuf or to make contact of any kind with him. Counting the members of the Queen's Guards and Guardsmen, Duke Antonio Leon's men, Lady Francesca's household, and sundry soldiers there were about fifty people making the journey.

Cass's attention lighted on a horseman who was cantering down the line from the forward position. Several officers had already ridden past, but something in this man's bearing struck her as special, though she could not think why. As he approached, Cass recognized the uniform of the Queen's Guardsmen, complete with the close-fitted helm, with its Roman-style vizor open, glinting in the sun. Light chain mail provided upper body protection. Over the chain mail was the doublet that Cass and Thea had admired on Sebastian when he was in full uniform. The doublet contained the royal insignia, the black castle tower of Castile with the blood-red lion of Leon rearing on its rampart. Cass raised her eyes to the man's face and gasped.

"Alan!"

Cass's expression barely had time to change from wide-eyed shock to a smile of delight, when it changed again, this time to a flush of humiliation and anger. Alan passed by his sister with no sign of recognition. She turned in disbelief and watched him ride to the rear.

"Did you see that?" she demanded of Thea.

"I could hardly miss it when you shouted his name. Maybe you embarrassed him," said Thea, trying to console Cass. "And did he not look handsome in the Queen's uniform, nearly as handsome as Sebastian."

Cass's irritation softened a little, but she burned with curiosity about Alan's new status. Despite these concerns the ladies soon found themselves enjoying the journey. The weather was clear and mild, as is usual even in winter in this part of Al-Andalus. The road was not only protected but was kept in good repair by local nobles, acting under the King's Peace. Along the way, the countryside was cultivated and wore the blush of fertility. A few oranges and lemons still shone blissfully in the December sun, while pale green olive trees looked refreshed after having yielded their fruit to the harvesters. They passed numerous bustling farms and villages, fresh and white in the sun, and they passed an occasional town, walled in for extra defense or as a show of pride in its size and wealth.

It was at one of these towns that they halted gratefully on the afternoon of the first day. They had not come far, as it was customary to travel a shorter distance the first day so the travelers could gradually adapt to the demands of the journey. Cass and Thea were preoccupied attending Lady Francesca, and attending to their own saddle sores. After these tasks they ate a few mouthfuls and were soon asleep.

By the afternoon of the second day, the ladies knew that Alan intended to avoid them for the entire journey unless they could do something to force his hand. Messages sent through Sebastian to Alan and to Yusuf went unanswered. Sebastian had in fact learned the reason for Alan's behavior, partly from Alan, but mostly from his friends among the Guards. But he could not bring himself to tell Cass or Thea. Perhaps he felt that it was not his place. The two ladies were becoming increasingly anxious. Cass's irritation with Alan returned, but it was now mixed with worry. Both ladies were further distressed with Yusuf's plight. It made them wretched to see him ride the entire time with his hands tied to his horse's saddle, and with the bridle held by one of his bodyguards.

"Alan has not gone near him since the journey started," said Cass with disgust. "He is going to hear from me tonight…I hope." Because of her insistence, Sebastian did finally overcome Alan's reluctance. Alan agreed to meet with his sister that night.

There was a stir in the ranks as a few of the more experienced travelers pointed out the town that marked the end of their second day's journey and the place where they would spend the night. As they neared the town its castle, set royally on the top of a hill that appeared to be of solid rock, caught the attention of Cass and Thea. The castle, whose occupants had seen them coming while still a half day away, stood sentinel over the town. "Come in peace or beware," it seemed to say. Beyond the castle the land became gradually more hilly. Part of the town and all of a large building, a monastery as it turned out, nestled into the protective foothills. Under the wing of this monastery the travelers would find protection that night, though not all of them were to find much rest.

The monastery was the traditional stopping place for the second night of the journey from Seville to Cordoba. Traditional also was a modest celebration for the travelers, who would be less weary than on the previous night. With the Queen present, the celebration would provide more than the usual hardy fare. The brothers of the monastery had a reputation for hospitality as well as for some of the best wine cellars in the province. In the twilight, after a plentiful meal of bread and honey, bits of lamb in a savory sauce, deep red wine moderated by water, and, of course, olives, the younger people sat around a bonfire that crackled in the square outside the monastery. The more sedate travelers—Lady Francesca included—had eaten indoors, in the dining hall listening to devotional readings. They now joined the others in the square outside. Thea was much in demand, as usual, for her recorder music and her storytelling. With everyone thus preoccupied, Cass and Alan were able to meet in relative privacy just beyond the circle of light.

For several moments. sister and brother stood, staring at the fire from a distance. The sound of voices was faint. Cass did not know how long they stood that way, but she was startled by the sound of Alan's voice when he began. His voice was toneless and haunted.

"Please just keep looking over at the fire, Cass." Cass obeyed. Alan sounded so dejected that she wanted to comfort him. Her anger, which had been rising and falling over the past two days, now disappeared altogether. "When I left you three nights ago," Alan began, "after we told you about Yusuf having to leave, I tried but could not find him anywhere. I asked, but no one had seen him for hours. After curfew Julian came to ask me if I knew where he was. Yusuf should have been on duty several hours earlier. He had not asked to be relieved. Julian decided to go to Alzarad. He came back very shortly with word that Yusuf and Maricarmen had run away.

"Alzarad knew, as soon as Julian told him that Yusuf was missing, what must have happened. At first I was glad and hoped they would somehow make their escape. If anyone could do it they could. I thought of how easily they could hide in the gardens. And then it dawned on me that they would be wise to do just that and then slip over the palace wall after the initial search for them failed. It would be a desperate plan, but it could work. And it might have if...."

Alan's voice broke off. He put his head in his hands, then cleared his throat to regain control of his voice. Cass wondered what could cause such grief. She again controlled her urge to take him in her arms. She waited. What she heard next chilled her as though she had been plunged into icy water.

"I betrayed Yusuf. I told Julian what I suspected."

"Why?" was all that Cass could say.

"Julian knew how close we were. He guessed that I might know something. He asked me. I was about to say I knew nothing. He cut me off. He said the Queen was much agitated. Both Maricarmen and Yusuf were under her protection. She was upset with them but also concerned for their safety. She knew what her own people might do to a Christian woman traveling with a Muslim man. That worried me, but I would still have probably told him nothing, but Julian knew what would win me over.

"He said that the Queen would regard it as a sign of particularly loyalty to her if anyone helped her find them quickly. He did not have to say any more. And he was himself completely sincere about what he thought best for everyone. I told myself that he was right after all. But underneath, I knew I traded my friend for my own gain."

"I took them where I was sure we would find Yusuf and Maricarmen. I can still see their frightened faces—like young rabbits frozen with fear." I was the one who pulled back the wall of vines. Already I was regretting my actions, but when I saw how roughly the Guards pulled Yusuf from their nest, I woke up. I did this to him."

"That is when Yusuf saw me. He was confused for a moment when he saw me. Then he knew. He said, 'why?' as the Guards dragged him past me. His face looked like I had just spat on him."

"Julian ordered him to be taken to the dungeon near the fish pond. To that horrible place. I could not believe it. Just for trying to run away. That is when I realized that was not the reason for this treatment. It was because he was a Muslim running away with a Christian woman. Maricarmen was standing nearby with a Palace Matron and two Guards. She looked terrified, but not for herself. She kept saying, 'Please, not there. Please, not there.' I actually tried to stop them then. I pleaded with Julian. He just put his hand on my shoulder and told me not to worry. 'It is just for tonight.' Before I could say anything more he had one of the Guards walk with me back to the barracks and even remain with me until I calmed down."

"He came to see me later. He treated me with greater respect than ever before. I hate to admit it, but I was flattered. He knew exactly the right words to use with me. 'Loyalty to the Queen above friendship is an act of honor and will not be overlooked.'"

"Before the usual time for rising, Julian appeared, solemn but smiling. 'There is no time now for formalities. They will come later. The Queen has personally approved your appointment and wishes you to put on her uniform immediately.' I was so dazzled that I completely forgot my guilt feelings. Or maybe I felt guilty but unable to refuse the Queen. I do not know now. I put on the uniform."

"I have hardly slept since. Every time I drift off, I see the startled and frightened faces of Yusuf and Maricarmen in the torchlight. And in the firelight I see the face of Bladen with an empty smile looking on. Have I brought her back? Or has she never left?"

Cass had been torn between anger and pity toward her brother. His seeing the face of Bladen chilled her. It also startled her into turning her thoughts back to their mission and to the fact that Bladen was a formidable enemy. She made some quick calculations. "Alan, I am not going to accuse you, and you cannot just go off by yourself and be consumed by your guilt. That is just what Bladen wants, to break us up or even worse, to set us at each other's throats. We have to try to put matters right. I want you to promise me that you will do exactly as I say. I will send word to you through Sebastian." Alan agreed without question. It gave him some relief to obey Cass's orders.

During the journey the next day, Cass repeated to Thea what Alan had told her.

"I did not know who to feel more sorry for, Yusuf or Maricarmen, but now it turns out that it must be Alan," was Thea's sad response. "How can we rid ourselves of Bladen?" she asked, "and where has Maiden been?"

"We cannot get rid of Bladen. She can and will defeat us if we give her the chance, the way Alan …." She stopped, then resumed. "Our mistake is that we keep forgetting that she is in our midst. We might be able to set matters right again, at least partly. Cass told Thea of her plan, a gamble that they could easily lose, and for several different reasons. She assigned Thea the parts that she and Sebastian would have to play. "Play your recorder tonight. Improvise whatever song or tale you can, for as long as is needed," Cass concluded.

The companions hardly spoke for the rest of the day. That night was the last night of the journey, and, as Cass knew full well, would provide the only chance to enact her plan. The travelers stopped for the night at a hacienda, a large ranch very near Cordoba. They could easily have made it to the city by sundown—two messengers in fact had gone ahead to announce their approach—but it was customary on such important occasions to spend the night resting and preparing for a grand and festive entrance the next morning after breakfast. The Cordobans would also be alerted and have time to make final preparations to receive their most royal of guests in fitting fashion.

Lady Francesca's household was particularly busy settling their mistress down for the night, so excited was she to arrive at her new home. This task accomplished, the Matron said goodnight. Cass led Thea to the large yard, triangular in shape, formed by the main house and two lesser buildings, servants quarters and storage space, wherein most of the squires and Guards were quartered. A dozen or more Guards and Duke's men sat around a crackling fire. Among them was one Queen's Guardsman, Sebastian. Yusuf, the prisoner, was curled up about ten feet from the fire. He was just on the edge of the circle of light, close enough so that the Guards could keep an eye on him . Yusuf was nestled close to a pile of brush for protection against the night breezes. He snuggled warmly under a blanket.

As they approached the gathering, Thea warned Cass, "your elbow is showing outside your cloak. Better keep covered." The two ladies looked at each other and smiled. Cass made sure the helm was out of sight. Fortunately the plan called for a cheerful expression. They greeted the men around the fire.

The men welcomed the visitors heartily and with respect. They appreciated the company and, with Thea present, they anticipated some entertainment to hasten the hours of their watch. Thea and Sebastian soon began playing their part. Thea sang one of the favorite songs of Spanish soldiers, which quickly captured their full attention. It was about the betrayal of the Christian army to the Moors by one of the Christians' own nobles. But this treachery was offset by the loyalty of two captains, sworn brothers, who held off the enemy until the main army could escape. The two heroes died in the distant mountain pass. The Moors did them honor and buried them there side by side. While Thea alternately sang and recited verses of her song, accompanied by Sebastian's strumming on the lute, Cass slipped away into the dark. She crept to the pile of brush, pausing for just a moment by the sleeping Yusuf and then proceeded further into the darkness and behind the brush. Here she stopped and whispered some instructions to the waking Yusuf who had been waiting for her.

Cass had left word for Alan, directing him where to find her that night as soon as he was off duty—beyond the storage house, behind a small hill. Alan was already waiting for her when she rounded the hill, but when she moved closer, he saw that someone was with her.

"Yusuf!"

"Halán Idriss, my friend" replied the young Moor. He then embraced the Queen's Guardsman.

Cass inhaled deeply and let the air out slowly through pursed lips in front of inflated cheeks. For Alan, Yusuf's four words acted like hot coals burning and purifying his sickened conscience. They hurt deeply. And they gave him new life. He quietly shed tears on Yusuf's shoulder and tried to kneel before him. Yusuf would not permit him to do that.

"Until I arrived here," said Yusuf, I did not know if I came to spit in your face or to embrace you. When I saw your face, it was not one to spit in."

The three of them huddled, speaking in subdued tones. Even in Alan's whisper Cass could detect a lilt that reminded her of their days of playing hide and seek in the palace gardens. What was said was of little importance at that moment—hopes, promises, questions, encouragements. That Yusuf had forgiven Alan was all that mattered. Both felt the beginnings of a healing. Some part of them might never heal completely. Neither would be quite the same. None the less they had never been closer. That night, Cass guessed, Alan would have no nightmares and no visions of Bladen.

When Cass finally reappeared by the fire, Thea and Sebastian promptly finished off a tune. Accompanied by Cass they took their leave of a slightly startled but grateful audience of Guards who had nearly forgotten that Cass had been there before. They assumed that she had come to bring the others to their quarters inside.

When they were arrived safely by torchlight in front of the main house, they found Alan waiting for them. Thea looked closely at Alan to see for herself how the plan had worked. Satisfied, she next asked Cass, "Why did you not come back sooner? Yusuf was back for ages before you came."

"What do you mean?" asked Cass. "We just sneaked him back in a few minutes ago."

"Then tell me who it was who answered when the soldiers insisted on checking him and I thought for certain they would find only the helm and some rags under the blanket?" As soon as she had said "helm," Thea smiled broadly at Cass. "Of course! Maiden!" Cass took the helm out from under her cloak and held it up to eye level. There was Maiden, smiling from her perch, looking quite pleased with herself.

"Permit me at least the freedom to sleep, please," she said in a perfect imitation of a slightly grumpy Yusuf. She then disappeared from the helm and reappeared in her normal size.

"Hmpf." She frowned at Alan. She did not sound as forgiving as the others had when she addressed him. "Wear that uniform as a reminder of your act of betrayal, the price you accepted for your friend's capture. It is in my mind that you may one day be able to redeem your selfish act with that uniform. But had Yusuf not forgiven you, I would have had to return you to your own time and home. That would have imperiled you and your companions and even the quest itself." She looked at Cass and Thea as she said this.

"Yusuf has done well, fortunately for all of you...and, I think, for his own people," she added. "I wish his reward could be reunion with Maricarmen, for her sake and for his, but I fear that is not to be. By forgiving Halán he has grown much. I am sure he has also forgiven his father and the Queen. They acted according to their lights in an age which is getting darker at present. Maricarmen too will come to realize this and will be forgiving, eventually."

"All of you now, to bed. Bravely done," she said looking at Cass, "and you played your parts with skill and emotion," she said, her eyes flickering at Thea and Sebastian. "And welcome, My Lord Sebastian, to the Companions of the Necklace." She favored him with a slight bow. Sebastian, to his credit, managed to return a graceful bow despite his having been completely enchanted by Maiden. She looked a final time at Alan, nodded as one might to the survivor of a battle, and said simply, "Halán Idriss." Then she was gone, but in the air was a sudden warmth and the scent of lilacs.

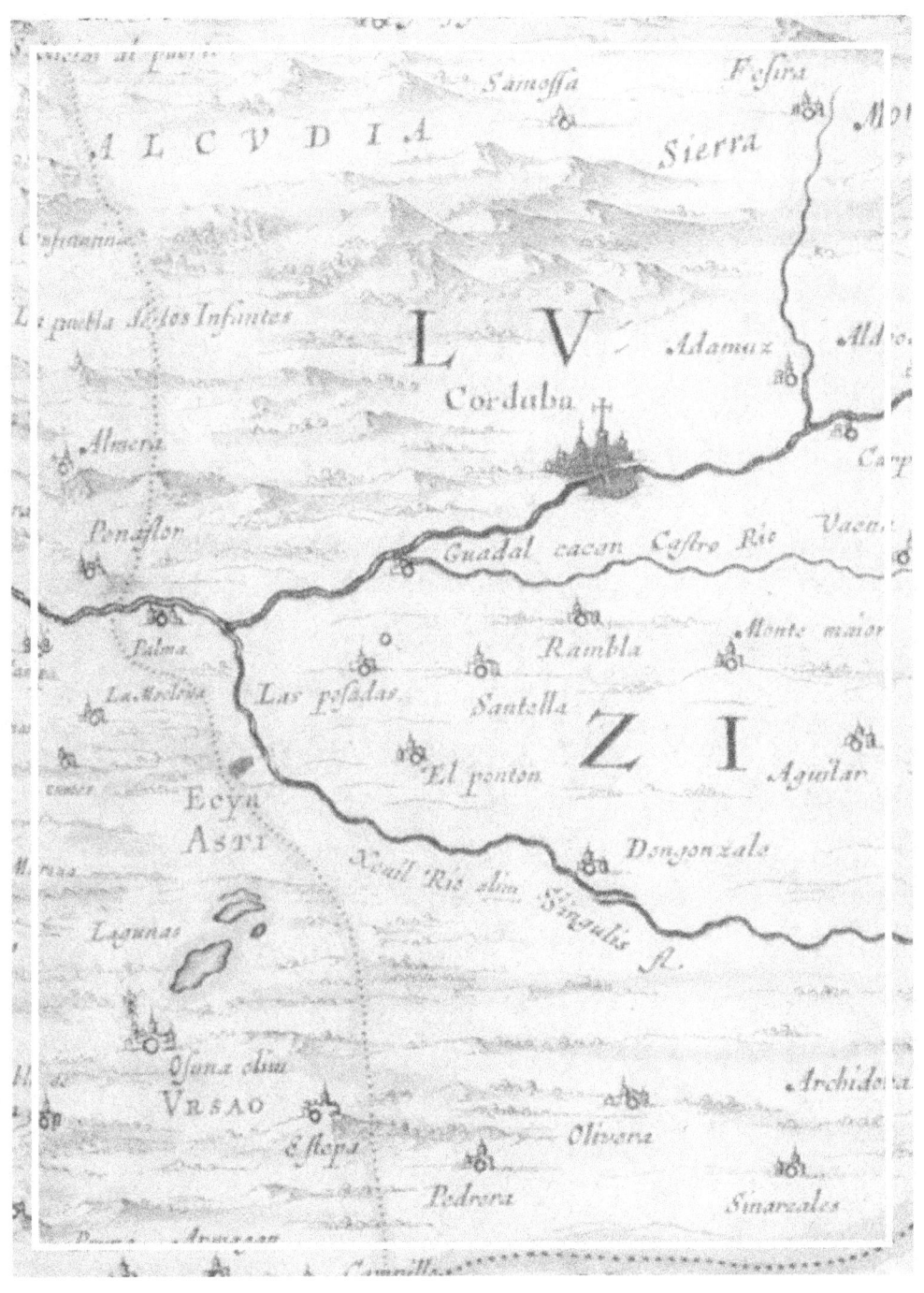

Now as they came over the final hilltop, they were greeted by a
story-book picture of a royal city ... Cordoba.

# Chapter XVI

# Cordoba

Their first close up view of the city of Cordoba spellbound the companions. They had glimpsed it briefly from afar from the top of a hill the day before. From that distance the city had seemed little more than a dark lowland patch beyond still more hills to be crossed. They had lost sight of it completely when they descended into the valley where their host's hacienda was located. Now as they came over the final hilltop, they were greeted by a story-book picture of a royal city.

A square minaret similar to the one in Seville towered over the Great Mosque-Cathedral of Cordoba, known to local inhabitants simply as the Mezquita. The Mezquita and the minaret dominated this famous city, once known as the Baghdad of the Western Caliphate. As the double file of horses and riders began its down-hill ride, the height of the minaret surrendered to the sheer size of the Mezquita. As she looked down on the still-distant rooftop of the Mezquita, Cass was impressed but also puzzled. The size of the roof impressed. Its rectangular shape occupied the space of a few city blocks in Philadelphia. What puzzled her was what appeared to be a series of A-shaped rows on top of the roof. She discovered later that these were part of the structure's architectural genius. Alan's duties allowed him a brief but appreciative assessment. His soldier's eyes moved from the mosque and minaret to a lesser tower, which he correctly guessed was part of the palace-fortress, the Alcazar of Cordoba. From here he looked for and quickly found the turreted towers and walls of the fortified city. Thea, for her part, was too enchanted by the scene before her to settle for long on any one detail. She looked from tower to mosque to palace to walls and back again in an attempt to absorb as much as she could. "What a glorious sight, the pages of a medieval picture book come to life," she announced to Cass and anyone else within hearing.

As the entourage approached the bottom of the hill, the scenes of the city all but disappeared, hidden by the walls of Cordoba. The road led to the southwest corner of the city and to its Seville Gate. A growing crowd lined the approach from the Seville Gate all the way to the first half-mile stone. Country-folk swelled the ranks of city-dwellers. The travelers' excitement mounted as they heard the calls and cheers of the people.

"Looks like a warm welcome for the Queen," called Cass, raising her voice above the increasing noise. Thea turned to reply but just then caught sight of Sebastian riding down the line toward them, issuing orders. She considered teasing him about his serious expression, but she changed her mind. As he got nearer, she experienced a Sebastian that she had not yet gotten to know, the Officer of the Queen's Guardsmen.

"Close up the line," ordered Sebastian, now shouting over the increasing din from the people. "Keep your horse's head close to the tail of the horse in front. Two-by-two, within arm's reach of your partner." He saluted Cass briefly as he passed along the line. Thea tried unsuccessfully to hear Sebastian's commands, but she needn't have worried. A Guard on her side of the line now issued emphatic commands. If they failed to close ranks, they could get separated from the group, or people in the crowd could get trampled, or both.

They barely had time to follow the orders when they were

nearly hemmed in on both sides by the crowd. Up ahead they could hear shouts: "The Queen! Long live Queen Isabella." The people were all smiles, their expressions mingling admiration, curiosity, and welcome. Some bowed or curtseyed. Others, dressed in sturdy homespun, waved and called greetings.

Cass became aware of a cluster of people on her side, standing a little to the back of the welcoming crowd. They were talking excitedly among themselves and seemed to be gesturing at her. She would have dismissed that notion, except that they were now looking directly at her, most with wide smiles, a few attempting a detached reserve. She couldn't help but take note of them. They were dressed in Arab style, but they seemed somehow different. A young girl, perhaps ten years old, left the side of an elderly gentleman in the group and began making her way toward Cass through the crowd. The crowd, however, seemed little inclined to make room for her. Cass called out, asking people to let the girl through, but only those in front heard her. So she stood up in her stirrups and gestured to the people to make a path. They did so, smiling with surprise and with a few friendly calls of "lady knight." The young girl, with midnight eyes and raven hair—eyes and hair like Cass's own—approached and presented her with a bouquet of wild flowers.

"Welcome, Lady. Yahweh bless you," said the girl to Cass. Cass thanked her and would have asked her name, but the girl had quickly disappeared back into the crowd.

"What a lovely little girl," thought Cass, as she strained unsuccessfully to get a further glimpse of her. The entourage pressed on and the crowd was getting denser. "And how lovely these," she said aloud to herself, gazing at the flowers. Now others clamored for her attentions. More young girls and maidens were welcoming her with flowers. Some handed them to her. Those who couldn't get close enough, called out as they threw them to her. Looking over to Thea, Cass saw that her friend also had her hands and arms full of flowers. And a young man was at that moment shyly presenting a bouquet to a beaming Thea. Sebastian later told them that it was fortunate that Lady Francesca was far enough ahead so that she could not see them. Other than the Queen herself, Cass and Thea received more flowers than anyone else. Cass particularly treasured the bouquet of wild flowers from the raven-haired girl.

As they neared the gate, flushed with pleasure and excitement as well as some embarrassment at being the object of the emotional outpouring of the people, Cass turned again to Thea. "I have always enjoyed watching parades but never thought I would be in one," she said, or rather shouted.

"I have marched with the band in parades, but never with a crowd this large or joyful," responded Thea. "They love the Queen, her Guards, and her Ladies. And now, here comes the gate."

"And here is Sebastian," said Cass.

"And Alan," said Thea. I think we have an escort of Queen's Guardsmen.

The two Guardsmen had somehow slipped in behind them in the line or march. "Greetings," called Alan and Sebastian together from behind.

Both ladies smiled back to them but then turned their attention to their riding, as the horses clattered onto the drawbridge and thence under the great Arabian arch of the gate. Only when she noted the thickness of the walls during this brief lull did Cass remember Yusuf, somewhere at the back of the line, a prisoner. As it was, Cass and Thea had to pay ever closer attention to their riding. They now proceeded in single file. The streets had narrowed, becoming barely wide enough for one horse at a time and the foot soldier that now accompanied each lady rider. People crowded into doorways or leaned well out of windows or over balconies two and three stories above the street.

The cheering crowds finally, but reluctantly, released their visitors at the gate leading to the Alcazar, where the Queen would reside. Though wide here, the street still provided privacy. It was lined on one side by a high wall and on the other side, the ladies both guessed judging from the smell, by the royal stables. Just beyond these, their horses stopped, and their mistresses gratefully dismounted. Before they parted from Sebastian and Alan, the ladies had the pleasure of hearing from Sebastian how Alan had persuaded Duke Antonio Leon to allow Yusuf to ride with the Guards in his squire's uniform. As grooms led the horses away, attendants ushered the visitors through yet one more gate and to their quarters. Or rather first to Lady Francesca's quarters, since their lady, of course, needed a change of clothes.

"Well, I hope I do not have to put up with all those crowds getting so close at my wedding," she said by way of greeting her two Ladies In Waiting.

She need not have been concerned. The wedding would be elegant certainly but, by royal standards, unusually small. It was a matter of timing. They had arrived on December 23, and Lady Francesca would be married on December 31, between Christmas Day and Feast of The Three Kings on January 6. The Church frowned upon having a wedding so close to either of these major holy days, but the Bishop of Cordoba had readily agreed to the exception.

Queen Isabella had explained to the Lord Bishop that she must leave at dawn the day after the wedding, January 1, 1492. Her timely departure, she explained, was to join King Ferdinand for their grand entrance into Granada. He envisioned, approvingly, of how it was going to be staged.

"The Queen sets out for Granada on the first day of the New Year, leaving Cordoba, accompanied by a large contingent of her Guards and Guardsmen. She joins the King and the main body of the Spanish Army already massed in the Vega of Granada, the rich farmlands that had supplied the Moors of the region with an abundance of food for nearly seven hundred years. The Catholic Monarchs together, at the head of the victorious Conquistadors, arrive in sight of the gates of Granada January 5, 1492, but they do not enter the city. They encamp overnight outside but in full view of the city. There on the morning of January 6, they accept the surrender of Boabdil El Chico, the last Moorish King in Al-Andalus.

Only then, and with great ceremony, do they make a triumphal entry and take possession of Granada." The Bishop was pleased. Gradually the rest of the court learned of the plans.

The companions learned of them from Ibrahim Leonides on the day before Christmas. "Disgraceful," complained Cass loudly. "The Catholic Monarchs plan to exalt Christianity—and themselves—by humiliating Islam and the Caliph."

No one disagreed, least of all Alan. "This is terrible," he said, "and I will have to be there to witness it. I was planning to tell you all after Christmas. My request for leave has been denied. I will have to be with the Queen's Guardsmen when they enter Granada."

"You said you would persuade the Queen to give Alan leave," said Thea, turning quickly to Sebastian.

Sebastian looked definitely uncomfortable. "I did not succeed," he said. "I thought I had made a perfect request. Alan would be needed here to be chaperone to Lady Theadora and Lady Cassandra during the brief holiday from their duties as Ladies In Waiting. The Queen agreed that a chaperone was needed. I am afraid that she appointed me instead." Before either Cass or Thea could reply Alan spoke out. "At least some good does come from all of this. I will try to be of some help to Yusuf until he is freed to rejoin his father and the rest of his family in Granada. I can at least be of some comfort to him at such a painful time. Maybe I can even atone in a small way for what I did to him and Maricarmen."

Thea was prepared to agree that perhaps this arrangement was for the best, but she waited to hear what Cass would say. Cass, to her—and she was sure Sebastian's—relief, broke into a broad smile and hugged Alan, who happily returned the hug. "I will miss you, little brother, but, yes, I can forgive the Queen. And you too, Sebastian," she added. "The Queen has perhaps shone some sensitivity to at least one Moor," she concluded.

While Lady Francesca had initially pouted about the small

scale of the wedding, she quickly entered into the festivities on her wedding day. Cass and Thea found the wedding much to their liking. The chapel, a favorite place of the Queen's, was off on a side street but just a short walk from the Alcazar. It was very old, perhaps five or six hundred years old, a charming Christian Arab church with elaborate arabesque arches. The entrance led into a small, sun-filled garden. The inside walls and domed ceiling were covered with glazed, dark-blue tiles decorated with stars and little suns. Cass and Thea stood close by their lady during the ceremony. Lady Francesca smiled happily, as did her two Ladies in Waiting.

Lady Francesca's husband-to-be had charmed the two ladies, although they joked, in private, that he had one of those excessively long names—Don Enriquez Garcia Muñoz-Cabrera de Cordoba. He insisted, however, to Cass and Thea's surprise and approval, that they call him simply Don Enriquez. This they did, except, of course, when Lady Francesca was near. She would have been shocked by anything less than "My Lord Muñoz-Cabrera," but she could not dampen the spirits of her Ladies. They were about to enjoy a holiday.

On the evening of their arrival in Corboba, Don Enriquez had announced to them that after the wedding and until after the Feast of The Three Kings, Doña Francesca would require only the presence of her new personal attendant. Her Ladies In Waiting were free to do as they liked. For Cass and Thea this meant that from the wedding on December 31 until after The Three Kings on January 6, they would remain at the Duke's Palace, the Alcazar. They would be his guests and could come and go as they pleased, within the expected limits of Spanish Ladies, of course. Duke Antonio Leon had approved of this arrangement. In addition he had offered his secretary and chronicler, Ibrahim Leonides, to be their host and guide to Cordoba. The ladies would have Sebastian as chaperone and Ibrahim Leonides as guide.

Sebastian promptly began his new duties at the banquet immediately following the wedding ceremony, sitting between the two Ladies in Waiting. After the meal and the departure of the Queen and other notables from the banquet, he invited Cass and Thea to accompany him on a walk around the large courtyard of Don Enriquez's palace. As they were leaving, Ibrahim Leonides approached. He wore the colorful livery of his master the Duke, so the ladies were not surprised when he made a formal bow, sweeping his fashionable floppy hat before them.

"Well met, My Ladies," he greeted Cass and Thea, who smiled back and bobbed curtseys. Omitting the sweep of his hat, Ibrahim Leonides then bowed to Sebastian. "Allow me, sir, my name is Ibrahim Leonides, and whom do I have the honor of addressing," he inquired.

Sebastian had, of course, seen Ibrahim Leonides in Seville and heard much about him from Cass and Thea, but this was their first formal meeting and therefore of some importance. Sebastian hesitated but just for an instant and then replied, "please, call me Sebastian."

Ibrahim Leonides nodded, visibly pleased by this friendly informality. "Are you not from Seville, Lord Sebastian? May I know your surname," requested Ibrahim Leonides. "Perhaps I know of your family." Cass and Thea recognized that Ibrahim Leonides was being both gracious and a little bit mischievous. As the Duke's chronicler and collector of noble gossip Ibrahim Leonides would certainly know of Sebastian's family and noble lineage. It dawned on them that he was inviting—perhaps requiring would be more correct—that Sebastian formally introduce himself.

"Sebastiano Francisco Romero Santamaria, at your command," responded Sebastian with a slight but gracious nod to Ibrahim Leonides. He glanced at Thea and Cass, betraying a becoming flush that spread from his neck to his face. They had never heard his full name.

"My Lord," said Cass, unable to suppress a smile as she curtseyed to Sebastian.

"That is beautiful," said Thea admiringly, conveniently forgetting that it was one of those "long important-sounding names" she enjoyed mocking.

"And a prominent name indeed," noted Ibrahim Leonides. "Your guard and host," he announced to the ladies, "is of the blood of Conquistadors, one of whom accompanied King Fernando the Third when he captured Seville from my ancestors—and Dhu Khiffil's—centuries past. That is if I am remembering my facts correctly," he added, looking at Sebastian.

"I am honored," said Sebastian, "that my family is known by such a distinguished chronicler as yourself. You are, if my sources are correct, a learned and honest, though skeptical man."

"Touché," declared Cass, recognizing that Sebastian was taking the offensive in the verbal tournament.

"Well said," responded Ibrahim Leonides with a chuckle, looking at Cass. To Sebastian he said, "You have done your research. I suspect the blood of diplomats also flows in your veins. Very likely from the Romero side."

"That will be quite sufficient for the compliments," intervened Thea, seconded by Cass. "We were just going for a walk—excuse me, a promenade," she said. "Will you join us, Ibrahim Leonides."

As they walked, Sebastian and Thea in front, Cass and Ibrahim Leonides behind, Cass could hear Thea questioning Sebastian about his family. He told her that he was the oldest of five children. He had three younger sisters the eldest of whom was close to Thea's age. She would be married after Easter.

Sebastian and Thea were getting too far ahead for Cass to hear, so she took Ibrahim Leonides' arm and hurried him along. She heard enough to guess that there were at least two sisters and a brother still living at home. The home, Cass gathered, had considerable lands and herds of cattle. Cass and Ibrahim Leonides were now practically on the heels of the others and could hear them clearly.

"Do you have bulls?" asked Thea excitedly. She had barely heard his "of course," when she launched into a short history of the bull-dancers of Crete in ancient times. "They were acrobats. They could take hold of a charging bull's horns and do a somersault onto its back or completely over it. Just amazing!"

When Thea paused, Sebastian was finally able to ask her about her family. Thea replied in detail and without hesitation. Ibrahim was again slowing down, but Cass could hear enough of Thea's chatter to understand that she was introducing Sebastian to her family. Her mother's death giving birth to Thea. Her closeness to her father who had died two years ago when she was fourteen. The many German and Irish aunts, uncles, and cousins, the Leiterman-mans, her father's family, and the Griffins on her mother's side. Living with one or other of the Leitermanmans in Philadelphia during the school year, with one or other of the Griffins in Queens, New York in summers. "All a bit overwhelming, which is not a complaint." She spent much of her time at school where she was in the band and her favorite activity was modern dance. "The bull-dancers were the modern dancers of olden times." Cass noticed how Sebastian nodded as he hung on her words. It did not seem to matter that he could not have possibly understood "playing in the band" or "modern dance" or "Queen's, New York."

Cass was startled by Thea's next words, realizing that she had been caught eavesdropping. "Cass has been my dear friend and anchor in the good times and the not so good. She still is," she concluded, glancing back at Cass. Turning in her direction, Sebastian smiled and bowed to Cass. Cass returned his smile, at the same time blushing up to her eyes.

Partly to cover up her embarrassment and partly because she had been ignoring him, Cass turned to Ibrahim Leonides and let the others go on ahead. "When you met Sebastian back there the two of you had quite a duel with words," she said.

"I hope I was not too forward with Lord Sebastian," he replied.

"No, you were most diplomatic," replied Cass, "and Thea has wanted to know about Sebastian's family for ages but has not found the proper time. Your questions gave her the opening she needed, which I rather expect you intended."

"You, Lady Cassandra, are most observant," replied Ibrahim Leonides, "**and** your comment emboldens me. There is something I have been wanting to ask you for some time, if you will permit me. It is in part, I think, of a personal nature."

"I have just eavesdropped on Thea's family story, so I should not object to questions of a personal nature," replied Cass readily.

"Thank you," said Ibrahim Leonides. "In my family we have many legends about our esteemed ancestor, Dhu Khiffl, whom you have so wondrously met. One of the legends clearly involves you and your companions, but it contains a puzzle. It is the legend, which you are in fact living, of the three travelers from another time and place. One traveler is a Frank, that is, a Christian. Clearly that is the Lady Theadora. The other two travelers are traditionally referred to as being of mixed Jewish and Arab blood. One of the two has a Muslim name known only to a few, which I presume is Lord Alan, known to a few as Halán Idriss. The other must be you. The puzzle, of course, is that you and your brother identify yourselves as Jews and have never mentioned being part Arab. Is the legend mistaken in this?"

"I think it must be, but I am not sure," answered Cass after some hesitation. As you say, Alan has an Arab name, two in fact. Maiden has only ever called him Halán. Then Dhu Khiffil himself added the second Moorish name of Idriss, the Wanderer. Still, I cannot imagine that either I or Alan has Arab blood. My father the historian was—is—most particular about our Jewish family tree going back hundreds of years. Of course, I have always found that to be a little strange since he is against organized religions, including Jewish, and he has refused for years to discuss our family history other than its being so old."

"Perhaps the deeper question is would you welcome having Arab ancestors as well as Jewish?" asked Ibrahim Leonides. He used his serious-chronicler tone.

"I hope so," began Cass, but then she stopped and thought

before continuing. "I cannot really say. I do not know much about being a Jew, much less about being part Arab, or how my Jewish part would feel about having an Arab part. How should I, as a Jew, feel about being part Arab, either in this century or my own twentieth century?"

"Oh, you do have the makings of a courtier," exclaimed Ibrahim Leonides. "Answer the question with a question. Ah, but I am still ahead of you, although just a little bit. You will recall that you first spoke about your Jewish ancestry the night we met in Seville. You regretted then that you did not know what being Jewish meant for you, and you have just done so again. You may find me presumptuous, but I have secured you a teacher. What better place than Cordoba to discover what it means to be a Jew. You would find no better teacher, that is, of course, if it is your wish."

"That explains it. The beautiful girl who gave the flowers and asked Jahweh to bless me," exclaimed Cass. "I should be upset with you for not asking me first, but I am not. You were right. I do want to know for my own sake as well as for our quest, which clearly has something to do with my being Jewish. Now I hear that I might also be part Muslim Arab, another reason to first understand being a Jew. When do I begin lessons?"

"First we get you better acquainted with Cordoba, which we begin tomorrow. After that we—you—begin as Stephen's pupil. I should let you go to get your rest, but, like your father I am a historian, and as such, I ask your indulgence to pose one further question." Cass had barely said yes when he went on.

"You have told me much about the magical necklace. It was made by a Jew over 1600 years ago in Al-Andalus. At the outset it led to an important conversion to the Jewish religion. It later saved at least one Jewish community of Al-Andalus. It works its magic only for a Jewess, such as you, assisted by the djinni of the necklace. You come from a time in the future when your father and Lady Theodora's fought in a war that ended a most brutal persecution of the Jews. Could it be that your quest is about the survival of the

Jews of Al-Andalus?"

Cass thought for some time as they continued to walk. Finally she said, "Is it enough just to survive?"

"Do not underestimate it," answered Ibrahim Leonides, "but in any case, you may be better able to answer that question after your lessons with Stephen. They walked on for a while longer, not speaking. Ibrahim Leonides broke the silence, this time in a tone that signaled the conclusion of their conversation. "You have heard at court, I trust, the tales of heroes on their quests," he said, "and any hero worth her salt knows that acquiring self-knowledge is part of her quest." He smiled. "Now I definitely have kept you over long, myself as well. My wife will be worrying. Fortunately we live nearby. I will come for you and the others tomorrow morning for your introduction to Cordoba—past and present."

"You are married!" Cass had become used to surprises from Ibrahim Leonides, but she could not resist chiding him for not mentioning before now that he was married. "Well, we must meet her, and perhaps she will join us on our holiday," she concluded.

"Tomorrow you will meet my Lucía, though about joining us on our adventure, well, you can ask her. What I do know is that you and she will have lots of questions for each other," said Ibrahim Leonides, rather mysteriously thought Cass. He escorted her back into the palace and then took his leave. "Until tomorrow, My Lady."

# Chapter XVII
# Tales of Cordoba

The Duke's chronicler was waiting at the palace for the three companions after their breakfast early the next morning. He led them to his house, or rather to Lucía's house. It had been her mother's and her mother's mother's home. It would be her daughter's, when she decided it was time for one. Ibrahim Leonides called it the House of Light, "Casa Lucía." It was located about half way between the Alcazar and the Christian Arab church where Lady Francesca's wedding had taken place. The house was quite large, especially for just two people, and it was picturesque. It was stone, two stories, and filled with windows with shutters that opened and curtains that pulled back to let in the light. The house had settled and protruded slightly into the cobblestone street, reminding Cass of a pregnant woman. In the back of the house there was a well-tended garden of flowers and vegetables.

Lucía met them at the door. "Welcome," she greeted them warmly, inviting them to make themselves comfortable on one of the cushioned benches and stools. They had barely done so when biscuits, grapes and cool glasses of a fruit drink appeared. Cass and Lucía were soon chatting like old friends, while the others at first listened and then gradually joined in. Lucía was perhaps thirty and attractive with typical Andalucían features: light olive skin and dark brown eyes and hair. She wore her hair pulled straight back and tied midway in a bright red bow. An apron covered a good portion of her light tunic. She seemed to glow with energy and cheerfulness. Her conversation was punctuated frequently and spontaneously by a musical laughter that reminded Cass of Maiden.

"No, I certainly would not wish to mix with the nobility the way Ibrahim Leonides does. They spend their time being noble instead of being productive," she chuckled in response to one of Cass's questions. "And at the Duke's palace one must always be on her best behavior while doing nothing."

"What do you do here, then?" asked Cass, intrigued by this woman who spoke about the nobles as though they were overgrown children.

"I am a jeweler. My workshop is upstairs. Ibrahim Leonides does his writing down here. Best that way for both of us. We meet in the kitchen area and the bedroom." Lucía paused, smiling at Cass. "Lord Sebastian," she called over her shoulder, "your charges should not have to stay at the Alcazar where they have to be on their best behavior all the time. What sort of holiday is that? They should come and stay here, and you also, if you like."

Sebastian spoke up quickly. "I doubt that I could get permission," he said, "but I do not know why the ladies on holiday could not accept."

"Then that is settled," declared Ibrahim Leonides. We shall leave shortly to begin your acquaintance with Cordoba, but first I believe Lady Cassandra may have a pressing question or two for my Lucía." He smiled at Cass. As he had expected, Cass's eyes had widened when she learned that Lucía was a jeweler. He knew that only Cass's politeness had restrained her from immediately asking her about the necklace.

"I am afraid that you read me like one of your books, Ibrahim Leonides," responded Cass. Wordlessly she lifted the necklace from under the ruffles of her dress so that Lucía could see it.

Lucía moved closer to Cass to examine the necklace. "As I expected," she pronounced, "the legend is true. The necklace of the Sunstone and two Skystones," she whispered.

"You know of it?" asked Cass.

"Yes, but until now I knew of it only from the magical stories. Every jeweler in Al-Andalus knows the legend in one form or another. In Seville they boast of it as their own, but there have been rumors that it was seen here in Cordoba by one of our elder sisters who is still alive. I never thought I would see it." Lucía touched the Sunstone as reverently as she might have touched a saint's relic.

"You know all the legends…and the stories?" asked Cass.

"I am afraid that I must disappoint you there," answered Lucía. "Ibrahim Leonides has already told me what you told him about the necklace, which is a great deal. I have only one piece of information that you might not yet possess. Once the Jewish female becomes the bearer of the necklace, she remains its mistress until she dies."

"Nothing will happen to Cass as long as I am alive," interrupted Thea protectively, as though to break the spell of Lucía's words. Thea blushed and looked down at her hands. Cass smiled at her and then looked at the necklace pensively.

"Amen," said Ibrahim Leonides. "And now," he went on, "while it is still morning, let us embark on our journey in Cordoba?"

"Each of you take some grapes and biscuits with you," instructed Lucía. "Tomorrow I will pack a food basket for you."

Everyone happily obeyed. As they were about to leave, Cass asked Lucía, "Are you coming with us? Please do. I doubt that we will encounter any noblemen."

"No indeed," laughed Lucía. I am happy that you will have such a knowledgeable guide as my husband, and such a protector as this one," she said looking at Sebastian. "No, I will be able to get twice the amount of work done with him out of the house. We will have plenty of time to talk later. Now off with all of you. Oh, and, husband, you need not narrate the entire history of the city this first day."

Ibrahim Leonides had been anxious to begin, but now that the moment had arrived, he was hesitant. "I thought we would begin at the Mezquita, but let me list the major sites so you can choose for yourselves where to start," he said. "The Synagogue ... The Baths ... The Waterwheel ... The Roman Bridge ... The Minaret ... "

Cass interrupted to help him. "Shall we go to the Mezquita, as you intended at the outset, and you can tell us something about it along the way. As Lucía said, we need not rush to see everything in one day."

"Yes. Very good idea," seconded Thea.

"Please, lead the way," encouraged Sebastian.

"Then, follow me," said Ibrahim Leonides happily. "You will have to excuse me. As my Lucía says, she is my wife, and Cordoba is my mistress—the only one I could wish for or that Lucía would permit." He and Cass walked ahead, with Thea and Sebastian close behind so that all of them could hear his explanations as they went.

"The oldest part of the Mezquita is built on the site of the Basilica of San Vicente, a Christian Church, which was originally the site of a Roman Temple. When the Moors first took the city, they claimed one-half of the church for Muslim worship, as was their custom. When the numbers of Muslims increased rapidly, mostly through conversions, the Emir had to buy the Christian half from the Christian Arabs to make room for the larger numbers. They tore down the church and built this mosque, the Mezquita. It grew like a city, getting bigger and adding the new styles of each new age. It remains the largest mosque outside of Damascus. Even though it was converted to a Christian church more than a century ago, everyone continues to call it the Mezquita, the Castillian word for mosque."

As their guide led the way and spoke of the past, the companions followed along, listening and looking. While still at a distance from the Mezquita their eyes were drawn to the tall, square minaret off to their left. As they came closer to their destination, their attention moved to the massive outer walls of the mosque looming up in front of them and dwarfing the neighboring shops and houses. They could just see the tops of the tallest palm trees peeking over the walls of the mosque's garden. The Mezquita seemed to cover acres of ground.

Ibrahim Leonides paused in his explanations and announced, "Here we are." They stood in front of the tall wooden doors set into a large gate. They were open wide in welcome. "This is the Gate of the Palms," he explained, "named for obvious reasons."

"It is just like the orange grove outside the Cathedral of Seville," observed Cass.

"Where we met Brother Bartolomeo on our first day in Al-Andalus," added Thea. "How long ago was that?"

"About a hundred years ago," answered Cass, with an impish grin.

"There were not so many palm trees in Seville," said Thea.

"They help shade the orange trees in the very hot, dry weather," said their guide, but come, we shall enter the Mezquita itself through the Gate of the Palms."

They moved through the sunny garden and another door into the coolness inside. Just past the entrance they were welcomed by glowing lights. The interior was brightened by numerous oil lamps fastened to pillars. They stared at countless rows of arches on top of arches that were on top of pillars. The rows extended as far as one could see until the lights finally shrank to pinpoints. The companions had never seen such arches.

"Striped," said Cass in a low voice.

"Beautiful," added Thea in the same tone.

"Yes, and very dramatic," affirmed Ibrahim Leonides. "The white blocks, made from limestone, alternate with red bricks of the same thickness. The first builders started the pattern. Those who enlarged the mosque over the next two centuries wisely remained true to the same pattern." He paused to allow the companions to take in the amazing sight before continuing his description. "The higher arches support the wooden roof of the mosque. Wooden beams fastened on either side of each arch meet to form a peak. The wooden roof is supported by these beams.

"That explains the A-shaped rows on the roof that we saw from a distance. They actually shape the roof," exclaimed Cass. "Oops, sorry for the interruption," she added.

"Not at all," replied their guide, "and quite correct. There are eleven original roofs, or A-shaped rows, each supported by the double arches and their pillars. In the newer section, built four hundred years ago, there are eight additional such aisles of arches. The part we are in is seven hundred years old," he said with obvious pride. He was rewarded by the appreciative exclamations from all three of the companions.

Sebastian walked over to one of the pillars, as though drawn to it. He patted its surface, much as he would his horse's shoulder. The pillar felt smooth like his horse, but it was cool to the touch. He kept his hand on the pillar for some moments. Around his hand the marble was pale but with a blush of pink. "It is almost as if it is alive," he mused. "But they are so slender. How can they support the roof?" he asked.

"Roman engineering," answered Ibrahim Leonides promptly, "developed further by the Arabs. Now, come and see the most beautiful part of all." The group followed their guide, who was careful to stay in the same aisle as the one they had entered initially. He did not want anyone wandering off into the maze of pillars and arches. As they walked, he explained to Sebastian, "the pillar that you were touching is Roman, probably from the original temple. Later the Arabs, and later still the Franks, added more. They were scavengers of pillars from everywhere, including Greece and Byzantium."

Ibrahim Leonides paused, realizing that he had lost his audience's attention. They had just passed the more recent Christian chapel and were approaching what seemed to be a large niche in the east wall. It was ablaze with gold. Their guide watched the faces of his guests. He was pleased by their wide-eyed astonishment. "This is the Mihrab," he said. "Every mosque has one, though none so elegant as this one. It is where Muslims keep their sacred scriptures, the *Koran*, for services." He spoke reverently. The others stood as though entranced. It seemed to them that rays of light came from within the Mihrab. Thin layers of beaten gold leaf decorated the alcove and the surrounding surface. Cass, Thea, and Sebastian all instinctively inclined their heads in a mark of respect for what was clearly something precious, something sacred.

"Here the Imam led the worshippers in prayer," commented Ibrahim Leonides. "Then he would read a passage from the Koran and they would discuss it." The companions continued to contemplate the Mirhab, while he spoke. "Just imagine. Here the great philosophers, Alfarabi and Avicenna, prayed. And here the learned Algazel prayed, when he was not writing treatises against Alfarabi and Avicenna for putting as much faith in Greek philosophy as in Mohammed. Later still, Averroes, the philosopher and scientist, humbly bowed to Allah in this very place." The names were not familiar to the companions. Still, they struck them as both poetic and magical.

They were startled out of their reverie when a door, previously invisible to them, opened next to the Mihrab. A little bell rang, and a server and priest appeared from within, on their way to the chapel for mass. Guide and companions quietly retraced their steps. Thea and Sebastian bowed in the direction of the altar where the priest was beginning the service.

When they emerged into the Garden of the Oranges, the sun was hours past its noonday point. They had totally lost track of time.

"We may be able to return another day," said Ibrahim Leonides, "to visit the newer part of the mosque, the part built by the Grand Vizier Almanzor in the tenth century. There is a legend that says that Allah was displeased with the Moors, with Almanzor in particular, for enlarging the mosque at that time. The numbers of worshippers did not require more space, so the expansion must have been for reasons of pride, and not piety. The Grand Vizier it seemed wished to leave behind a monument to his own greatness. As punishment Allah permitted the great Caliphate of Al-Andalus to be broken up into a number of small kingdoms shortly after the death of Almanzor. This was a serious loss for the Muslims because it gave hope to the Christians from the north that they could re-conquer Al-Andalus. Thus it happened that instead of remembering Almanzor by the name he gave himself—The Victorious of Allah—he is today remembered as the one who weakened and betrayed the Caliphate of the West."

By now the group was mingling with numerous other late afternoon strollers. It was hardly any colder than it had been in the Mezquita, but the ladies and Sebastian pulled their cloaks tighter. It had been warmer in Seville.

"Sebastian and I are going to return to the palace," announced Thea. "I am too cold, but you two go on if you like."

When they later spoke about what happened that afternoon, Cass could not remember if she had heard Thea's announcement or not, or whether it would have made a difference. She and Ibrahim Leonides were ahead of Thea and Sebastian and continued walking along the spacious main road in the opposite direction from the Mezquita and the Alcazar. "Do you believe the legend?" she asked. "Was Allah punishing Almanzor and the Moors of Cordoba?"

"There usually is a truth behind such a legend," answered her companion. "Almanzor's ambition was boundless, and he was completely unscrupulous. He seduced and became the lover of the favorite wife of Al-Hakam, the Caliph, the man to whom he had pledged his loyalty. He used his influence over his lover to gain power at court. Then when Al-Hakim died suddenly, Almanzor succeeded in becoming the new Caliph's Grand Vizier and counselor. Eventually he ruled the kingdom through the Caliph. To solidify his power he won the support of many of the strict Muslim religious leaders of that time by ordering that the Christians and Jews of Al-Andalus convert to Islam or be put to death. The Koran, of course, forbids this because, like Muslims, they are people who follow a sacred book. Fortunately for everyone the Grand Vizier's ministers conveniently failed to carry out his command."

"Unfortunately Almanzor did not live to suffer Allah's displeasure in person. The Moors of Cordoba would suffer it centuries later as a direct result of Almanzor's pride. When Almanzor conquered the Christian city of Campostella in the north, he rubbed salt into the Christian wounds. He made Christian captives carry the church bells from Santiago to Cordoba. The distance was so great, and the bells were so large that it took hundreds of Chirstians more than a year to get them to Cordoba—to be used as oil lamps in La Mezquita. Each bell, inverted, held enough oil to light the entire building for weeks, even months. When the Christians re-conquered Cordoba, they made Muslim captives carry the bells back to Campostella by the same tortuous route."

"In short," concluded Ibrahim Leonides, "Almanzor's memory is not a happy one for either Christians or Muslims."

"Understandably," exclaimed Cass, "but I think it is past the time that I should be returning to the palace. It is getting dark, and we seem to have lost Thea and Sebastian."

"We can take a short-cut through the Jewish neighborhood," said her guide, "and just stop at Stephen's house long enough for me to introduce you."

As they entered the street on which Stephen lived, Cass wondered if coming here at dusk was a mistake. The street was dark, narrow, and twisting. Only a few oil lamps lighted the way. They seemed to create as many shadows as they shed light on the street. As they came round a curve, Cass was at first relieved to hear laughter, boisterous as it was. She quickly realized something was wrong. The laughter was more like jeering and was coming from five or six men who had who had surrounded two figures, one an elderly man, the other a young girl. Even without being able to see their faces, Cass knew instinctively that the young girl was the same who had greeted her with flowers on the approach to the city.

The man was the elder relative or guardian. She hurried forward to help the couple against the bullies attacking them.

The attackers were too busy pushing the elder around the circle and making fun of him to notice the approach of the lady and her companion. They sneered and brushed the young girl away when she tried to stop them. Cass strode up to the men, despite Ibrahim Leonides's attempt to hold her back, and shouted loud enough to be heard above their noise.

"What are you doing? In God's name, and the Queen's, stop this instant."

Ibrahim Leonides, who was regretting not wearing the Duke's livery, had now taken his place next to Cass, but his face looked as pale as the white marble pillar in the mosque. The men at first stared at Cass with a mixture of confusion and fear. They could see that she was a lady who was connected to a wealthy or even a noble family. One of them explained, almost apologetically, that she shouldn't worry, that they were having some fun. "It's a Jew and his little bitch's all," he said.

Cass was too infuriated to be frightened, even though she could tell that the speaker had been drinking and was slurring his words. Some part of her brain told her that very likely all of the bullies had been drinking, but the rest of her brain, and her emotions, were directing her actions. "How dare you! Let them go immediately, or I will inform my Lady Francesca. Better still I will notify one of the Queen's Guardsmen," she said.

"Why would you do that?" whined another of the men.

"Maybe we should just go," said a third.

But the first speaker had gotten over his initial surprise and fright and became bolder. He had seen that the lady's companion was frightened. He put his face in front of Cass's, just inches away, and repeated his friend's question, "yes, why would you do that? You a Jew lover? Maybe I should report you to one of them that burns Jews." He turned to his friends. They were clearly less frightened now and still surrounded the elder, though the girl had disappeared. "Maybe the fine lady would like a kiss," he said to renewed laughter.

The speaker turned back suddenly and pulled Cass to him. Ibrahim Leonides tried to pull Cass away from him, but two of the bullies took hold of him. Cass finally realized the danger she was in. The man had one arm around her shoulders, while he groped for her breasts with his free hand. She could not avoid his sour-beer breath as he grunted in anticipation. Then he and Cass were both jolted sharply. The man's anticipation changed to surprise, and he gave a gasp of pain, letting Cass go and hugging his right side with both arms. Cass now saw a small, hooded figure on hands and knees immediately behind the man, gesturing. She responded instinctively, shoving the man with all her might. He stumbled backward over the hooded figure, crashed to the cobblestones, and lay there stunned and moaning. Everything had happened so quickly that the rest of the bullies simply gaped. Cass now gambled. She reached under her outer mantle, as though going for a knife that women occasionally wore at their side.

"Let him go," she commanded. The bullies hesitated. With her heart pounding and hoping that the wobble in her legs was not visible, Cass moved slowly with a determined scowl toward the two men that were holding Ibrahim Leonides. "Let him go!" She reached out and pulled the elder away while keeping her other hand under her mantle.

The other two bullies released Ibrahim Leonides. They all started to move off into the darkened street. Cass managed one more brave-sounding order. "Take that scum with you," she said, pointing to the speaker who still lay moaning where he had been toppled.

"That will not be necessary. Arrest these men. Take them to the Alcazar and lock them in the dungeon." It was Sebastian's Officer's voice. Cass whirled around in time to see him and four pike-wielding foot soldiers hurrying up to take charge of the bullies, who were now looking like frightened dogs expecting a beating.

The soldiers prodded them sharply on their way.

Sebastian began to apologize for having left Cass unprotected. "I neglected my duty…," he began, but stopped abruptly. He caught Cass before she crumpled in a heap on cobblestoned street. She had kept up her fierce appearance as long as it was needed. Now she allowed herself to collapse into Sebastian's arms. He lifted her and held her for several moments.

"You can put me down now," said Cass finally. "Just a little shaky, but I will be fine."

"You just fought off this gang of thugs. You deserve to be a little shaky. I was sick to my stomach after my first battle, which was not even a battle, just a little skirmish." Sebastian had an added note of respect in his voice as he addressed Cass.

"Yes, and I am sorry to say that she had to do it single handedly," spoke up Ibrahim Leonides humbly. "It was all I could do not to run away."

"Which you did bravely," said Cass. Then she turned and nodded to the young girl, who stood respectfully a few paces away with the elder. "This is the one who turned the tide. You are very brave … and resourceful," Cass said, addressing her directly. "My name is Cassandra. What is yours?"

"I am Sarah, and this is my grandfather Stephen. We were late returning from the synagogue, when we ran into those men. They and others just like them come into the neighborhood regularly to have their fun by mocking and shoving us around. We have learned a few tricks that we use when we have to." She could hardly repress a smile. "Like the way I rammed the one who was attacking you by hitting him with my head, like a goat." Sarah's voice quickened with excitement as she spoke to Cass as though no one else were present. "Do you really have a knife, or were you bluffing? I think you were bluffing, but you were the brave one, and you saved us from a beating. Thank you, My Lady, she added, as an afterthought."

"My granddaughter is, as you see, a tigress, but excuse her for all the questions. She is a bit headstrong, in more ways than one," he said fondly, rubbing Sarah's head. "I am Stephen ben Isaak, and we are in your debt, dear lady, yours and my friend's for bringing you here, imprudent though that may have been." He smiled at Ibrahim Leonides. "Those ruffians were bad ones, the worst of the lot. I was teaching rather later than usual, I confess. We should have been home sooner." He winced slightly as he took Cass's hands into his own.

"You are hurt. Let us help you," said Cass.

"Only bruises. I shall tend to them shortly, as we are quite near home."

Cass insisted that they accompany Stephen and Sarah. Stephen agreed and indicated the way to their house. As they walked along, Ibrahim Leonides asked Stephen in a partly-teasing voice, "Should you be your own physician?" Even if you are the best physician in Cordoba," he added, speaking proudly of his friend in the hearing of the others.

Stephen gave a slight bow of thanks. Cass, however, decided to hurry them along. She took Stephen by one arm. Sebastian immediately took the other. "No more talking," said Cass, "until we get you home. Come."

"Yes, My Lady," piped up Sarah, as she slipped her hand into Cass's free hand.

When they arrived at their house, Stephen invited them to come in, but Cass said, "Another time." Then noticing Sarah's look of disappointment, she added, "I promise. In fact...." Cass hesitated for a moment and then continued. "Ibrahim Leonides and I were coming to see you when we found you being attacked. I would like to learn about being Jewish," she said without further explanation.

Stephen looked at her searchingly for a moment. "I will send word to you," he said, to let you know if it is safe." He gave no further explanation.

As Cass, Sebastian, and Ibrahim Leonides walked toward the palace, Cass asked, "When Stephen spoke about it being safe he was not simply referring to the bullying was he?"

"I am afraid not," answered Ibrahim Leonides. I am also afraid that I have been imprudent, as Stephen mentioned. I should not have encouraged you to learn about your Jewish roots here just now. Cordoba is too dangerous at the present time."

"I would wager that Maiden has been whispering in your ear. If anyone is to blame it is she, and I agree with her. I am quite sure it must be here and now that I learn about being a Jew," answered Cass, without hesitation, "for my own good and for the quest. I shall not back out now."

"Excuse me," said Sebastian, "but I share Ibrahim Leonides's worry, Cassandra. I do not understand all of these religious identity matters myself, not fully, but I do know that you could be in great danger if you meet with Stephen. Everyone assumes, because you are Lady in Waiting to Lady Francesca, that you are a Christian."

"Precisely the point," said Ibrahim Leonides. "If you were discovered to be a Jew now, you would be considered a 'converso,' meaning ..."

"Meaning that I am a Jew in secret, pretending to be a Christian in public," interrupted Cass. I have heard of conversos, but I am not one. I have never pretended to be a Christian."

"Not by design," said Sebastian, but you must have realized what everyone thought.

"But it never came up. No one asked me."

"No one would," replied Sebastian. "You were appointed by the queen herself. Besides, every one of us in Al-Andalus has a Jew or a Moor or two somewhere in their family tree, but no one talks about that, or asks about it. That includes me, or it did until I met you and Theadora and Alan."

Cass wanted to ask Sebastian more about these hidden ancestries, but Ibrahim Leonides returned to his argument against her taking lessons from Stephen.

"When that horrible man attacked you back there, he was joking when he threatened to report you to 'them who burned Jews.' He knew, or thought he knew, from the way you were dressed and acted, that you were a Christian. What he was actually referring to, however, were the inquisitors, though he would not know them by that name. And the Jews they burn are the conversos."

"Well, then, we will just have to do as Stephen said. I will go when it is safe," said Cass. "Tomorrow," she added as they arrived at the palace gate.

Ibrahim Leonides sighed but bowed graciously to her. "I will call upon you on the morrow," he said. "We have much yet to see in the city. Until then, My Lady. And you, My Lord Sebastian."

When he arrived at the palace the next day, Ibrahim Leonides conveyed Lucía's greetings and her insistence that Cass and Thea stay with them for a few days. This second invitation was welcome and the move quickly accomplished. When the companions and their guide arrived at the house, Lucía would not be satisfied until she had gotten a full account from Cass of what happened the night before. At the end of Cass's story, Lucía hugged her, saying, "you could have been raped and killed, but thanks be that you were protected—and that you are a woman warrior." Lucía dismissed Cass's objections about her role in defeating the bullies. "Ibrahim, my love, do not forget the basket of food. Now off with you all. I have much to do, and remember to be back here early for dinner." She looked pointedly at her husband.

The three companions, much to their guide's delight, were unanimous in requesting that they start out the day by returning to the Mezquita to visit the new part and revisit the old. They were less in awe of the mosque this second day, but no less impressed by it. Like the original section, the Almanzor addition cast its spell with the arches of alternating red and white stone set upon marble pillars. Cass tried to imagine the famed church bells from Santiago filled with lamp oil. "Where would they have put the bells," she asked.

"The oldest tradition says that they were hung face-up like cups, from selected arches. Six or eight of them would have illuminated this whole section." Ibrahim Leonides, prompted by Cass, repeated the story of the bells as the group walked among the pillars and arches.

They once again visited the Mirhab, which was on their way out, and once again they came under the spell of its shimmering gold. As they moved to leave, Cass, who had finally figured out her directions, said, "I thought Muslims always faced the east, toward their holy city of Mecca, when they worshipped, but the Mirhab is on the south wall."

"Very perceptive," said Ibrahim Leonides. "The probable explanation is that the Moors simply followed the old foundations of the church of San Vicente. The most suitable wall faced south. They would have considered it disrespectful to tear down walls and deface the old church. Either that or their engineers had a poor sense of direction," laughed their guide.

They left the Mezquita by another route through the Garden of Oranges, past the fountain, to the old minaret, now a bell tower. As they climbed the steps of the tower, following them in their circular ascent, Cass and Thea were reminded of another tower. "We climbed the Giralda, the minaret in Seville, chasing after two children—your ancestors, the grandchildren of Dhu Khiffil," said Thea to Ibrahim Leonides. "You remind me of him," she added, except that you do not speak in verse."

"Ah, his talent is legendary," replied their guide. "Would that I had a portion of it. Here we are at the top. A feast for the eyes awaits you." Cass and Sebastian followed him through a doorway to a narrow walk with a protective, waist-high wall around it.

"Sebastian, give me your hand," pleaded Thea. She was still standing inside the doorway. "I am petrified of heights," she explained, "so I will keep my eyes closed, and Ibrahim Leonides, please describe what I am not seeing as I hide behind Sebastian."

Which is what they did. Ibrahim Leonides pictured the scenes for Thea's imagination, starting from the east section of the tower walk and moving to his left until they covered all four sections.

"All Cordoba is laid out below … The Old Walled City … Newer dwellings and markets beyond … Great roads coming and going in all directions … Travellers approaching from the North, perhaps from far away Toledo … The noble ruins of the summer palace built for his favorite concubine Zahara by the Caliph of the West."

Even Thea risked looking at the ruins of Zahara, at first with a squint and then with wide eyes as she listened. "At one time the Palace of Zahara became the main meeting place for the court of the Caliph. It was filled with silks and carpets from the east and gold from Africa. Artists, poets, and scientists from all over the world were welcome and were rewarded with dinars for their works. Ambassadors visited from Rome and Damascus, Baghdad, and Constantinople. The Khazari came, a mysterious people from some unknown part of Asia. They were known only in legend until Hasdai, the Caliph's Jewish physician and counselor, made contact with them. The entire nation of the Khazari had converted to Judaism, but no one knows how."

Ibrahim Leonides moved to the end of the west section of the walkway and pointed. "That tall building near the public baths is the most important government building in Cordoba, more important than the Alcazar. It is the information center of Al-Andalus with messages coming in and going out constantly even beyond the kingdom. Questions, answers, requests, commands." Ibrahim Leonides looked past Cass and Sebastian and noticed that Thea's eyes were tightly shut once again. He moved around the corner to the south side of the tower.

"We have almost finished," he said for Thea's benefit. "There is the Guadalquiver River that flows from here to Seville. The great bridge that crosses it was built by the Romans a thousand years ago, rebuilt by the Moors centuries ago, and is maintained now by the Christians. They hire Moorish architects and engineers, of course, just as they do in Seville. Imagine. Over that bridge passed great Romans, like Seneca the philosopher. Over that bridge passed the Jewish philosopher Moses Maimonides when he left his beloved

Cordoba, city of his birth, for the last time. He was fleeing from the Muslim reformers who feared his teachings. In fact he too feared his teachings because they sometimes went against his own Jewish beliefs. He left Cordoba and went to Jerusalem to restore his faith."

"Ibrahim Leonides, what is that huge wheel?" asked Thea, who had once again opened her eyes but tightened her grip on Sebastian's hand. "There to the right of the bridge. You can see it even above the Alcazar and the Mezquita."

"That is the water-wheel built by the Caliph Abdul Rakman the Third to move water up to the Alcazar. From there it flowed to the mosque and other public buildings. The Romans brought water to Cordoba by digging wells and building aqueducts. They tapped the water sources. The Moors added the water wheel that could actually pump water faster and farther."

"This water wheel is famous throughout Al-Andalus, but no one has been able to duplicate the construction and make it work," said Sebastian. "I'm afraid that knowledge has been lost."

"And now," said Ibrahim Leonides, "that we have seen these wonders of Cordoba from afar, which do you want to visit first?"

"First, I believe is the lunch that Lucía sent along with us," observed Cass, "and then a short rest." Thea and Sebastian promptly seconded Cass.

"Oh. Yes, of course," responded their guide slightly disappointed at the delay.

They did visit most of these wonders later that day and on the days following, except for Cass. As matters turned out she had to miss about half of the sites. A messenger from Stephen found them in the Garden of the Oranges where they were enjoying their picnic lunch prepared by Lucía. He told her that she was to begin her instructions, what Stephen called her Jewish baby steps. These started that afternoon and continued on the two following afternoons. It was because of her lessons that the companions missed visiting the ruins of Zahara. That would have required a full day, and Thea and Sebastian refused to be without her for such a long time. Cass loved the lessons, and Stephen was amazed at her quickness.

Cass was about to discover who she was.

# Chapter XVIII

## Essie

C ass's baby steps quickly lengthened into youthful strides propelled by her thirst for information and Stephen's guidance. She particularly loved the stories of Abraham and Sarah, of Moses, of Esther, and especially of King David and his songs. She did tell Stephen that she was surprised at the martial tone of the Psalms. She questioned Stephen about everything he told her from the Jewish Scriptures, from the teachings of Moses and the Prophets, Amos and Micah being her favorite. Stephen also asked questions, about Cass's family, about her previous adventures in Al-Andalus, and about the necklace.

So quickly had Cass absorbed Stephen's teaching that by the third session he decided that it was time to acquaint her with the synagogue. Cass was delighted. She was surprised to see that the Jewish Holy Book was placed in a niche and revered much like the Koran was in the mosque. When they returned to Stephen's and Sarah's house, Cass asked if she would be permitted to attend a service. Stephen had hoped for exactly this request when he took her to the synagogue. He was pleased that he did not have to make the suggestion. She could come to worship the next day.

She was ready.

When they were back at the kitchen table, which doubled as Stephen's work space, Cass looked at her teacher with an expectant smile, ready to add to her growing knowledge about being Jewish.

"It is time for you to hear of a Jewish hero of our own here in Cordoba, and not from ancient days but from only a few centuries ago." Cass felt that Stephen was looking at her extra closely as he started his narrative.

"It was in the tenth century that the famed ruler Abdul Rakman the Third became the Leader of the Muslims in Spain. Abdul Rakman the Third was a good Muslim. In fact he was the first to declare himself to be the Caliph of the West in Cordoba and equal to the Caliph of the East in Baghdad. This meant that he was the protector of all the Muslims, not only of Spain but also of any nearby territory that was closer to Cordoba than to Baghdad. A great many Muslims looked to him as their guardian. He was so conscious of their needs that at first he seemed to have forgotten about the other people of the book, the Christians and Jews. He paid attention to them only when he needed tax money or when a Muslim complained about them. They had to pay dearly in both cases. Taxes and complaints became so numerous that the Jews believed that they soon would have nothing left with which to pay, except their lives."

"This is when the Jewish hero arrived. She simply appeared among the Jews one day. 'My name is Essie,' she said. 'I too am a Jew, and I was sent to help you, I think by an angel.'"

"Grandmother Esther!" Cass had to cover her mouth with both hands to stop herself from laughing or screaming, or both.

"Yes, so I have come to see," answered Stephen. "I hoped so from the moment I received the message about you from Ibrahim Leonides. When I saw you in the royal procession entering the city I felt in my heart that you were the one. Seeing the necklace convinced me, but I wanted to hear you say what you just did."

"What did she do?" asked Cass excitedly.

"As I was saying," replied Stephen. "Her story may be instructive."

Cass sighed, struggling to calm herself. "Yes, of course. Sorry. I am listening," she said after a moment.

Stephen continued. "Abdul Rakman's agents, always on the lookout among the Jews, brought word of this stranger who appeared out of nowhere. They spoke of her liveliness, her laughter, her beauty. The Caliph promptly insisted that she be brought before him. He was immediately smitten by her beauty and captivated by her fearlessness before even him. When he asked her if she were not afraid of him, she laughed and replied that she could disappear as suddenly as she had appeared in Cordoba. When he asked her where she came from, she said simply, "I am from the future." The Caliph, not to be outdone in cleverness, said, "That is when, not where." Essie smiled. "I came here from Seville. I came to Seville from the New World." "Then tell me of this New World," said the Caliph. "I will, My Lord," agreed Essie."

"Essie moved into Abdul Rakman's palace that very day and became his second favorite concubine after Zahara, his favorite."

"Oh, my. Grandmother!" exclaimed Cass. It would not be the last time she would make this exclamation. She apologized again for the interruption, and Stephen continued.

"Most nights the Caliph called for Essie to join him in his chamber. She would tell him of the marvels of the New World. As time went on and Essie's visits to Abdul's chambers continued on almost every night, the condition of the Jews in Cordoba improved considerably. The Caliph in fact wondered how it had happened that he had neglected them. He became friendly even with Christians."

"Zahara, however, the Caliph's favorite, soon became jealous. She worried that Essie, so strong and healthy, might bear Abdul a child, possibly a son, and thus become Abdul's new favorite. She had as yet not been able to have a child with Abdul. The Caliph and Essie were both aware of Zahara's jealousy. Essie also learned from the Jews that the Muslims who used to bully and threaten them were starting to grumble about the Caliph becoming friendly with Jews and Christians. They took their complaints to Zahara who foolishly listened to them. Some of the Muslims had already been enemies of the Caliph. They added logs to the fire of Zahara's envy. Essie reminded Abdul that his political enemies had tried once in the past to murder him. She had been told of this by the Jews, who said the attempt was by two female assassins. The Jews warned Essie to beware of Zahara and the grumbling Muslims."

"Not long after this warning it happened that Essie indeed realized that she was pregnant with her and Abdul's child. When she told Abdul, he was delighted. They celebrated but decided to keep their joy to themselves until Essie should begin to show that she was with child. Zahara, however, saw the happiness in Abdul and Essie and began to suspect the reason. She spoke with two Muslim leaders who were among those who complained to her about the Caliph and his Jewish concubine. The Jews, who were watching out for Essie, discovered that the two Muslim leaders were planning to kill the Caliph. They told Essie, and Essie told Abdul, who uncovered the plot. He had the two Muslim leaders imprisoned. Zahara repented and confessed her treachery. The Caliph would have had her imprisoned and possibly hanged, but Essie pleaded with him to forgive Zahara.

"But Essie knew how proud and how foolish Zahara was. She feared for Abdul and for her unborn child. Essie told Abdul that she would have to disappear back to the New World, that only there would their child be safe."

"Oh, my!" exclaimed Cass.

Stephen paused for a moment, looking at Cass. Cass returned his look, wide eyed with wonder. "Go on, please," she whispered.

"At first Abdul refused to hear of Essie leaving him, especially since she said she might never return. He pleaded with her at least to send their child to him. Essie told him in a sad voice that she could not make such a promise. If the child were a girl, Zahara would kill her or die trying. Abdul loved Essie so much that he finally agreed to let her go. He also promised that in her memory, and for their child and their child's children, he would continue to protect the Jews."

"Essie returned to her New World and was never seen here again. But the Jews of Cordoba celebrate every year how she was their angel in the Caliph's court. We have a tradition that a descendent of Essie will one day return in another time of great need."

"That has now happened," said Stephen, smiling at Cass.

"Grandmother Esther and the Caliph," exclaimed Cass. "And my mother, their daughter ... I am ... ."

"A Jew of Arab nobility, the granddaughter of a Muslim Caliph," said Stephen.

Cass could say no more. She hugged Stephen, and they laughed together. It was not long, however, before Cass's tone changed from joyous surprise to anxious concern. "But what can I do to help my people? I am a Lady in Waiting to the wife of a minor nobleman, and if she knew I were a Jew, she would send me away. I have no powerful friends. And I certainly have no one important to marry. It seems I lack my grandmother's powers, including her attractiveness."

"Just your being here has already lifted our spirits. I was not alone in wondering if you were the one to be sent by Essie—and the Most High—a young Jewish woman travelling with Queen Isabella, and from Seville. The fact that you were Lady in Waiting to the wife of Don Enriquez only added to our wondering. Don Enriquez and his family have been friends to the Jews of Cordoba for many years. But, My Lady Cassandra, no one is expecting miracles." Stephen paused. He looked a bit worried but then went on. "Yet I must confess that every Jew is looking to you for some word or sign, some indication of what you intend. If it brings you any comfort, for my own part, your presence among us has already fulfilled the people's hopes and restored their faith."

"It does bring me comfort," responded Cass with a smile and a bow.

"Come to the synagogue tomorrow," said Stephen. "Sarah will be waiting for you outside. She is very excited that she will be your guide for our modest Sabbath service in the synagogue. But do not come alone. I have been told that those bullies have been seen again in the neighborhood."

Cass began to object to this precaution, but Stephen insisted, and she agreed. "Sebastian has been assigned as body-guard for Thea and me, and has had very little to do so far except be a tourist with us. Speaking of Sebastian, I must meet him and the others at the House of Lucía. I think I am already overdue." Cass gave her teacher another hug.

"Peace with you," said Stephen.

"With you, peace," replied Cass.

# Chapter XIX

# The Caliph, The Queen, The Physician, and The Bishop

When Cass returned to the House of Lucía, she found the others already there, as she had expected. Barely able to contain herself, she took Thea up to their room and there revealed the story about Grandmother Esther being Essie, a Jewish hero of the past. Thea greeted the news with amazement, excitement, hugs and tears. Cass only wished that Alan could have been there to share the joyous moment. A little later Cass shared the story with Sebastian, Ibrahim Leonides, and Lucía. Ibrahim Leonides was delighted both for Cass and for the accuracy of his family's legends about the travelers from the future. He, of course, gave Dhu Khiffl full credit as poet and prophet. Sebastian rose quite solemnly, bowed deeply, and addressed Cass as "Princess," which she was. Lucía toasted Essie as the original woman warrior of Lady Cassandra's family.

The only slightly negative note to the evening meal was that Sebastian had received word from the Duke. The Ladies-in-Waiting were expected to arrive at their new home and duties two days hence. Even that news could not dampen Cass's excitement, both about Grandmother Essie, as she now referred to her, and her attendance at the synagogue the next day. The companions would miss the House of Lucía. They would, however, continue in close contact, since Sebastian would remain as bodyguard whenever Thea or Cass needed to go out. The Duke insisted upon rendering this service to his Queen. The companions promised Lucía, at her insistence, to make Casa Lucía their second home. The group settled into a mood of quiet contentment.

That was when Ibrahim Leonides spoke. What he said would have profound consequences. "I have a proposal."

"We should visit the Cordoba of Abdul Rakman the Third, Lady Cassandra's grandfather. My Lady, you and the necklace could take us there as it once took your grandmother." His proposal was greeted by an attentive silence, which he interpreted as positive, or at least not negative. He waited. Everyone looked from Ibrahim Leonides to Cass, and waited.

"Why?" asked Cass. She was excited but hesitant.

Ibrahim Leonides had anticipated that question. "We have experienced the wonder-filled sights of our—that is, my—Cordoba, capitol of Al-Andalus. Impressive as the city is today, we can hardly imagine its past glories, especially during the reign of the great Caliph Abdul Rakman five centuries ago. It would reveal the flowering of Spain's greatness at the peak of harmony among Muslims, Jews, and Christians."

"The *convivencia*," exclaimed Cass and Thea simultaneously. Lucía vigorously nodded her approval. Only Sebastian remained quietly reserved.

"Cass, we could visit your Grandmother Esther, I mean Essie," said Thea excitedly.

"I just had the same thought," replied Cass, "but I do not want to get in the way of her mission. It might not be a good idea for us to meet. Besides, I have already learned from Stephen what she accomplished." Thea assented. Cass looked at Ibrahim Leonides, who also was smiling in agreement with her. "Something tells me that you already have an idea about the details of this journey."

"I have often dreamed of it," replied Ibrahim Leonides. "Imagine this. We are present in Cordoba on the very day that the Christian Queen of Navarre brings her grandson, the deposed King of Leon, to this city. They have come to the Caliph, a Muslim potentate, for medical and military help. On that day the sun of Al-Andalus is at its zenith."

"That does sound exciting," urged Thea. Ibrahim Leonides had re-awakened her holiday mood. Thea looked encouragingly at Cass but avoided looking at Sebastian, having sensed his disapproval of the idea.

Cass still hesitated. She was intrigued. Where better to witness the *convivencia* in action, as Ibrahim Leonides pointed out. Might not it provide clues about their own mission. "What will the djinni of the necklace say about a history excursion, should we ever hear from her," she asked half seriously. "I think we may have been distracted from our mission of late by our holiday. I regret that Alan would not be here to share such an experience. I miss him."

"I think it is too dangerous, especially without Alan," agreed Sebastian.

Thea looked at him, hesitated, and then spoke. "But we are quite certain now that our Cordoba is at the heart of our quest, and, as Ibrahim Leonides says, it was at its zenith on the date he is proposing. Unfortunately Alan will not be back by tomorrow," she added. "I doubt that he would want us to miss an opportunity of such significance."

"Significant for your search for your Jewish roots," contributed Ibrahim Leonides. "Hasdai ibn Shaprut, of whom I have spoken, was the counselor who negotiated bringing the Queen and her grandson to Cordoba. And I am convinced that he did it to add to the renown of Al-Andalus. He was the most famous Jew of the age, and the hero and protector of Jews throughout Al-Andalus and beyond, even to Bagdad." He had played his trump card. Now he looked at Cass and waited.

Cass could not help but smile at both Ibrahim Leonides and Thea. "The two of you should have made fine counselors to the Caliph or the Queen. You might even have persuaded Maiden." She frowned slightly, as though this thought troubled her. "She told us that we had to learn to rely on ourselves." Her frown disappeared. Thea knew that Cass approved. Cass looked at Ibrahim Leonides, who was trying to conceal his anxiety of uncertainty.

"You say that this Hasdai negotiated between a Queen and a Caliph. Who knows. Perhaps we could learn from him how one persuades a queen." She looked meaningfully at Sebastian, giving him the chance to speak.

"I do not know if Maiden would approve or not, but I have been charged by the Duke de Cordoba and by the Queen herself with the safety of the two Ladies in Waiting. I know what the Duke and Queen would say if we proposed visiting the Cordoba of Caliph Abdul Rakman the Third, providing they believed me. Our history regards him as the Muslim prince most feared by Christians in all of Al-Andalus."

"Most feared but most respected," interjected Ibrahim Leonides, who then added a diplomatic, "My Lord Sebastian."

"It is a chance for Cass to see and possibly even meet her grandfather," said Thea quietly.

"I confess that the chance to see the great Caliph and his realm is very tempting," admitted Sebastian. He nodded to Cass.

"So be it," concluded Cass. "We leave after breakfast in the morning."

Ibrahim Leonides, who would have preferred to leave immediately, resigned himself to a sleepless night. He wished for the others to "Sleep Well."

The next morning no one asked who had slept well as they gathered around the table. The food was practically ignored. After the brown-crusted loaves, still warm and dripping with honey, the nervous conversations—to which no one paid any attention—trailed off. Lucía brought the large bowl of water. She stepped away, but stayed close to watch. Cass closed her eyes.

"Ibrahim Leonides, describe Cordoba as it was on the day the Queen of Navarre entered the city."

The chronicler, again, was prepared. "The warm spring weather has arrived. The sun is half way to its peak. The air is filled with the scent of jasmine and roses and orange blossoms. It is Tuesday, the major market day of the week. It is a special Tuesday, the one that comes just after Easter and during Passover. The streets are brimming with crowds of people who are spilling into and out of doorways. This is the day in the year 960 of the Christian era that I believe Hasdai would have chosen. He wanted as many people as possible to witness the greatness of Al-Andalus."

"Thank you," said Cass. She opened her eyes. She instructed the others. "Dip both hands into the bowl. Rinse them gently but do not dry them." She did the same. "Now the three of you join hands and gather round me. The ones on either side of me hold onto my mantle." When everyone had followed these instructions, Cass reached back and undid the wolf catch of the necklace. Then she re-fastened it.

The four companions found themselves caught up in a festive swirl of humanity.

"A carnival," thought Thea.

"Fiesta," guessed Sebastian aloud.

"The Queen must be in town indeed," laughed Cass lightly to herself.

"We are here," announced Ibrahim Leonides triumphantly, quite loud enough to be heard over the din. "Cordoba … .market day … tenth century. Stay close together."

They moved with the crowds, jostling and mingling with people of every description. There were swarthy Berbers, brown-skinned Africans, olive-complected Arabs, pale Northerners. There were slaves from Frankish lands, from Africa, and from the East. Most of the women were covered except for their hands and feet and their dark, dark penetrating eyes. The streets were wide and lined with stalls where merchants and farmers sold their wares. And you had to watch where you stepped or you might find your foot either under the hoof of a camel or burro or else in their droppings.

"Stop on the other side of this gate," shouted Ibrahim Leonides. He had just caught sight of the Mezquita over his right shoulder and gotten his bearings. They did manage to get out of the human mainstream and gather a little way beyond the gate. The crowd was less dense here in the vast open market area outside the city walls.

"This is certainly the Great Market," trumpeted their guide. "Much larger than our paltry affair. Everything is on a grand scale. So many more people. More everything. Cordoba is one of the largest and most advanced cities of the world at this time. And we are here. We are here," chanted Ibrahim Leonides. "Wait here while I inquire if this is the day we hope it is."

"Cass, we must explore this market," said Thea as they waited. "The whole known—and unknown—world must be here with all their goods."

"Would someone tell me what is happening. I seem to understand everything people are saying, but I know that they come from many different lands." No one had remembered to explain to Sebastian this power of the necklace to make all tongues intelligible.

The ladies laughed. Cass explained as Sebastian's eyes—and mouth—opened wider in amazement. "And I think you make a handsome Arab," observed Thea. Sebastian examined what he was wearing.

"This is the day. This is the day," repeated Ibrahim Leonides excitedly. "No one knows exactly when, but it will be today. They have stayed overnight in a hacienda nearby. We should go round to the northern gate so we will be able to witness the entrance of the Queen and her son."

"Can we just walk quickly through the market first, or on our way," requested Thea.

Ibrahim Leonides agreed, but reluctantly, and he 'ahemmed' nervously.

The market revealed its diverse riches to the companions. The visitors from the future—two futures—agreed that they had never experienced anything comparable. Innumerable amusements vied for their attention. The snake charmers and the hawkers announced magical potions and objects of mystery. The preachers and the performers—jugglers, actors, clowns—called to them with messages of wisdom or simply of fun.

They came upon a different area where they were surprised to find medical practitioners. Dentists were pulling teeth and replacing them with custom-fitting false teeth while people sat patiently. Some pressed gold fillings into the teeth of the wealthier clients. Oculists ground lenses and fitted eyeglasses on customers. Physicians bled their patients or applied leeches to their bare backs, necks, and faces.

"These market doctors did—still do—fine work," said Ibrahim Leonides. "Not everyone can afford the private physicians or even the barbers who perform the operations in the city. But come, we should be getting into position to watch the great event. No, Lady Theadora, do not touch the dog!" he shouted as he saw what Thea was about to do, but he was too late."

"Ahhh! Ouch! It bit me on the hand," cried Thea. Sebastian moved swiftly with his dagger to kill the animal, which only made Thea feel worse. "Did you have to kill it," she lamented.

"Yes, he did," said Ibrahim Leonides. "Dogs are the plague of the market place. Their bites are poisonous. Sit down and be still. The Master of the Market will want to have someone examine the dog."

Even as Ibrahim Leonides spoke, a crowd had gathered. Only a few minutes later the people respectfully made way for an official, of high rank to judge by his clothes and the insignia on his turban. He was followed by four soldiers. The official waived to one of the market physicians who seemed to have been awaiting this signal. He came quickly to examine Thea's hand, now wrapped in a bloody kerchief. He next went to the dog and examined the color of the saliva still oozing from the dead animal's mouth. He then pronounced the dreaded word that was in everyone's mind: "rabid."

While the physician worked, the Master had studied this group of visitors to his market. He correctly guessed that the younger man was a soldier out of uniform, judging from the way he had dispatched the dog and now stood guard beside the seated woman. The woman was certainly a northerner and probably a Christian. The other two were less identifiable but had the looks of a high-born woman and her counsellor. "The Caliph will not be pleased if a Christian noble lady has been attacked by a mad dog in his Great Market, on this of all days." He spoke briskly to two of the soldiers who left to carry out his orders. Then he turned to Thea.

"Young mistress, I apologize most humbly for this outrage." Thea could see that he was genuinely distressed. "We will get you to a physician who has a reputation for curing mad-dog bites. You are not to worry at all." He stood up and nodded to the others, but he was not smiling.

"That man is truly worried," Cass thought and promptly became seriously anxious herself.

"Here we are," announced the Master as the two soldiers returned with the riding chair and an additional soldier who seemed to be in command. "Carefully," the Master ordered, as they helped Thea onto the chair. "I cannot accompany you myself," he told Thea, "but the soldiers and my sergeant will take you. May Allah be with you."

The four soldiers, with the sergeant leading and making a path through the crowds, carried Thea quickly but with never a bump to the house of the physician as directed by the Master. The sergeant had barely knocked on the door before the physician took command. "This way. Quickly. Set the carrying-chair down," he instructed the soldiers, "and bring her carefully to the next room. You," he said to Cass with penetrating eyes and the briefest of smiles, "might be of some help. The rest of you stay out here."

Cass hurriedly thanked the soldiers and followed the physician, who was beginning his work. He mixed some ingredients into a glass of what appeared to be orange juice and had Thea drink it. "We must remove your outer garments," he said to Thea, "but move as little as possible. We will be your muscles." Thea attempted a smile and followed his directions. "We must avoid her getting a chill," he said to Cass. "Here are blankets and here are water and cloths to bathe her when the fever gets high." Cass settled into her role of assistant physician. She noticed that Thea had relaxed and even seemed to be dozing.

Cass was too busy to ask a lot of questions, other than, "You will be able to cure her, doctor, will you not?"

"Please, do me the honor of calling me Abu Yusuf, as all my friends do. As for your friend, the bite is a bad one, but she is strong and young. She will have considerable pain, but I think she will be all right, although she will have to stay here overnight to recover. The poison that entered her blood from the dog has the ability to breed somehow in her body. So we have to get it out of her. And we start by letting some blood. Do not worry," he hurried to say, noticing Cass's startled expression, "I do not bleed patients blood-less. We need only to void the blood near the wound. Luckily the Master of the Market was at hand. He and I have learned that if the victim remains calm and unmoving, the poison does not travel far."

Cass smiled at Abu Yusuf, a smile that conveyed her relief and her admiration. She made conversation to keep herself calm. "I would guess that the Master learned this lesson from you. Have you written down your findings about mad-dog bites?" asked Cass, as she dabbed the perspiration on Thea's forehead. She was mentally replaying the scene of Thea's misfortune; it was Ibrahim Leonides who had insisted that Thea not move.

"Oh, yes, we make notes always on our observations and pro-cedures. People do not always pay attention—the Master of the Market is exceptional as are a few others—but perhaps someone in the future will benefit. Sometimes you have to be dead before people think you are wise," he chuckled. "That should be sufficient bleeding. Now the remedy."

He picked out a phial from among several on a nearby shelf. "We bathe the wound in this liquid, so ... and ... so. Now we wrap her hand with clean linen, just so. Now, rest her elbow on your leg, holding her forearm upright. Every few minutes put the arm down. Add about ten drops of the liquid to the cloth over the wound. Then raise the arm again and repeat the cycle until the liquid is used up. This procedure helps speed the medicine in pursuit of the poison. I have already given her some of the same medicine diluted in the orange juice."

Abu Yusuf watched as Cass followed his instructions. He smiled, nodded approvingly, and went into the outer room where Sebastian and Ibrahim Leonides anxiously waited for word about Thea. Abu Yusuf put them at ease as much as possible. "I believe she will recover fully," he said. "I will let you know when she wakens."

When he returned to his patient, Cass had just put the last of the drops of medicine on the cloth. She was sniffing tentatively at the cloth bandage. "It has a strong aroma, but it is not a bad smell, some curative oils distilled from natural herbs and plants. The taste also is not unpleasant," said Abu Yusuf.

"She is sound asleep," said Cass. "What besides the curative oils did you put into the orange juice?"

"Ah, I think you have the makings of a physician's apprentice," he replied. "Yes I gave her a sleeping potion mixed with the oils and a few drops of the Seder wine. She will rest and gather her strength. She will need it for her battle with the poison. The remedy helps, yet it but assists the body's self-healing."

Cass looked intently at Abu Yusuf as he spoke. She noticed for the first time that he was wearing eye glasses. She was surprised but then she remembered the oculists in the Great Market.

At that moment Thea moved and moaned slightly. "The battle has begun," pronounced Abu Yusuf. He went to get a fresh phial of oils and a fresh bowl of water and a clean cloth. "I will take care of the drops and arm if you will keep the fever down with the cloth and water on her forehead, face, and neck. We must see that she does not take a chill."

Thea struggled against the poison for nearly two hours. Cass alternated between bathing Thea to keep the fever down and bundling her in blankets to prevent chills. Thea became more restless and moaned more often. She groaned loudly when Cass moved her in an attempt to make her more comfortable. Sebastian, alarmed, called from the other room. "How is she? What can I do?"

"Stay calm," ordered Cass, without feeling that way herself. Sebastian knelt and prayed aloud the Latin prayers he had memorized as a youth. Even Ibrahim Leonides, the skeptic, supplied the "Amen" to the prayers. He also kept muttering that it was all his fault. Sebastian was still kneeling and Ibrahim Leonides still pacing when Abu Yussuf returned. He was smiling.

"The fever has broken. She is weak but resting. You can come in for a short time."

Sebastian knelt by Thea's bed and looked into her weary but happy eyes. His own eyes were glistening. "I was never before so frightened in all my life," he said to her.

"The rest of us could be in another century for all they know," said Cass, smiling, to the others.

Ibrahim Leonides, looking over Sebastian's shoulder at Thea, said, "This day would no longer have been the greatest day of Al-Andalus if worse had come of this wound."

"Ibrahim Leonides has missed the great event," Cass explained to Abu Yusuf.

"And what event is that?" inquired Abu Yusuf.

"The entrance of the Queen of Navarre and her grandson," replied Ibrahim Leonides, coming to stand with them. "But, truly, the great event of this day is Lady Theadora's recovery, which you, Master Physician, have brought about."

Abu Yussuf nodded his thanks for the compliment, after which he said, "but you have not missed the entrance of the Queen and her grandson. That will happen later, not long before dusk. That was one condition that the Queen insisted on. She hopes that at least some of the people will tire of waiting all day, but I do not think so."

"Can it be, but how do you know this," asked Ibrahim Leonides.

"Because I am the one who arranged for their coming to Cordoba. I am Hasdai ibn Shaprut."

"But you said your name was Abu Yusuf," said Cass, not understanding.

"It is. My full name is Abu Yusuf Hasdai ben Ishaq ibn Shaprut. Which is why my friends call me Abu Yusuf, and here is one of my friends. As though on cue, a man with a dark beard and wearing a brown robe with a thick chord around his waist, had just appeared in the open doorway. His face expressed curiosity but not surprise at finding the surgery room so full of people. "Come all of you, except my assistant. I will introduce you in the front room. To Cass he said, "join us when our patient is resting again."

In the front room, Abu Yusuf introduced everyone to the new arrival. "Brother Nicholas has come from Constantinople to help me translate the most important medical work ever written. It has an elaborate title, but I call it simply *The Book of Medicine*."

"*On the Ingredients of Medicine*, by a Greek of ancient times named Dioscorides, to be more precise," said Brother Nicholas as he bowed, or rather bobbed, briefly, revealing his monk's tonsure. Despite the streaks of gray in his short and otherwise dark hair and beard, his face was youthful and lively, with darting eyes, ruddy cheekbones, and a longish, narrow nose. Even in his thick robe, his appearance and motions gave the impression of a restless songbird hopping about on a limb, about to take flight. He nodded to each person in turn, registering everyone's names.

Ibrahim Leonides wished he could tell these men about being from the future, and he especially wanted to tell them about how many people had been cured, how many lives had been saved over the centuries thanks to their translation of the names of the herbs and other medicines from Greek into Arabic. But he feared that he would thus raise more questions than could be answered. He contented himself with saying simply that he and his companions had come from Seville to see the Queen and her grandson, but that they also had wanted to find out more about the work of Hasdai—Abu Yusuf—and Brother Nicholas.

"Ibrahim Leonides is an important chronicler," noted Sebastian. Ibrahim Leonides was pleased and only slightly embarrassed. But it was a fortunate compliment. Both Abu Yusuf and Brother Nicholas bowed respectfully to the chronicler, Brother Nicholas several times in quick succession.

"Without the chronicler," said Abu Yusuf, "the philosopher can think wondrous thoughts, but no one will remember them."

"Without the chronicler," said Brother Nicholas, "the scientist may discover marvels, but if no one knows how or why, they will be forgotten or, even worse, misused. Abu Yusuf, I believe our chronicler friend should witness more than just the grand entrance."

"I agree, Nicholas. After the procession, bring Ibrahim Leonides and my assistant with you, through the tunnel. A chronicler in disguise present at the official but secret meeting of the Queen and the Caliph," he exclaimed with delight. "Perfect. And now, Nicholas will explain the arrangements."

The arrangements were that Brother Nicholas would remain with their new guests. Abu Yusuf had "palace-related duties," for which he had to leave. "Stay close to Nicholas, Chronicler, you and my assistant both, he cautioned," as he moved toward the door. "We do not want to lose either of you," he added on his way out.

"We will watch the royal procession from our roof," Brother Nicholas said. "They will enter the city from the north. By and by they will leave by the West Gate for the Summer Palace of Zahara a few miles away. There they will be the guest of the Caliph. The "by and by' is the fun part. They will cross the city square, pass by the Mezquita and so come to the edge of the Jewish neighborhood and the West Gate. That means they will pass right in front of this house." Everyone in the room voiced their approval and applauded this news.

Brother Nicholas gave instructions for carrying Thea up to the roof on a cot to watch for a short period. After the procession had passed, Ibrahim Leonides and Cass would accompany him to the secret meeting.

"That sounds very mysterious and inviting, Brother Nicholas, but surely I must stay with Thea," objected Cass.

"No, I pray you," said Sebastian, "You have done everything for her, Lady Cassandra, while I stood helplessly by. Please allow me the honor of caring for Thea."

Cass frowned, sighed, and smiled in succession. Sebastian long since dropped the formal address, until that minute. "If I return and find the patient worse, you, My Lord Sebastian will pay dearly." Her tone was teasing, but not without a serious edge.

Sebastian bowed solemnly to her. "My Lady."

"That is settled then," said Brother Nicholas, rubbing his hands together briskly. He had smiled but showed no surprise when hearing "Lord" and "Lady." "Now, let us move Theadora to the roof. I think I can hear shouts in the distance."

By the time they were all settled on the roof, they could hear crowd sounds. The procession must have reached the city square and would be on its way to the Mezquita. The surge of sound became louder and more insistent. From their rooftop perch the watchers caught glimpses of banners flapping and lance points shining as the procession made a left turn onto their street.

The crowd flooded the street as people surged ahead of and in back of the royal visitors. The first of the Christian knights were now in sight. Sparks of sunlight glanced off their helmets and chain mail, ricocheting in all directions and nearly blinding the watchers. Beyond this first rank of knights came a herald dressed in the purple and gold of Navarre. He was shouting something. Only a few words reached the watchers as he passed below. "Make way... her Royal... Lords... way!"

Now a second even more splendid rank of knights clattered by. These were dressed more for show than for war. Their tunics were emblazoned with the shield and crown of Navarre. The people waved. Their shouts and cheers rose to a crescendo. "The Queen, the Queen." Queen Toda of Navarre passed below, seated side-saddle upon a dancing white Arabian stallion. She was dressed simply but was unmistakably a Queen, her graying hair brushed upward to form a natural crown.

And walking beside her, humbly holding onto her stirrup, was undoubtedly the fattest person Cass had ever seen. His red mantle had enough material in it to make a tent for four. In fact he looked like a walking tent, with his head as the ornamental top of the tent pole. The wide brim of his floppy hat actually bounced off his rounded apple cheeks. He was puffing, but strode along with determination. Cass later learned that he had, at Abu Yusuf's recommendation, walked a portion of each day all the way from Navarre, from northernmost Spain in the shadows of the Pyrenees Mountains, to Cordoba in the bright southern plains of Al-Andalus.

The people shouted, "El Gordo! ... Sancho El Gordo! ... Sancho the Fat One." The young Lord, however, behaved like the king he had been and hoped to be once again. He smiled and waved. He had won the peoples' hearts and, finally, their admiration. They continued calling out "El Gordo," but their tone had changed from ridicule to praise.

And just behind the Queen and El Gordo rode none other than Abu Yusuf whom the people all along the route had been greeting, not just as a Royal Counselor, but as a prophet. Here in the streets of the Jewish neighborhood, the cheers mounted in intensity. "Al Nasi, protector ... Al Nasi, Prince of the Jews." Without realizing she was doing so, Cass shouted herself hoarse, waving her arms and dancing in place. When she could shout no more, she laughed and cried and danced. The rest of the procession was a blur of more knights, Christian and Muslim. Cass noticed that Brother Nicholas had laid a kindly hand on her shoulder and wondered how long it had been there. Thea had already been returned to the surgery room. It was time for Cass and Ibrahim Leoinedes to accompany Brother Nicholas to the secret meeting.

The wave of people had quickly receded before the late April twilight. Thus Cass and Ibrahim Leonides had no difficulty in following Abu Yusuf's caution to stay close to Brother Nicholas. The rest of Abu Yusuf's advice, "ask no questions," was more difficult, at least for Cass. She assumed the same was true for her chronicler friend. Both of them, nonetheless, followed Abu Yusuf's advice. They made their way easily through the streets toward the West Gate through which the Queen and El Gordo had passed. They were not going to the gate, however. Brother Nicholas lead them aside, to a small wine shop built up against the west wall. The strong metal bars of the shop's gate were chained tightly. Cass was startled when she heard owl sounds. She almost laughed aloud when she realized they were coming from Brother Nicholas.

A woman, her face hidden by her veil, approached silently. She opened the iron gate, let them in, and then re-locked the gate. She motioned for them to follow. They descended a narrow stone stairway, single file, each holding onto the mantle of the one in front. The darkness was complete, but their guide seemed to be moving with confident steps. Then they stopped. Cass could hear the woman move off, but then stop again. She heard a few taps, like a hammer against stone. As though in response, a torch flared up, then settled into a steady, reassuring beacon. Cass sighed with relief, realizing how anxious she had been. Still, she wished the woman would speak. She began to think of stories she had read about slaves whose tongues had been cut out so they could not betray the secrets of their masters.

And this tunnel was clearly a secret. Cass already guessed, correctly as she later discovered, that the tunnel connected the city with the Palace of Zahara. No doubt it was also an escape route for the Caliph's family and perhaps also a passage for his spies and other secret contacts. "Like us," thought Cass. She noted that the tunnel was cut through stone, for the most part, or lined with stones and beams. "Nothing fancy here," she mused, "but well made." The floor was gravel. Periodically she caught drafts of air from above and saw grates in the ceiling. "The Moors are great engineers." She remembered Ibrahim Leonides's high praise. "They learned from the Romans." These thoughts comforted her, but she remained conscious that they were probably now deep under the ridge of hills that ran from the city to the Palace of Zahara, and that there was barely room to stand up.

It seemed like hours before the tunnel finally began a gradual ascent that brought them to another set of steps. They emerged into a moonlit night. Cass shuddered a bit, not so much from the cooler air as from the discovery that they were in a cemetery. It was a very old cemetery. When she looked behind her, she realized that they had just come out of a tomb. It was a crumbling Roman mausoleum, covered partly by the hillside, partly by the vines. When she turned back again, she saw their guide's silhouette. She was without a torch, entering another equally decayed mausoleum. She whispered for them to follow.

"Well at least she can speak," thought Cass, as she grimly followed her into the tomb. This time the passage was mercifully short, and their guide had lighted another torch when it would not be seen from outside the tunnel. In its light Cass soon saw what looked like a solid wall blocking their passage. The guide, however, merely felt along the wall for a moment and then gave it a push. It swung open, and she motioned for them to pass through. "Thank you," said Cass to the guide, who rewarded her with a "shush," but then a fleeting smile.

The change was remarkable. They entered a large, bright, comfortable-looking room, one that was meant to be lived in, thought Cass with relief. When she had a further look after her eyes adjusted to the light, she gasped. Hangings of spun silk and of brocaded cloth softened the stone walls. Layers of overlapping carpets covered the floor. The carpets provided many varieties of reds and purples that complimented elaborate designs of gold leaf. Braziers with glowing coals showing through artful designs in the metal of moons and stars warmed the room with both light and heat. Reclining on a couch, Roman style, was Abdul Rackman the Third, Caliph of the West. He looked handsome and was dazzling in his white robes and turban.

His couch was located near the center of the wall opposite where Cass and the others entered. He was watching a stately gray haired woman, whom Cass recognized from the procession as Queen Toda of Navarre. The Queen was pacing rapidly back and forth a little in front of him as she addressed the Caliph. Standing at a discreet distance from the Caliph's head, to Cass's left, was Abu Yusuf, looking elegant in courtly robes. Cass fancied that he was just close enough to place himself between the Caliph and the Queen quickly if necessary. On another couch, near the Caliph's foot, sat El Gordo. Cass could not tell if he were reclining or sitting up straight since he filled the entire couch with his bulk.

The Caliph motioned to Brother Nicholas and his companions, when the Queen was not blocking his view, for them to be seated on some cushions near Abu Yusuf. Ibrahim Leonides and Cass followed Brother Nicholas's example and slipped quietly over to the cushions, taking care to stay out of range of the pacing Queen. Cass sat next to Brother Nicholas, Ibrahim Leonides just behind them. From their new vantage point Cass now saw a lady, clearly an attendant to the Queen, close to El Gordo's couch. There were no introductions, although the Queen's Lady nodded briefly to Cass and made a slight bow in the direction of Ibrahim Leonides and Brother Nicholas. Neither of them seemed to notice this politeness, however, as they were focused intently on the Queen and the Caliph.

Only now did Cass notice another figure, dressed in Arab style, but all in black, and with a gold chain around his neck, holding a large, jeweled cross. He stood slightly removed from the Queen and her lady. He looked on intently. It struck Cass that there were no guards of any sort in sight. She turned her attention to the speakers.

"But my dear Aunt, it is not as though you were dragged through the city as slaves or captives. Everyone knows that you are here for my cousin's weight-reducing treatments, and that you are my guests and my kinsmen."

"Humph, you call me Aunt and guest. Why then do you parade us through the main street of Cordoba. That was a gross display of power before all your people. You should be ashamed. And as for 'kinsmen,' if your mother, my dear sister, were still alive and knew how you make war on her people, she would be incensed at you."

Cass was impressed by the vigor of the Queen's attack on the Caliph. The Caliph was on the defensive. "Queen Toda is a good debater," Cass realized.

"My Lady Aunt," responded the Caliph evenly, "I will keep in mind what you say about warring on my mother's countrymen. And if I have offended you personally, I apologize. My intent was not to bring shame upon you or cousin Sancho. I wanted to bring joy to my people that they might witness the greatness of Cordoba and the mercy of Allah."

"To say nothing about the might and mercy of Abdul," retorted Toda.

"I will admit," said Abdul a little gruffly, "that it does not hurt for the people to be reminded of who is the Caliph of the West. They sometimes forget."

"May I say, Your Highness, that the affection that you and my Lord Sancho kindled in the people today may be useful in further-ing friendship between Al-Andalus and Navarre," said Abu Yusuf.

"If I may add to Abu Yusuf's keen observations, Your Majesty, you may not have noticed, but among the crowds today were a large number of Christian Arabs. I have been meeting with their leaders for the past two days. They came to do you and your son homage." The speaker was the man in black.

"You see, Aunt Toda," said Abdul Rakman, "it is you who have won my people. I do believe that they would rally to your cause, should cousin Sancho decide to win his rightful position as heir to the throne of Navarre, now held by another."

"And what would it take for their Caliph to allow them to do that," asked Toda, who was intrigued by this veiled proposal but also suspicious.

"Only your request. I would send you mounted knights and archers at my own expense and require nothing in return."

"As King of Navarre, I would, of course, be in a position as mediator and even ally, cousin, should any of my Christian neighbors decide to attack you. I expect that the Bishop of Constantinople might also be of assistance should your cousin the Caliph of the East decide to challenge your right to the title of Caliph." All present turned in amazement to stare at Sancho el Gordo, who apparently had just spoken for the first time that evening.

Cass again got the feeling that she was watching a play in which she was a very minor character. The major characters had just been circling around each other, looking for an opening, like hawks looking for prey. Now it seemed that the least likely hawk had found the mark.

"Thank you, Sancho," said the Queen, who was not quite as surprised by his cleverness as were the others. Turning to Bishop Recemoundo, to whom Sancho had just referred, she went on. "I am pleased that you are here, and I thank you for your kind words about your Christian Arabs. I believe you welcome not just Christian Arabs but also Muslims in your kingdom of Byzantium and its great city of Constantinople. Would they follow you and their emperor if you were to join a Spanish Alliance of Christians and Muslims, of Navarre and Al-Andalus?"

"Diverse as its citizens are," replied the Bishop, "all are loyal to Byzantium, which means to the Christian Emperor. That includes not only Christians and Muslims, but many others as well. We have a growing number of Jews." The Bishop bowed to Abu Yusuf. "Constantinople, and thus Byzantium itself, is the crossroads of

East and West, of Africa and Mongolia. Many find a home there."

Cass immediately thought about how wonderfully different a place Byzantium must be from Spain, certainly from the Spain of Queen Isabella. She dared not turn around but could imagine a broad smile lighting the face of Ibrahim Leonides.

"And so, My Lady Aunt, I thought the Bishop and his Lord the Emperor might be able to assist us by encouraging your fellow Christians to behave themselves and keep to their own parts of Spain."

Queen Toda had taken a seat next of her son on his couch. She sat on the edge so she would not be enveloped by Sancho's flowing robes and great bulk. She frowned at her nephew, but only slightly, and addressed Bishop Recemondo. "And what, Lord Bishop, could we do to earn your assistance?"

"Encourage, or at least allow, your Muslims, your Christians, especially your Christian Arabs, and your Jews to come to Constantinople. We will welcome them, and they will help us to remain in power ... for a time at least. A hundred years, maybe more. When the Arabs and their Islamic cousins, the Turks, conquer us, as is inevitable, they will show mercy, recognizing so many of their own in our midst."

Cass was electrified. "Could that be my mission," she wondered. She would have liked to ask the Bishop and the Caliph if she could lead the Jews out of Spain into Byzantium, but, of course, she was thinking of 1492, not 1092. Still, she remembered the Bishop's words: "They will show us mercy." "Will it welcome the Jews of Al-Andalus four hundred years from now?" Cass wondered, squirmed a little in her seat, not used to observing the action without participating. This was about to change.

Two serving women were being ushered into the hall by the Caliph's Chief Steward. Cass noticed that they were covered more than usual, with an extra scarf around their heads that left only two narrow slits for their eyes. She thought that this was strange. That thought led to another worrisome one, Stephen's story about an assassination attempt. "Could they be the two women assassins? There are no Royal Guards close by. Could someone be trying to block this Muslim-Christian alliance," she wondered. Her heart began to pound. "This is crazy, but can I take that chance? Oh, my. Yahweh, help me."

"Stop!"

Everyone turned to stare at Cass, who had jumped to her feet as she shouted her command. There was complete, shocked silence. "There is a plot to kill the Caliph," she announced.

The Caliph himself was the first to speak. "That is a very serious accusation. Explain yourself, please." He was studying Cass with an intentness that unnerved her if only for a moment but long enough for the Caliph to repeat his command, with a frown of skepticism.

"I was warned by someone I trust completely that two women would try to kill you, My Lord. With your permission I will search them and question them."

"Nonsense," said the Chief Steward. "These women are here at my bidding and at the request of the Lady Zahara to bring refreshment to you and your guests, Oh Wise One. They bring only tea and fruit as you can see."

"Abu Yusuf, what do you say of your young friend?" asked Abdul.

"That she is sensible and intelligent," replied the physician. "Also that she is named Cassandra, which is the name of the soothsayer of Greek history and story." He smiled slightly but reassuringly at Cass.

Cass's mind was racing. "Why was Lady Zahara not here, especially with a Queen, a Crown Prince, a Bishop, and the Caliph and his Physician all gathered. She would have come herself to arrange the refreshments. So the Chief Steward must be involved."

"The serving women must come with me into the tunnel, but I will need help," she said, "including this man," indicating the Chief Steward. "Are there Royal Guards nearby?" she asked the Caliph, remembering to add, "Your Highness."

"Brother Nicholas and I will be your Guards," volunteered

Abdul Rakman. Brother Nicholas was on his feet and moving toward the servant women in an instant.

"And the Lady Barbara will assist you. You will find her the equal of any Guardsman, stated Queen Toda." Lady Barbara moved quickly to stand by Brother Nicholas with the women. Cass was both pleased and worried. "If I am wrong, it is your fault Grandma Essie," she thought, "so help me now."

"Please open the passageway," she said to the Chief Steward, who looked at her with hatred. Cass led them a little way into the tunnel where she called a halt. She noticed that the Caliph remained at the entrance, with the Chief Steward. She asked Lady Barbara to help her search each of the women in turn while Brother Nicholas stood guard.

"Arab assassins stabbed their victims, at least in the stories I have read. I hope they were accurate," thought Cass. But neither she nor Lady Barbara found knives, large or small, hidden underneath the women's robes. She began seriously to worry. She looked toward the Caliph who was not smiling. The Chief Steward, standing next to him was, but that quickly changed. The serving women were adjusting their veils and robes when Lady Barbara asked them why they needed the extra veils and such long hair pins. "Show us," ordered Cass.

Others later had to explain to Cass what happened next. She remembered being pushed aside roughly and crashing into the wall of the tunnel. She was dazed but could hear shouting and screaming. She had just struggled to her knees when someone slammed into her, and this time she heard nothing more.

She came to with Abu Yusuf bending over her, looking concerned but relieved to see her awake. He smiled. "You gave us a fright, My Lady Assistant. You will be sore for a while and have a headache, but I have remedies for those. You are alive, and so are the Caliph and the Queen, thanks to your warning and quick thinking."

Cass looked at him. When she tried to make sense of what he

was saying, her headache got in the way. Gradually she noticed and recognized the others standing close by. Ibrahim Leonides folded his hands before him and bowed to her. Brother Nicholas approached. "I beg your forgiveness, Lady Cassandra, for pushing you into the wall, but the assassin was just about to plunge her poisoned hair pin into you."

"He saved your life, My Lady," said Lady Barbara, who joined Brother Nicholas.

"And Lady Barbara saved mine," said Brother Nicholas, looking at the Queen's Lady. "Thank the lord that you were there. You are clearly trained to be more than a Lady in Waiting, unless that means waiting for trouble." Brother Nicholas beamed at Lady Barbara. She blushed and avoided his eyes, keeping them on Cass. Cass, whose head was now clearing, noticed the red cheeks as well as the sparkling blue eyes and the blond hair that tumbled around her face. Her veil and head dress had come off.

"Thank you both," said Cass. Then she saw the Caliph standing at a little distance looking concerned. "My Lord, you are all right?" She started to sit up, but Abu Yusuf held her shoulders firmly to the couch.

"No sudden movements, Lady Cassandra," he insisted.

"You are to remain on my couch for as long as needed," said Caliph Abdul Rakman. The others moved back as he and Queen Toda came to Cass's side. "I do not fully understand how you knew they were assassins," said the Caliph, "but I thank you and Allah for sending you to me to save my life and the Queen's."

Cass reflected often on this moment later on, and what it meant to her personally, to Grandma Essie, and to the quest. All that she could think of at the moment was to say, "Oh, My Lord, My Lady, thank goodness."

"The eloquence of directness," said the Queen. "I like it, and thank you Cassandra, both a Lady and Seer it appears. I would have you in my court, but the Caliph and Abu Yussuf have already made prior claims for you. Lady Barbara would like to have you as an ally in protecting us."

"Perhaps Lady Barbara can at least sit next to our deliverer as we all share a proper meal," announced the Caliph. "We will need nourishment to complete our deliberations. It is clear that they are no longer secret."

Ibramin Leonides and Lady Barbara sat on either side of Cass during the meal. As the food was being served, Lady Barbara told Cass that both assassins had died at their own hands, rather than allow themselves to be captured. "Trained assassins rarely can be captured," explained Lady Barbara matter-of-factly. "That is part of the bargain they make with those that hire them. The Caliph, however, will have their heads hung on the palace walls as a warning. The Chief Steward tried to stab himself, but the Caliph prevented that. He will be questioned, and will eventually reveal other names before he dies." Cass found her new friend fascinating. She wanted to know how she became the Queen's bodyguard. But the business part of the meal limited further conversation, other than whispered questions and explanations between the two ladies.

Two major agreements were enacted. Until recently Cass would not have thought either of them as being remotely possible. In the first one, a Frankish Queen, a Byzantine Bishop, and a Caliph of Al-Andalus pledged to support one another in case any one of them were attacked—by Christian or Muslim. In the second, the Caliph's physician, a Jew, pledged to help El Gordo, a Christian, to lose enough weight to resume his throne as King of Navarre.

The Caliph announced that the meeting was concluded. "And now," he said, "I must ask my deliverer what she would request of me in return for saving my life. I have no doubt that the poisonous needles would have done their work on me had she not discovered the plot. What would you, My Lady?"

Cass seemed to have been preparing for this. "My Lord I ask only that you welcome at your court another lady who will look very much like me. She will be someone close to me. I do not know when she will come, but I think that you will not have to wait too long. She will have a strange tale to tell about a New World, but I pray you, welcome her for me. You will not regret doing so."

Abdul looked at Cass intently. "I promise that I will do so and gratefully so. Is there anything else?"

"I would ask the Lord Bishop a favor if I may."

"That is, of course, up to the Bishop, but I … ."

"Gladly, Lady Cassandra. But for you the treaties just made would not have happened. I and my people are grateful. Also from what I have witnessed, I confess that I am curious to know what you will ask. You seem to have knowledge of things unknown that may prove to be both good and useful. I promise that I will honor your request if it is within my power."

"Thank you, Lord Bishop," replied Cass. "You also seem to have knowledge of the future. You expect that our Kingdom of Byzantium and its great city of Constantinople will be captured by new Muslim peoples in the centuries to come. I too believe this. I also share your hope that these new Muslims will be as enlightened and tolerant as many now are here in Spain. So, my favor is this. Will you establish an academy, a place filled with books where scholars and students of all beliefs can learn from each other."

"And so that Jewish philosophers and scientists and poets will become the excellent public face of the Jews in Byzantium, especially Constantinople. Brilliant," said Bishop Recemondo.

Cass bowed slightly, acknowledging the compliment. "Perhaps Abu Yusuf and Brother Nicholas will contribute their notes on curing mad-dog bites," said Cass with a smile. She concluded in a much more serious tone. "I know such a place will be a beacon for centuries, and I fear, no, I know that my people, Spanish Jews, will sorely need that beacon centuries from now."

Cass's speech had arrested everyone's attention. No one spoke for several heartbeats when she finished, but then all started voicing their approval, to no one in particular. It was a form of applause. Bishop Recemondo spoke again.

"You have not disappointed me, My Lady Cassandra," he said.

"I will start such a place of learning. You have my pledge, and may your people find a safe haven in Constantinople in this future you speak of. I should not be surprised if they were to be led by a Lady Prophet with a Greek name."

"We will establish such an academy here as well," said Abdul Rakman, bowing to Cass. "I should be saddened to lose any of my Jews," he said seriously. With a smile he added, "even you Abu Yusuf Hasdai ben Ishaq ibn Shaprut, my friend."

"Thank you, My Caliph. And now, I fear, My Caliph, I must see that Lady Cassandra and her friends are returned whence they came," said Abu Yusuf.

As they all began to leave, Cass wondered to herself if Abu Yusuf could come with them back to the future to persuade Queen Isabella not to expel the Jews or the Muslims from Al-Andalus. That would be a bold move she thought, but sadly she realized that not even such a miracle would keep the candle of *convivencia* burning in Spain. "But it did burn for a time here, and brightly too," she knew.

# Chapter XX

# The Synagogue

"Thanks be that you are back. I was just praying for your safe return. It will soon be dark." Lucía was sitting at the table with her hands folded. She opened her mouth to say more, but then noticed Thea looking pale and leaning on Sebastian for support, with Cass close behind. She hurried to help.

"I am well enough," Thea said, "but tired. I should sit down, but Sebastian and I want to hear all about the Secret Meeting. A Queen, a Bishop, and the Caliph, and we missed it."

Lucía thought Thea must be delirious and was about to suggest moving her into the next room, when Ibrahim Leonides, who was just coming in the door behind Cass, explained the situation. "The most incredible events took place this day," my Love. "The one Lady Theadora just spoke of is the secret political meeting of nobles, but it is a lengthy story, my dear, and there is much else to tell. I believe we should first make everyone comfortable, especially Lady Theadora."

They arranged cushions and blankets to prop up Thea in a chair. Lucía brewed tea and served it with biscuits. Then the travelers to the tenth century told Lucía all of their adventures. Everyone contributed, agreeing most of the time, but not always. Cass and Ibrahim Leonides described the dramatic meeting of the Caliph, the Queen, and the Bishop and the assassination plot. Thea and Sebastian recounted the attack by the mad dog, Thea's treatment by Abu Yusuf assisted by Cass, and Sebastian's vigil watching over his Lady's recovery. These were the highlights. Then they enlarged on particular details. They seemed to want to continue the adventure by memory.

"Before the mad dog's attack I was in a dream world," reflected Sebastian. "I had never seen so many people nor so much activity anywhere. Our chroniclers have not done justice to the Cordoba of the Caliphate."

"I never knew such great markets existed," noted Thea, "where you can get your teeth pulled and then get new teeth and a new set of clothes, all while you wait. And modern medical attention, I should add."

"I do not think any chronicler could do justice to Abu Yusuf," offered Cass.

"Nor to Brother Nicholas and *The Book of Medicine*," said Ibrahim Leonides.

Before long Lucía's head was filled with a list of recurring characters: Abdul Rakman, Recemondo, El Gordo, Toda, Assassins, Chief Steward, Barbara.

"A final word about Abu Yusuf and Brother Nicholas," said Cass, "and then we should take pity on our hosts and retire to bed. On our way back through the tunnels they asked many questions. They are curious observers and, of course, very clever at drawing conclusions. It was not long before they guessed that we were from the future and were speculating about our mission, without our telling them in so many words. They even knew of Maiden. They referred to her as the healer djinni. And they had heard of a necklace of mysterious powers."

"Neither Abu Yusuf nor Brother Nicholas was very happy with what we told them about the future, but I did get to tell them of the good that their translation of the ancient *Book of Medicine* continues to do," reflected Ibrahim Leonides.

"They both gave each of us their blessing as we were about to leave them," observed Sebastian. "Blessed by a Catholic priest and a Jewish elder." He smiled at Cass.

"When he put his hand on my head for his blessing," said Cass, "Abu Yusuf told me that he too had had to find his own way to his Jewish roots. He was glad, he said, that I was discovering mine. His final words I remember exactly: 'May the God of Israel and of Judah remain always with you and keep you steadfast in your faith.' I would have liked to have told him that our mission is now clear to me. Well, maybe not all of it, but I am sure that we are supposed to help the Jews get to Byzantium, even to Constantinople itself when they are expelled from Spain by Isabella and Ferdinand." Cass paused and looked at Thea and Sebastian. "At least, I am sure that that is what I am to do. I will have to tell Stephen."

Thea started to say something, but Lucía spoke first and forcefully. "Oh! You have just reminded me. A message came today from Stephen. He wanted to tell you that you are to be at the synagogue for the Sabbath service tomorrow at noon time. Be there early. Sarah will be waiting for you, the messenger said. Also Lady Francesca sent a messenger. She expects you back the day after tomorrow as early as possible and certainly before dark."

"Then tomorrow will be a busy day indeed," said Cass with a smile as she thought mainly of going to her first Sabbath service.

"That means it is time for everyone to be off to bed," ordered Lucía, "or breakfast will be too early for some of you."

Before they went to their rooms, Thea spoke to Sebastian. Rather she looked at him but really was speaking to the whole group, especially Cass. There was a note of anxiety in her voice. "Perhaps Sebastian should bring some extra soldiers from the palace when he accompanies Cass to the synagogue."

Cass, however, protested. No extra soldiers would be necessary. "Sebastian is a Queen's Guardsman. No one would dare bother us."

Everyone recalled these words later.

"Enough," said Lucía. She helped Thea out of her chair and ushered her on her way to bed. No one protested. It had been a very long day.

Sebastian arrived well before noon the next day. Cass was already waiting for him. He could tell that she was anxious to leave for the synagogue. After a brief greeting to the others, accentuated by a bow to Thea, he and Cass took their leave. They arrived early, but found Sarah already waiting excitedly. She was with an older woman by the outer gate that opened onto the small patio of the synagogue. Sarah was shifting, or rather bouncing, from foot to foot.

"Quickly," Sarah called as soon as she saw Cass, "we have to get up to the balcony before the service begins, or we will have to wait below where you cannot see anything."

The older woman introduced herself as Devorah. She greeted them sedately in comparison to Sarah, but warmly and welcoming. She showed Sebastian where he could wait in the patio until the service was over. He would be able to hear the prayers being chanted. Then she led Cass, who was being tugged by Sarah, through the inner gate and up a wooden stairs to an inner balcony. As she moved from the stairway onto the balcony Cass found herself in the midst a dozen or more women of various ages, though there seemed to be a good proportion of younger women and girls. They seemed in festive spirits, chatting animatedly. As Cass followed Sarah the few steps across the balcony, the women paused in their conversation to welcome her. She had the feeling that she had been expected. Sarah brought her to the low wall under a wide archway at the edge of the balcony. The sight that now greeted Cass delighted her.

Her first impression was of a square hall, modest in size and appearance at the base, but rising up in beauty for three stories. "Like the elegant courtyards of the Alcazar of Seville," she thought. The lower walls were covered with glazed aqua-blue tiles. The middle walls were decorated with elaborate plaster designs of interlacing vines and stars and diamonds all delicately colored in blues and blue-greens. Cass was standing directly opposite this middle area, enabling her to examine the artwork more closely. She saw that among the artful designs were passages of writing in a large, elaborate Hebrew script. Above this area were small arched windows. The noon-day light shone so brightly through these windows that the many oil lamps of the synagogue were not needed. Still some of them had been lighted and added a cheerful touch. Above the windows were wooden panels that swept upwards still higher to form a dome. The wood was decorated with golden suns and silver moons and stars that caught and reflected the light from the windows.

Directly below the balcony where Cass stood, near the east end, were eight or ten men and boys. One of the men waved to her. She recognized Stephen. He and most of the others were standing, but a few rested quietly among the three rows of plain benches. In the midst of those standing was a short, portly gentleman who seemed to be entertaining the others with a humorous story. He wore a large shawl that covered his head and draped over his shoulders and upper body. He was the center of attention.

"That is the Rabbi," said Sarah, seeing where Cass was looking. "He loves to tell stories, often funny ones."

At the opposite end of the hall another group of eight or ten men milled about. In the center, between the two groups, was a raised area upon which rested a table with a simple cloth covering. Several objects were arranged on the table. Among these were an unlighted candle and a small dish of oil on which floated a single tongue of flame.

"Do you like it?" asked Sarah, who had, with barely repressed excitement, been watching Cass's eyes devouring the scene.

"Beautiful beyond words," replied Cass.

"What do you want to know about? I am your guide," Sarah said.

"Well, what is that red lamp for, in front of those curtains below us to the right?"

"The eternal light of God's dwelling place, here in the synagogue, and in all of us." Sarah paused to let the effect of her well-learned lessons sink in and then continued. "The curtains cover the chamber that holds the Ark, which contains the scrolls of our holy book, the Torah. The Ark is in the east wall, the direction of Jerusalem where the Great Temple was. We say our prayers and read from the book facing that wall."

"And what is the fancy arch and niche on the west wall, opposite the Ark?"

"That is where the person stands to lead the prayers or to read from the Torah. He is called the Lector. If he is going to read passages from the Torah scrolls, he and two other men carry the scrolls from the Ark in procession to the Lector's arch. At today's service, the Closing of the Sabbath, we do not read from the book. That is because the Closing is supposed to be after dark, and in olden times it was feared that the Lector might make a mistake in the reading. Nowadays it is too dangerous for us to have any services after dark. Instead we have the prayers and the Havdalah, the public Sabbath Closing, right after mid-day. Tonight at sundown we say prayers at home for the Closing. But the Havdalah here at the Synagogue is my favorite of all our services," concluded Sarah with delight.

"And who is the person going to the platform?"

"That is the Lector. He will start the prayers." Sarah put a finger to her lips to indicate no more talking.

The Lector began the service, reciting from a booklet that, from a distance, looked to Cass like a thin song book. She noticed that the men and boys each had a similar booklet. The Lector shifted to a singing or chanting voice, with the men and boys responding, also in song. Cass noted that some of the songs were in very formal patterns while others seemed almost improvised. In both cases much of the phrasing seemed to be in an antique style. She did not follow all of the words but clearly caught three repeated sets of contrasts: the Sabbath is a time of worship, not of business;

light opposes darkness; Israel is unlike any other nation.

Cass was reflecting on these ideas when Sarah whispered with anticipation. "Now is the Havdalah. Watch."

Someone stepped forward. He first lit a long, thin taper from the tongue of flame in the dish of oil. With the taper he lit the ritual candle on the table. The Rabbi now approached the table. He recited prayers, first over a large silver goblet, then over a metal object twice the size of the goblet. This object looked like a miniature castle tower, but, like the goblet, it had a stem. He handed the tower goblet to someone in the congregation who then left the hall. The Rabbi blessed the candle with the words, "divine light," and "light of God's law." Cass now saw that the candle was actually two intertwined candles, one purple, the other ivory, with two wicks that joined in one bright light.

While Cass was reflecting on what the candle might mean, the Rabbi drank from the goblet and then passed it to the man closest to him. This man drank and passed it to a man or boy near until all had shared its contents. "Wine" Sarah whispered to her. While the goblet was being passed the Rabbi and a several others sang prayers; the rest sang responses to the prayers. Cass noticed that the men and boys smiled as they greeted and passed the goblet to their neighbor. "This is a group that enjoys being together," she thought. Cass had never considered having fun as part of a prayer service. Meanwhile the woman to her right turned to her and wished her a good week ahead and sealed the wish with a hug. Then Cass was engulfed in hugs and good wishes, given and received.

Hardly had these greetings concluded before Sarah tugged on Cass's sleeve and held up to her the tower goblet. As she took it in her hands, a sweet aroma engulfed her, bringing a smile to her face. She sipped the wine. Sweet. She passed it to the woman who had first hugged her. When the passing of the goblet was over, and Cass was certain that she had hugged every woman and girl in the balcony, she descended hand in hand with Sarah, to the vestibule below. The men and women were rejoining their spouses and family members and wishing one another a happy week.

Stephen approached Cass and hugged her. "Peace," he said, "and a blessed week for you." He handed her a small metal cylinder and told her it held a tiny prayer scroll. "Hear, O Israel, the Lord our God, the Lord is One," he quoted to her. "I hope we can continue your lessons," he said when she told him she was returning to Lady Francesca.

"Oh, yes," promised Cass. "In fact I have something very important to talk with you about. I may have learned how I am to help the Jewish community, but I will need your guidance and your help."

Devorah now approached her, accompanied by two other women. "We wanted you to have this memento of your visit with us, hopefully the first of many visits." She handed Cass a small scroll rolled up and tied with a silken ribbon. "It is a poem," she said, "the first that we know of by a Jewish woman. Writing poetry is not just for men." Devorah paused and smiled at Stephen. "The poet wrote it for her husband when he left Cordoba on a long trip."

Cass embraced the woman gratefully. "Can I read it now?" Devorah nodded, pleased with Cass's request and obvious delight. Cass read Aloud:

*Will her beloved remember his gazelle? When he departed she*
*Was holding their dear son in her arms.*
*He put the ring from his right hand on her left hand, and she put*
*Her anklet on his arm.*
*While she took his veil as a keepsake, he took hers as a*
*Memento.*
*He would not stay in Sepharad even if he were given half the kingdom*
*by his master.*

"Sepharad is the Jewish name for Spain," volunteered Devorah. The poet's husband was probably a court diplomat from the East.

"I will treasure this always, both of these," she assured Devorah. To both of them she said, "this poem I think contains a message for me. And now I must find Sebastian." She took her leave of everyone, except Sarah, who accompanied her out to the patio. There Sarah reluctantly turned her over to Sebastian, but not until Cass assured her that she would see her again as soon as it was safe to do so after returning to Lady Francesca's. Sebastian said little but was aware of how elated Cass was, despite having to leave.

"Were you tired of waiting for me," asked Cass as they left the patio and began their walk toward the House of Lucía. "Well, I am anxious to get back," he answered truthfully, "but I was content listening to the music… so different from ours in style, but not so different in meaning."

At that moment soldiers emerged suddenly from a half shaded sidestreet. They quickly surrounded Cass and Sebastian. "Pardon this intrusion, my Lord Sebastian. We are here to arrest this converso woman, by order of the Duke at the request of the Holy Office."

# Chapter XXI

# The Inquisition Begins

It took all of Sebastian's military discipline to appear unruffled by the words "converso" and "Holy Office." He returned the Captain's salute and told him that there was surely a mistake, which he would look into. "No mistake," was the only reply. "Then I will go with you," announced Sebastian. Cass was surprised and then simply irritated at the soldiers' intrusion on the sense of joy that she had just experienced. She wondered a little at Sebastian's concern. She did have a moment's pause when she got a glimpse of the leader of the bullies that had attacked Stephen and Sarah and then threatened her. He hopped about just outside the ring of guards, trying to get a glimpse of her. She remembered him threatening to report her as a Jew lover. She dismissed the worry. "Who would pay any attention to such a person?"

Sebastian accompanied Cass, overruling the Captain's objection. He resolved that none of the soldiers should even come near her. Cass remained unworried as she marched next to Sebastian between two ranks of soldiers. They continued along for some time, going north, paralleling the west wall of the city, until they arrived at the Church of St. Dominic, whose bell tower had been the minaret of a former mosque. They were taken to a room on the second floor of the tower.

Sebastian hardly looked around the room. "We will get you out of here. I will go to the Duke. I will go to the Queen if necessary. You know how she cannot refuse me anything," joked Sebastian. Cass recognized that his joviality was forced and that he was trying to reassure her. She only sighed and shrugged. This was all simply a great bother about nothing.

"Tell the others not to worry and that I will join Thea at Lady Francesca's later, in a couple of hours," she said to Sebastian, who was then ushered out of the room. The door was shut and locked. Left alone, Cass took stock of her dreary surroundings and decided that they would do even if she had to stay more than a couple of hours. "I am imprisoned in a tower," she mused aloud to herself, as she examined the bare stone walls of the six-sided tower. She walked over to the heavy wooden door. It opened outward. She noted in particular that it had an opening at eye level that allowed someone to look in after sliding aside a thick metal bar on the outside. There was no sliding bar on the inside. "Not much privacy," thought Cass as she turned back to the room. Near the center of the room were a table and three chairs. To her left was a low wooden bed, little more than a few wooden planks. Directly ahead ten paces was the lone window. Four or five paces to the right of the window was a hole in the floor where two of the walls came together. "Not even a commode," thought Cass. "Even less privacy."

She was a little startled by a knock at the door, followed by the door being unlocked and opened. A man entered. He wore a black cape that rested on his broad shoulders and reached down his back to his ankles, just above his white religious robe.

"God be with you," he said.

"I hope so," replied Cass, "and with you," she added, softening her tone. The priest's physical appearance reminded her of one of Thea's Leiterman cousins. He was moderately tall and even in his priestly robes looked athletically trim. His hair was brown and curly, his eyes bright and blue. "He could be a Frank," thought Cass. Suddenly from her childhood memory came the expression, "caped crusader." Cass could not completely repress a smile, which did not go unnoticed.

"My name is Felipe Guzman, a priest of the Order of Preachers," said her visitor in formal tones. I am your chaplain. I am here for your spiritual needs. Is there anything I can do for you now?" He looked and sounded both solemn and concerned. The wrinkles on his forehead stood out against his smooth skin. "I am instructed to ask if you would like to make your confession to me," he said. "It would be for the good of your soul, if, of course, you are ready to do so."

"No, thank you," replied Cass, recognizing the priest's sincerity within his polite formality. "I do not suppose I can request a counselor for my legal needs, can I?"

"No. All such needs will be taken care of by the Inquisitor. He will be wholly impartial. All you need do is tell the truth and justice will be done." He sounded to Cass much like a young beginning teacher she had once had. She would have smiled, except that she found his answer worrisome. She tried to shrug off the feeling but did not succeed. "Well, then, at least you can tell me the procedure, just in case I am still here after Lady Francesca hears of my arrest," she said, persuading herself that she would soon be released. The priest's next words, however, were more than just worrisome. They frightened her.

"Doña Francesca has been informed. She and Don Enriquez have agreed to assist the Holy Office in these proceedings. They have already granted the Inquisitor one interview. Doña Francesca praised Lady Theadora's Catholic behavior but did not do the same for you. Don Enriquez spoke highly of you and noted that you were chosen by the Queen. He acknowledged, however, that he knew little about you. I must advise you that your situation is serious. As for the procedures of your trial, you will hear from the Inquisitor shortly."

He now had Cass's full attention. She sensed the danger. She walked over to the window and stood facing it, hardly noticing that the glass was too thick and milky to see through. She recalled the warnings that Ibrahim Leonides and Sebastian had given her about people thinking that she might be a false convert from Judaism to Christianity. She remembered how concerned they were. At the time she had dismissed their concerns. Her going to Catholic services was fulfilling a duty expected by Lady Francesca. She was never a make-believe Christian. She turned to face her chaplain. "What exactly are the charges brought against me? And what should I expect to happen?"

Father Guzman had barely moved at all. He remained, as he had been, standing in the middle of the room, his arms crossed under his scapular, part of his religious habit that reminded Cass of a very long, wide white scarf. "White on white," crossed Cass's mind. As she looked at him, he shifted his eyes and looked deliberately at the ground as he told her the accusation. "The charge is that you are a converso."

"What does that mean," asked Cass of her chaplain. She knew but she wanted to hear the precise definition. The priest looked surprised at the question but answered.

"It means that you have fallen back into the error of Judaism after becoming a Christian, and that you are keeping up only the appearance of being Christian to avoid discovery and death."

"How can such a lie be proved?" For the moment Cass overlooked the last part about "discovery and death," but she had registered it.

"I have inquired, and there is evidence. You are lady in waiting to Doña Francesca, giving her and others, including the Queen, the impression that you are a Catholic. Now you meet with Jews. You have today attended synagogue. A complaint has been made that you threatened the life of a Christian simply for making a harmless joke about Jews in their presence.

"Nonsense. Your witness is a bully and a liar."

"I wish to be clear, my Lady, in answer to your question about what to expect. The Inquisitor need not prove anything. If you are innocent, you will need to prove it. If you are guilty you should confess and repent. I have told you the accusation and the evidence, as far as I know them."

Cass began pacing back and forth between the door and the window, trying to clear her mind. "How am I going to prove that I could not be a converso because I was never a Christian?" she wondered. "I have no evidence. I cannot tell them that I am from the future and that I am a citizen of a country that has not the least conception of what a converso is and where no one would care anyway. A country in a continent that will not be discovered until later this year. Who would believe me? If anyone did, they would accuse me of being a witch."

Aloud she said, "And what if I cannot prove that the charges are false? "

"If you confess and are absolved, you will be burned at the stake as penance, but your soul will be saved. You will be cleansed and go straight to heaven."

"You cannot possibly believe that," said Cass.

"It is what the Church teaches," replied the priest. His forehead again showed what Cass interpreted as worry wrinkles. Cass paused in her pacing. She looked in disbelief at Father Guzman. "He truly believes that," she thought. Her hand went involuntarily inside her cloak to her chest. For the first time in many days, she needed to touch the necklace for reassurance. "I will escape from here as soon as this frightful priest leaves," she decided at first, but as she calmed herself, she changed her mind. "With the necklace I can leave whenever I choose," she reminded herself. I should not run at the first sign of danger. I just saved the life of a Caliph. I should be able to handle this. Perhaps I should see what it is the Holy Office does to Jews."

She looked at Father Guzman. He was watching her closely, as though studying her. "Well, Father, I will hope to prove my innocence, that I am not a converso. When does the inquisition begin?" she asked calmly.

Now it was the priest's turn to be surprised. When he spoke, Cass heard a note of admiration in the surprise. He answered politely. "You will be met by the Inquisitor this evening. Perhaps you will want to rest for a while before then. I will leave you for now." He motioned to the bed. He bowed to Cass, turned, and left. Someone locked the door behind him.

Cass decided to take his advice and sat on the wooden bed. "A pallet," she said half aloud this time. She was content that it had no straw or blanket. They would have been full of lice and who knows what else. She sat for a few minutes. The room had darkened considerably since she had first entered. She could feel the air getting colder and remembered that Lucía had wanted her to wear a shawl under her cloak, but she had just laughed and remarked on how sunny it was that morning. She lay down. "Just for a moment," she told herself. Her last thought before falling asleep was that she should use the necklace to escape before it was too late.

"Strip down to your under-things." The loud, harsh voice awakened Cass like a splash of ice water. She had lain down and fallen asleep, but now she was suddenly wide awake and staring up at a repulsive face leering at her from an arm's length away. The owner of the face held a candle whose light formed a circle that linked Cass's face with his own. His greasy hair hung down past his chin, framing a red face riddled with pock marks and white pustules. His mouth hung open, showing a thick tongue and two blackened teeth. He hardly moved back when she started to get up, causing her to brush against him. He was huge, at least six feet tall and grossly fat.

"Strip down to your under-things," the figure repeated harshly, leering even more now that Cass was standing.

Another voice broke in. "No, first I want the object she has around her neck under her cloak or perhaps under her dress." This was Father Guzman, whom Cass now saw behind the figure. She quickly reached for the necklace, but it was too late. The guard grabbed her wrists in a grip so tight that Cass went to her knees. "Hold her while I take whatever that is. She was touching it before when she was worried. It must be some sort of Jewish talisman," said the priest.

"Please, I will take it off for you," begged Cass. She was again close to panic but in control enough to try to outsmart this pair of jailers. But the priest was too quick and more observant than she had given him credit for. He easily found the necklace and removed it, while Cass gasped. The guard released her. She remained on her knees, rubbing her wrists to get the circulation going again.

"Strip down to your under-things," said the guard for the third time.

"Calm down," she mentally commanded herself. She looked round for the priest. "Father Guzman, I appeal to you as my chaplain to give the necklace to Lord Sebastian or Lady Theadora. It was my grandmother's. Please," said Cass as she got slowly to her feet. The priest did not reply, but Cass thought he was a little mystified, maybe embarrassed, at not finding a "Jewish talisman," but rather an antique and expensive-looking necklace. "Thank you," she said as calmly as she could.

"Do as you're told. Stop bothering the chaplain," shouted her guard.

"Guard, you may calm down. You need not bully her. I was mistaken about a Jewish trinket," said Father Guzman, but the guard simply shrugged.

"Take everything off except what you wear next to your body," commanded the guard. "Everything else I take. After I search you, that is," he added with a guttural laugh.

Cass took off her cloak, remembering that Stephen's prayer cylinder and Deborah's scroll poem were in the pockets, as the guard grabbed it from her and handed it to Father Guzman. The priest found the cylinder and the scroll almost immediately. "These, My Lady, look to be Jewish items," he said.

"Are you my jailer or my chaplain," she shot back. The guard abruptly drew her full attention as he impatiently began removing her dress and undergarments with filthy hands. She fiercely pushed the hands away and undressed herself. Had she been able to see her chaplain's eyes, she would have recognized that her shot had hit its mark.

She had no time for such thoughts now. Cass had hardly removed her outer clothes, except the thin shift next to her skin, when her jailer pulled her to him. He held her close in an ugly embrace as he began feeling along every inch of her body.

"Stop," Cass screamed repeatedly, but the guard continued patting and pawing her. Cass had to fight against a feeling of nausea as he pinched and squeezed, all the while breathing heavily. His breath smelled of the decaying bits of food lodged in his rotting teeth and gums. Cass heard Father Guzman call out "Guard," but she was sure the guard never heard a thing. She finally screamed, "Father Guzman, for god's sake." A moment later the guard called out in surprise. The priest, with a soldier-like move, had caught him around the neck and wrestled him to the ground on his back. The priest was kneeling on the man's arms while sitting on his chest. He had both hands now around the guard's neck. "Move and I will crush your throat," commanded the priest. The guard stopped struggling and stared wide-eyed at the figure on his chest. "When I let you up you will take what you need and leave immediately," said the priest.

When the guard had gone, the priest helped Cass up and wrapped her in her cloak as he guided her to her bed. "Thank you," Cass managed to say through her weeping.

"That guard is a disgrace," he answered in a tight voice.

Cass lay down on the pallet. She was bruised in spirit and body. She wept hot, angry tears as she lay shivering from shock and disgust. Father Guzman knelt down next to the pallet. There he remained, quietly praying. Cass finally stopped shaking and was able to quiet herself. She looked at the chaplain, noticing the worry lines on his forehead. When he saw that she had calmed down he stood up. He dropped his eyes and crossed his arms under his scapular. "I will report that disgraceful guard to the Chief Inquisitor. I will try to be here as much as possible to be sure that he does not again commit such acts against you."

Cass sat up on her pallet, holding her cloak close about her for warmth and modesty. "He took my things?" she asked him. He nodded that he had. "Everything? The necklace too?" she asked more anxiously.

"Please, we do not have much time. Another guard will be here shortly with some food before the Inquisitor comes. I am confi… hopeful that he will be different."

Cass stood up. He had not answered her question about the necklace. That gave her some hope. She looked more closely at her chaplain. His face was easy to read. The worry creases on his forehead had deepened and met other worry lines at the inner corners of his eyes. "I can see that you are not pleased with what is happening here. Why is that?"

Father Guzman became flustered and looked nervously at the door. "Kneel down beside me as though we were praying together." He spoke quickly and in a low voice. "I let the guard take the scroll and the cylinder for the Inquisitor. I do not have enough experience to know whether or not they are Jewish, but I think that they are. I had no choice. They might be important as evidence. I believe you that your necklace is something personal from your grandmother. For that reason, and because it has no apparent Jewish connection, I will give it to your friends. If they are brave enough to show themselves, I will entrust it to them." He again looked at the door. "The evening guard is coming. I dare not stay longer now. May God protect you."

Cass was warmed by the priest's words. He was kind, more than kind given his beliefs. She knew that he thought she was guilty of being a converso and that she should confess and accept death to save her soul. But he was clearly a person of honor. He was willing to be her link to the others, even though doing so was probably against some rule. She realized that one of her worst fears was losing contact with Thea and Sebastian and Ibrahim Leonides and Lucía. Most importantly she felt that Fr. Guzman would give Thea or Sebastian the necklace. Surely one of them could get it to her. She found further comfort in the fact that Father Guzman took his role as chaplain seriously. She could still see with her mind's eye the guard with his back on the ground and the priest on top of him with his hands on his throat. She did not know yet what was in store for her, but because of her chaplain she felt less afraid.

Cass did not feel threatened moments later when the evening guard barked and waived at her to back up as he banged a cup of water on the table, spilling half of it. "No food, just water. That's fitting for you this evening." The guard's grin was worse than his scowl. Cass took a tentative sip of water and then quickly drained the cup. She had not had food or anything to drink since leaving Lucía's house that morning. "Thank you," she said as she handed the empty cup back to the guard. He snatched it from her hand. Resolved not to be bullied, Cass calmly sat at the table. She could feel the guard's eyes on her, until the door opened and the Inquisitor entered the room, followed by his assistant.

"On your feet," growled the guard at Cass. "Bow to his Excellency." Cass stood. She wanted to back away from the table but forced herself to stand still, facing the Inquisitor. His face reminded her of Bladen's, "except that his was still human, not quite empty of expression" thought Cass. She did not find that entirely reassuring. Her composure might have vanished, except that Father Guzman re-entered just behind the Inquisitor and his companion.

She was reasonably composed when she heard the Inquisitor speak. "I am Father Blanco. You know Father Guzman. This is my assistant and secretary, Father Perez. He will also be the recorder." Like Father Guzman, the two priests wore the garments of the Order of Preachers, the black cape, or mantle, over the white scapular and robe. The Inquisitor and his assistant sat at the table, which the guard had quickly wiped off with his sleeve before he left. Cass and Father Guzman were left standing. "Father Guzman, stand behind me," he ordered. "Lady Cassandra, stand behind Father Perez, facing me." He paused while his orders were being followed, and then began again. "Father Guzman has just been telling me that you were mistreated by the guard earlier this evening," said the Inquisitor. He looked at Cass as he spoke. "Father Guzman acted wrongly in interrupting the guard's search of you. Father will, of course, do penance for that. He is young and a nobleman so he must be excused for some things. Interfering with body searches and not turning over personal items are two examples. But we must be understanding. Now he wishes to be a scholar and to teach at a university, perhaps here in Spain at Salamanca. He will have little stomach for his brief prison ministry, I fear, but he will learn something here about applied theology, I trust." He then addressed Father Guzman directly but still with his back to him. "You will repent of your action, and you will stay for my questioning, will you not, Father Guzman, and when we leave you will give me the necklace?"

At first there was no response, but Cass knew what her chaplain's answer would have to be. She could hear her heart beating. "Yes, father, I will stay. I am sorry."

"And ... ," said the Inquisitor.

"And I will give you the necklace." He was about to add something, but the Inquisitor cut him off.

During the Inquisitor's criticism of him, Cass had watched the change in Father Guzman. He listened to the Inquisitor while staring at his back. Surprise, even shock was followed by the now familiar worry creases, and finally the lowering of the eyes and crossing of his arms under his scapular. He was defeated. Or he was repentant. Cass was not sure which. Perhaps he was both at once. It did not matter. She and her chaplain, for different reasons, were completely at the mercy of the Inquisitor. She felt abandoned, but she resolved that she was not going to be intimidated like Father

Guzman.

"Do you have any other complaints?" the Inquisitor said, speaking now to Cass.

Cass could not tell if he were being ironic or serious. She doubted that the question was a serious one but decided to treat it as such. "Yes, two items were taken from my clothes."

"I know," responded the Inquisitor, "a mezuzah with your Jewish prayer inside and a poetry scroll. We will have to keep the mezuzah as evidence. You may have the poem back. Father, make a note of that. Anything else?" His voice was hollow, empty like his face.

"What will happen to my necklace?"

"Strictly speaking, all such possessions of a convicted converso belong to the Holy Office when the death sentence is carried out. However, if it is of no value to us we may return it to your family once you have identified it. Anything else?"

"Who is my accuser?"

"That we never reveal. Now, if you have finished, I will begin the questioning. You are the woman known as Cassandra, the Lady in Waiting to Lady Francesca, wife of Don Enriquez Garcia-Muñoz de Cordoba?"

"Yes."

"You are from the Province of Seville?"

"I do not know how to answer that."

"Why not?"

Cass thought for a moment, then drew a deep breath. "I have been told that my family is from Al-Andalus, but I am not sure where exactly. No one ever told me that. I have not been in contact with my family for some time and have been under the protection of various people, most recently the Queen, and now Lady Francesca."

"Is your family Jewish?"

"Yes, though they do not practice any religion."

"None of them is a convert to Catholicism except you?"

"None of them is a convert to my knowledge, nor am I. Like my parents, I have never practiced any religion."

"How is it that the Queen took you under her protection and elevated you to a position reserved for nobility?"

"I have some influential patrons."

"And who might they be?"

"You would have to ask the Queen. I am not sure how she chose me."

"And you deny that you are a Christian?"

"Yes."

"And you deny that you are secretly a practicing Jew, while pretending to practice Christianity in order to gain advancement."

Cass considered the accusation. "I was not given a choice about being a lady in waiting. I did as I was bidden. I never claimed to be a Christian, nor did I make any of the outward signs of being one. I attended Mass with the household because it was expected of everyone. I never went to communion or confession or made the sign of the cross. I have never been baptized.

The Inquisitor looked up at Cass's final statement. "You cannot prove that. On the contrary, your behavior suggests that you were Catholic. The Queen, Lady Francesca, everyone believed it. Yet now you have been attending the synagogue and defending Jews. Can you deny that?"

"I have become interested in the religion of my people since arriving in Cordoba. I want to learn about it…and, I hope, to practice it… and to defend my people. As for everyone thinking I was a Christian, I am sorry if I mislead them. If I had wanted to keep my being a Jew secret, I could have done so. I have gone to my teacher and to the synagogue openly."

"I could almost believe you," said the Inquisitor. "You are clever, hiding behind the Queen and unknown persons of influence, but that will not work. You are trying to protect your parents who no doubt are, like you, conversos. Will you sign the confession to that effect? Before you answer, I must warn you that if you refuse, you will be tortured and then brought back for more questioning. That will continue until you confess."

What mostly shocked Cass was how matter-of-factly he said this, especially that she was to be "tortured." She simply stared at the Inquisitor. There was nothing more to say.

"Very well, then. Father Perez, note that the converso prisoner named Cassandra refused to sign the confession. She will be subjected to the water torture immediately. We will not waste time with words." Cass continued to stare at the Inquisitor but now her eyes were glinting. Anger cleared her mind.

"Do not count on saving time," she said firmly. The Inquisitor ignored her words.

"Perhaps at our next meeting you will be less clever and more truthful. I will want to know who your parents and influential guardians are, not the Queen, you understand, and I will want a signed confession." As he rose, his assistant hastened to the door to call for the guard. They left without another word or glance at Cass. Father Guzman followed them.

When they were gone Cass sat down heavily on the edge of her pallet. She fought against the rising panic and hysteria. She had no idea what the water torture was. She would try to prepare herself for whatever was to come. She focused her mind on the Sabbath Service at the synagogue. She envisioned the red light that stood before the curtains of the sacred Ark. "Eternal light … Divine presence… God's dwelling place." She held fast to the image of the red light, and she repeating the phrases over and over. When the two prison guards came for her and took her to a different room where they tortured her, she kept her mind on the red lamp that signified the Divine Presence. She saw it even as she gagged on the linen strip that she could not help but swallow with the water. She saw the light flickering as the ropes bit into her wrists and ankles when she struggled against swallowing and breathing in more water. After an eternity of pain, the light began to fade. She was drowning.

Cass made a final desperate effort to focus on the light. It flickered twice and then held steady. Inside the light a tall building took shape. It was the Giralda of Seville. At the foot of the tower there was a man in a brown robe. Brother Bartolomeo! He was walking toward the orange grove, head bowed in thought. He paused suddenly, turned and looked directly at Cass, his face breaking first into a broad smile and then into a worried frown. He squinted. His eyes filled with tears, but then he smiled again though not so widely. He extended both arms toward Cass in an embrace and a blessing as the tears streamed down his face.

The candle began to flicker more weakly. Cass was about to let it go out, but she once again felt a presence. She broke through a wall of pain to focus on the light. It steadied itself. It brightened. Inside it again was the Giralda, this time high up by the highest open arch. There was Dhu Khiffle. He was calling out the prayer. He was far away, but Cass could hear the prayer. It sounded like a poem. She struggled to hear it. "God, Allah, the Master of the Universe/ Blessed be the One in song and verse." He had hesitated ever so slightly before the last word. He waived from the tower toward Cass. Then it was the candle waiving, but it did not fade. It brightened still more.

Cass came to back in her room, choking and coughing and spitting out water while struggling to breathe. Her throat felt like she had swallowed a knife. Father Guzman had placed her on her stomach and was moving her arms forward past her head and then back to her sides. "I think that is the last of it," he said. "God grant that it is." He gently dried Cass's head and face and tried to soak up the water from the wooden boards of the bed. Cass moaned as he helped her to roll over on her back. She again lost consciousness. The light was flickering but bright. Distantly she felt the soreness of her throat, swollen from the rough cloth, and her nostrils, bruised from the wooden pegs. She gradually returned to consciousness and reluctantly surrendered the vision of the red lamp. At last she noticed Father Guzman next to her bed, holding her wrist. His face betrayed his agony of compassion. Cass tried to speak but cringed at the pain it caused.

"Do not try to speak now," warned Father Guzman. "Those fools nearly killed you last night. The Inquisitor will punish them, but he must have told them that your case was urgent for them to have tortured you so long and so severely. But today is the Feast of the Three Kings, so there can be no torture or questioning … today." Cass made a motion to speak, but Father Guzman quickly but gently placed two fingers of his right hand on her lips, as though blessing her. "Not yet. Rest for a while."

When she next awakened, Father Guzman was still at her side. He knelt next to her, reading from a prayer book by the light of a candle on the table behind him. "It is night out already," thought Cass. The priest noticed her opened eyes. He rose and went to the table where he picked up a bowl and wooden spoon. Cass tried to lift herself on her right elbow, but her stomach churned and head throbbed, causing her to fall back.

"I will raise your head just a bit," said Father Guzman. "Just hold the cold soup in your mouth and move a little bit of it to the back of the throat, slowly." After a few excruciating failures that brought tears to the corners of Cass's eyes, she was able to work some of the thick, orange-colored liquid down her throat. The coolness relieved the burning. Cass guessed that the cold soup contained wine and some narcotic. The swelling must have gone down quickly; she could breathe more easily and with less pain.

"Thank you," she whispered hoarsely.

"You are doing well. Swallow as much as you can, but slowly," replied Father Guzman. "There are some matters we must discuss, but first I have news for you. "Your friends have been quick to act on your behalf. Lord Sebastian left for Granada immediately after your arrest to inform your brother and the Queen. Lady Theadora told me this. She came to my early Mass this morning to celebrate the feast of the Three Kings in the church below." Cass looked up and was surprised to see Father Guzman actually making eye contact with her, and with a slight smile. "Lady Theadora revealed her identity to me when she asked me to hear her confession before

Mass. She is a devout Christian. She plans to attend Mass every morning while you are here. You are fortunate to have her and Lord Sebastian as allies. Lord Sebastian will ask the Queen to intervene somehow for you, though I doubt that the Queen will do that. No matter, though, because I have thought of ... ."

"Could you get the necklace from the Inquisitor? Give to Thea?" Her voice was little more than a raspy, halting whisper, but the priest heard.

Father Guzman looked truly contrite. His voice lost its excitement, and the worry signs appeared on his brow as he spoke. "Forgive me, My Lady. Please try to understand. I have myself just confessed and done penance for protecting you against the guard and withholding the necklace. The Inquisitor warned me that my help was to be spiritual, not material. Otherwise I would be endangering your soul ... and my own."

"I must have the necklace." Cass tried to push herself up on her elbow but fell back with a groan.

"That is not possible, but I have a plan, My Lady, that could save you in both body and soul," said Father Guzman with a note of pleading in his voice. "That is the important matter I wish to discuss with you. I followed the interrogation closely last evening. I also read the notes taken by Father Perez. I believe that you are sincere in what you say. If you can convince the Inquisitor that you never were baptized, then you are not a converso. You might then be pardoned for posing, or seeming to pose, as a Christian. You are from the country and clearly not acquainted with the ways of court."

"And how could I prove I was never baptized?" asked Cass. The priest smiled slightly. Her skeptical tone assured him that the soup and treated wine were having a beneficial effect.

"It would take two steps. First, if the Lady Theadora, who has shown a most Catholic devotion, could testify that she is confident that you have never been baptized, she could help you considerably. She is a particular friend of Lord Sebastian's and remains the ward of Don Enriquez and under the protection of Duke Antonio Leon.

"Thea—Lady Theadora—could testify to that in good conscience," replied Cass with a surge of hope. "We have often spoken about my lack of a religion. What is the second step?"

"As you have told the Inquisitor, my Lady, you are Jewish but not a practicing Jew, at least not until very recently. If you were to decide to become a Christian and be baptized, the Inquisitor must look more favorably on you. Combining Lady Theadora's testimony with your request for baptism would, I believe, persuade the Inquisitor to dismiss the converso case against you and anyone connected with you."

Cass's face slowly clouded over. "Father, I have just discovered my true faith. Surely you ... would not want me to renounce it."

"But are you certain, My Lady, of your new-found faith? Is it possible that you can have such conviction in so short a time? Are you so sure that you can sacrifice your life, and perhaps even the life of your brother of whom Lady Theadora has spoken to me, on such a brief acquaintance with the Jewish religion?"

Cass looked at Father Guzman for some time, considering what he had just said. Then she shook her head. "You will be a good teacher, persuasive and sincere. But I have searched since I can remember, wanting to believe ... now I do. I could not turn away now. Nor would my brother ... wish it."

"My Lady, I pray you to reconsider. Your Judaism is still fresh and untested. You have not even been formally received."

Cass looked at her chaplain pensively. "Perhaps you will accomplish with your kindly persuasion what the Inquisitor could not, so far, by torture," said Cass. "You could be right and my newfound faith may be just a fancy. I do not wish to die, for ... nothing." She closed her eyes tightly, trying to see the red light again, but she did not see even a flicker. "Pray for me to do what is right, Father. Ask my friends to pray. I will need their help ... meet the Inquisitor tomorrow."

Father Guzman stood up to go, feeling that he had overtaxed

Cass. He nodded. "I will, My Lady." He gently coaxed the last of the healing drink into her. "You rest now but please consider what I have said." He bowed and quietly left.

Cass lay back on her pallet, bewildered and exhausted, unmindful of the sour-smelling dampness of her clothes and her cloak. She began to surrender to the merciful effects of the wine and narcotic. Her thoughts started to trail off. "Perhaps being a religious Jew is just a romantic dream, a wish for what has been missing in my life. Maybe I could fill the same need by becoming Christian. Then I could work for the Jews, maybe influence the decision about Jews. Can not help if I am dead or in prison. What about Alan?" She slept.

Long before first light Cass was already wide awake, again debating within herself. The last hour or more of sleep had been made restless by stark images of the torture. She dreamed of the pegs being forced into her nostrils, the linen gag causing painful swallowing, the choking, not being able to breathe. But in the midst of the nightmare, another image reappeared. She saw the red lamp, its flame flickering but constant before the Ark. The flame grew in her mind and from inside it she heard Abu Yusuf's blessing: "May the God of Israel and Judah remain always with you and keep you steadfast in your faith."

Now, in the pre-dawn hours, she struggled again between her dread of the torture and her devotion to her new-found belief. "Belief in what," she wondered. "God? An ideal of Judaism only a few days old?" She feared the torture. She desired her faith. One was very real; the other a mystery. "Where is Maiden? I need her more than ever. What am I to decide? What of the quest, the Jews? Have I failed? Thea and Sebastian could help me. As a Christian, together we could help the Jews. Thea used to quote an English lawyer saint, something about loving God with our intellect as well as our heart. Help me now, lawyer saint."

She prayed another prayer, the one she had just recently learned: "Shema Israel. Hear, O Israel, the Lord our God, the Lord is One."

But other thoughts interrupted the prayer. "Ibrahim Leonides is Christian just to please his masters. Why should I not do the same, so I can do good?"

"Hear, O Israel, the Lord our God, the Lord is One." The words repeated themselves in Cass's mind. Her heart ached. "God, why now, why do you give me this faith now, when it would kill me?"

Cass received no answer to this question, nor, she finally realized, did she need to. She remembered Abu Yusuf's words about the "gift of faith" and sharing it with others. She finally lay on her pallet and quietly rested. A few more tears ran down both sides of her face, but she knew what she would do, and her mind was at peace. Lines from Devorah's poem-gift came back to her.

*He put the ring from his right hand on her left hand, and she put her anklet on his arm;*
*While she took his veil as a keepsake, he took hers as a memento.*

The thud of the key in the lock scared away her thoughts. The morning guard brought in her breakfast of a cup of water and a wooden bowl of bean paste. Cass was grateful that he said nothing. The first guard, the vile one who had searched her, had not returned since then, and the others had been almost respectful, as was this one. She succeeded in sitting up, though she needed to grip the edge of the pallet to steady herself. She mixed some of the water and paste and managed to eat a few mouthfuls. Her throat throbbed with the effort, but she could taste the beans and felt that they were nourishing. She lay back down. When Father Guzman arrived a little later, he felt guilty awakening her from such a peaceful sleep.

"You will need a few more mouthfuls to get you through this morning's questioning," he said. Cass sat up and did as he asked. He was pleased to see her looking better.

Cass ate all of the bean paste and then announced, with only a slight tremble in her voice, "I think I am ready."

"You have thought about what I said? You have come to a

decision?" asked her chaplain.

"Yes," answered Cass. "I tried to convince myself that I could ask for baptism in good conscience, or even in a state of sincere doubt—one of your phrases, Father—but I have discovered who I am, a Jew. I cannot, even if I wanted to, turn my back on that discovery. I think I must have been looking for it all my thinking life."

Father Guzman nodded and sighed. "I feared as much, as did the Lady Theodora when I spoke with her this morning. She used the same words you just did, that you would not turn your back on your people or your faith. She also said, however, that you must not give up. I was to remind you of a saying. You are to find a way 'to serve God wittily in the tangle of your mind,' but she did not explain what that meant. Do you know?"

Cass laughed even though it hurt her throat terribly when she did so. "Yes I do. That is what her lawyer saint, the one I told you about, said. He was on trial for his life and he was looking for a way not to lose it and still keep his honor. Tell Thea that I am grateful for her message and intend to follow the advice."

"Lady Theodora also reminds you that she remains anxious to testify that you were never baptized."

"I will not ask her to do that. You and I both know that it will probably not help prove my innocence without my asking for baptism. The Inquisitor might even accuse Thea for admitting to friendship with a converso."

"I am afraid you could be right," said her chaplain. "Then what is your plan? I know you have one." His voice was grim and his face unsmiling, but his eyes told Cass of his admiration and that he would do whatever was possible for her.

"Since I cannot endure the water torture again, I will confess, but on my own terms. I will say that I have returned to the Jewish faith and practice but that I continued to pose as a Christian for my advancement. These statements are true enough, in a tangled way. My mother's mother was a devout Jewish woman, even a leader among her people. I am returning to that faith and, if I am able, would try to be worthy to be such a leader for my people."

"I will admit that I gave the impression of being a Catholic, another tangled truth. I can agree that in some ways, maybe subconsciously, I was acting like a Catholic to avoid complications that would get in the way of my search, the quest."

"I will not confess to ever being baptized. I will not even mention baptism. The Inquisitor and others will draw the baptism conclusion for themselves."

"Good so far," said Father Guzman, as though her were tutoring her. "What will you tell him about your parents being conversos? And about your unknown benefactor?"

"I will say that my parents are from the land across the water where English is spoken. My parents live there still. The Inquisitor will naturally think I am speaking of England. I believe that some wealthy and influential Jews still remain and practice their religion there."

"My benefactor is the easiest of all. She is my guardian angel, an old friend of my mother's mother. She is the one who arranged for me to be Lady Francesca's Lady in waiting. She has numerous contacts both here in Spain and abroad. Unfortunately I have not heard from her for ages and have no idea where she might be at present."

"This is all true about your guardian?" asked her tutor in wonderment.

"All literally true," answered his pupil, with a satisfied smile.

"Very good. Now I have a most difficult question for you. If the Inquisitor accepts your confession, and we are not sure that he will, but if he does, you are ready to be burned at the stake?"

"Yes and no. First, a strong no. If you could somehow get the necklace back from the Inquisitor, I assure you that I can escape. It would take too long to explain how at the moment, but I assure you it is so." Father Guzman was about to reply, but she held out her hand for him to wait.

"Second, yes, I could accept being burned at the stake more

readily than being put through the water torture again. I believe that the victims suffocate from the smoke before the flames get to them. Still I would much prefer to escape with my necklace. I am not a hero, Father." Cass shivered at the vividness of her memory of her near death by slow, painful drowning. "If I do not sign the confession I will be tortured again. If that happens, I will agree to any terms. That could mean involving others, including Stephen and Sarah and certainly my brother and possibly Lady Theadora, even Sebastian. Who knows what else I could confess to? No I would much rather control my own fate."

"And if the Inquisitor does not accept your confession, and threatens to torture you anyway, what will you do?"

"You are a thorough instructor, for which I am grateful. I pray that I do not face that decision. I think it an unlikely one. The Inquisitor may reject my signed confession by itself." Cass paused a moment and gave her confessor a look that told him he was in for a surprise. "But he will most likely accept it along with my oral confession to you." She hurried on before Father Guzman could object. "He is a businessman, and his business is to get me to confess and thus to save my soul, while at the same time giving a public display of faith for Christians and a warning to Jews. He will be confident of my soul when he knows you will hear my confession."

Father Guzman looked at her sharply. "I do not understand. How can you refuse baptism on principle but agree to make your confession as a Catholic. I would not be party to a sham confession, nor would you. If you are willing to make a true confession, why not be baptized and save your life?"

"It would not be a sham confession, although it would not be confession as you or Lady Theadora normally think of it, with, what do you call it, absolution. But I do wish and ask, whatever happens, that you will let me confide in you and that you will give me a blessing before I die, if I have to die. I should think we can both do that without compromising our beliefs. Baptism on the other hand would be a betrayal of what I now believe. And that would not be a very good example for Sarah, would it?"

"The mind of a lawyer," said Father Guzman, marveling at her. "But in this case you are wrong. Your signing the confession and then being burned at the stake will show that you have repented of your error in leaving the Church and secretly returning to Judaism. Sarah or Stephen, or the other Jews of whom you have spoken will not know that you have remained steadfast in your Jewish faith."

"They will know when they know how the confession reads," Cass replied confidently, "and you will be my witness to that."

Cass looked fondly at her confessor and new teacher. He in turn could hardly repress a smile of satisfaction. "I doubt that I will find a student at Salamanca or anywhere else to equal you, My Lady. I had hoped for a different outcome, but I cannot believe that what you are doing will in any way endanger your soul. Just the opposite. Therefore I will do everything I possibly can to find your necklace and get it back to you. If necessary I will hear your confession, or rather your confidences."

Cass was about to give father Guzman a modest but hearty hug when they heard keys jangling at the door. The guard entered and announced the Inquisitor and his secretary.

The meeting with the Inquisitor went as Cass had predicted. The Holy Office, through the Inquisitor, accepted her confession with the condition that she also confess verbally to Father Guzman. The Inquisitor's secretary wrote as she dictated. Then she signed. She would be executed in two-days' time to complete the saving cleansing of her soul.

# Chapter XXII

## Rescue Plans

C ass spent the day before her execution date in a reasonably hopeful manner despite several major disappointments. The Inquisitor had refused her request to see Thea. She continued to feel abandoned by Maiden. No one seemed to have heard any word about Sebastian's attempt to contact the Queen on her behalf, or his expectation to find Alan. She still hoped that Father Guzman would find the necklace, but he had so far been unable to discover its whereabouts. He had given it to the Inquisitor, now much to his regret. He was far from giving up, but time was growing short.

Still he stole some time to visit Cass. She took consolation in his presence and took advantage of it to make what they both agreed was a good confession. She told him about the necklace and about Maiden, and about some of their adventures. She spoke of not being a helpful big sister to Alan, about getting Thea caught by the Romans in Italica because of her curiosity, and about how totally stupid she had been not to have escaped immediately before he took the necklace from her. She told him of her doubts about fulfilling her quest. Father Guzman was not as surprised as she thought he might be by her revelations. He told her that early on he had realized that she had a mysterious past. "I was quite sure of it when you said, in all truthfulness, that you were from across the water in a place where English is spoken. As for Maiden, I have been taught to believe in angels since I can remember anything, and I have seen such angels in manuscripts such as your Brother Bartolomeo illuminated."

He listened carefully and asked many questions. He asked in particular about Hasdai ibn Shaprut—Abu Yusuf—about whom he knew a fair amount. He was familiar with the translation Abu Yusuf and Brother Nicholas had done of the famous Greek book of remedies called the *The Book of Medicine*. He also disclosed another reason for his interest in Abu Yusuf, one that surprised Cass but bound them still closer.

"My ancestors, like yours, were Jewish, in my case up until about a century ago," he explained. "They were not particularly distinguished as far as I know. In fact several generations of them were agents for the slave trade in Cordoba, the basis for the Guzman family wealth and, later title of nobility. Now I am confessing to you it seems. There is one member of the family, however, who, from what you have told me about Hasdai, was a nobler sort. He was a merchant who supposedly carried letters from Hasdai ibn Shaprut to the Khazars in the East. That is a family story that most historians reject. They say that the Khazars are a myth and never really existed, but you have discovered differently. I am happy to hear that, especially because the merchant ancestor is the one that first brought honest wealth to our family."

Cass spoke about her hopes for helping the Jews of Cordoba get to Constantinople, that is, Stephen and Sarah and others who wished to go. Father Guzman shared Cass's excitement about that great city of many peoples and religions. "Those who are able to get to Constantinople or elsewhere in the New Muslim Empire will be most fortunate," said Father Guzman.

"Yes, I agree, thanks to Bishop Recemondo and the others" said Cass. "So I thought that helping them to get there might have been my mission, but if I am not able to escape with the necklace, how will I be able to help?"

"The necklace! God forgive me," exclaimed her confessor suddenly, "and you, My Lady. We have talked too long. I must return to my search. It is near the supper hour. I will leave you now. You will have some good food for supper, what is supposed to be your last meal. I believe it will be brought to you by Father Perez himself. After you have eaten try to get some rest. I will return when I can."

Cass agreed that he needed to go but even so was sad to see her chaplain leave. Father Perez did bring her supper, a stew that consisted of vegetables and a few cubes of meat. He also brought her wine and water. Next to her cup she found the poem scroll. After she had eaten she walked, or rather paced, for some time. She tried to concentrate on getting her people to Constantinople. She would enlist Sebastian and Thea and, of course, Ibrahim Leonides. And Alan. Cass felt a stab of longing as she thought of her brother, and that she might never see him again. To compose herself, she read her poem repeatedly. And she prayed for guidance as well as deliverance. The poem and prayers helped. Her candles dimmed and went out. She realized it was late and that she was very tired. She lay down and fell immediately into a sound sleep.

At just about that time, something after midnight, two members of the Queen's Guardsmen, just arrived from Granada, were challenged by the night watch. Sebastian fortunately managed to persuade the watch to open the gate without doing a closer examination. Alan carried written orders from the Queen, allowing him to return temporarily to Cordoba, which would probably have overridden any suspicion that he too might be a converso like his sister. Sebastian still did not want to take any chances. In order to keep Alan's identity a secret, the two Guardsmen avoided the palace of the Duke. They went rather to Casa Lucía and by the darkest alleys. Alan was impressed that Sebastian was so confident of finding his round-about way there on such a dark night as this and despite his nearly exhausted condition. Sebastian had ridden night and day and into the next night to get back in time.

They were welcomed warmly by Lucía and Ibrahim Leonides. To their surprise and delight they found Thea also there. She had gotten leave to spend that night and the next at Lucía's home. She was grateful to Lady Francesca, who had started to ask her the reason for her request, but then thought better of it. She granted it with an almost kindly tone. Thea and Father Guzman had agreed that Lucía's house seemed to be an almost charmed safe-place and therefore the most desirable place to meet. Cass's chaplain would be the bearer of news. He might also have to bring the necklace there if he could not smuggle it into Cass's cell. Either way, of course, he had to regain it first.

"Thank God you are here," said Thea to the new arrivals. "Cass is sentenced to be burned at the stake the day after tomorrow. I have been terribly afraid that you would not get here in time." She stopped and looked fixedly from Alan to Sebastian. "What did the Queen say?"

"She could spare me only a few moments, but they were enough to convince me that it was hopeless. She will not interfere with the Holy Office. I knew they were powerful, but I could not imagine that she would not intervene to save someone under her protection. I am truly sorry," he concluded as he took both of Thea's hands into his. "The Queen herself wishes it could be otherwise and has sent Alan to be a consolation to his sister."

Thea hardly heard anything after Sebastian's "I am sorry." She gripped his hands tightly. "This is impossible. How can this be happening?"

"But what about the necklace?" asked Alan. "Why has she not used it to escape already?"

"That is the worst news of all. The Inquisitor has it," answered Thea.

Lucía took command during the shocked silence. She knew that there would be a flood of questions and emotions that would lead probably nowhere. "You cannot do anything until you have all sat down and had some nourishment." She took the road-stained cloaks from Sebastian and Alan. "Sit," she repeated. She handed the cloaks to Ibrahim Leonides. She brought water and towels for the two travelers. Before they had finished cleaning up she had provided water and wine, bread and cheese. "Keep the towels. Eat," she said as she removed the basins of used water. Sebastian and Alan picked at the food mechanically at first and then more attentively as they realized that they were famished. The others joined them. The tension eased. Thea and Ibrahim Leonides took turns explaining Cass's situation. They began discussing possible rescue plans for Cass.

When she had allowed them enough time for talk, Lucía again took command. "Of course Alan must stay here where he is safe. We have heard as much from Sebastian." She gave him a warning look, when Alan began to protest. "Best to stay out of sight, even with the Queen's letter." Looking at Sebastian, she added, "you are also welcome to stay with us, but I doubt that you are in any danger." Sebastian said that his presence in the city will have already been reported, or soon would be, and that he should leave shortly for the Duke's palace where he would be expected. "Then perhaps you should go now. You will all need rest if you are to be of any use to Lady Cassandra," said Lucía.

When Sebastian was gone, Thea turned to Alan who sat looking both exhausted and worried. "Tell us how our friend Yusuf is and about Granada, if you are not too tired."

Alan smiled slightly. "All right, I will, but first I am happy to tell you that the surrender by the Moors was not humiliating the way the Bishop of Cordoba and maybe even the Queen initially had hoped. Instead of making a Grand Entrance by the victorious Christians with bells and trumpets on the Feast of the Three Kings as originally planned, Boabdil El Chico and his Royal Guards left with honor before the King and Queen entered. I am sure it was Ferdinand's doing, but the Queen went along. They stayed with the army on a hilltop close enough to the gate to watch the Moors march out. Boabdil noticed and was not to be outdone in courtesy. He rode his horse half way up the hill, dismounted and saluted. Ferdinand rode down to him, dismounted and embraced his old enemy. The troops on both sides cheered."

Thea saw the tears welling up in Alan's eyes and held his hands. Alan smiled through his tears. "Only after the last of the Royal Guards were out of sight did the King and Queen give the signal for Army of Castille and Aragon to march, in respectful silence, into Granada."

Alan paused briefly and then went on. "Now to your question. Our friend Yusuf, who was treated as little more than a servant in Seville, turns out to be from one of the oldest and most prominent Arab families of Granada. They consider being an architect and a builder, like Yusuf's father, an honor. Unfortunately his family, like most other Muslims, has lost practically everything they had in Granada. They had almost lost their self-esteem until Yusuf returned. I have met Yusuf's family and spoken with them. They are already looking to him as their leader. He will be a good one. They will need him. Everyone there is convinced that after the Jews are expelled, the Muslims will be the next to go, regardless of the surrender treaty that allows them to stay. I promised them that if I could, I would go with them to help them wherever their journey took them."

"But how so?" said Thea. "That will split us up. Cass surely will not leave the Jews, nor could I," said Thea, who then looked down. "Nor, I think, could I leave Sebastian."

Alan smiled as broadly as he had when he and Sebastian first arrived at the House. "I think, My Lady, we have all already guessed at the roles you and Lord Sebastian will play," he said. "I am confident that the two of you will be protectors of Jews and Muslims, those who will be leaving and those who stay." He put a reassuring hand on her shoulder. "We may all three be going in different directions to fulfill our quest. That is, after we rescue my sister from prison." Alan's reassuring smile shifted into a wide yawn that he tried, with no success at all, to stifle. That was Lucía's sign to usher everyone to bed.

Sebastian escorted Thea to church the next morning. After Mass the two of them, along with Father Guzman, came back to Lucía's house for breakfast and to discuss their plans. Sebastian took a quick liking to the priest. He was simple and devout, and he was their ally in helping Cass. The last point, of course, ensured that Alan would like him. The gathering was brief, although Ibrahim Leonides managed a short summary of the court gossip about Father Guzman and his family. Before becoming a priest the young Felipé Guzman had been an accomplished Squire, who had served his military apprenticeship. He was quite a lively bachelor, and destined for knighthood. The young priest bowed modestly, but he promptly directed everyone's attention to the fact that he still had not discovered the whereabouts of the necklace. He had explored the Priory of the Order of Preachers, next to the Church of St. Dominic, including the Inquisitor's own room. He was convinced it was not there. If he failed to find it and to "borrow it," as he put it, he would simply have to persuade the Inquisitor to give it to him. He would devote the entire day if need be to this task, after a visit to Lady Cassandra.

Sebastian meanwhile would speak to several of the soldiers, including those who had accompanied the Duke de Cordoba to Seville to join the Lady Francesca and escort her to her wedding. He knew that at least a few of the Duke's men would give a sympathetic ear to Cass's cause. Cass had shared in Thea's widespread popularity at the Court of Seville. The soldiers heard about and approved of how Cass had cleverly mended the breach between two friends, one a Queen's Guardsman, during the trip to Cordoba. They admired her. And they admired and highly respected Lord Sebastian.

The other 'conspirators,' as they now thought of themselves, would have to wait patiently until they could all gather that evening to make their final plans. Alan had pleaded to be allowed to go in disguise to explore the site of the execution, known as the Plaza of the Faith, where the Inquisition burned the converso Jews. He was promptly outvoted for his own protection. He conceded when Sebastian pointed out his own familiarity with the site and that he would inspect it further that day. They would meet again that evening at the supper hour.

Ibrahim Leonides and Lucía went about their normal activities, as much as that was possible, so that the house would retain its sense of order. Thea spent most of her time trying, with moderate success, to keep Alan calm. She reviewed with him several times what had happened in Cordoba while he was gone. Alan wanted to know every detail. He was, of course, astonished and delighted, especially by the news of their Grandmother Esther or rather Essie. He wished he could have been with Cass when she went to the Synagogue service. Thea had been able to pick up details of the service from Sebastian and from Ibrahim Leonides. Ibrahim Leonides had met secretly with Stephen, though only once. They had been able to share information with each other, but they also agreed that any further visits would be too dangerous. Anyone connected in any way with Lady Cassandra might be being watched. The Jewish community would re-double its prayers for her.

The news, when they all gathered at Casa Lucía late that afternoon, was mixed. Sebastian had judged correctly about the Duke's men. He had enlisted a dozen of them. They were all trustworthy and good soldiers. His examination of the Plaza of the Faith had given him some ideas about how best to deploy them. Father Guzman was, however, visibly distressed. He had discovered the location of the necklace and practically despaired of obtaining it. The Inquisitor had it on his person under his robes. He had no intention of giving it to anyone except perhaps to the Head of the Holy Office, Torquemada himself. The others could only groan when they heard this.

"I pleaded with him," said Father Guzman. "I said it had belonged to Lady Cassandra's grandmother, a practicing Jew in good standing with the Church. Relatives might still be found. The Inquisitor looked at me as though I were a fool. He shook his head and said nothing. I made one last try and asked if she could wear it one final time since it was so precious to her. The Inquisitor showed me that he had a strong leather cord around his neck. 'I have it,' he said, 'in a leather pouch held next to my heart by these stout leather cords. It will not leave my person until I see the Head of the Holy Office himself. But since you have been so cooperative, I might show it to you during our period of recreation after dinner.' Then he left."

"Then I will go with you to see him," said Thea. Father Guzman simply stared at her, but the others turned expectantly and waited for her to explain. "I have been given a gift for telling stories, some made up, some factual, but all entertaining and at times persuasive. I wish to try to persuade, and maybe even entertain, the Inquisitor."

"Impossible," said Father Guzman. "Even if he would agree to meet with you outside the cloister this evening, which I doubt, he will never agree to give you the necklace. All you would accomplish is to endanger yourself by too close an association with a former converso."

"You and Cass have protected me far too much, and without asking me, I might add. I will do this," Thea replied decidedly.

"The only other alternative is for us to get to him and take the necklace by force," said Alan. Sebastian nodded his agreement.

Father Guzman looked at them, shaking his head negatively. "I have more bad news," he replied. "The Priory always asks that extra prison guards be posted there and at the tower the day before a burning. In fact more prison guards than usual have been on duty all day today in both places. The Holy Office is worried that Lady Cassandra has friends, both Christian and Jewish. The only practical chance to rescue her will be when she is taken from the prison to the Plaza of the Faith, or at the Plaza itself."

"I must try tonight," repeated Thea firmly.

"The Lady Theadora indeed has an unusual talent," said Ibrahim

Leonides, speaking for the first time on the matter. "I have heard both her songs and tales. Do not underestimate the power of the storyteller to enchant."

Father Guzman sighed. He looked around the room. Seeing only heads nodding in agreement with Ibrahim Leonides and Lady Theadora, he voiced the phrase a debater uses in such cases. "I concede."

"Is there some way you could smuggle the necklace into Lady Cassandra?" asked Sebastian, "assuming Lady Theadora could get the Inquisitor to give it to you."

"The Holy Office trusts no one, including me. Prison guards watch every move I make when I visit her. If I attempted to smuggle it to her and failed, you would never see it or me again," said the priest, looking at Sebastian.

"Then we will make two plans right now, before Lady Theadora and Father Guzman leave," said Sebastian, addressing the whole group. One plan will presume that we have the necklace, the other that we do not."

The conspirators listened closely as Sebastian outlined the two plans. When he finished, he looked at the group around him. "Suggestions? Questions?" he asked. "Alan?

"No."

Sir Priest?"

"None, My Lord."

Everyone nodded agreement with Sebastian's carefully outlined plans. Ibrahim Leonides and Lucía put the food on the table. They ate standing. When they finished they said their farewells. Thea left with Father Guzman. She would return later that night. Sebastian left to contact his men among the Duke's soldiers. He too would return later that night. The others wished them good luck.

# Chapter XXIII

# The Act of Faith

C ass arose and dressed as the first birdsong marked the pre-dawn of the day of her execution. She had not slept, unless it were for a few restless moments and then only from sheer emotional exhaustion. She wept when she thought of never seeing her parents or Alan again. She remained resigned to whatever her newly discovered God decided for her. That seemed more and more to mean her death. That frightened her, but she worried as much or more about her friends. She knew they would try to rescue her. She welcomed the thought, but she did not want any blood shed over her and had said so to Father Guzman. Her anxiety increased when Father Guzman arrived. He was paler than normal. His complexion reminded her of a bleached sheet, in sharp contract to his black mantle. She wanted to speak, but his eyes counseled silence. Close behind him were the Inquisitor and Father Perez. "So this is it," she thought. She stood up straight, receiving them like a noblewoman. "Graceful," thought her chaplain, something she managed, even in the simple ankle-length, gray woolen dress and pair of sandals the guard had given her the night before. She had eaten no breakfast and had only wetted her lips with the cup of water on the table.

"You have confessed?" asked the Inquisitor.

"Yes," replied Cass. The Inquisitor looked to Father Guzman, who nodded his agreement.

Then let us begin," said the Inquisitor.

The soldiers were already standing at attention in front of the church. A dozen of them had formed two ranks to escort the prisoner. At the head of the procession was the anonymous executioner. He wore a long black hood that reached from a peak above his head all the way to his shoulders, completely covering head and face. He wore robes like a monk's and carried a processional cross. At the back of the procession the Sergeant at Arms directed Cass and the others to their places between the two ranks of soldiers. First came Cass accompanied by Father Guzman, then the Inquisitor and Father Perez. The Sergeant brought up the rear. The soldiers and their Sergeant were impassive, business-like. Any novelty about their task had worn off with repetition. According to law the soldiers were provided by the civil authority, in this case the Duke, but they were, as usual, handpicked by the Inquisitor of the Holy Office. The Sergeant gave the order to start.

The Plaza of the Faith was only a few minutes' walk, but the cross bearer moved slowly, deliberately. People had been milling about. They quickly made way for the procession and then closed in behind to follow it. The Holy Office, Cass knew, wanted a show and an audience. Word would have been spread so that the people could witness the "Act of Faith" by the repentant sinner. In reality most people watched out of curiosity. Some shook their heads sadly or wept in sympathy. A few called out insults. Cass heard them. Her senses were heightened.

They had hardly begun when Cass saw her accuser, the bully who had attacked her and later turned her in to "them that would burn Jews." She braced herself for his insults as he stepped toward them from the crowd. Instead what she heard was, "Lady, forgive me." Two soldiers pushed him away roughly with a stern warning. "I do forgive you," she called to him over her shoulder. Father

Guzman looked briefly in the direction Cass had called and then looked at her. Cass recognized the admiration in his expression and managed a nervous smile. "I think I must have sounded much more in control than I am. Please stay close." He nodded a quick assent.

The procession turned onto the street that led to the Plaza of the Faith. It was a short but wide street, about as wide as a good sized courtyard, but little more than a hundred and fifty paces long. It made for a grand entrance to the Plaza which was already crowded with people. Cass took note of everything about her destination. She could see the stone wall at the far end of the Plaza. A short distance in front of the wall was what at first looked like leafless trees that had been knocked down by a storm. Nearing the Plaza, she saw that the 'tree branches' were covering an elevated platform. In the center of the platform stood a tall, heavy wooden stake fashioned from a tree trunk. A little closer and she could see the narrow path to the stake. "That is my execution pyre." She knew that she was "the central character of a spectacle," but she felt more like part of the audience that was filling the Plaza and the side streets. It was as though she were about to witness her own burning.

As the procession entered the Plaza itself the crowd parted, revealing a ring of soldiers, evenly spaced every few yards, facing the people. The soldiers held a rope to mark the limit of the crowd's approach, for safety and security. As the procession approached, the the rope was lowered temporarily to allow it to pass. It entered an open space and continued for a half dozen paces and stopped before a second ring of soldiers, this one facing the pyre, shoulder to shoulder. The Sergeant called out an order. The soldiers in the path of the procession moved in formation to make an open passageway. The Sergeant directed Cass and Father Guzman to follow the cross bearer and the two leading soldiers. The soldiers who had brought Cass took up positions re-closing the circle. The Inquisitor and Father Perez had remained in the open space between two circular ranks of soldiers. From here they could witness the execution at close hand but yet at a safe distance. The Sergeant and two of his men continued on behind the cross bearer with Cass and Father Guzman to a set of wooden steps next to the platform. The stage was nearly set.

The cross bearer—executioner stopped on the first step, turned and nodded to Cass and Father Guzman. The Sergeant and his two men moved a short distance away to give Cass a moment with her chaplain. She turned to him. He put his hands on her head to give her his final blessing. He spoke in a low voice for her ears alone. "May the God of Judaism and of Christendom and of Islam bless you and receive you, if that is His will. May He otherwise yet find a way to deliver you." Cass smiled calmly. She understood that he still thought she had a chance to be rescued, but she had fully accepted her sentence now.

As she turned to start up the steps, she noticed the bucket of glowing coals next to the steps. She turned her thoughts inward, to seek the flickering red light of the Ark. She quickly found it. She barely felt the two guards chaining her to the post. She did not notice branches piling up around her, waist high, or fire crackling, or smoke beginning to rise. Cass focused inwardly. She was completely unaware now of the crowd of watchers in the square whose attention was fixed on her, none more so than Thea's.

Thea was dressed as a woodsman, a forester. "Like Robin Hood," she thought to herself, but with a few important differences. She wore a scarf that wound snugly around her neck and covered the leather pouch that held the necklace. She had shortened the pouch's leather ties so that it sat high on her chest below her adam's apple. She had also made a mental apology to the Inquisitor for cutting up his property. She wore skin-tight gloves to keep her fingers nimble but protected. In her left hand she held a hood, folded up, ready to cover head and face. She had managed to work her way up to the restraining rope at a positon where she could see the platform steps. Cass and the procession passed close enough to her that Thea could easily have called to her if it had not been too risky. She carefully watched as the execution proceeded so that she could time her role precisely. While she waited she flexed her body, preparing. She moved up on her toes, like a ballerina, then back down on her heels, and then she repeated the motion, over and over, all the while concentrating fixedly on picking the shortest path to Cass. When the smoke neared Cass's face and she began to cough, Thea put on the hood and went into action. She slipped under the rope.

What the startled crowd nearby saw was an unexpected figure, resembling a huntsman, take quick running strides directly at the inner circle of soldiers. Their surprise gave way to astonished gasps. They saw the runner, without hesitating, reach his hands onto the shoulders of two startled but statue-like soldiers and vault over them in a somersault, and come down running. He dashed across the remaining space to the wooden steps. The Inquisitor turned and stared fixedly at the runner in bewilderment. He quickly came to himself and started shouting to anyone who would listen, mainly to Father Perez, the Sergeant and his two soldiers. "Stop him! Stop that man! He is going for the prisoner."

Before the Inquisitor had even finished his outcry, Thea was at Cass's side. She feared that she had waited too long. Cass was not breathing. Thea began to push on her chest and then breathed mouth to mouth. The Sergeant and his men were heading for the steps when two soldiers, wearing hoods, intercepted and quickly disarmed them. Their hoods protected them from the fire and also hid their identities. They took defensive positions at the steps, clearly intending to stop anyone from interfering with Thea.

The situation in the Plaza quickly became chaotic. The shouting crowds had pushed into the roped-off area. Most of the soldiers guarding the platform now turned to help their comrades hold back the crowds. The Inquisitor, waving his arms and shouting, finally got a handful of soldiers to respond. They were pushed back, as much by the flames and smoke as by the two defenders who were better prepared for the flames. Father Guzman joined the attacking soldiers to persuade them that it was too late to do anything. He all but ordered them back to their ranks along with additional soldiers who were coming to their aid. He encouraged them to help bring the crowd to order, which in fact several officers and their men were beginning to succeed in doing.

The Inquisitor realized that little or no further counter-attack was coming. He turned to the scene on the platform and was re-assured but puzzled by what he saw. He could not see how the would-be rescuer and two renegade soldiers would have time to free the prisoner from her chains, much less help her to escape. Smoke mixed with sparks of fire was swirling around the prisoner and the rescuer. The prisoner seemed to be unconscious. The rescu-er was trying to attach something around her neck. For a moment he thought of the necklace but quickly dismissed the idea. "They will both perish," the Inquisitor decided. As he held this thought, one of the two defending soldiers climbed onto the platform next to the rescuer. He reached out to help steady him. As he did so the pyre began to cave inward toward the stake. It crashed into an eruption of sparks and tongues of fire followed by billowing smoke. The crowd groaned as one and moved back instinctively.

"They have gotten their show," thought the Inquisitor with some satisfaction, although he was somewhat bothered that many in the crowd seemed to have sympathized with the daring rescuer and the prisoner. He also wondered about the remaining renegade soldier. Instead of running from the killing flames, he was trying desperately to get closer, but several soldiers managed to seize him and drag him forcefully away. "Good. We will have another pris-oner to interrogate," he thought. The Inquisitor turned back to wait and watch for the fire to burn down enough so that he could see the remains of the prisoner and the two rescuers. When he was finally able to examine the ashes, he was disappointed. Search as he might he could not discover evidence of any of the three bodies. He insisted that the soldiers find any kinds of remains. "Bones or a weapon," he urged, "or any kind of jewelry." He refused to leave until the ashes of the fire had been sifted repeatedly. They found nothing. Finally he dismissed the soldiers, claiming that he was satisfied and left. Father Perez followed.

# Chapter *XXIV*

## Out of the Ashes

Sebastian, overcome by smoke and bleeding freely from half a dozen wounds, had been brought to Casa Lucía by some soldiers guided by Ibrahim Leonides. The Duke de Leon had sent his private physician to tend to him. It was his own soldiers who had reported to the Duke about Sebastian. They simply said that Sebastian had fought valiantly during the attempted rescue of the condemned converso. They were the same soldiers who had skirmished at the Plaza of the Faith and who had dragged Sebastian away from the flames. They were the soldiers who had helped carry out Sebastian's plan to make sure that the Thea, the runner, would have time to get to Cass with the necklace.

For two days Sebastian lay on a makeshift bed on the first floor near the dining area. In addition to his wounds he was suffering from shock at seeing Thea and the others disappear into the fire. For those two days he did little more than stare into space fixedly, while Lucía and the physician tended to him. His several visitors came and went or watched and spoke to one another in whispers. The regulars at Casa Lucía were all there the next day when Sebastian looked around as though waking up for the first time since arriving there. He sat up with some with help from Lucía. He recognized them all. Father Guzman, Ibrahim Leonides and Lucía, Stephen and Sarah. He read the relief in their faces and was grateful. Sarah walked over to him and handed him a bouquet of daisies. "I picked them on the way over, Lord Sebastian. I guessed today was the day you would return to us. What has happened to Lady Cassandra? And to the others? Do you know?"

The adults gasped a bit, and Stephen apologized for Sarah, but it was clear that Sebastian wanted to talk, as did they all, about what had happened but hadn't yet dared to. Sebastian looked at the faces now in the room. He was bewildered but felt alive for the first time in days and even wondered if he dared have any hope. He looked at Sarah. "I wish I did know, Mistress, but I do not." He again looked around the room. "Perhaps," he began, then stopped and waited.

"I can help a little," said Father Guzman. He explained how Thea had gotten the necklace from the Inquisitor, but only after a number of complications and almost too much time. The attempt to get the necklace had begun well. "Had I not witnessed the event, I would have thought that Lady Theadora had cast a spell on the Inquisitor. Instead it was the power of her words and her manner that worked the magic. The Inquisitor only reluctantly at my insistence came out of the cloister to speak to her that evening before the burning. She did not exactly tell a story. She persuaded as might a lawyer. She spoke of how a series of Jewish women, like Biblical heroes of old, preserved the necklace and its good works over the many centuries since it was made in Roman Days. She described in brief how one was helped by a Brother of the Order of Saint Augustine and how many were helped by an angel, and some even by Spanish noblemen. When she finally had the Inquisitor nodding his approval, like a proper debater she drew her conclusion. Since Cassandra the Converso was the last of the Jewish women bearers of the necklace and had confessed, she should at least be allowed to see it one last time.

The Inquisitor accepted the conclusion with just the slightest hesitation. He began to remove the leather pouch holding the necklace from around his neck, and that is when the hooded figure appeared. It stumbled out of nowhere straight into the Inquisitor, who backed away off balance. The two of them caught each other spontaneously, a natural gesture, but it was almost like an embrace. Surprisingly it was a woman's voice I heard making apologies. She added something further in a whisper before they parted. Lady Theadora and I both heard the repeated word 'beware.' She hurried away as we approached. It all happened in a matter of moments, but the damage was done. The Inquisitor seemed a little confused, which is most unlike him. He said that he would have to give further thought to lending Lady Theadora the necklace to show to the prisoner."

"I was speechless, but Lady Theadora was equal to the challenge and improvised. She spoke gently and very briefly, once again of Biblical heroes and angels and noblemen. She paused, looked smilingly into the Inquisitor's eyes and said, 'do not forget to bring the necklace with you, Good Father, when you meet us after early mass in the morning.' She then knelt before the Inquisitor and asked for his blessing. He gave her his blessing, but first he waved his hand before his eyes as though he were clearing his vision, or brushing away a fly. After the blessing he helped her to her feet and said, 'of course' and then 'goodnight' as he left us. He would lend her the necklace the next morning. This meant, of course, that there would be but little time for Lady Theadora to prepare for the rescue, but we had no other choice."

"After mass, as we waited for the Inquisitor, Lady Theadora told me to be on the lookout for the same woman from the evening before. She was right. We approached the Inquisitor as he was leaving the cloister. Just before we met, Lady Theadora looked over her shoulder. Without saying a word, she pushed me into the path of the woman. I collided with her as she was hurrying to pass us to get to the Inquisitor. I apologized to the woman, but she only stared at me. Her hood had fallen back. I have faced the enemy on the battlefield with less fear than I felt then. Her look was without human expression. It seemed that we stood that way for many minutes, but it must have been only a few seconds, just long enough for Lady Theadora to get the necklace. My Lady took me by the arm as though nothing unusual had happened, and we left."

"Your Lady would have made a good soldier," said Sebastian solemnly.

"Who was the woman? Did she disappear? Was Lady Theadora as brave as Lady Cassandra?" Sarah would have continued her questions, but her grandfather put his hand on her shoulder to stop her.

Sebastian answered the last of her questions. "No one could have been braver than the Lady Cassandra." Turning to Father Guzman he said. "Now I understand why she was late arriving with the necklace in the Plaza of the Faith. Was she too late?"

The question hung in the air for several seconds, until Ibrahim Leonides replied. "I watched from a distance, a little behind some of your soldiers, My Lord, at the main entrance to the Plaza. I can only guess, but what I saw makes me believe that Lady Cassandra must have regained consciousness long enough to direct the necklace as Lady Theadora placed it around her neck. That was at the same moment that Halán Idriss reached out to support Lady Theadora, just before the pyre erupted and collapsed. We know from some of your soldiers that no bones were found."

"I can confirm that," said Father Guzman. "I stood beside the Inquisitor until the ashes were examined. There were no bones nor weapons nor the necklace, though these facts were never revealed. The official account, given by the Inquisitor, is that the prisoner and two of the three rescuers were consumed by the fire."

"They must have all three disappeared together," said Ibrahim Leonides, "but where to, or in what condition, I cannot say."

This last comment was greeted by the group with a thoughtful silence. Father Guzman then looked with his slight smile at

Sebastian. "The other would-be rescuer, according to the official word, meaning the Inquisitor's, will be found, imprisoned, and tried as a converso. Oh, yes, and the Inquisitor sends you, My Lord, his compliments for your reported bravery and his hope for a speedy recovery."

"But what of their mission?" asked Ibrahim Leonides. Will they return to accomplish it?"

"We believe that Lady Cassandra has accomplished all that we could ask, and more," observed Stephen.

"Yes, she has," insisted Sarah. "We will never forget her ever. She is a Jew and a hero and . . . . " She had to stop as her eyes welled up with tears.

"As my granddaughter suggests, she is an example to us." Stephen looked at her proudly. "Our community has for too long been frightened and confused. Lady Cassandra has given us the courage to take action. She spoke to me of the City of Constantinople, where Jews might be welcomed. She was going to help us to get there, but now maybe Sarah and I can take her place." He gave Sarah a hug, which also enabled her to dry her tears against his robe.

"I agree, my friend, about Lady Cassandra's mission, though I will sorely miss her if she does not return, but what of Lady Theadora and Halán Idriss? Is their role in the mission also now complete? Will they find a way to return?"

"Only if Lady Cassandra survived and can bring them," noted Stephen. Again, thoughtful silence prevailed, and longer this time.

"May I suggest that we meet here at this same hour of the morning every day as long as we are able," said Lucía, who had been listening attentively. "I know all three of the companions well enough to expect that we will have one or more visitors before too many days pass. I am hoping for three visitors." The others agreed immediately. Her expectations were fulfilled, or partly so.

Two days later, on the fifth day after the burning, shortly after the group had gathered, a windstorm broke suddenly. It stirred up the dust and particles of sand on the dry streets until the large drops of rain cleared the air and washed down the cobblestones. The storm stopped as suddenly as it had arisen. There was a knock on the door. Two hooded figures appeared in the doorway. Strangely their cloaks showed no evidence that they had been in the storm. As they entered the room, they pulled back their hoods. Sarah immediately ran forward arms wide to embrace Cass and Thea. She hardly noticed seconds later that she was in the middle of a crush of hugging adults.

Lucía, of course, took charge, and finally guided everyone to the table. "No questions, no explanations," she commanded, "until the travelers have had refreshment. Also us," she added. For once, however, she was overruled. She got as far as bringing water and rolls. Cass and Thea did take a drink of water, but as each dutifully reached for a roll, they took pity on their friends, noting their anxious and expectant faces.

Cass began. "First of all, we are all three alive and well, but that did not happen easily. We returned to the future, to the house of Alan, my parents, and me in the city of Philadelphia in the New World. My thanks to all of the "conspirators," she said gesturing widely to all in the room. "I forced poor Thea and Alan to repeat every detail as many times as I could until they refused."

"Cass had stopped breathing and lost consciousness," said Thea, "from the smoke. I was able to breathe some oxygen into her lungs, but I could not rouse her. I screamed into her ear to think of her house. In her sub-conscious she must have been aware of the fire and smoke. That made her think of the fire in Alan's attic laboratory, because that is where we went, from one fire to another. Luckily for us firemen were already in the house, and we were rescued. They were able to get Cass breathing again and gave her oxygen. They got us to a hospital, but Cass almost died there."

"I spent many days in the hospital," explained Cass. The doctors said that there had been some earlier damage to my lungs, before the fire. They guessed that I had had pneumonia. When my parents told them that I had never had pneumonia or any problems with my lungs, the doctors said that pneumonia sometimes can occur without the person being aware of it."

"The water torture," exclaimed Father Guzman.

"Yes," said Cass as Thea nodded. "Something else that the firemen and the doctors could not understand was why both Alan and Thea had some pretty bad burns, especially Thea … .

"Even though the fire had never reached us in the attic where we were. Oops, sorry, Cass."

"Thea has taken over my role of finishing other people' sentences," said Cass with a short laugh and a little intake of breath. "My lungs are not as good as they used to be," so I am glad for the assistance."

"We just let them guess about where our burns came from," said Thea. "We had enough explaining to do as it was."

"And Thea had the most difficult explanations of all," said Cass.

"After we knew that Cass was going to get better," said Thea, "the three of us spent a lot of time puzzling about what we were going to do next, after we had let you know we were alive, that is." She paused and looked at Cass. Cass took her hand. The group stirred for the first time since the ladies had begun their narrative. Cass noticed the anxious look on several faces and the barely repressed excitement on Ibrahim Leonides' expression. She came directly to the point.

"Thea, Lady Theadora, has decided to spend her life here in Spain, starting now in 1492. Alan, Halán Idriss, will spend part of his life here and part in the future, as will I. As we speak, he is in Granada with the family of Yusuf. He has embraced Islam and will help the Muslims. I will continue my education as a Jew, if I am allowed, and will go to Contstantinople with whomever among the Jews wish to make the journey. These are our decisions. We hope they meet with your approval," she concluded with what sounded more like a question than a statement.

Chairs scraped back; a few fell over as everyone rose as one and, for the second time embraced the travelers and one another.

Sebastian came immediately to Thea who forced herself to look directly into his eyes, despite her uncertainty about his response. He was from a prominent Spanish family of the high nobility. She was no one, and she had practically just proposed to him. She need not have worried. He knelt before her and offered her his hand if she would have him, unworthy as he was. Of course, he knew she had already said that she would.

After Stephen and Sarah hugged Cass, Stephen told her how glad he was that they would not have to try to replace their guide. Sarah kept her arms around Cass's waist as though she would never let go. She did let go, however, to make room for Ibrahim Leonides and Lucía, who embraced both Cass and then Thea, when Sebastian finally released her.

"And now, I beg your forgiveness, but I have so many questions that my mind cannot contain them all much longer," said Ibrahim Leonides."

"Only after we have some proper refreshments to celebrate," interrupted Lucía, "and for this occasion, that will include a glass of our best sherry." This time she prevailed.

Toward the end of the meal, Ibrahim Leonides rose to make a toast. "As the present chronicler of the Royal Court of Cordoba and of its Eighth Duke, Antonio Leon, I ask that you join me in a toast to the valiant companions of the necklace. To their Quest, fulfilled and on-going." All except Cass and Thea stood, raised their glasses, and repeated the toast. "And now to the questions," said Ibrahim Leonides hopefully, but before he could speak further, Sarah spoke out.

"Did you make the storm happen?" asked Sarah?"

"Maiden," answered Cass and Thea together. "You first," said Thea.

"Yes, Maiden appeared. Re-appeared, I should say. It happened one day while we were talking at our house. We used the attick, of course, for privacy. The three of us had just decided that I was well enough for us to return here. Suddenly the shadowy corner of the attick moved, and Maiden was with us. We were thrilled, but I fear we scolded her a great deal even though she had told us that we had to be on our own during those final days. We asked her what would have happened if the rescue had not succeeded and we had all died. 'I think you know,' she answered. 'It would have been a different ending and fulfillment.' The pupils of her eyes flickered, reminding us of the fire. 'Come,' she said. We hurried to embrace her. Maiden is the one who made the storm, Sarah. In fact she made two different ones, one to carry us to Granada and one to bring us from there to here. Those were memorable journeys."

"She took us with Alan to Granada in a thunder storm. We were surrounded by bolts of lightning," said Thea. "She brought Cass and me here sailing on currents of wind above dark clouds bursting with rain."

"Ohh!" exclaimed Sarah's with eyes wide.

"I personally think she was showing her joy and relief that we were still alive, without having to actually say so," said Thea. She looked fixedly at Sara and added, "It occurs to me that I have a good idea of who would have become the next bearer of the necklace had the rescue failed."

Cass had been noticing Ibrahim Leonides fidgeting as Thea spoke. "Ibrahim Leonides, your hands have been trying to speak for you I think," she said.

"A thousand pardons, My Lady," he replied, "but you are indeed perceptive. "How came Halán Idriss to decide on Granada, and will he realize his mission there?"

"You have asked two questions," said Lucía with a teasing hint of reproof. Everyone laughed, but these were questions the ladies expected.

"You first," said Cass.

"We have been busy," stated Thea. "We all went together, with Maiden, to Granada before coming here. Cass and I had decided to go there with him even before Maiden reappeared. Alan wished to see all of you, and he sends his greetings, but he is worried about

Yusuf. Cass and I visited with Yusuf and Alzarad. We saw the conditions there. Alan is right to be worried. The Moors are suffering. They expect that they too will soon be expelled from Al-Andalus, their earthly Garden of Paradise. Already they are being forced to give up their homes and move to less desirable parts of the city or even to the rural parts of the Province of Granada. Alan can help. He has returned to the Queens Guardsmen. Cass by the way is now truly in harmony with her necklace. She was able to time Alan's return to his unit so that he was never missed."

"Alan will be able to protect Yusuf's family and at least some of the other Muslims while they prepare to leave," continued Cass. He might even be able to persuade the Queen to send him with them as her envoy to the Ottomans. Yusuf, with Alan's advice, has decided to take his family and followers to Izhtar, Stephen. Izhtar is also in the new empire of the Ottoman Muslims. It is only a few days journey by horse or mule from Constantinople, so he will practically be your neighbor. I'm sure Alan could also be of help to the Jews, should they need it, especially if he becomes one of the Queen's envoys.

"Speaking of that," continued Cass. "Yusuf showed us a proclamation that the Sultan of Constantinople sent to the governors of all provinces of the Ottoman Empire when he heard of the Jews being expelled from Spain. I can remember the words just as they were written. They were 'not to refuse the Jews entry, or cause them difficulties, but to receive them cordially.' I saw a copy of it." Cass was beaming and thinking to herself that the Caliph of the West, Abdul Rackman, would approve.

While Cass was occupied with her thoughts and catching her breath, Thea asked Ibrahim Leonides, "Have we answered your two questions?"

Ibrahim Leonides silently smiled, closed his eyes, and bowed his "yes."

"I am afraid, My Lord Sebastian," said Thea with a wry smile, "that the Sultan of Constantinople does not have a high opinion of our Catholic Majesties of Spain. Another saying of the Sultan is now circulating in Granada by word of mouth. According to one of Yusuf's cousins, when the Sultan heard of the expulsion of the Jews, he asked, 'How can you call this King Fernando a Wise Man? He is impoverishing his own country and enriching mine.'

"One last word about Alan," said Cass. "You will appreciate this, Father Guzman. I had told him that you, like another friend of ours, Brother Bartolomeo, had been a soldier before becoming a priest or brother. That thought struck him. He said that after his usefulness as a diplomatic Queen's Guardsman is over, he may study to become an Imam."

"I understand that and wish him well," said Father Guzman, "but warn him that it takes time to unlearn behaving as a soldier."

"I have seen evidence of that, to my good fortune," laughed Cass, remembering how he had pinned down her jailer.

"As have I," said Sebastian, "as you were pretending to be a frightened priest while holding back the soldiers from attacking me."

"So you saw right through me. Are you saying that I am not much of an actor," asked Father Guzman.

"Yes," answered Sebastian. "But do not worry. Lady Theadora and I will have need of your talents as a priest more than as either a soldier or an actor."

"At your service, with pleasure," said Father Guzman.

"I must ask one question," said Lucía. "How can you three companions leave your country, your time, and most of all, your families?"

"You first," said Cass.

"This was difficult. As I think you all know, I am an only child, and both my parents are dead. Still some of my extended family will miss me, and I did not want to worry anyone. I told my oldest and favorite aunt that I had decided to leave, perhaps for good. She knew my mother and me the best of all the relatives. She gave me a hug and said she knew I would leave them but not quite so soon.

She said if ever I needed a roof over my head, I would be welcome, but I think she knew we would never see one another again. As for living here in the past, that is a dream for a lover of history like me. I have heard that there are some good books to be read here."

Thea looked at Sebastian, as everyone laughed. Then she turned to Cass. "Your turn."

"Alan and I will both return to the future from time to time. Our family has pulled together. While I was in the hospital I told my father about living my Judaism. He had been so worried that I might die that he hugged me and said he was just happy that I was alive. In his typical contrary way, he decided that Alan's joining Islam somehow balanced my practicing Judaism. My mother, as usual was way ahead of me. She already knew a great deal about the necklace. She saw that I was wearing it when we were rescued and guessed where we had been. She and Grandma Esther, Essie that is, had shared more than I had realized. When I told her about helping to save Abdul Rackman, she became quite emotional. She excused herself and left the hospital room. When she came back, she told me she had gone to the Chapel of St. Joseph to give thanks, that from my mother, the agnostic, non-practicing Jew. Her father's life had been saved by her daughter. She also asked St. Joseph to protect us, since she fully expects that we will return to the Spain of the past. She made two requests. Alan and I should be with them as much as the necklace permits, and we should have daughters. They will also visit and bring any brothers along."

"Could you live in both times, or at least seem to?" asked Ibrahim Leonides.

"Just for a while," answered Cass. "I am planning on making that journey to Constantinople with you. But I cannot go back and forth indefinitely. Alan and I will both have to make a decision where our permanent home will be. I expect the necklace will let me know when the time has come for a final decision."

"Stay with us when that happens, Lady, "pleaded Sarah. "Here, please," she added only slightly less urgently. Stephen did not attempt to restrain her.

"I cannot speak for Alan, or even for myself with complete certitude," replied Cass. She looked at those around her, her eyes lighting on Stephen. She thought fleetingly of her Quaker friend Robert and smiled. Then she took Sarah's face between the palms of her hands and looked into her eyes. "Whatever happens, here is where I found myself," said Cass to Sara.